Ro...   ...nean

Jennifer Faye

Siblings Annabelle and Luca DiSalvo have
grown up in the gilded shadow of royalty.
Now they're breaking free of palace protocol
to find their own happy-ever-after!

The Millionaire's Royal Rescue

Lady Annabelle's father doesn't approve of her
globetrotting ways. He thinks a job will teach
her some responsibility, but it gets her tangled
up with renowned tycoon Grayson!

Married for His Secret Heir

Earl Luca needs to settle down and produce
an heir. An unexpected arrival from his
past seems to be the answer, but the journey
down the aisle is far from smooth!

For more royal romances
from sunny Mirraccino read

A Princess by Christmas
The Prince's Christmas Vow

Available now!

MARRIED FOR HIS
SECRET HEIR

BY
JENNIFER FAYE

MILLS
BOON

First Published in Great Britain 2017
By Mills & Boon, an imprint of HarperCollins*Publishers*
1 London Bridge Street, London, SE1 9GF

© 2017 Jennifer F. Stroka

ISBN: 978-0-263-92306-3

23-0617

Our policy is to use papers that are natural, renewable and recyclable products and made from wood grown in sustainable forests. The logging and manufacturing processes conform to the legal environmental regulations of the country of origin.

Printed and bound in Spain
by CPI, Barcelona

Award-winning author **Jennifer Faye** pens fun, heart-warming, contemporary romances with rugged cowboys, sexy billionaires and enchanting royalty. Internationally published, with books translated into nine languages, she is a two-time winner of the RT Book Reviews Reviewers' Choice Award. She has also won the CataRomance Reviewers' Choice Award, been named a TOP PICK author and been nominated for numerous other awards.

For Caitlin

From one book lover…
to another :-)

PROLOGUE

Paris, France

IT SHOULD HAVE been the most amazing night of her life.

Elena Ricci swept her long blond tresses over her shoulder as she stepped backstage at the Paris fashion show that had just concluded. She should be on cloud nine, but instead worries brought her feet back down to earth. With a borrowed diamond necklace and matching earrings now returned to the jeweler and her crystal-embellished gown returned to the designer, she was ready to call it a night.

"Are you heading straight to the party?" a female voice called out behind her.

Elena turned to find a young woman smiling at her. Try as she might, Elena couldn't put a name to the face. "No. I'm going to pass on it."

"But you have to go," the beautiful young woman with flowing black hair said. "As the face of the line, you're like the guest of honor. Tonight is your night."

"I'm sure you'll all have fun without me. I'm just not up for a party."

"Ah, I bet you have other plans." The young woman flashed her an I-know-what-you're-up-to smile. "I'm sure he'll be worth it."

He? There was no he. The last guy she'd had the misfortune of dating had been a liar and a cheat. Elena had sworn off men after that debacle. Who needed the hassle?

"There is no guy," Elena clarified.

"Really? Then who's the man waiting for you at your station?"

Elena didn't bother answering. She just started walking. If it was Steven, she was having security escort him out.

She'd told him in no uncertain terms to get out of her life. And she'd meant it.

When she neared her station, the man had his back to her. "I told you I didn't want to see you again."

The man turned. "Is that the way you greet all your friends?"

Heat rushed to Elena's face. Before her stood the Earl of Halencia, Luca DiSalvo, her childhood friend. "I'm sorry. I, uh, thought you were someone else."

"I think I feel bad for the other guy."

"Don't. He doesn't deserve anyone's sympathy." She rushed forward and gave Luca a hug, finding comfort in his strong arms. And there was something else—a warm sensation that set her stomach aflutter. But she refused to examine the reason for her elated reaction.

The truth of the matter was, she'd grown used to shoving aside her emotions when it came to Luca. Their friendship meant the world to her, and she wouldn't do anything to risk it—even if it meant they would never be more than friends.

He pulled back and smiled. "That's better."

She looked deep into his tired eyes. There was something bothering him. This wasn't just a casual visit. Luca didn't do those. For him to come here unannounced, it meant something had happened—something big.

"What is it?" she asked. "Is it your father?"

Luca shook his head. "It's my mother."

"Your mother?"

Luca drew in a deep breath. "They caught her murderer. Actually, my sister did. Can you believe it? After all these years, it's finally over."

Elena wasn't sure how to react. On one hand, she was relieved they'd solved the crime, but she also knew how tough the years following the heinous crime had been on Luca and his estranged family. She couldn't imagine how he must be feeling at this point.

After the murder, Luca had withdrawn from everyone around him—including her. When he'd finished high school, he'd moved away. Soon after, she'd done the same and moved to Paris. Their friendship dwindled to an occasional phone call or an annual visit over coffee at a small café when Luca was in Paris on business.

Over the years, she'd told herself not to take the distance personally. It was Luca's way of dealing with the unimaginable grief. But she couldn't deny that losing the close connection with her best friend had hurt—a lot.

A million questions bubbled up within her. And yet she remained quiet as he gave her the highlights of how Annabelle had caught the murderer. The story was truly stunning.

"Annabelle just phoned me." His gaze didn't quite reach Elena's. "And I just needed to tell you." He paused as though considering his words. "I guess if I'd been thinking straight, I should have realized your mother would tell you."

Elena reached out and briefly squeezed his hand. "I'm glad you're the one who told me."

"You are?"

She nodded. "I'm so sorry this happened to you and your family. I hope the murderer's capture will help in some small way."

"Me, too."

There was something different about him. Instead of the usual cool aloofness that he wore like armor, he was uneasy, and there was a glimmer of vulnerability in his blue-gray eyes. Had he come here for yet another reason?

Refusing to let herself imagine that Luca was ready to become a part of her life again, she busied herself. She bent over and slipped on a pair of bright white tennis shoes with pink laces. Now that her makeup had been wiped away and the glittery, gauzy creations had been returned to the clothes rack, she felt like herself. Plain old Elena.

When she straightened, she found Luca staring at her. Her heart thump-thumped. She swallowed hard. "What is it?"

"Nothing. I was just looking at you."

Worried that she'd missed removing some of the sparkly blue eye makeup they used to make her up as a fairy for the new magical fashion line, Elena turned to the mirror. She didn't see anything but her own complexion. Her cheeks were a little rosy from the cleanser, but it was all her in the reflection. So why had Luca been looking at her so strangely? She shrugged it off.

"Can I persuade you to stay long enough to eat?" She hadn't eaten a bite all day. She'd been a nervous wreck about the show, and now that it was over, she was ravenous. "Or we could get one of your favorite pizzas from Pierre's and take it back to my flat."

"Your flat?" Luca shook his head. "Not going to happen. I hear you have some exciting news." He moved to the end of her makeup table and retrieved a champagne bottle. "We have to celebrate. It's nonnegotiable."

She wasn't sure either of them was up for celebrating. Before she could vocalize her protest, Luca popped the cork and Elena watched as pink bubbles rushed down the side of the bottle. Luca reached for a champagne flute and filled it up.

"For you." He held the glass out to her.

She accepted it. Luca was certainly acting out of character. Her gaze lowered to the glass as the pink bubbles rose and popped. If Luca and the designer of the line Elena now represented only knew of the mess she'd made of her private life, they wouldn't help her celebrate being chosen as the new face of the Lauren Renard line.

Elena felt like a fraud. They all thought she was so good—so deserving. But she was none of those things. Her judgment was way off where men were concerned. She'd been too trusting—too open—and in the end, she'd been lied to in the worst way. Now she didn't trust herself or men.

"Elena?"

She glanced up. Her gaze met Luca's. Tears suddenly rushed to her eyes. She blinked repeatedly, refusing to unleash the turbulent emotions that had been threatening all day.

"Hey, none of that." Luca raised his glass. "This is a moment for celebrating."

Elena forced a smile to her lips and lifted her glass.

Luca held his glass close to hers. "To the most amazing, wonderful tomboy I've ever known. And I might add that you clean up pretty good, too."

Her mouth gaped as their glasses clinked together. "That's not fair. I haven't been a tomboy since we were kids."

His eyes studied her. "I have one question for you."

"You can ask it, but I reserve the right not to answer." A nervous shiver rolled through her stomach. Had he heard about her romantic debacle? She groaned inwardly before taking another drink of champagne—a much bigger drink.

"When did you become so beautiful?" Luca's gaze caressed her, leaving her insides aflutter.

Heat rushed to her cheeks. "Be careful, Luca. If I didn't know better, I might think you were flirting with me."

"I am."

Her heart lodged in her throat. What had come over him? Luca was a constant flirt, but always with every other woman in the room. And now she didn't know how to react to him.

Luca grabbed the champagne and refilled their glasses. "Drink up. I'm taking you out on the town tonight. I'm going to show off the hottest lady in Paris."

He thought she was hot?

Maybe he was referring to the blush that had engulfed

her face. She resisted the urge to fan herself. Instead, she gulped another mouthful of bubbly.

Luca was far too sexy, and he was saying all the right things to sneak right past her meticulously laid defenses. If she wasn't careful, this evening was going to blow up in her face.

She swallowed hard. "But I'm tired—"

"Trust me. What I have in mind will wake you right up." He winked at her.

Her heart skipped a beat. She didn't know what to say. Instead she busied herself with another sip of champagne. As the alcohol hit her empty stomach, she realized that it wasn't her wisest idea and set aside the glass. "It's not that big of a deal."

"Of course it's a big deal. It's a huge deal." He smiled at her like he had something in mind. He'd been giving her that look since they were kids playing in the fields of wildflowers on the palace grounds in Mirraccino, and she knew it meant he had mischief on his mind. "We have to celebrate. And I have the perfect idea."

Why did it suddenly feel like Luca's reaction to her new role for the world-renowned Lauren Renard line was over the top? After all, Luca was an earl. He was royalty, for goodness' sake. His father was the Duke of Halencia. And Luca's mother had been the sister of the King of Mirraccino. Elena knew that her accomplishments didn't come close to stacking up to Luca's impressive lineage.

"Luca, it's really not that big of a deal." Heat rushed to her cheeks.

"Quit being so modest. You worked hard for this." He walked over to her and put his arm over her shoulders. "I'm proud of you. Just wait until my sister hears about this. In fact, she was just asking about you."

"She was?" When he nodded, Elena said, "Tell her I said hi."

"I will. Right after I tell her about you being world famous and the face of her favorite clothing line."

In truth, being the face of such a renowned line was truly a turning point in Elena's career. She wouldn't just have her face on the middle pages of a magazine. She would now dominate the covers. Her calendar would be filled with photo sessions. Finally, she was no longer just the daughter of the King of Mirraccino's secretary or the tomboy who followed Luca all around the palace grounds and played football with him until long after the sun set. She was now a successful international model—for however long it lasted.

"But after your news, I'd really understand if you didn't want to make a big deal of it."

"Indulge me," Luca said.

"What's that supposed to mean?"

"It means while you were taking your final stroll down the catwalk, I was on the phone."

"And? You were finding out the location of the next hot party?" She had no doubt there were parties with so many notable people in town this week for the line reveal, but that just wasn't her scene.

"There's only one party on my mind." He looked at her rather intently.

Her heart raced. "Luca, when did you become so mysterious?"

"Mysterious?" There was a glint of mischievousness reflected in his eyes. "I've been accused of a lot of things, but never that."

"Well, then out with it. What plans did you make?"

"Trust me. You'll find out soon enough."

She moved to retrieve her purse and turned back to say something when his lips landed on hers. That wasn't supposed to happen. Her heart jumped into her throat. So why wasn't Luca pulling away? Why wasn't she?

Maybe if she had held still just a moment longer, his

kiss would have landed on her cheek. Yeah, that was probably it. But now that they were in this awkward situation, neither moved. Could he hear the pounding of her heart?

Over the years, she'd wondered what it'd be like to feel Luca's mouth pressed to hers. But she'd never, ever thought that it would actually happen.

And then his lips moved over hers, tentatively and slowly, as though figuring out where they went from here. Her pulse raced, and any rational thoughts slipped out of reach. At last, her dream was coming true.

Her purse slipped from her hand as she reached out to him. Her fingers slid beneath his gray sports jacket to the black T-shirt beneath. As her palms slid over the defined contours of his chest, a moan swelled in the back of her throat.

Oh, yeah... This kiss—this moment—was so much better than she'd ever imagined. She definitely approved of this change in Luca.

His arms wrapped around her, pulling her close. Need, wonderment and eagerness consumed her. The rush of emotions was more intoxicating than the bubbly they'd just shared.

As their kiss intensified, his tongue slipped past her compliant lips. She leaned in closer, pressing the length of her body against his. If this was a dream, she didn't want to wake up.

A whistle followed by applause from the stage crew had her reluctantly pulling away. She wasn't sure what she expected to find when she gazed into Luca's face. Perhaps disappointment or regret, but instead he was smiling at her. It was one of those smiles that made his eyes twinkle.

"Are you ready to go?" Luca whispered into her ear, sending goose bumps racing down over her body.

"Um...yes."

"Good. I want to make this a very special evening for you."

It was already special. That kiss had been so unexpected and so much better than she'd ever imagined. This was a different side of Luca, and she liked it—she liked him—a lot.

After retrieving her purse from the floor, she slipped her hand into his and they rushed out the door. She refused to second-guess this decision. It was her one chance to be something so much more than Luca's friend.

At last, he'd seen her as a desirable woman.

CHAPTER ONE

Nine weeks later, Mirraccino Island, the Mediterranean

SHE'D HEARD IT said that you can never go home again. Maybe she should have heeded that warning.

Elena stared at herself in the full-length mirror in her bedroom at her parents' modest home on the royal estate of Mirraccino. This trip had not been her idea. It had come about rather suddenly when her mother broke her leg.

Her mother had called to say that she couldn't get around on her own, and since Elena's father was needed at the palace, her mother was home alone all day. As their only child, it was up to Elena to return home. And though the timing wasn't ideal with the start of the new campaign for the Renard line, Elena had worked feverishly to reschedule all of her appointments. She was more than willing to help her mother, who'd always been there for her.

But unbeknownst to Elena, her mother had exaggerated her condition. The fact that her mother had played on Elena's emotions was unusual, so she let it pass without comment. The truth was she didn't make it home often enough.

Don't think about it. Not this evening.

She hadn't even unpacked yet when her mother had handed over an invitation printed on heavy cream stationery sealed with a deep purple royal crest. A little confused, Elena had opened it, surprised to find that she'd been invited to Lady Annabelle's engagement festivities. The invitation had said the event was to be intimate and to dress casually.

Now, two days later, she'd tried on every single dress she'd brought with her from Paris at least twice. Some were too revealing. Others were too flashy. And some were too formal. What exactly did one wear to dinner at the palace?

She'd never been in this situation before. Although she was the daughter of the king's private secretary, she wasn't the type who received invitations to royal events. And this wasn't just any party. It was a weeklong series of events. And her mother had taken it upon herself to post an acceptance on Elena's behalf.

Knock. Knock.

"Come in."

Her mother smiled as she entered the room. Her long dark hair was pulled back and tucked up at the nape of her neck. Only powder accentuated her natural beauty. "I just wanted to see if you needed any help getting ready."

"I'm the one who should be asking if you need anything."

Her mother waved off the concern. "I'm fine."

"Isn't Father home yet? I thought he might stay with you while I'm out for the evening."

The smile slipped from her mother's face. "I don't see your father much lately."

Elena had noticed her father's increased absence. "What has him so busy?"

"The same thing as always—the king."

"Oh." Elena knew from growing up that her father kept his work to himself. And that was probably why he was the king's most trusted employee. "I'm sorry. I had hoped the king would be back to normal by now."

"I had hoped the same thing. Nothing has been right since they arrested that murderer. The news hit the king really hard."

"I'm sure it was quite a shock to learn there was a murderer wandering through the palace all those years."

Her mother shuddered. "I don't like to think of it. Your father saw that criminal every day. Just the thought—"

"Don't go there. It's all over." Elena hoped to reassure her. "Father is safe."

Her mother sent her a weak smile and nodded.

Elena turned back to the full-length mirror. She'd finally settled on a little black dress. It wasn't anything special. But the black suited her mood. She'd been sullen and reserved ever since her night with Luca. It had been just one more mistake on her part—a total error in judgment.

The only right decision she'd made was agreeing to be the face of one of the world's hottest designers. The work was now coming in droves. In fact, there were so many requests for appearances and photo shoots that she couldn't do them all. But once word got out about her condition, it would all end.

She was pregnant with Luca's baby.

Pregnant. The word still sounded so foreign to her.

She'd always kept track of her cycle—a little tick mark on her day planner. With the hectic schedule of a new campaign, she hadn't noticed right away that her timely cycle had suddenly drifted off course. But referencing her day planner to schedule future shoots, she'd stumbled across the missing tick mark. Her heart had clenched before panic ensued.

Four home pregnancy tests later, her worst fears had been confirmed. She was pregnant with Luca's baby. At this point, only Elena and her doctor knew the truth. And for the moment, that was how it'd remain.

"Is that what you're wearing to dinner?" her mother asked, studying Elena's black dress. A decided frown came over her face. "Don't you have something more cheerful?"

For some reason, her mother's disapproval decided Elena's attire for her. "I like this."

"You're awfully skinny." Her mother clucked her tongue disapprovingly. "While you're home, you need to eat more.

Thin is nice, dear. But when a man wants to wrap his hands around you and—"

"Mother, stop." She couldn't believe her prim and proper mother was talking about a man having his hands on her. It just sounded so wrong to hear her mother talk about sex. *Ew!*

"Really, Elena. I didn't think you were a prude, especially with those sexy outfits you model."

"I'm not a prude. It doesn't mean I want to talk about—about that—with you."

Her mother smiled. "I didn't think people your age were so shy talking about sex."

"Enough. You're really making me uncomfortable here."

"Okay. Okay. I'll stop."

"Thank you."

Ding. Dong.

Elena looked at her mother. "Are you expecting anyone?"

"Not that I recall."

"I'll get it." Elena made a move toward the door, immensely grateful for the interruption.

Her mother held up a hand. "You stay and finish getting ready. I'll entertain your date."

"I thought you didn't know who was at the door?"

"I, ah, just remembered." Her mother's gaze avoided hers.

"Really? That's interesting, because I don't recall making a date."

"I know, dear. That's why I arranged for one. After all, you don't want to show up at the palace all alone."

Stunned by her mother's matchmaking, Elena stood slack jawed as her mother used her crutches to maneuver out of Elena's bedroom. She even pulled the door shut behind her.

Elena didn't know what shocked her more—her mother's agility or the fact Elena had a date that evening and her mother hadn't even told her the man's name. At least with her mother doing the matchmaking, Elena knew the man would be honest and a gentleman.

The only problem was Elena didn't want a date. She was perfectly happy going to the palace alone. This wasn't the good old days when it was unseemly for a twenty-five-year-old woman to be seen in public without an escort.

She had to put a stop to her mother's meddling. After all, she'd returned to Mirraccino to take care of her mother, not the other way around.

Elena glanced back at the mirror. She turned, giving a side view. Would anyone be able to tell she was pregnant? She didn't think so. She wasn't far along. And so far she'd been able to avoid the dreaded morning sickness. A little nausea now and then and being a bit more emotional than normal were her only symptoms.

She turned away from the mirror and slipped on a pair of platform stiletto heels adorned with crystals. The added height to her five-foot-ten stature always gave her a boost of confidence. The peekaboo toes would give a glimpse of her pedicure. Thankfully, she'd had a nail appointment just before she left Paris. She'd hoped it would lift her spirits. It hadn't.

She pulled open the bedroom door and headed downstairs. "Mother, I—"

The words died in her throat. There, making chitchat with her mother, was Luca. Her heart lurched into her throat. How could this be? Luca never visited Mirraccino. And yet here he was, smiling and laughing with her mother.

He looked incredibly handsome with his dark hair cropped short on the sides and back while the top was a bit longer. He wore a charcoal suit that amplified his already broad shoulders—shoulders where not so long ago she'd rested her head. She squelched the thought as fast as it came to her.

Sans a tie, the top two buttons of his white dress shirt were unbuttoned, revealing a glimpse of his tanned chest and the gold chain that held his St. Christopher medal. He'd been wearing that necklace—a gift from his mother—almost as long as Elena had known him. She knew it meant a great deal to him.

He looked like he was ready to step onto a runway in Paris or Milan. He was certainly photogenic enough. He had it all—the looks, a title and money. He wanted for nothing. Even though he'd settled down with a job in the financial sector, she knew he traveled routinely. With his home base in Milan, he often traveled throughout Europe to the States and then to Australia before he started the expedition once again. And he certainly never lacked for companionship.

She should have known that Luca would be her mother's idea of an appropriate date. Her mother would like nothing better than to have her marry into the royal family. But Elena had made it clear that would never happen. She'd had enough of men. They only wanted one thing. Once they got it, it was game over and they were on to their next conquest.

Not so long ago, Luca had been the love 'em and leave 'em type. And the aftermath of their night together hadn't convinced her that this particular leopard had changed his spots. It was best that she trod carefully where he was concerned.

"Hello, Elena." Luca placed a practiced smile on his face, but there was a flicker of something dark in his eyes. In a blink it was gone, leaving her to wonder if she'd imagined it.

"Hi. I…I didn't know you were back on the island."

"I was told by my sister that if I didn't make an appearance for her engagement celebration, she would track me down and it wouldn't be pretty when she found me."

"I can imagine your sister following through on that threat."

"Me, too. So here I am."

"And since your appearance was last minute," her mother interjected, "Luca kindly agreed to be your escort. Isn't that right, Luca?"

His Adam's apple bobbed. "Yes, that's right. It looks like we're both without dates this evening."

"But that doesn't mean my mother should have imposed on you." Elena sent her mother a pointed look.

"I didn't." Her mother feigned innocence.

Elena's gaze narrowed on her mother, not believing her. "And I suppose Luca is now psychic and knew I'd be here this evening without a date?"

Elena could feel Luca's gaze on her, but she refused to face him. She was already embarrassed enough. How could her mother do this to her?

"I was just trying to help," her mother said. "Luca came round the other day to check on me. He'd heard about my accident, and he wanted to make sure I was okay."

It sounded innocent enough, but how that translated into a date was another story. "And that's when you hatched this scheme to impose on his kindness."

"Young lady—" her mother's voice took on a sharp edge of indignation "—I don't now, nor have I ever, hatched a scheme. I merely mentioned that you were flying in to town."

"And I suggested that we go to the dinner this evening—together." Luca was no longer smiling.

He was mad at her? She was only trying to undo her mother's meddling. She was certain her mother had more to do with this arrangement than she was letting on. Wait. Had he just said he was the one who'd wanted to go to the dinner with her?

Elena's gaze shifted to Luca. But it was like he had built a wall between them, and she wasn't able to read his thoughts. Drat! She felt as though she was standing on shifting sand and she just couldn't get her footing. The best thing to do was let him off the hook, gently.

"I appreciate your thoughtfulness, but you don't have to bother," she said, watching his eyes grow darker. "I don't mind going to the palace by myself."

"What about the palace?" Her father stepped through the doorway in his standard black suit, collared white shirt and black tie.

"Luca came to escort Elena to the dinner at the palace." Her mother beamed. "Isn't that wonderful?"

Her father's face was pale and drawn. Dark circles had formed under his eyes from being on call for the king at any hour of the day or night. Elena wished her father would set some boundaries in his life, but he insisted that his duty was to the king, and he could not be deterred.

Everyone stood quietly waiting for her father to speak. It wasn't like him to be so quiet. Usually he would tell her to have a good evening and be on his way.

"Are you all right?" Elena asked her father.

"I'm fine. Just a little tired." Her father moved to stand in front of Elena. He leaned forward and pressed a feathery kiss to her cheek. "But I'm feeling better now. How could I not with my wonderful family around me?"

Elena's mother nodded toward Luca. "Aren't you going to say anything to our guest?"

Her father grunted as though he'd forgotten. He turned to Luca. "Don't do anything to hurt my girl. Or else…"

Her father didn't finish the threat, but Luca's rigid stance and the firm line of his lips said that he'd gotten the message.

"I'll go clean up for dinner," her father said and moved toward the stairs.

"Shall we go?" Luca asked.

Elena had to try one last time to call off this awkward

date. "As I was saying before, I really don't mind arriving alone."

Luca sighed. "Ah, but see, I do mind. I hate showing up at these family events alone. There will be questions about who I'm dating, if it's serious and if I ever plan to settle down and get married. I'd rather avoid all that."

So she would be doing him a favor? By what? Being his decoy? A shield?

No. No. No.

She wasn't comfortable with any of those titles. Elena had enough of her own secrets. She didn't need to be drawn into anyone else's drama.

The past few months in Paris had consisted of making one bad decision after the other. It had gotten to the point where she had no faith in her own judgment. And now that she was pregnant, she had to make the right decisions. There was an innocent baby counting on her. She had mixed emotions about her unexpected condition. How could she tell Luca she was pregnant when she didn't even know how she felt about it?

That was why her mother's request for her to return home couldn't have come at a better time. She had hoped some downtime would clear her head. At the time, she'd had absolutely no idea that Annabelle was having a big celebration or that she would include Elena in the festivities.

Her gaze landed on Luca. He looked uncomfortable and anxious to be anywhere but here. Things had definitely changed between them. Where there had once been an easiness, there was now this crackling tension. If she needed any confirmation that they could never go back to how they used to be, this was it.

Tonight, she would be nervous enough being a guest at the palace. She really didn't need the added awkwardness she felt around Luca. If only he wasn't so insistent on being a gentleman and escorting her.

"I'm not quite ready to go." When he didn't say anything, she added, "I don't want to make you late."

"I don't mind waiting," he said. "It'll give me some more time to talk with your mother."

Her mother smiled. "And I just made a fresh batch of those amaretto cookies that you enjoy."

"They're my favorite," Luca said. "And I haven't had them in a very long time. You really are the best in the kitchen."

Her mother shook a finger at him. "You have grown up to be quite a flatterer. I'll just go get you a few."

"If you don't mind, I'll join you."

Her mother nodded and set off for the kitchen with Luca following closely behind. Elena stood alone in the entryway. What exactly had just happened?

CHAPTER TWO

LUCA COULDN'T TAKE his gaze off her.

Had Elena always been this beautiful?

Thankfully she'd turned her head to stare out the car's window at the passing fields of wildflowers while in the background the setting sun painted the sky with streaks of orange, pink and purple. But tonight Luca was in no mood to appreciate nature's beauty.

In the weeks since he'd last seen her in Paris, he'd convinced himself that everything about their evening together had been blown out of proportion by the champagne. He just couldn't accept that he was attracted to his childhood friend. He couldn't allow that to happen, because they could have no future.

He wasn't into commitments.

Not now. Not ever.

But there was something about Elena that pulled at him...even to this day.

And then he remembered how he'd woken up the morning after they'd made love and heard Elena sniffling. The sound had ripped him apart. No one had ever cried after spending the night with him. And the fact that it was Elena, of all people, made the situation so much worse.

He hadn't moved for an indeterminable number of minutes. Her muffled sobs had sliced through him. Clearly she'd thought their night together had been a mistake. Unable to think of anything to say to comfort her, he'd continued to breathe deeply as though he'd still been asleep. Each breath had been painful, as his entire body was tense. The memory was still so crystal clear.

He had done that. He had made Elena cry. And he felt awful.

If only he hadn't let things get out of hand. But he'd thought she'd been having a good time. Still, he should have resisted kissing her. He should have made their friendship the priority. If he'd been thinking clearly, he would have realized there would be no coming back from holding her all night long.

He swallowed hard as the limo glided through the estate to the palace. The ride only took a couple of minutes, but with Elena so close to him, time seemed to stand still. For the first time, he wasn't sure what to say or what to do.

Boy, he'd really messed things up between them. He resisted the urge to rake his fingers through his hair. He needed to look his best for the professional photos his sister would undoubtedly insist upon.

On second thought, this date is not a good idea.

Not good at all.

"Are you sure about this?" Elena asked.

"Yes." *Liar.*

She arched a brow. "You don't sound certain."

This was where he should reach out and squeeze her hand to reassure her, but instead he didn't move. He didn't trust himself to touch her. The images of their night together were still in the forefront of his mind.

He'd really mucked things up. The truth was he didn't want to be Elena's escort, but when her mother had mentioned Elena's return to the island, he'd been caught off guard. And when her mother had mentioned the party, Luca had spoken without thinking.

And now, well, all he wanted to do was sweep Elena into his arms and pick up right where they'd left off back in Paris. He wanted to feel her eager lips beneath his— ready and willing.

He halted his thoughts. This wasn't like him. When he ended a relationship, he moved on without looking back.

With Elena there had been no moving on. Since that night, no other woman had interested him.

When he closed his eyes, it was Elena's face he saw. It was the memory of her lips that tormented him. How was he ever supposed to get her out of his system?

So he didn't dare look at Elena right now. He refused to act on those desires. She'd made it abundantly clear that she regretted their night together—no matter how hot and steamy it had been.

He just needed to focus on something else—anything else. His mind drew a blank. Perhaps he should start a conversation. Yes, that was a good idea. But what should he talk about?

"I was surprised to hear you were back on the island." There—that sounded normal enough.

She shrugged. "I didn't have much choice, considering I thought my mother truly needed me."

"I take it she exaggerated her injuries?"

Elena nodded. "By the sound of her on the phone, she was on death's door."

Luca smiled. "I can imagine."

"What does that mean?" Elena suddenly sounded protective of her mother.

"I just meant that your mother would do anything to get you home."

"And how would you know? You're here even less than I am."

He shrugged, not certain he wanted to admit that he talked with her mother often enough. At first, Elena's mother had concocted any excuse possible to call him, but as time went by, he got used to hearing from her. He actually looked forward to it, because she would fill him in on all of Elena's accomplishments.

"I just remember how she used to be—always wanting you to stay close to home."

Elena shrugged. "She finally accepted that my future wasn't in Mirraccino."

"Speaking of which, how did you get time off from your new campaign to fly here?"

Elena glanced away. "I…ah, had a break in my schedule."

There was something more she wasn't telling him, but he didn't push. If she wanted him to know, she'd tell him when she was ready. The fact she was even speaking to him, he took as a positive sign. Maybe there was hope for their friendship after all.

The car pulled to a stop in front of the palace. Though he'd been staying here since he arrived a couple of days ago, he didn't want to attend this dinner any more than Elena. But he refused to disappoint his sister. He'd already hurt her enough by leaving home and allowing extended gaps between visits. He knew Annabelle wanted her family reunited, and now that their mother's killer had been caught, she thought it would fix everything.

It wouldn't.

Luca had witnessed too much. Experienced too much. And he couldn't be the son that his father needed—and perhaps deserved.

But now that Annabelle was getting married, hopefully she'd stop longing for the family she'd lost. When a family member was murdered, it seemed for the most part that families reacted in one of two ways. The horrific event either drew them together—the family against the world. Or it splintered them apart—each finding their solace in a different way. His family had been the latter.

Luca's car door swung open, interrupting his thoughts. It was for the best. He didn't want to dwell on how he'd disappointed his sister repeatedly over the years. Tonight was to be a celebration. And he would put on his biggest and brightest smile, which shouldn't be too hard since their father, the duke, was not to be in attendance. Tonight was an informal gathering of friends and some family. Annabelle wanted her groom to meet the people who had meant a lot to her while she was growing up.

An enormous wooden door with brass fixtures swung open. An older gentleman in a black-and-white tux stepped outside to greet them.

Elena put her hand on Luca's arm, pausing him from getting out of the car. She leaned over and whispered, "That's so strange."

"What is?" Luca glanced around, but he didn't notice anything amiss.

"That the butler is there to greet me—well, us. That's never happened in my whole life."

Luca smiled and shook his head. "I'm glad it makes you happy."

"It does."

Luca alighted from the car and turned back. He held out his hand to help Elena to her feet. "So what do you think?"

"I think that no matter where I go, this palace is the most beautiful building." Her gaze focused on the palace and not him. "What do you think? You've traveled even more than me. Have you ever seen anything so amazing?"

Luca turned to study the expansive building. He had honestly never really looked at the place. He was embarrassed to admit that he'd taken the centuries-old palace for granted. Over the years, it'd been expanded upon, which included the addition of the towering turrets. Though once used to keep an eye out for approaching enemy ships, they were now more a decoration and painted with stripes of yellow, pink, aqua and gold.

"It really is remarkable," Luca said, his gaze straying to Elena. "A beauty unlike any other that I've ever found."

Just then Elena glanced at him, and he turned away. Did she know he was no longer talking about the palace?

He hoped not. He didn't want to give her the wrong idea. They'd had their chance together—as brief as it might have been. There was no way of recapturing it. He refused to even consider it. Okay, maybe he had considered it, but he wouldn't act upon his desires.

Even if their lovemaking hadn't made her cry, they didn't belong together. He couldn't make her the promises she deserved. And he wouldn't have any woman waiting around for him when he had absolutely no intention of making a commitment.

Therefore, it was best that he shove aside those tempting images of her in his arms with that wanton desire reflected in her eyes. He swallowed hard. Could they ever be friends like before? He was feeling less assured about that with each passing moment.

The butler stood aside. "Welcome, Miss Ricci. It's good to have you back."

"Hello, Alfred. It's good to be back."

Luca held out his arm to Elena. She paused and looked at it as if she wasn't sure what to do. Boy, he really had messed things up between them.

"Go ahead," he encouraged. "I promise not to bite."

A small smile lifted the corners of her very desirable lips. She tentatively slipped her hand into the crook of his arm. When an unfamiliar sensation pulsed up his arm and settled in his chest, he stilled his body. He refused to give any indication that her touch affected him. Because it hadn't. Not really. It was just nerves. He was just worried about doing something to drive his best friend even further from him.

"Are you ready?"

Elena nodded.

Her face was void of emotion. He knew that look. It was her working face—the look she wore when she was strutting down the catwalk in some amazing outfit. He couldn't rightly describe any of the fashions she wore, because when he googled her, he was always caught up by the beauty of her face. It didn't matter what hair color or stylish cut she was sporting—ever since their night together, he'd been captivated by her.

He took sure strides up the steps to the open palace door. Inside, there was a host of palace staff to greet them and escort them to the dining room. It was odd, considering Luca had been running through this palace with his host of cousins since he was in diapers. That seemed so long ago now.

A flash went off, momentarily blinding Luca.

Elena came to a standstill. She released his arm. "The press is here?"

"Not that I know of."

Elena took a step back. "I should have expected this. Coming here was a mistake."

Luca glanced around. The photographer moved out of the dining room. "It's not the press. It's a private photographer. My sister is sentimental and wants to have pictures to remember these events."

Elena's worried gaze met his. "You're sure?"

He nodded. "Since when did you become so shy? I thought the camera was your friend."

"You thought wrong." And with that Elena brushed past him and headed into the dining room.

What had just happened? His radar was going off. Something was definitely amiss. And it frustrated the heck out of him that he'd wrecked their relationship to the point where she wouldn't even open up to him.

He rushed to catch up to her. "Tell me what's bothering you."

"Nothing."

"If it's nothing, why won't you even face me?"

She didn't stop. "It's nothing," she called over her shoulder. "Just drop it."

"Tell me what it is and I'll fix it if I can."

She stopped and turned to him. Wearing an indifferent expression like a mask, she said, "I don't know why you think I need help."

Luca reached out and grasped her arm before she could wander off. "I know things aren't right between us, but I also know you really well, and no matter what you say, I know there's something wrong—something big."

Elena yanked her arm from him. "You should concentrate on your sister. This is her big night."

As though his sister had heard her name mentioned, she rushed over to them. Annabelle's face was aglow with happiness. "Elena, I was so excited when I heard you were back on the island." She reached out and they quickly hugged. "Thank you so much for coming."

A strange sensation coiled through Luca as he watched the easy smile light up Elena's face. Elena certainly hadn't done that when she'd spotted him at her mother's house. In fact, her reaction had been quite the opposite.

He didn't know why he let it bother him. There were plenty of other women out there who would be happy to have his company. If only he had the slightest bit of interest in those other women.

He inwardly groaned with frustration. He turned away and went in search of something to drink. He wasn't really thirsty, but it was certainly better than watching Elena make nice with everyone—everyone but him.

He had to quit letting her get to him. He needed to withdraw. Wasn't that what he'd promised himself after his mother's murder? To keep people at a safe distance?

That was why he'd packed up and moved away from Halencia and Mirraccino. It hurt too much when people he cared about were torn from his life—whether by murder, grief or something else. He just couldn't go through that again.

And though he'd missed his sister and Elena while he'd been traveling, he'd been able to distract himself. He was always on the go. A new adventure. A new challenge. That was exactly what he should do now—set off on a new expedition. But he couldn't. Not yet.

Until the week was over, he had to make the best of this situation. And then he would be gone. He would return to Milan. He would make plans for some daring feat and forget all about these unwanted emotions.

CHAPTER THREE

AT LAST SHE was an invited guest.

Elena had never thought the day would come when she would be invited to the palace. It was the final confirmation that she'd gone from being a nobody to a somebody. She was no longer the shy child who was left out of all the elaborate royal birthday parties and the other celebrations Luca and his sister attended.

After waiting a lifetime for this moment, she was surprised to find it wasn't nearly as satisfying as she'd imagined. Truthfully, she wasn't enjoying herself. She was in no frame of mind to take part in such a celebration. Her life was a mess, and she had a feeling the worst was yet to come.

At dinner, Luca had been seated at the other end of the extremely long table. There was no chance of him probing her with his eyes—searching for answers to his unspoken questions. The problem with hanging out with her former best friend was that he could still read her like a book. And she just wasn't ready to open up to him.

During the dinner, she'd witnessed Annabelle's bubbly happiness. It was then that Elena made her decision. She would delay telling Luca about the baby until the end of the week. By then, the celebration would be over and the fallout from her announcement couldn't ruin this happy occasion.

The delay would be best for everyone. Until then, she'd have a chance to figure out her life plan and to find the right words to soften the blow for Luca. Not that she wanted anything from him—that she'd decided. But he was the father of her baby, and he deserved to know the truth.

She glanced around, finding Luca engaged in a conversation with Prince Demetrius. This was her chance to quietly slip away from the party. After all, who would notice?

Besides possibly Luca. But they'd been doing their best to avoid each other all evening. So perhaps he'd be relieved to realize that she'd gone.

Luckily, having spent her youth avoiding the guards and servants, she knew her way around the palace. She slipped into the hallway. A quick check both ways let her know that the coast was clear. Her gaze latched on the French doors at the end of the hallway. Although freedom was within reach, she forced herself to walk at a reasonable pace.

She inhaled a deep breath, hoping to calm her rising nerves. All she wanted now was to escape the curious looks and the inevitable questions regarding her showing up as Luca's date. When her hand grasped the brass handle, she glanced over her shoulder. So far, so good.

She let herself out onto the patio that was surrounded by the royal gardens. She looked left and then right. All alone. She breathed her first easy breath all evening. Whatever had made her think that coming here would be a good idea?

She moved to the far end of the patio and leaned her palms against the cold concrete balustrade supported by dozens of tiny pillars. The entire palace was a work of art. And just now the gardens were aglow beneath the full moon. It was breathtaking—

"There you are." Luca's voice came from behind her.

The breath caught in Elena's throat. She'd been so close to making a successful escape. Why had she stopped? Maybe because she knew this would be the last time she would be welcome at the palace. Once word got out about all her ill-advised activities, no one would want her around—most especially Luca.

Steeling herself, she leveled her shoulders, plastered a smile on her face and turned. "Luca, I didn't hear you approach."

"And I didn't hear you say anything about sneaking off into the night." His dark brows were drawn together.

"Who said I was sneaking away?"

"I did. And you were."

The smile was getting harder and harder to maintain. "Really, Luca? Sometimes you imagine too much."

"Don't try to brush me off. I know you, Elena. You put on a pretty good show this evening for the other guests, but I can see you aren't happy."

"Of course I'm happy. I'm honored that your sister still thinks so highly of our childhood friendship to invite me to such an event."

"Annabelle likes everyone." And then, as though he realized how that might sound, he added, "But you meant a lot to her, especially when our mother died."

Elena had tried her best to be there for both Luca and Annabelle, but he'd pushed her away. It was as if overnight Luca had built a wall around himself and no matter how hard she tried, there'd been no scaling that wall. Eventually she gave up.

"I don't belong here," Elena said.

"What? Of course you do."

She wasn't going to argue with him. Her gaze strayed to the sweeping steps that led to the garden. "I made an appearance, and now it's time that I go. Please tell your sister I had a good time."

Luca crossed his arms over his broad chest. "Tell her yourself."

The abruptness of his comment caught her off guard. "I…I will." A written message would be so much easier than a phone conversation where inevitable questions would arise. "I'll drop her a note tomorrow."

"This isn't about you fitting in. It's about us. Isn't it?"

She met his unwavering gaze. "Why would you think that?"

"Because I really screwed up in Paris. It was all a big mistake. I wasn't myself that night. And if you give me a chance to make it up to you, I swear it'll never happen again."

The more he tried to explain, the more his pointed words poked at her hope that they'd get past this awkward stage. But now she knew the unvarnished truth. And it was worse than she'd thought.

Having no response for him, she turned to continue walking.

"You can't just walk away," he called out.

Why did he have to keep pushing? He wasn't going to like anything she had to say. It was best to keep moving. She took another step.

"Elena, what is it going to take for you to forgive and forget?"

She turned, catching the frustration written so clearly on his face. "You don't understand. The past can't be that easily erased."

"What are you saying?" He stepped closer to her. "Elena, what is going on?"

Elena pressed her lips together. She'd said far more than she'd intended at this juncture. And now she'd aroused Luca's suspicion. There was one thing that Luca excelled at and that was ferreting out the truth. If she didn't get out of here soon, her secret would be out. And this royal scandal—the earl having a baby with a commoner, the daughter of the help— would be the talk of the palace and beyond.

She knew it would happen sooner or later, but she'd been hoping for later, after Annabelle's moment in the spotlight. After all Annabelle had been through tracking down her mother's murderer and then being held at gunpoint, her friend deserved this bit of happiness.

"I'm not leaving here until you talk to me," Luca said. "So out with it."

"I just meant we can't pretend that night didn't happen."

He didn't say anything for a moment, as though he were

considering the sincerity of her statement. "I understand. But I don't want to lose our friendship."

Before she could say a word, the sound of voices and approaching footsteps interrupted. Elena glanced past Luca and spotted Prince Alexandro alongside another of Luca's cousins. The prince glanced up and surprise flashed in his eyes.

"I'm sorry. We didn't know anyone was out here," Prince Alexandro said. "We'll go."

"No. Stay. You aren't interrupting anything," Elena hastily responded.

The prince's gaze moved between her and Luca. "You're sure?"

Luca hesitated and then nodded.

"Good," the prince said, approaching them. "Luca, we need you to settle a disagreement."

The men quickly got into a heated discussion about the upcoming European football season. Elena immediately tuned out the conversation. She wasn't a sports fan unless it was auto racing. There was just something about a hot guy and a fast car. Her mind immediately conjured up Luca in a sleek racecar. The image definitely worked for her. But just as quickly as the image came to her, she dismissed it.

With the men now deep in conversation, Luca had his back to her. She took advantage of the moment to follow through with her original plan to steal away into the night. Trying to act as casual as possible, she quietly strolled down the steps and entered the garden.

When she reached the other side of the garden, she slipped through the gate and entered the open field illuminated only by moonlight. At last, she was free.

With her hand splayed over her midsection, she said, "Don't worry, little one. We'll tell your father. The time just has to be right."

* * *

A late-night phone call was never a good thing.

In Luca's case, it always meant that his life was about to take a turn for the worse. He doubted tonight would be any different.

"Father?"

"Luca, you answered." Surprise rang out in his father's voice.

Was he that bad at accepting calls from his father? Perhaps. He had started to avoid his father's calls because the man kept hounding him to step up and take his place in the family business—a position Luca didn't feel comfortable assuming.

"Are you all right?" Luca asked, rubbing the sleep from his eyes.

"I'm coming to Mirraccino first thing in the morning. We need to talk."

"Is that code for you want to discuss how I'm wasting my life? If so, you're wasting your time—"

"I'm serious, Luca. It's imperative that we talk." There was a weariness to his father's voice that he'd never heard before. And it concerned Luca more than he'd expected.

"Can't you just tell me now?"

"No. We need to do this in person. And don't tell your sister. She'll find out soon enough, but for now she deserves to enjoy her engagement."

"Understood."

"Good. I'll see you first thing in the morning. Don't sleep in."

"I won't."

When they disconnected, sleep was the very last thing on Luca's mind. His father was far from melodramatic. In fact, after his mother's murder, his father had been the only calm person—perhaps too calm. At the time, Luca had resented the fact that his father hadn't fallen to pieces. In that moment, he'd been certain his father didn't love his mother. Not like he should have loved her.

That was the moment when Luca pulled back from everyone. Convinced that love was just an illusion, he'd refused to become a victim of romance and happily-ever-after. Because when the haze of lust lifted, someone would walk away and someone would get hurt.

And as much as Luca believed his father had not loved his mother, as the years slipped by, his doubts set in. His father never moved on with his life. He never remarried. Luca wasn't even sure his father dated. If he did, he used the utmost discretion. And the few times that Luca had returned to their home in Halencia, it remained the same. His mother's belongings were still where she had left them. It was so easy to pretend that she was just out for the day. It made Luca wonder if he'd misjudged his father. Had his father loved his mother in his own way?

Sleep was elusive for the rest of the night as Luca stared into the darkness. He knew as sure as the sun would rise that his life was about to change dramatically. It left him restless.

And then there was the matter of Elena.

She'd gotten away from him tonight. He didn't know what was bothering her, but he intended to find out. It wasn't like Elena to act so mysteriously.

Tomorrow there was a picnic. He wasn't sure what else Annabelle had planned for the day, but he was certain it wouldn't be boring. Nothing about the day would be mundane, because he had every intention of once again escorting Elena to the event. It would give them a chance to finish their prior discussion.

There was something going on with Elena, and he felt driven to find out what had this international fashion model cowering from the cameras. Perhaps it wasn't any of his business, but the worried look reflected in Elena's eyes haunted him.

He might not have been around much in the past few years, but he was here now. By helping her, he might be able to assuage some of his guilt over losing control in Paris. If he did, perhaps they could part on good terms.

CHAPTER FOUR

THE NEXT MORNING Luca paced back and forth in the palace library.

It was time he let his father in on his life choices. Luca couldn't help but wonder what his father would think of the fact that he'd gone back to school and received his degree in business management. He knew he was destined to run the family's citrus business one day. And he wanted to be prepared. In fact, for the past several years, he'd been working his way up in an investment firm in Milan.

Perhaps he should have told his father all of this sooner. He'd intended to, but it never worked out. Every time they got together, they argued. His mother used to say that they butted heads so much because they were so much alike. Luca had always taken it as an insult. He had never wanted to believe that he was as stubborn and infuriating as his father—

"Luca." His father's voice came from behind him.

Being so deep into his thoughts, Luca hadn't heard his father approach. He turned toward the doorway. "Hello, Father."

"At last we talk. You really ought to get a new phone so your messages don't get lost."

Luca had noticed the messages, but he kept putting them off for one reason or another. "I've been busy."

His father's dark, bushy brows drew together. "Humph... How can you be busy?"

Luca inwardly groaned. Did his father always have to think so little of him? And then he realized that it was partially his fault. His stubborn pride had kept him from revealing to his father that he'd followed the path his father had wanted him to take in the first place.

Luca cleared his throat. "What did you need to talk about?"

"Is that how you greet your father?"

"It's not like we're the mushy type. That's Annabelle's area."

His father broke out in a hearty laugh, surprising Luca. He had absolutely no idea what he'd said that was so amusing.

His father quickly recovered his composure. "Apparently you've spent as little time around your sister as you have me. Let me enlighten you so that you are not shocked this week. Your sister has grown up into a strong woman and a bit of a spitfire."

That would explain the adventure she'd gone on to track down their mother's murderer. "I'll definitely keep that in mind." Still not comfortable in his father's presence, he said, "Now, what did you want to talk about?"

His father's formidable presence melted away as his face seemed to age almost instantly and his broad shoulders drooped a bit. The duke closed the library door and headed for the tray of coffee and biscuits that had been left by the staff.

His father busied himself pouring a cup of coffee. "Would you like some?"

"I'm good." Then as an afterthought, Luca added, "Thanks."

He wasn't used to his father being thoughtful. This meeting must be serious. And right now, he was too wired. Adding caffeine to the mix would be a mistake.

After his father fixed his coffee with some sugar and a bit of cream, he turned. He took a long swallow before returning his cup to the saucer. "You need to move home."

Luca's body tensed. That was it? No explanation. Nothing but an order. Throwing around his authority was so typical of his father. But he must have forgotten that Luca was no longer a child to be bossed around.

"No." If his father would talk to him differently, he'd explain to him that he already had a job with responsibilities.

His father's eyes flared with anger. "You don't understand. You don't have a choice. It's time you stop partying and live up to your responsibilities."

"And if I don't?"

"You'll be cut off from your funds."

This was where he had his father. "If you hadn't noticed, I haven't touched that bank account in years."

His father's mouth gaped. A second passed before he regained his composure. "I…I didn't know. How are you getting by?"

Luca knew that he could continue to keep his father in the dark, but what good would that do? After all, he wanted to prove to his father—and himself—that he had changed. This was a good starting point. "I'm an account manager at an investment firm."

"You are?" His father leaned back against the table as though for support. The news appeared to have knocked him off balance.

Luca couldn't deny that he found a bit of satisfaction in being able to surprise his father. "Yes. I went back to school, earned my degree and I've been based in Milan ever since. But my work takes me around the globe."

"I see."

No *I'm proud of you.* Or *I'm happy for you.* His father seemed to absorb the news as though he'd just been told there was rain in the forecast.

"Well, I'd like to say that it's been great catching up, but we never were good at casual conversation. So if that's all, I should be going." Luca turned to the door.

"Wait. You can't go. Not yet." His father's voice took

on an ominous tone, causing Luca to turn back. "You need to know…"

When his father's voice faded away and his gaze centered on the coffee in his cup, Luca became suspicious that there really was a problem. His father never acted coy. Whatever it was had his father acting out of character.

"I need to know what?" Luca asked.

His father's hand shook just a bit as he turned to place the coffee cup on the table. When he turned his attention back to Luca, his eyes were dark and unreadable. "The family business is failing."

Failing? The grove of lemon trees had been in his family for five generations. It was a tradition. It was their history.

Luca had to be certain he understood his father. "And this is why you want me to move home?"

His father sighed. "I'm not getting any younger. It's time I pass the torch to you and step down. But before I do this, I need to know that you're up to the challenge. Are you ready to settle down and do the work necessary to save our business and our home?"

Sure, he'd been gone for a long time, but in all honesty, he never meant to be gone forever. His home in Halencia was where he planned to settle…eventually. He'd just never thought anything would happen to it. He always imagined it'd be there waiting for him when he was ready to accept his destiny.

But now his father was looking to him for help. What did his father think Luca could do that he hadn't already done himself? Luca didn't have any answers, but he did know this was his chance to prove to his family that he was someone they could count on.

After all, they had world-renowned lemons with a delicate taste and low acidity. Surely there had to be a market for them. They'd never had a problem in the past.

It would be so easy to turn his father down and go back

to his comfortable life in Milan. After all, he hadn't created the problem. It wasn't his responsibility to fix it.

But this was the first time his father had ever turned to him for help. How could Luca walk away from that? He was certain his mother would plead with him to let go of his pride and help his father.

It wouldn't be easy moving back to Halencia. His father might talk of retirement, but Luca knew his father wouldn't do it. The business was all his father had left. It was in his blood. So how would Luca work side by side with such a stubborn man?

Before he made up his mind, they needed to get a few things straight.

"Why do you want my help?" Luca asked, needing his father to admit that he needed him.

"I…I just told you."

"No, you told me the company is in trouble, but you didn't say why you turned to me."

His father hesitated. "Fine. I need your help. I can't do it alone. Is that what you want to hear?"

Luca nodded. "Yes, it is. And there's one more thing."

"I'm afraid to ask."

"Then just listen. If I succeed, you'll sign over the position of president to me."

His father's dark brows gathered and his mouth opened, no doubt to protest.

"You did say that you were planning to step down, didn't you?" Luca knew as sure as the sun was going to rise tomorrow that unless an agreement was in place, his father would never step down. Once the company was back in the black, his father would no longer have a reason to hand over the reins.

His father sighed as he shrugged his shoulders. "Okay. You'll be president if you succeed."

"And you'll put this all in writing?"

The duke's shoulders grew rigid as his bushy brows drew together. "My word isn't enough for you?"

"Let's just say, this way there will be no room for misunderstandings."

His father studied him for a moment. "The Luca who left here years ago never would have asked for such a contract."

"I was young then. And my mother had just died. It's not fair to throw that in my face—"

"Slow down. You didn't let me finish. I was going to add that I am impressed. You've grown up to be a man who isn't afraid to stand his ground, even against his father. I just hope you have that much resilience and guts when it comes to turning around the business."

"I will. Trust me."

Luca hoped he sounded more assured than he felt at that moment. His entire future and his family's legacy hinged on him pulling together a new business plan. And it was just starting to sink in that this endeavor might be much more important than proving himself to his father.

He had just signed on to save their home—the place where his ancestors had lived for generations. The place that was filled with memories of his mother. The thought tugged at his heart.

And at the moment, he didn't have a plan. He had to come up with one fast. And it had to be good—no, it had to be great.

At last her mother was resting.

Elena breathed a sigh of relief. Her mother was far too active. It was difficult to get her to stop and elevate her ankle like the doctor had told her to do. And her mother looked wiped out. She'd said her ankle throbbed at night and it kept her awake.

Today, Elena had promised to sit with her to watch an old black-and-white movie starring Cary Grant. Her mother seemed pleased with the suggestion, seeing as her father wasn't one for movies. He'd rather play checkers or cards to pass the time.

It was only a matter of minutes into the movie when her mother drifted off to sleep while sitting upright on the couch. Elena put a throw blanket over her and was on her way to the kitchen for another cup of coffee when there was a knock at the door. Not wanting her mother to wake up, she rushed to the door and opened it.

There, standing before her, was Luca in a blue button-up shirt with the sleeves rolled up, white shorts and boat shoes. He looked as if he'd just stepped off the deck of a luxury yacht. Dark sunglasses hid his eyes from her.

She ran a hand over her hair, realizing that she hadn't bothered to do much with her appearance that morning. "Luca, what are you doing here?"

"I thought we could walk together to the picnic."

"But last night—"

"You left before we finished our conversation. So are you ready to go?"

"I'm not going."

"You can't back out. It's a weeklong celebration and everyone on the invite list is expected. I was told this personally. Apparently my sister thinks I might skip out on her. So if I have to go, you do, too. And that includes the dinner and dance on Saturday."

"Your sister must be so excited." What did one even wear to such an affair? She wasn't certain, but she guessed frilly hats might be involved. She didn't own any.

"I'll give my sister credit for bringing together all our childhood friends. It was a good idea. And don't worry, the dance isn't a full-on ball. I imagine she's saving that for the wedding. Anyway, are you ready to go?"

He had to be joking. She glanced down at the ratty T-shirt she'd found in her old dresser as well as a pair of cutoff jean shorts. "Um, no. I'm looking after my mother. She had a rough night."

"I'm sorry to hear that. We could always stay here? I'm sure Annabelle would understand."

"But I wouldn't." Her mother's voice was immediately followed by the tapping of her crutches.

Elena turned to her mother. "But I'm here to take care of you."

"I can take care of myself. And if you go, perhaps I can take a nap without being interrupted."

"Sorry. I didn't mean to disturb you." Luca at least had the decency to look embarrassed.

Her mother waved away his worry. "I'm glad you stopped by. I remember a time not so long ago when you and my daughter were inseparable."

Was her mother trying to set them up again? Heat rushed to Elena's face. Of all the times for her mother to try to play matchmaker, this was the worst.

"That was a long time ago, Mother." Elena hoped to dismiss that subject.

"Not that long ago by my standards. You two got into all sorts of mischief. I was never sure which one of you was the instigator. I think you took turns, but regardless, you were always a mess by the time you got home. I can't begin to tell you how many outfits you ruined with mud. I was certain that one day you two would end up together—"

"Mother…" Elena lowered her voice, willing her mother to stop.

Elena didn't know if it was the embarrassment or something else, but suddenly her head felt a bit woozy and her stomach lurched. She pressed a hand to her forehead, hoping to settle her head. This wasn't good. Not good at all.

At least it wasn't the cramping she'd experienced just after she'd learned she was pregnant. That scare had sent her running to her ob-gyn. The doctor assured her that everything was normal, but she'd agreed to do a sonogram so Elena could see it with her own eyes.

The sight of her own itty-bitty baby with a heartbeat had brought tears to her eyes. She'd had them print out a photo that she carried in her purse everywhere she went. She was surprised she hadn't worn out the photo from holding it so much.

"Elena, are you feeling all right?" Her mother sent her a worried look.

Elena willed her body to cooperate. If only it would listen. "Sure. I'm fine."

Her mother studied her. "I don't know. You're a bit flushed and you haven't been eating much. Maybe you should stay home today and rest. I could call my friend and tell her that we'll play cards another time—"

"Nonsense. I'm fine. Nothing to worry about."

Her mother sent her a look that said she didn't believe her. With her mother, it was hard to say if the news that Elena was pregnant with the earl's baby would be welcome. It would either make her mother extremely happy or horrify her that it hadn't happened in the proper manner.

"There you go again," her mother said. "You look like you're about to pass out."

Why did her mother have to pick now, of all times, to make a fuss over her? Elena swallowed hard. "It's just a little warm in here."

"Warm?" Her mother's frown increased.

Elena chanced a glance at Luca, who was unusually quiet. He was staring right at her as though also trying to determine what was up with her. She just hoped that after their time apart his keenness at reading her thoughts would be skewed. After all, surely he wouldn't be able to figure out her condition just by looking at her.

Perhaps an outing was best. She was anxious to avoid

her mother's questions. "I really need to change my clothes. I don't want to be late."

Once upstairs and with the bedroom door closed, Elena took her first easy breath. It wouldn't be long now until her mother figured out that she was pregnant. And then what? Did she fess up that it was Luca's baby? Her mother would insist on a wedding. And that wasn't going to happen. Neither Elena nor Luca was interested in marriage. As it was, Luca had been doing enough backpedaling after their night together to make it clear that he didn't want more than friendship with her.

So where did that leave her? Saying she didn't know the father of the baby? No. That so wasn't her. And anyone who knew her would realize it was a lie.

That left her with refusing to divulge the father's name, saying he wanted nothing to do with her or the baby. But was that how Luca would truly feel? Would he turn his back on them both and walk away?

The Luca she'd known all these years would never do such a thing. No, he would stand by her out of obligation. But how would that work? She would make him miserable, and vice versa. Talk about a mess.

Elena switched into a dressy pair of shorts and a cotton top. She stopped in front of the mirror and decided to pull her hair up into a ponytail. She couldn't believe that in the midst of everything she was going on a picnic with Luca.

Five minutes later, she returned to find her mother and Luca deep in conversation about Annabelle's fiancé. They both stopped talking and turned to her.

"I'm ready," Elena said.

"Are you feeling better now?" Her mother sent her a concerned look.

"Yes. You're the one who needs to take it easy. I feel really bad about leaving you again."

"Nonsense. I'll be fine." Her mother smiled.

She and Luca said goodbye to her mother and headed outside. Once the door was shut, Elena said, "Sorry about that. You know how my mother can be."

"So there's nothing to her worries?"

Drat. Now wasn't the time to get into her pregnancy. It would wait until the end of the week, just like she'd planned. "No. I am not sick. I promise."

Luca arched a brow. "But something is wrong. I can feel it. Are you sure you're up for the picnic?"

She nodded. "It sounds like a lot of fun."

He paused as though evaluating her sincerity. "I still can't believe my sister is taking this long walk down memory lane with all these activities that we did when we were kids."

"I think it's sweet. She gets to share a bit of her past with her fiancé, and it's a way of saying goodbye to that part of her life before she sets out on a new journey."

Luca's smile broadened. "You got all that out of my sister's invitation?"

Elena nodded. "I think it's quite original and a lot of fun. Has she said what she's planning for the wedding?"

"She said the engagement is the fun part and her wedding will be formal. The best part, she said, will be the honeymoon."

"I like the way your sister thinks."

"And how about you?" Luca asked. "Have you met anyone special?"

"No." The answer came out too quickly and too vehemently. She inwardly groaned. "You know how it is with work and traveling. I hardly have a minute to myself."

Luca's inquisitive gaze was full of questions. "Is that the only reason?"

He was referring to their night together. She wasn't about to let him know that it had meant more to her than it should have. "Of course."

He nodded and looked away.

And then she knew exactly how to jerk him out of this train of thought. "The way you're questioning me, I'm starting to think you've been spending too much time with my mother."

"Ouch. That bad, huh?"

She smiled and nodded. "I'd rather talk about this picnic."

"Someone in your line of work probably doesn't eat much."

"Oh, come on. You know me. I love food."

He gave her an appraising look. "You sure don't look like it. You have all of the curves in just the right places."

A tentative smile pulled at her lips. "Well, thank you. I think. I'm just fortunate that I have a really fast metabolism, because there's hardly a thing I don't like."

He didn't say anything. They continued to walk along the dirt path to the bluff, and the silence dragged on. So much for their conversation.

She glanced over at Luca. She was surprised he hadn't chastised her for disappearing on him last night. Perhaps that was why he'd grown quiet.

"It's a beautiful day," she said, trying to break the tension.

He glanced up from where he'd been studying the ground. "Uh, yes, it is."

"Your sister seems to be having a good time this week."

"Uh-huh."

"I haven't been on a picnic since I was a kid."

"Uh-huh."

She doubted he'd heard a word she'd said. "I was thinking of cutting all my hair off."

"That's good."

She wondered what he'd say to this. "I'm thinking of dyeing it purple."

"Wait." Luca stopped walking and looked at her. "Did you say you're dyeing your hair purple?"

She smiled and nodded. "Wondered if you'd notice."

It was then that she realized she was smiling. That was something she hadn't done in what felt like forever. Her life had taken so many twists and turns in the past couple of months that she'd forgotten what it was like to unwind and enjoy the sunshine on her face and breathe in the sea air.

"I'd certainly notice something like that." Then concern filled Luca's eyes. "Please tell me you're joking."

She wasn't quite ready to quit teasing him. "I don't know. It'd certainly be different."

"Trust me, you don't have to go to those lengths to be unique."

She wasn't sure she liked that comment. "What exactly does that mean?"

He held up his hands as though to fend her off. "No offense meant. I was just referring to the way you left Mirraccino and made a name for yourself. Not many people achieve such notable accomplishments."

"You act like that's such a big deal. It's not like I'm an earl."

"I was born into that title. It had nothing to do with me. You, on the other hand, worked hard and earned a prestigious place as the face of the famous Lauren Renard line."

His words meant a lot to her—more than she'd expected. "Thank you."

Luca reached out, grabbing her hand. When she stopped walking and turned to him, he said, "Listen, I know I really messed things up in Paris, and I'm sorry. I don't want to lose our friendship."

With all her heart, she wanted to believe him—believe that their friendship was strong enough to overcome any obstacle. But that night had changed everything. And how would he feel toward her once he learned she was carrying his child?

She pulled her hand away. "Things are different now. We're not kids anymore."

"What's that supposed to mean? Are you saying you never want to see me again?"

"It means…" In that moment, she got choked up. She glanced away, not wanting Luca to see the unshed tears in her eyes. Darn pregnancy hormones. "I can't do this. Not here. Not now."

He placed a hand beneath her chin and lifted until their gazes met. In his eyes, she saw strength, but more than that, she saw tenderness and warmth. She latched on to that and found that between his touch and his gaze, her rising emotions had calmed.

Being this close to him had her remembering their brief Paris affair. Her gaze dipped to Luca's mouth—to his very tempting lips. What would he do if she leaned forward and pressed her mouth to his?

As if in answer, he turned away and started walking.

She stifled a sigh. If only things were different.

She rushed to catch up to him. The truth was in this particular moment, she didn't trust him. He'd said and done things with her in Paris that he now wanted to conveniently sweep under the rug. Was that how he'd feel about this supposed friendship once he found out they were to be linked for life?

She didn't know what to believe. She'd thought she'd known Steven, and she'd been horribly wrong about him. Now she didn't trust herself to make good decisions where men were concerned.

If he'd known she had been considering kissing him back there, he didn't let on. And that was fine by her. She'd had a moment of weakness. It wouldn't happen again.

CHAPTER FIVE

WHAT WAS GOING on with Elena?

Nothing had been the same since they made love. And he was left feeling—feeling…ugh! He didn't know how he felt, except confused and frustrated.

The rising sound of excited voices drew his attention. Today's guests consisted of the same group from dinner the prior evening minus the twin princes and their spouses. They all had prior engagements that they couldn't cancel. His sister took it all in stride. That was one thing Luca admired about his sister, her ability to handle the curves life threw her way with a minimum of fuss.

He wished he could be that way around Elena, but she got under his skin. She made him experience emotions he didn't want to feel and provoked him to act out of character. No one had ever had that sort of effect on him.

It was then that Luca noticed she was speaking with Alec, Luca's cousin. She smiled and toyed with her ponytail as it fell down over her shoulder. She was engaging and charming with his cousin. The thought of her being drawn into Alec's arms had Luca's jaw tightening. What was up with that?

The scene unfolding before him shouldn't bother him. After all, this was what he wanted, wasn't it? It wasn't like he wanted to romance Elena. The night they'd shared had been a mistake. Nothing more.

He turned away, refusing to keep watching. What Elena chose to do and whom she chose to do it with was absolutely none of his business.

He made his way over to his future brother-in-law, Grayson Landers. Luca was pleasantly surprised and relieved to find his little sister had chosen a really good guy. As they talked about Grayson's growing cybercafé business, Luca found himself periodically gazing in Elena's direction. She'd seemed to relax and unwind now that she'd moved away from him. The thought slugged him in the gut.

With lunch cleared, Annabelle let them know that it was time for games. A large white tent and a gentle breeze offset the warmth of the sun. But it was the heat he experienced when he was close to Elena that worried him. So when the guests set aside their hard lemonade and iced tea sangrias in order to play badminton, Luca made sure he played the opposite side of the net from Elena. And when it was time for bocce ball, he stood in the background sipping on a tall glass of ice water.

He had to keep all his wits about him, because something had happened back in that field—something intense had coursed between him and Elena. And it wasn't good. He knew what it was like to hold her in his arms, and now he wanted more. It wasn't logical. It wasn't realistic. But the desire was there every time they were within each other's orbits.

But even if she did want him, he could never be the sort of man she needed. He just couldn't commit himself to a lifetime of unhappiness. He'd watched it with his parents. They put on a good show for people, but they were very different behind closed doors. He forced away the memories of the secret arguments he had overheard as a child.

Annabelle had been too young to have noticed these things or else she didn't want to acknowledge that their parents' marriage had been far from perfect. And Luca had no intention of changing that for her. Their mother's murder had devastated both of them. Whatever comfort Annabelle found in her memories of their family, she deserved. They'd all endured far too much for one lifetime.

Once the badminton and bocce wound down, Annabelle

clinked a butter knife against her lemonade glass. Silence fell over the small group. "Okay. Everyone gather round."

Luca had an uneasy feeling as he took a seat at the large round table. His sister was up to something because she had a mischievous smile on her face. Every time she looked that way, he knew he was in trouble. It was just then that Elena drew a chair up next to his.

"Are you having a good time?" He didn't know why he'd asked. It wasn't like he really wanted to know if she was enjoying his cousin's company more than his.

She nodded. "Surprisingly, I am."

Annabelle again clinked her glass with her butter knife. She waited until she had everyone's attention. "I hope you all are having as much fun as I am. Thank you for joining in the celebration this week. And now it's time for a blast from the past."

The impish expression had yet to leave his sister's face, making Luca even more concerned at what she might be up to. Past experience told him he wasn't going to like it. He braced himself for what she said next.

She picked up an empty wine bottle and placed it on its side in the middle of the table. "Remember this?"

Remember what? Where was Annabelle going with this? He turned a questioning gaze to Elena. Her eyes widened, and then she turned a worried look his way. His gut knotted up tight.

"I can tell by the puzzled look on my brother's face that he doesn't have a clue." She looked directly at him. There was a gleam of devilment in her eyes. He was doomed. She continued, "It's called spin the bottle, Luca. Except that my version is a mix between spin the bottle and truth or dare."

His sister was always one to be creative with the rules. That was probably how she got herself in serious trouble with a killer. Thank goodness Grayson had been there.

The thought of his sister facing down their mother's killer shook Luca to the core.

And then guilt settled in. He should have been there to protect her—not that his sister ever needed anyone to play hero. She had a stubborn and independent streak, just like their mother. But that didn't lessen his guilt for not being there—for not uncovering the killer himself. Perhaps he had been gone far too long.

But now that he'd spoken with his father, things were changing. If all worked out, he would be around more for his family. But that didn't mean he had to stick around for this walk down memory lane.

He knew exactly how his sister would play the game— she would make people squirm. And he wasn't having any part of it. He started to get up to leave when Elena reached out, placing her hand on his arm.

She leaned over and whispered, "Please don't go."

His body tensed as he was torn between leaving before this day went horribly sideways and doing as Elena asked. It wasn't like he owed Elena anything. In all honesty, he wasn't even her official escort. He'd merely walked with her to the picnic. He knew he was just making up excuses in order to leave without a guilty conscience.

Then his gaze lifted and met Elena's. The worry was still there. No. It was panic. Why was she so upset about the game? Then again, who was he to question her when all he wanted was out of there?

He leaned toward her. It was then that a gentle breeze picked up and with it carried the not-too-sweet scent of jasmine perfume. He inhaled a little deeper. Every time he smelled that scent, he thought of Elena. She'd started wearing that perfume as a teenager. For some reason, he'd thought now that she was a famous model she'd have switched to a more trendy fragrance. Was it possible that everything about her hadn't changed?

And then, remembering he was supposed to say something, he whispered in her ear, "Come with me."

"I can't leave your sister's party."

"Sure you can. Come on."

"Luca, be serious. Everyone will notice."

He knew she was right, but that didn't mean he wanted to sit here and play a child's game. "I don't want to do this."

Elena squeezed his hand. "It'll be all right."

His fingers instinctively wrapped around hers. It was such a simple act, and yet his heart was racing. He loved the feel of her hand in his. His thumb stroked the back of her hand.

And then he remembered that they weren't alone. They had an audience that included his very astute sister. Thankfully the table and the white linen tablecloth hid their clasped hands from view. But not wanting to take any chances, he forced himself to release Elena's hand.

"Since I'm the bride, I'll go first." Annabelle smiled as she gazed directly at Luca.

He resisted the urge to shift in his seat. He would not be outmaneuvered by his little sister, and especially not over some childish game.

Annabelle spun the bottle. It circled round and round. Each time it neared him, the breath caught in his lungs. And then it started to slow down. His body tensed.

Thankfully the bottle didn't point at him. But it did point to Elena. He glanced her way, and she looked as pale as a ghost. Oh, no. This wasn't good. He wanted to tell her that she should have listened to him when he suggested they leave together, but he resisted.

Annabelle beamed. That was never a good sign. He wanted to speak up and tell his sister to back off, but before he could utter a word, his sister said, "Okay, Elena, you're first. Truth? Or dare?"

Elena looked horrified that she'd just been caught in his sister's crosshairs.

Luca leaned forward. "Annabelle, I don't think this is a good idea."

That was probably the wrong thing to say. His sister's eyes lit up. "Oh, come on, Luca. Loosen up." Everyone's gaze moved back to Elena. Once again his sister said, "Truth? Or dare?"

A moment passed as everyone waited for Elena to decide.

"Dare," she said so softly that Luca wasn't sure what she'd actually said.

"What was that?" Annabelle asked.

"Dare," Elena said louder.

Annabelle pressed her lips together as she made a show of making up her mind. She was having too much fun with this. Her gaze moved back and forth between him and Elena. What was she thinking? Surely she wouldn't—

"I dare you to kiss my brother."

Elena's mouth gaped, but nothing came out.

"Annabelle, enough is enough," Luca said.

"Tsk, tsk, brother." His sister shook her finger at him. "Since when did you become the serious one? I thought you enjoyed fun and games."

"But this is different—"

"Really? How so?"

He could feel all eyes on him now. What had he done? Was everyone going to guess that he had a thing for Elena?

Before he could find a way out of this mess, Elena leaned toward him. She grabbed the front of his shirt and pulled him toward her. What in the world?

The next thing he knew, Elena's lips were pressed to his. They were warm and so very sweet. His eyes drifted shut as a moan swelled in the back of his throat. Did she know how excruciating this was for him? Did she know how many sleepless nights he'd spent thinking of their lovemaking?

Remembering that they had an audience, he squelched the moan. It took all of his self-restraint to keep his hands to himself. He longed to crush Elena to him. He ached to feel her body next to him with their hearts beating in unison.

If they were alone, he'd kiss her slowly and gently at first. He'd let the hunger and desire build. And just when neither of them could take it anymore, he'd deepen the kiss. Just like before...

They'd been so good together.

It was like they'd been made for each other.

A moan started low and grew. Oh, yeah, her kisses were as sweet as berries and held the promise of so much more. If he were to pull her closer—

Elena pulled back.

And as quickly as the kiss began, it ended. His eyes opened to find her frowning at him. It would appear he'd lost his touch, and along with it he'd lost any semblance of a good mood.

CHAPTER SIX

"ELENA, WAIT!"

She didn't stop. She didn't slow down. In fact, Elena made a point of picking up her pace. The last thing she wanted to do now was deal with Luca.

She'd forced herself to remain at the party until it was over, but she'd made sure to keep her distance from Luca. She didn't trust herself around him. That kiss had reminded her of their night together. And that wasn't good. She had to keep her wits about her.

Steven and Luca weren't the first men in her life who had said sweet nothings to sway her to let her guard down. The others had been photographers, models and other men in the fashion industry. She'd done well navigating her way between the truth and the lies—until Steven.

She'd thought she'd known Steven. He'd seemed so sweet and charming when she'd met him in the Paris café. When she'd dropped her phone, he'd picked it up for her. A bit of casual chitchat led to him asking her to join him for a cup of coffee. From there they'd had dinner. To say it was a whirlwind relationship was putting it mildly. Maybe that was why she'd held back. Maybe there was something in the back of her mind that had said it was all too easy.

She wasn't used to things coming to her easily. Sure, she'd been raised on the royal estate of Mirraccino. But she was raised as an employee's child—someone who was forced to keep to the shadows. When there were grand functions, she had watched them from afar. She'd never had any illusions that she was anything but the help's daughter— a nobody.

When she'd moved to Paris, there was no modeling job waiting for her. She'd waitressed until she had enough money to have a portfolio made and then she started making the rounds of the modeling agencies. No part of her journey had been handed to her. But she'd never regretted any of it. She'd learned a lot and grown as a person.

So when Steven seemed more than willing to let their relationship escalate quickly, she'd put on the brakes. He'd been dropping hints about the future—their future. It had all been happening too easily—and too fast.

When their photo had been taken by an investigator his wife had hired, the whole truth about Steven came out. They had been caught kissing near the Arc de Triomphe, but luckily that was all they'd done. It was what she'd told Steven's wife when the irate woman had confronted her. No matter what Elena said, the woman refused to believe that it was a kiss and nothing more.

Elena had tried to explain how Steven had lied to her about himself and hidden the fact that he was already married. His family had conveniently been on vacation in Australia visiting his in-laws while he'd been sweet-talking Elena.

By the time Luca had arrived in Paris, Elena had been at her lowest. And Luca had been so vulnerable—so open. She'd let her guard down—perhaps too much. Obviously too much, or she wouldn't be pregnant.

She inwardly groaned. She shouldn't have chosen the dare. She could still feel Luca's lips on hers. She knew how easily his kisses could make her forget her common sense. The events of that night came crashing back to her. And the part that stuck out the most was how their night in Paris had all started with a single kiss.

And look where it'd landed them. But of course Luca didn't know yet. She was trying so hard to keep everything light and fun until the week was out, but at every turn Luca was making that increasingly difficult. Just like now. Couldn't he just let her go? Didn't he understand that she needed some alone time?

His fingers reached out, touching her shoulder. "Hey, slow down. What is this, a race?"

She came to an abrupt halt. She spun around and faced him. "What was that kiss back there?"

"A dare issued by my sister." He paused. Suddenly his eyes widened. "You surely don't think I put her up to it, do you?"

Elena crossed her arms. "I'm not sure what to think."

"Sure you do. We're still best friends. Just like always."

"Not like always. Things have changed."

"You keep saying that, but we don't have to let one night ruin a lifetime of friendship." His eyes pleaded with her.

"Why don't you understand that the bell can't be unrung?"

"I think you're making too much of things."

"Really? Then how would you explain that kiss?"

"What about it? It was a dare. A game. No big deal."

"This is me you're talking to," Elena said. "You can't lie to me. I was on the other end of that kiss, and you kissed me back."

He shook his head, not wanting to admit that there was something going on between them. "You're making too much of it."

"And you're working too hard to deny there was something to that kiss. Now why would that be?"

He ran a hand over the scruff lining his chiseled jaw. "It must just have been instinctive. After all, I'm not used to women literally throwing themselves at me."

Elena sighed. "Well, your sister saw that the kiss was more than a friendly peck. You know she's going to make something of it."

"Not if we don't let her."

Nervous laughter escaped her lips. "Have you met your

sister? No one tells her what to do, and that includes her big brother."

Luca's lips settled into a firm line. Apparently he didn't find it amusing. She didn't blame him. This whole thing was getting sticky. Maybe she should just fess up now about the baby.

But what did she say? Did she just blurt it out? No. It had to be handled delicately.

"Luca—"

"Elena—"

They both spoke at once. Both surprised, they stopped and stared at each other.

"Ladies go first." Luca looked at her expectantly.

Suddenly her nerve failed her. She needed more time. She had to think of the right words. "You go first. You look like you have something important to say."

He glanced at his phone. "I have to get to a meeting with Prince Demetrius."

"Oh." She noticed how he used the word *meeting*. "Do you two have business together?"

"I hope so." Then a guilty look came over his face. "Would it be all right if I left you here?"

"Seriously? You're worried about me walking home alone in broad daylight while on the royal estate—"

"Okay. Okay. I get the point. I just didn't want you to think that I was ditching you."

"I'll be fine. Go have your meeting. I hope it goes well."

He started to walk back to the palace, but then he turned back to her. "What was it you wanted to tell me?"

"It can wait."

"You're sure?"

"Positive." What they needed to discuss was going to take much longer than the couple of minutes that he had right now. And she was certain he wouldn't be able to think clearly after she told him. "We'll catch up later."

"You can count on it. Wish me luck."

"Good luck."

And with that he was gone. She was left to wonder what business he had with the crown prince. The last she knew Luca was into investments or some such thing, but what would that have to do with Mirraccino? And the last time they'd discussed his profession, he'd sworn her to secrecy until he told his father. So what exactly was he up to?

"I'm sorry—I can't help."

Luca stared at the crown prince, wishing he'd heard him incorrectly. This couldn't be right. He knew for a fact that Mirraccino was flourishing. So why was his cousin turning down his business plan?

"If it's the price," Luca said, "I'm sure we can negotiate it."

The truth of the matter was that he hadn't had near enough time to formulate any solid numbers. But the crown prince's schedule was kept quiet due to security concerns, and Luca didn't want to miss a chance to talk with him in person. His cousin was being groomed to take over the throne. And though Demetrius traveled often for diplomatic duties, he was also making business connections to keep Mirraccino flourishing.

Demetrius barely took his eyes off his young daughter. She was a toddler now, with a rosy smile just like her mother. She was into everything and getting faster on her toes each day. "It's not the price." When Princess Katrina landed on her diapered backside, Demetrius offered his hands for her to cling to while she got back on her feet. "This is just a really bad time. Perhaps we can revisit this in six months or a year?"

Luca had examined enough of the business's records to know there wouldn't be a lemon grove in six months, much less a year. It needed a large infusion of cash as of yesterday. But he refused to give up. If he hadn't let his ego rule his common sense, he would have returned to his home in Halencia long before now. He would have known the condition of his family's business.

"Perhaps I could speak with the king," Luca said.

"No." Demetrius frowned. Obviously he wasn't used to people not accepting the finality of his word. "My father is not seeing anyone."

Luca had noticed the king's absence since he'd arrived at the palace, but he'd thought his uncle was just feeling under the weather. "Is he okay?"

"I really don't want to discuss my father."

Princess Katrina toppled over on her backside once more, but this time she didn't laugh it off. She started slowly with a couple of unhappy grunts before it grew into a full-on cry. Demetrius immediately swung her little body up into his arms. "Is someone ready for a nap?" He shushed her before looking back at Luca. "I really am sorry. Now, I need to get this princess to her crib."

Luca watched the crown prince walk away. All the while Demetrius talked in soft, gentle tones that seemed to soothe his daughter. Luca wanted to be upset with him for immediately turning down his proposal without an explanation, but it was so hard to be angry with a man holding a baby in his arms.

Luca shook his head as he went to stand next to the elongated library window. He stared off into the clear blue sky. He couldn't imagine dividing his life between family and business. That was exactly what he'd been avoiding all this time—the complications.

He was so much better off alone.

CHAPTER SEVEN

THIS IS IT.

Today is the day.

Elena had awoken just as the sun rose the next morning. She hadn't slept well. Her thoughts wouldn't slow down enough for her to sleep more than an hour or two at a time. Finally she gave up.

By the time she stepped out of bed, she'd accepted that party or no party, she had to tell Luca about the baby. Keeping this secret was eating her up inside. They'd never kept secrets from each other until now. And this wasn't just any secret—it was gigantic and life changing.

She knew Luca had no intention of settling down with a family—ever. He said that families were too complicated and that love didn't last. She felt sorry for him. A lifetime was a long time to be alone.

She might have given romance a try and failed miserably, but at least she'd put herself out there. It bothered her that Luca wouldn't even try. What did that mean for their child? Would Luca insist on keeping their son or daughter at arm's length?

Elena hoped Luca would make an exception for his own flesh and blood. But he hadn't for his father or sister. Elena inwardly groaned. She'd been going in these endless circles all night. The only way to get some real answers was to speak to Luca.

After showering and dressing, she went downstairs to check on her mother. Elena found her in the kitchen about to prepare food for her invited guests. It appeared that Wednesday involved another card game.

Elena had her mother sit at the kitchen table while Elena set to work preparing a meat and cheese platter as well as a fruit and vegetable one. The whole time her mother filled her in on friends and family, who had married and who was expecting babies. Elena got the hint. Her mother was anxious to expand the family. She wondered what her mother would think if she knew the truth about Elena's condition.

"Are you sure I can't do anything else?" Elena asked as she placed the last platter in the fridge.

"No. You've done plenty by preparing lunch for everyone. Now, don't you have something to do this afternoon?"

"Mother, are you trying to get rid of me?" She eyed her mother, who suddenly looked flustered.

"Of course not. I'm not trying to get rid of you. It's just that there are four of us already. You would be a fifth person, and that wouldn't work well for cards."

"Okay." Something told her there was more to her mother shoving her out the door than setting her card game off balance. "Well, I should be going soon."

"Is Luca coming to pick you up?"

Elena rinsed off her hands in the kitchen sink. "Not that I know of." Of all the days she would welcome him picking her up, this would be the day he would skip out on her. "But I'm sure I'll run into him at the party. Unless, of course, you want me to stay home. I know you already have a foursome for cards, but I could take care of the food and clean up."

"That's sweet of you." Her mother reached out and patted Elena's arm. "But not necessary. You just go and have a good time."

Elena didn't know if she'd have a good time. Most likely it would not be a good day, but it was like her father taught her about peeling off a bandage—the faster you did it, the sooner the pain ended. Now it was time to yank off a very big bandage.

"I just need to get ready." Elena had changed outfits about a half dozen times. She couldn't tell if it was her imagination or not, but her clothes were starting to get snug—not that they'd been loose in the first place.

Elena glanced down at her stylish white cotton tank top, jean shorts and flip-flops with blue and white bows. The invitation had said casual dress. Maybe this was too casual.

Which meant once again rooting through her closet to put together just the right outfit—one that was casual but not too casual, dressy but not too dressy, and something that was comfortable, but again, not too comfortable.

"I'll be right back." Elena headed for the steps to the second story.

Twenty minutes later, she stared in the mirror at the coral sundress. It was actually one of the first designs she'd done. Designer Francois Lacroix had told her that she not only had to sketch her ideas but she also had to bring them to life. It wasn't frilly. It had a simple neckline with a beaded bodice that fit snugly. It was gathered just below the bodice and an embroidered hemline landed just above her knees.

She smoothed her hands over her midsection. She'd swear that she'd put on weight, but the scale in the bathroom said she hadn't gained an ounce. She turned to the side and puffed out her stomach, wondering what she'd look like months from now. They said your bustline expanded. She was looking forward to that part. Maybe then she'd be more than a padded B cup.

Everything about this pregnancy intrigued her, almost as much as all the unknowns and the forthcoming pain scared her. It might be easier if she had someone to go through it with her. Luca's handsome face came to mind, but she immediately dismissed it. He'd made it perfectly clear that he had no interest in extending his family line—title or no title. She'd never imagined that she'd end up a single mother, but sometimes you had to play the cards life dealt you—

"Elena! Elena, get down here." Her mother's voice was filled with urgency.

Oh, no! Elena rushed for the steps. Her mother must have reinjured herself. Elena had told her that she was doing too much, but her mother would not listen.

Elena almost missed the last step on the way down, but luckily she had her hand on the banister and was able to regain her balance. She rushed into the living room, where her mother was sitting in her favorite armchair.

"What's the matter?" Elena pressed a hand to her pounding chest.

Her mother's face was creased with frown lines. "This!" She turned the digital tablet Elena had gotten her for Christmas so Elena could see it. "Here. Take it. I can't look at it any longer. What are we going to do?"

Whatever her mother was going on about couldn't be nearly as bad as she was making it out to be. Her mother always did have a bit of an air for the dramatic. Elena took the tablet and gazed at the picture filling the screen.

It was an image of her…and Steven.

Elena's stomach plummeted down to her bare feet.

How could this be? They'd ended things the same day this picture was taken. She remembered wearing that exact outfit. This must be one of the photos the investigator had taken of them.

"Tell me it isn't true," her mother pleaded. "You'd never get involved with a married man. Right?" When Elena didn't say anything, her mother nervously chattered on. "I told your father that nothing good would come of you going so far from home. And now this. Well, what do you have to say for yourself?"

"Mother, I can't think when you keep going on like that. Just give me a second."

Her mother sighed but quieted down.

Elena scrolled down past the damning photo that was on a very popular tabloid website. The headlines read:

From Model to Home Wrecker!
Banking CEO Caught in Lover's Arms!
That Kiss Is Going to Cost Him Millions!

Elena's gaze stuck on the headlines as anger and humiliation churned within her. She forced herself to read the attached article. Word by painful word she choked down the lies and innuendo.

And the worst part was the press made it seem like that picture was new. It was more than two months old. She hadn't seen, much less talked to, Steven in that time. Nor did she intend to ever speak to him again. She'd been a victim here, but the press made it sound like she was a willing accomplice. She hadn't even known he was married. He'd conveniently forgotten to mention that part.

This was a disaster!

And it wasn't just her reputation that was on the line. It was going to affect her job, as her contract contained a morality clause. And when the paparazzi found out she was pregnant, they were going to jump to the wrong conclusion. It was like her life was a series of dominoes and now that the first one had fallen, the rest would follow. And it would end with Luca.

Luca!

She'd thought there would be time to speak with him. She'd thought she could break the news of her pregnancy to him gently. And now her best-laid plans were ruined. She had to get to him before he read these blatant lies.

"Well," her mother prompted, "what do you have to say for yourself?"

"I have to go." Elena turned to find her purse. She needed her phone. She had to call him. Had to warn him about the firestorm that was headed her way—and in turn their innocent baby's way.

"Go?" Her mother's voice rose to a screechy level. "Go where? We have to talk."

"I have something I need to do." Where was her purse? It had to be around here somewhere. She scanned the couch and the chairs in the living room. It wasn't there. *Think. Where did you leave it?*

Her thoughts were muddled and her pulse was racing. She was certain that all this stress wasn't good for the baby, but she wouldn't be able to calm down until she spoke with Luca.

She rushed to the kitchen. A quick scan of the house turned up her purse on the counter, where she'd placed it before preparing lunch for her mother and her friends.

"Elena, stop. You can't just rush out of here." Her mother balanced herself on her crutches in the doorway.

Elena paused at the front door to slip on her shoes. "I'm going. And you aren't going to stop me." Then, realizing that her mother was worried about her, she added, "Just concentrate on your card game. Don't worry about this. I have everything under control."

Her mother's face crumpled. Was she going to cry?

Elena hugged her mother. "I made a mistake. A huge mistake, and now it's coming back to bite me in a really big way. But it's not like the press is making out."

"Thank goodness. What can I do to help?"

"Forget you ever read that batch of lies." With her purse and phone in hand, she opened the front door. "I have something very important to do. Will you be all right?"

Her mother nodded. "Go ahead. I'm fine."

Elena rushed out the door and didn't slow down. She was a woman on a mission. She needed to speak to Luca before he read the headlines. Before he jumped to the wrong conclusion like the rest of the world.

Her fingers trembled as she reached for her phone. The display showed that she had three missed calls—all from

Lauren Renard. Elena's stomach knotted. The story was already making the rounds in short order. But Lauren would have to wait.

Right now, Elena's priority was Luca. She sought out his number on her phone. It rang once and went to voice mail. She disconnected and tried again. Once more, she was forwarded to his voice mail. She groaned inwardly.

"Luca, it's Elena. Call me when you get this message. It's important."

She disconnected the call. Where was he? And why did he have his calls forwarded to his voice mail today, of all days?

She could only hope he attended today's festivities. The invitation hadn't said what was planned for the day. It was going to be a surprise. Elena had to admit that initially she'd been quite intrigued with the mystery.

So far Annabelle had taken them on a fun trip down memory lane. Except for yesterday's spin the bottle game, Elena had enjoyed herself. Just the mere thought of that kiss yesterday sent heat rushing to her cheeks. She wondered if Annabelle was on to them.

Elena was still thinking all this over when she arrived at the far side of the palace. Before her stood a carnival, just like the ones they'd visited as kids. There was a Ferris wheel, game booths and food vendors. It was…it was amazing. Too bad she wouldn't get to enjoy any of it.

She walked around the small carnival, but she still hadn't spotted Luca. She couldn't imagine he'd miss it, not after he'd made the point that his attendance was mandatory.

"Elena, there you are." Annabelle and Grayson approached her. Annabelle wore a gleeful smile while holding cotton candy in her hand. "What do you think?"

It took Elena a moment to realize Annabelle was referring to the party and not to the nasty piece of gossip on the internet. "I think you've outdone yourself." Elena forced a smile on her face. "This entire week has been amazing."

"And it's not over yet." Annabelle reached for her fiancé's hand.

Elena did her best to act normal. "You're very lucky to have found someone so wonderful."

Annabelle blushed. "I know. Don't ask me how close I came to losing him."

"That wouldn't have happened." Grayson stared into Annabelle's eyes. "I know when I have a good thing. And you're the best."

"Aw…" Annabelle turned into his arms. She lifted on her tiptoes and pressed her lips to his.

Elena turned to walk away and leave the lovebirds alone—or as alone as they could be in the middle of a carnival. She really needed to find Luca.

"Elena, did you happen to see my brother?" Annabelle called out.

Elena turned back. "Actually, I was looking for him. I thought he would be here."

"I did, too, but he was distracted last night. He didn't even come down to dinner."

Oh, no. Had he heard something? Did he already know that she'd made a fool of herself in front of the whole world?

"So you haven't spoken to him since yesterday?"

Annabelle shook her head. "I wouldn't worry. It probably has something to do with my father arriving yesterday. Those two can get on each other's nerves."

"Well, if you see him, can you tell him that I'm looking for him?"

"I will. But before you go, I want to ask you something." Annabelle's expression grew serious.

"Um, sure. What do you need?"

"I, well, we wanted to know if you'd be in our wedding?"

"You want me to stand up for you?"

Annabelle smiled and nodded. "I know you're really busy now that you're a world-famous model, but the wedding is almost a year out. Please say that you'll do it. I know Luca would like it. A lot."

Elena wasn't so sure how to take Annabelle's last comment, so she just let it slide. "I'd be honored. Thank you for asking me."

Annabelle turned a triumphant look to Grayson. "I told you she'd do it. This wedding is starting to come together."

"I know it's going to be just as fabulous as your engagement," Elena said.

"Just not as fun," Grayson said.

"You'll just have to wait for the honeymoon." Annabelle sent him a devilish look.

Just then a man in a dark suit and sunglasses strode toward them. Elena guessed he was part of the palace security. She hoped nothing was wrong. But seeing as the man would want to speak with Annabelle, the king's niece, Elena was ready to make a quick exit.

"Looks like someone is searching for you." Elena pointed out the man.

"Oh." Annabelle frowned. "And here everything was going so well. I should have known it was too good to be true."

"Don't worry." Grayson rubbed his fiancée's shoulders. "Whatever it is, we'll get it straightened out and get back to the celebration."

Annabelle sent Grayson a worried look. "I hope so."

"I'll let you deal with it." Elena started to walk away.

"Ms. Ricci, could I speak to you?"

Elena paused at the sound of her name. An uneasy feeling inched down her spine. With great trepidation she turned to the man. "Yes?"

Out of the corner of her eye, she could see the surprised

look on Annabelle's face. Elena wondered if she was wearing a similar expression.

"Excuse me, ma'am. I was informed that you would be here."

"What can I do for you?"

"Ma'am, there are a bunch of reporters at the gate demanding to speak with you. What should we do?"

It felt as though the bottom had fallen out of her world. The article had just made the tabloid that morning and they were already seeking her out. She wondered what other information they had. She was certain that none of it would be good news.

"Did they say what they wanted?"

"No, ma'am."

Annabelle stepped up then. "Tell them to go away. Elena is my guest today, and she doesn't want to be hounded by the press."

"Yes, ma'am." The security guard pulled out his phone as he started to walk away.

"What do you think that's all about?" Annabelle asked.

"I...I have a confession." Elena's gaze dropped to the ground.

"That sounds awfully dire. Surely it can't be that bad."

Elena shrugged. "I guess it depends on how you look at it."

"I think I should go get another drink," Grayson said and slipped away.

"You don't have to tell me," Annabelle said.

"I do." Elena was so tired of keeping secrets. "There's a story in a tabloid and a photo linking me with a married man."

Annabelle's perfectly plucked brows rose, but she didn't say anything.

"It's not true. At least not like they are saying. I didn't

know he was married. He conveniently left that part out when we met. And it's been over for a while now."

Annabelle reached out and squeezed her arm. "It's okay. We've all made mistakes, but the paparazzi doesn't care about those mistakes unless you're an international public figure. I have a feeling this won't be your last time in the tabloids."

"I'd totally understand if you want me to go now. I don't want to ruin your party."

"Nonsense. You have to stay. We aren't going to let the paparazzi ruin our day."

"I don't think I'll ever get used to them."

"Me, either. We just have to stick together."

"Thanks for being so understanding." They shared a quick hug and then Elena said, "I think I'll go get a drink. It's a little warm out here today."

She moved away and spotted a lemonade stand. No doubt they'd used lemons from the DiSalvo lemon grove. They were the best. And she was thirsty. Hunting for Luca in the bright sunshine had her parched. And she didn't know where else to look for him…unless she was to search the palace. However, she doubted security was going to let that happen.

She stood in line for the lemonade. It seemed to be a popular stand. And she couldn't blame them. This was the best lemonade in the world. Not too sweet. Not too tart. It was just perfect. And any other day, she'd be excited to have some, but not today. Today she needed to find Luca before he stumbled across the lies and innuendos.

Once she had her refreshment in hand, she peered all around. He had to be here somewhere. But she couldn't spot him. She pulled out her phone and tried his cell. Again, it went to voice mail.

She'd just slipped the phone into her purse when she heard, "Elena, there you are."

She turned to find Luca approaching her. He was dressed casually in white shorts and a blue collared shirt with the sleeves rolled up. And she'd never seen him look more handsome. Of course, it helped that he was smiling right at her. He was like the sun, parting her clouds of gloom and doom.

He stepped up to her. "We need to talk."

"I know."

"You do?" Luca asked with a puzzled look on his face.

"Sorry. I thought you wanted to tell me about the press at the front gate."

He arched a dark brow. "No, but what are they doing here?"

She waved off his question, hoping he wouldn't make a big deal out of it. "It's nothing. We sent them away."

"We?"

"Your sister was here when one of the security guards stopped by. She instructed him to send the reporters away." And before he could question her further about the paparazzi, she asked, "So what did you want to talk to me about?"

Luca glanced around at the colorful tents. "It can wait until I win you a teddy bear at the ball toss."

So he really didn't know about the tabloid story. The breath that she didn't realize she'd been holding whooshed from her lungs. In actuality, she wasn't sure if this news made things better or worse for her. On second thought, it didn't do either. It just delayed the inevitable.

And then he paused and looked at her. She found herself staring into his blue-gray eyes. Some days they were bluer, but today they were a deeper gray. He had something on his mind. Just wait until he heard what she had to tell him. His eyes would turn dark and stormy.

"Elena, why are you frowning at me? I know I'm late to

the festivities, but you don't have to look that upset. What happened to bring the paparazzi here?"

She glanced around at all of the people they knew. This definitely wasn't the place to give him life-altering news. "I can't talk about it. Not here."

"Elena, there is obviously a problem. So out with it."

Just then her phone rang. She didn't even have to look at the caller ID to know it was Lauren again. She'd never called this many times in a row. With each phone call, Elena's hope of salvaging her job diminished.

"Do you need to get that?"

She shook her head. "It can wait. Can we go somewhere? Somewhere private?"

"Um, I haven't spoken to my sister yet, but she has enough distractions. I'm sure she won't miss me for a little longer."

They started walking toward the beach. All the while Elena searched for the right words. Was there such a thing? She hoped so.

"Elena? Hey, did you hear me?" Luca sent her a puzzled look.

"What did you say?"

"I said that you're really quiet today and you're starting to worry me."

He had no idea what was coming his way, and she felt bad for him. She didn't know whether to start with the tabloid story or the news of her pregnancy. Her stomach shivered with nerves.

Soon the worst will be over. It was the only positive thought she could dredge up, because her life was a scandalous mess.

CHAPTER EIGHT

WAS THERE ANY right way to say this?

Elena didn't think so. Maybe if they were a happy couple and madly in love. If that were the case, she'd do something cute—something memorable.

But in this case, she'd just have to settle for the blunt, honest truth.

They made their way down the long set of steps. She remained quiet, waiting until they were on the beach, where they wouldn't be disturbed. This conversation would be the most important one of her life. Once her feet touched the sand, she glanced up and down the beach, not spotting anyone.

"Okay. We're alone." Luca turned to face her. "What's bothering you?"

She gazed into his face. Her stomach started to churn again. And the words stuck in the back of her throat.

"Elena, you're really starting to worry me. Nothing can be this bad."

She nodded, trying to keep her emotions in check. "Yes, it can."

"Whatever it is, I'm here for you. You know that."

Her gaze rose to meet his. In his gaze, she found tenderness and warmth. She tried to impress that image upon her mind. She needed to remember this moment, because she doubted she'd see it again.

Where did she start? Did she blurt out about the pregnancy? Or did she start with the headlines? It was all such a mess.

She slipped off her shoes and started walking closer to the water. Letting the water wash over her feet always relaxed her in the past. She hoped it would do so again.

Luca walked beside her. He was quiet, as though giving her a moment to gather her thoughts. He was such a great guy. If he ever let down his guard, he'd make some woman a fantastic husband. It just wouldn't be her. They'd given it a shot in Paris, and it hadn't worked out. In fact, in the rays of the rising sun, it had gone from amazing to an utter disaster. The light of day had cast away all her silly romantic illusions and shed light on the stark reality—they did not belong together.

So what was she waiting for? It wasn't like they were a couple or even had a chance at a happily-ever-after. She might as well put it all out there and let the pieces fall as they may.

She stopped and turned to him. "This morning my mother found an article about me in the tabloids."

"And…"

She just couldn't look him in the eyes when she admitted the next part. She didn't want to see the disgust in his eyes. "And it had a picture of some loser kissing me. One of the headlines read, From Model to Home Wrecker!"

There was a slight pause as though he was digesting this news. "This is the guy you told me about in Paris?"

She nodded. "It's not true." She glanced up, willing him to believe her. "The whole thing is a twist of facts and lots of innuendo."

"I thought you ended things with him. That's what you said when I was in Paris."

"I did."

"Then how did they get a picture of you two kissing? And why is it showing up in the paper now?" Just as she predicted, his eyes were getting darker by the moment and clouds of doubt were forming.

Why did everyone in her life go for the worst-case scenario? Of course, the photo didn't help things. Before she could mount a reasonable defense, Luca pulled out his cell phone. And thanks to the beach being part of the royal grounds, the cell reception was excellent.

She wanted to beg him not to pull up the tabloid photo and article, but her pride resisted the urge. So what if he looked? It wouldn't change things. The tabloid was wrong. Surely he would see that. He knew her better. Knew that she would never knowingly cause problems in someone else's marriage.

She turned to stare out at the water. Usually she found it relaxing, but not today. Today all she could think about were all the mistakes she'd made in her life. And they seemed to be escalating this year. But that was going to stop. Here. And now. She had a baby to think about. She would do well by it.

She turned back to Luca. "There's more—"

"Did you read this?" His stormy gaze flickered to her and then back to the phone in his hand.

"It's nothing but lies."

"At the end, it says this jerk's wife filed for divorce. She's probably using this story as the basis for her multimillion-dollar settlement."

"And?"

He slipped his phone back in his pocket and stared at her. "Did you see this guy after you and I, well, after I visited you in Paris?"

"No. Of course not. Steven fooled me once with his flattery and lies. There's no way I would fall for his words again. I...I haven't seen anyone since you."

"And this story is the reason the press is at the palace gates?"

She lowered her head. "I had no idea they'd track me down here. I should leave Mirraccino."

"I can't think of any place better for you to be at this moment."

Her head lifted. "Really?"

"Yes. Here you have the best protection. No one will get near you. And eventually the paparazzi will get bored."

"I just don't understand why this is suddenly a story. I haven't seen Steven in almost three months."

His eyes momentarily widened, but then in a blink, his expression was unreadable. "Then I would say that picture suddenly appeared because the wife planted it, just in time for her to file for divorce."

"But the story made it sound like it just happened—as in yesterday."

"See, that's the thing. You were right here with me."

"Wait." She peered deep into his eyes. "You believe me?"

"Believe you? Of course I do. Why wouldn't I?"

She shrugged. "I don't know. I guess I'm just a bit on edge."

"Is this part of the reason you're in Mirraccino instead of in Paris, Milan or New York?"

She shook her head. "It has nothing to do with that story. In fact, there wasn't even a story until today."

"Then quit frowning. Everything will be all right. Give it one or two news cycles and the paparazzi will be on to another bit of sensationalized gossip." He reached out and pulled her into his arms.

She knew she should resist. She knew that things were complicated between them. But in that moment, she longed for the warmth and comfort she always felt in his arms. And so she let her body follow the pull of his arms.

Her chest pressed to his. Her arms wrapped around his trim waist. And her head landed on his broad shoulder. The stress ebbed away.

But then something happened that she hadn't been expecting. She breathed in his masculine scent, mingled with a spicy cologne. He smelled so good. She breathed in a little deeper. Oh, yes, she remembered being here—being held securely in his arms.

And it wasn't that long ago that they'd clung to each other like there was no tomorrow. Did he remember? Was that what he was thinking about right now?

Her whole body was alive with desire. It'd be so easy to turn her head just slightly and press her lips to the smooth skin of his neck. And then, realizing what she was about to do, she pulled away.

Luca gave her a puzzled look, and then he sighed. "Are you going to keep acting like this? Can't we just forget about what happened in Paris?"

She shook her head. "I can never forget."

"Sure you can, if you try. After all, we were friends a lot longer than we were lovers."

"Luca, quit trying to diminish it." That night had been very special to her even if it meant nothing to him.

He raked his fingers through his hair. "What can I do to make this better?"

"Nothing. Nothing at all."

"So that's it, we're always going to be awkward around each other? I can never put my arms around you to comfort you?"

"You don't understand. This isn't how I want things to be, but it's how they are."

"I don't understand. You're talking in circles."

He was right. She was being evasive on purpose. She was afraid to tell him that they would forever be linked.

"I'm pregnant." She hadn't intended to blurt it out, but at least it was finally out there.

"Pregnant?" Luca stumbled back a step as though the words had hit him with a one-two punch.

She nodded. The backs of her eyes stung with threatening tears. Darn hormones. She blinked repeatedly, refusing to play the emotional-woman card. She could get through the rest of this semirationally—she hoped.

His gaze searched hers. "You're sure?"

"Yes. I just saw the doctor last week for confirmation."

"Does he know? The guy in the photo?"

"Why would Steven know?"

"I would assume you'd tell the father, even if he's a total loser."

"I thought you believed me when I said it was only a kiss."

He shrugged. "People make mistakes. I thought maybe you were too embarrassed to admit it."

"First of all, he's not the father. Second, the baby's father is far from a loser. And lastly, I am telling him. Right now."

Luca's eyes momentarily widened. His lips pressed together into a firm line as the color drained from his face.

She'd never witnessed him speechless. He always had a quick comeback or a thoughtful comment. There was always something...until now.

The longer the silence dragged on, the more nervous she became. She had to do something, but what?

She knew this announcement was the last thing he'd expected to hear from her. "This was as much of a surprise for me as it is for you."

He shook his head as though he couldn't process it. He turned away and started walking—walking away from her. Just like he'd done in Paris. She'd let him go that time, but more than her broken heart was on the line this time.

She took off after him. "Luca, I know this is a shock. But we have to talk."

He stopped and faced her. The shocked look on his face told her just how caught off guard he was by this information. "Talk? Don't you think I deserve some time to absorb this information? After all, you've had how long?"

"A week or so. And I'm sorry I'm pushing this, but once the paparazzi finds out I'm pregnant, it's going to be a mess."

"Which won't be long, considering they're camping outside the palace gates." Luca turned and started walking again.

She walked with him. She hated having to push him, but the press was so close now. They were breathing down her neck—waiting for the next big headline. It was imperative that she and Luca do whatever they could to protect their child from scandal.

There was still so much to decide where the child was concerned. Would her child grow up here in Mirraccino? Doubtful. The only reason her parents lived on these amazing and sprawling grounds was because of her father's special affiliation with the king. If she wanted to move back to Mirraccino, she'd end up with an apartment in the city. Bellacitta was a thriving city that was a mix of old traditions and new technology. It certainly would be an interesting atmosphere to raise a child.

But she couldn't give up her future in Paris. If she remained there, her son or daughter would have the privilege of growing up in a city full of history, culture and endless ways to expand a young imagination. Luca could visit, or when she had time off, she could take their child to him. It would work out somehow.

But Luca wasn't helping her find any of those answers. She needed him to say something, or at least acknowledge what she'd told him.

She reached out, grabbing his arm. "Please, Luca, talk to me."

He stopped and faced her. "What do you want from me?"

"I don't know. I guess just to talk to me. Maybe to say that everything will be okay."

"Okay?" He ran his hand over the top of his hair, scattering the short, dark spikes. And then he expelled an audible sigh. "Just tell me one thing. Is it really my baby?"

Ouch! His question dug straight into her heart. Not so long ago, they'd accepted each other's words as fact without having to question. Obviously things had changed more than she'd ever imagined.

"I swear on my life that this baby is yours and mine. I didn't come to you expecting anything. I have enough of my own money to take care of the two of us. I just wanted you to know. It was the right thing to do."

"Then I would say, no, things aren't going to be all right. Those reporters at the palace gate, they are waiting for you and it has nothing to do with your work."

Elena's gaze lowered, and she shook her head. "They'll want some comment about the photo. But I didn't do anything they said. I went on a few dates with Steven. That's it. He told me he was divorced and lonely."

"How could you not know who he is?"

"He gave me a fictitious name, and quite frankly, I don't read the finance section of the paper. And he didn't give me any reason to doubt him." She worried her bottom lip as she internally berated herself. "I was such a fool."

"But smart enough not to sleep with him."

"Thank goodness."

There was one real reason why that wasn't an option for her. Steven didn't stack up to Luca. And though she tried not to, she couldn't help but compare everyone to Luca. Did that make her pathetic? She hoped not.

"And what will happen when they find out you're pregnant?" Luca looked worried. "The paparazzi is going to jump to conclusions, just like they did with that photo. They are going to tell the world that jerk is the father of my baby!"

There was so much emotion in that statement that Elena was caught off guard. Perhaps she'd been telling herself that he wouldn't care about the baby because he didn't care about her romantically—to soften his rejection. So where exactly did that leave them besides in a mess?

CHAPTER NINE

A BABY.

My baby.

Luca was having problems processing it all. A rush of emotions hit him like a tsunami. They swept away his breath and left him feeling unsteady.

I'm going to be a father.

Those were words he never thought he'd say. A tiny human was counting on him to get this right. Luca's gaze moved to Elena's still-flat midsection. It was so hard to believe there was a little human growing in there.

Luca raked a shaky hand through his hair. "Wow! This is a lot to take in."

"I know it is. Maybe I should go so you can think. Just know that I don't expect anything of you." She started to turn away.

"Wait. What?" Surely he hadn't heard her correctly.

"This mess with Steven, it's not your problem. I'll figure something out."

"Like what?"

She shrugged. "Maybe I'll just let the press have their say and ignore them. Eventually they'll catch on to a new story—a bigger story."

Luca shook his head. "No way. I refuse to let that scum be linked to our child."

"Like you can stop that from happening."

This was his moment to step up—to do the right thing. He'd never had anyone count on him so completely. The responsibility was enormous. He had no idea how to be a parent.

But he did know that no other man was going to take credit for fathering his child. No way! He refused to let that happen. He needed to head off the ensuing scandal. And there was only one way he could think of.

"We'll get married."

Elena shook her head in confusion. "I don't think I heard you correctly."

"Yes, you did. You and I, we're getting married."

"No."

"Yes. We have to. It's the only way."

Her eyes narrowed. "Did you just demand that I marry you?"

Had he? He supposed it might have sounded that way. Surely she had to see the logic of such a move. "This is what's best."

She shook her head. "No way. It's not what's best for me."

"Then think of our baby."

"I am thinking of the baby. And you forcing me into a loveless marriage isn't going to make any of us happy. Don't you remember Paris? That night—well, it didn't work out. Why in the world would you want to compound that mistake?"

"Because as you pointed out, this is about a lot more than you and me. There's the baby to consider. He or she will be the DiSalvo heir."

"Oh." The dejected look on her face told him that he'd said something wrong, but for the life of him he didn't know what it was.

"What does 'oh' mean?"

"Nothing. I'm just surprised."

"That I would want to marry you in order to protect our child?"

"I'm surprised that you would propose marriage at all. I thought you were a proclaimed bachelor."

"I was." He still wasn't comfortable with the idea of making a commitment. He hadn't had time to let it all settle in his mind. But time was running out before the press added two and two and got five. "Come on. Let's go."

"Go where?"

He sighed. Why wasn't she following this? "To get married. Once we do that, the problem is solved and the paparazzi will back off."

"Maybe it will fix one problem, but what about all the other problems it will create?" She shook her head. "I can't. I won't. I know you well enough to know that you don't want to get married, much less have children. I shouldn't have told you—"

"Yes, you should have. I don't know why you're fighting me on this. You have to see that I'm right."

"I don't see that. Just let me take care of this. You won't have to be bothered with me…or the baby. I'll go back to Paris and I'll refuse to name the father."

Was she even listening to what he was saying? She was going to compound this problem, whereas he planned to head it off from the start. "You'll just add fuel to the fire. The gossip will grow with every news cycle. By not naming me, it'll be like confirming that jerk is indeed the father."

She frowned. "Maybe you're right, but I can't do it. Binding us both to a…to a fake marriage, it just won't work."

He had to admit that she deserved better than to marry someone who couldn't love her the way she deserved to be loved. Perhaps he was broken inside. He hadn't chosen to shut down after his mother's death. It had just happened to him, like a raging case of the flu. No one wants it. No one expects it. And then pow! It hits you.

At least with the flu, you recover. Whatever happened to him the day his mother died, it hadn't gone away. His feelings just shut down—much like his father.

And so marriage had never been on his wish list. He knew it could become emotional warfare. All that emotional baggage wasn't something he wanted in his life.

But this was about so much more than what Elena deserved and what he wanted—there was now a baby involved. And this was no ordinary baby—it was the DiSalvo heir. His secret heir.

He cleared his throat. "Marriage is the only way I can think of to protect our child and give him or her a legitimate claim to their heritage."

Elena didn't move for a moment. And when she spoke, it was so soft that he had to strain to hear her. "Perhaps you're right." She paused as though gathering her thoughts. "On some level, your idea makes some sense—"

"Good. We have to do what is right for the child." He was finally getting through to her. He drew in a deep breath, hoping that everything was finally resolved. "Elena, I'm going to ask you one more time. Will you agree to marry me?"

"No." There wasn't even the slightest hesitation in her quick answer. She waved her hands, as though to chase away the idea. "I…I can't do this." A tear slipped down her cheek, and she swiped it away. "It's too much. Too fast. Too…wrong."

"Elena, don't do this. Don't do this to us—to our child."

This time it was Elena who took off down the beach, but she wasn't walking. She was running. Her long hair fluttered in the breeze.

Luca swore as he watched her run away from him. He'd never imagined if he proposed to someone she would run away in tears. Why did it seem as though he was always making Elena cry?

Part of him wanted to let her keep running until she wore herself out. And the other part of him wanted to go to her and comfort her. He was torn by the tumultuous emotions. And for a man used to keeping his emotions in check, this was a lot.

He realized that from this day forward, he would have

not one but two people to worry about—to protect. He knew just how unpredictable life could be, and he couldn't imagine living through another loss. His heart just couldn't take it.

And it didn't help that Elena was already a darling of the paparazzi. Her life was routinely on display for all the world to see—including potential stalkers.

However, his father would be thrilled to know the DiSalvo line would continue—someone to carry on the lemon grove. If there was still something to hand down. And that was Luca's fault. He shouldn't have let the distance between them become a yawning canyon with no footbridge to connect them.

But that problem was going to have to wait. First, he had to convince Elena to marry him. Knowing her as well as he did, she wouldn't make it easy on him.

And so he had to make it hard for her to turn him down.

He reached for his phone. This was going to take some work, but he would make her his bride in short order. And he would claim his baby—his baby. The words sounded surreal.

Life certainly did change on the spin of a coin.

Yesterday, he'd had a firm grip on his life. And today, he and Elena were having a baby.

And somehow, some way, they were getting married.

He'd make it happen. But it was going to take a little more forethought than he'd first envisioned. And he had no time to waste.

CHAPTER TEN

SHE WAS TRAPPED.

The paparazzi was camped out on the perimeter of the palace gates like leeches, just waiting to suck the life out of her.

Elena turned away from the roving cameras of the press. She'd been hoping that their fascination with her would end quickly, but that wasn't to be. It was open season on her life, and the reporter with the first exposé or telling photo would make a bundle.

And after speaking with Lauren Renard, Elena learned the painful truth—she'd been dropped from the fashion line. All her scheduled shoots had been canceled. Her contract was to be voided. And her name was on the lips of everyone in the know throughout Paris.

Without being spotted, Elena retreated to the royal gardens. Where she normally took solace in the serenity of the colorful blossoms and the gentle, perfumed air, today she didn't notice any of it. Her insides were tied up in knots. What was she going to do?

Luca's parting words kept repeating in her mind like a broken record.

Don't do this to us—to our child.

Normally, she'd blow off such a rushed, heat-of-the-moment proposal. No one would mean such a thing. After all, it wasn't like they were a couple. This pregnancy, it wasn't supposed to happen. *They* weren't meant to happen.

But a marriage proposal from Luca was different. He was not a man to throw around such words whether casually or in the heat of the moment. She knew him—or at least she thought she did. But everything had changed so dramatically between them since that night in Paris. Now, she questioned whether she'd ever known him at all.

Too restless to sit down, she started walking with no destination in mind. She moved past the garden gates and into the field of sunflowers. Blind to the world around her, she could only envision the *what if*s and *might have*s that this pregnancy had brought into her world.

She moved to the cliff overlooking the sand and sea. The breeze rushed past her, combing through her hair. Despite the beauty of this particular spot with the azure-blue sky, the sunshine dancing upon the water and the sailboat in the distance bobbing with each swell, all Elena could think about was that her life had come to a fork in the road.

The decisions she was about to make were so much more enormous than when she'd had to choose between attending college here on the island or pursuing a modeling career in Paris. To a young girl of eighteen who had led a sheltered life, venturing to a big city—even one as romantic as Paris—had still been a scary idea, especially when she knew absolutely no one there.

But now she had to make a decision not only for herself, but also for her child. The road to the left was one for just her and her baby. It would be them against the world. And if she took the road to the right, she envisioned herself holding her child's hand with Luca holding their child's other hand. Which was the right answer for all of them?

She started to walk again. Her head pulsed with chaotic thoughts of possible scenarios for her future. Her hand pressed to her midsection, feeling a protective instinct that she'd never felt before. She might disagree with Luca on numerous things, but there was one thing they agreed on. They had to do what was right for their child.

Their child.

The words stuck in her mind. As much as she wanted to make all the decisions about this baby, she couldn't.

They'd created this tiny life together, and it was only right that they share the decisions. It was her first solid resolution, and it felt right.

And then another thought came to her: she downright refused to be dictated to by Luca or anyone else. In that moment, it didn't matter to her one iota that Luca was an earl or that his uncle was the king. They would make decisions together—she would not bend to his will.

Elena stopped walking. Suddenly she was feeling a bit better. Her jumbled thoughts were starting to gain some clarity. Even the pounding in her head was starting to subside.

When she glanced around, she realized that she'd been drawn back to one of her childhood haunts. And it was looking none too good. The little cabin had been abandoned eons ago, but as kids, she and Luca had worked to patch up the roof with branches and leaves. They made it into their secret clubhouse.

She stepped inside and glanced up, finding most of the roof was now gone. So much for their repairs. She smiled at the memory of them working so hard together. Back then, it was so much easier for them to communicate.

Why couldn't life be like it used to be?

The sound of an engine cut through her thoughts. It was getting closer. Who in the world would be riding around out here at the far reaches of the royal estate? And then she realized that it was probably the security guards making their rounds.

She stepped outside to let them know of her presence, not wanting to alarm them. But when her gaze adjusted to the bright sunshine, she found that it was not a guard seated behind the wheel of the navy blue Jeep with the royal crest emblazoned across the hood. It was Luca.

He jumped out. "So this is where you ended up?"

"I…uh, was just walking."

"That's some walk. It's been a few hours since you left me on the beach."

"I had a lot of thinking to do." She wasn't so sure she wanted to get into it all now. "How did you find me?"

"After I checked your parents' place and the gardens, this place came to mind. You always used to come here when you were upset." He stepped past her and entered the cabin. He looked around before returning to her side. "I wonder if our child will find this spot and make it their clubhouse."

"I...I don't know." She supposed that it was a possibility when she visited her parents.

Luca moved to stand in front of her. "Listen, I'm sorry about earlier. I didn't handle that very well."

"You're right. You didn't." And surprisingly, she wasn't furious with him any longer. "How about we write it off to shock? You didn't know what you were saying."

"But see, that wouldn't be the truth." He reached out for her hand, but she stepped back. "I did mean it when I said we should get married."

She shook her head. "Not like this. I don't want anyone to marry me because they have to."

"It's not that way." He shifted his weight. "I could walk away, but I'm not."

Elena let out a nervous laugh. "I can hear it now. At one of your sister's parties, someone will ask, 'And how did Luca propose to you?' And I'll say, 'He fell on his sword to save me and my child from the monstrous press.'" She shook her head, dispelling the awful scene. "Not exactly the romantic beginning to a marriage that a girl would hope for."

His eyes widened as though a thought had just come to him.

She didn't want to know his new idea. It was best that they end things here while they were still speaking to one another.

She lifted her chin and met his gaze. "I should be going."

"Wait." He reached for her hand. "I know I messed things up when I proposed to you earlier—"

"You didn't propose." Her gaze narrowed. "You practically ordered me to marry you."

His mouth opened, but nothing came out. And then at least he had the decency to look a tad embarrassed.

As much as she'd like to tell him that his idea of them getting married was preposterous, she couldn't. She hadn't thought of any other way to protect the baby and pass on the proper legacy their child deserved. If she were to marry Luca, their child would fit in—unlike her, who was forever on the outside looking in.

Luca craned his neck, looking at their surroundings. What was he looking for?

"Of all the places with flowers on this estate, why couldn't there be some here?" he said with a sigh.

"Flowers?" It took her a moment to realize that he wanted to collect them for her. Her heart picked up its pace at the realization that he was trying to do this proposal thing properly. "I don't need flowers. But I do need us to come to terms."

"Terms? What sort of terms?"

"I agree with you. Our child deserves to have their legacy. But this will be a marriage on paper only."

"Are you sure that's what you want?"

Was he hoping that she'd change her mind? She couldn't quite tell by his tone. Or was he making sure she didn't want more from him than he was willing to offer?

"I'm sure. We'll have separate beds and separate lives."

"Not so fast on the separate lives. If we want everyone, including the paparazzi, to believe the baby is mine, we're going to have to present a happy front."

He was right. Still, she hesitated. Could she really agree to this arrangement? It was so cold and calculated.

Luca took a steadying breath and then dropped to his knee. He took her hand in his. And then he gazed up into her eyes.

"Luca, what are you doing?"

"Proposing. If you'll let me."

"But you don't have to—"

"I want to."

"And what about your sister?"

He frowned. "What does any of this have to do with Annabelle?"

"It's her week. You know, *her* engagement celebration."

"And?"

"And we can't let anyone know that we've gotten engaged. It'll overshadow Annabelle's moment in the spotlight."

"First of all, I'm not proposing an engagement. I want you to elope with me. Today. Right now. As for my sister…" Luca rubbed the back of his neck. "We won't tell anyone about our marriage until after the reception on Saturday. Okay?"

Elena's heart was pounding so hard that it echoed in her ears. "But—"

"Shush. Let me do this before I forget what I'm going to say."

She pressed a hand to her mouth, but her gaze never left his. This was it. He was going to propose and then they were to be married. It would all be done so quickly, so neatly. No fanfare. No frilly dress. No romantic moments.

And yet, she could not deny that it was best for their child. She could no longer put her needs and wants first. She was about to be a mother.

"Elena, we've known each other since we were little kids playing in the palace gardens. You've been there with me through the best and worst times of my life. Somehow it seems fitting that we are pledging to join our lives officially. I promise to always be there for you and for our child. Will you marry me?"

Tears ran down her cheeks. Instead of tears of joy, they were tears of sadness. This wasn't how she'd imagined this moment working out. And her pregnancy hormones were working overtime, making her a sappy mess.

He removed the ring from his pinkie. "I know you're expecting a diamond, but I didn't have a chance to get you one. I hope you don't mind if I use this as a temporary substitute under the circumstances."

She gazed down at the gold ring with his family's crest engraved upon it. Luca held it poised at the end of her finger. She couldn't believe that this was all really happening. It was like she was moving through a dream.

And then she nodded her head. "Yes, I'll marry you—we'll marry you."

He placed one hand over her still-flat abdomen. With the other hand, he slid the ring on her finger. It was a little tight, but it would do.

This was the beginning of a whole new future for her, him and their baby.

CHAPTER ELEVEN

THE HEAVILY TINTED town car eased out of the palace gates.

It appeared the paparazzi was off chasing another story. Elena breathed a sigh of relief.

But that was just the first hurdle. They still had to conduct a secret wedding. Just the thought of exchanging *I do*s with Luca made her stomach quiver. When she was a teenager, she'd imagined that one day they might marry. But that was when she was still young and foolish. After all, he was an earl, one day to become a duke, and at the time she'd been a nobody. Why would he have ever considered marrying her?

It wasn't until much later in life that she realized all of Luca's grumbling and resentment about the institution of marriage wasn't just a smoke screen to keep her at bay. He really meant it. She'd felt sorry for him. She couldn't imagine living such a lonely life and never allowing anyone to get close.

And now she was dooming herself to a loveless marriage. She banished the thought as soon as it came to her. There was no backing out now. Luca had made a flurry of phone calls. The arrangements were in motion.

Elena pressed a hand to her abdomen, thinking about their unborn child. At least their son or daughter would now be legitimate. They wouldn't be excluded and press their nose to the glass to see all the dressed-up people at the formal dinners and balls. That thought was what kept her quiet as the black town car ushered them through the streets of Bellacitta.

They'd already stopped at the jewelry store, the courthouse and the dress shop, and now they were headed to a little chapel just outside the city—a place where they would have the privacy to say their vows without the paparazzi lurking about.

She nervously played with Luca's ring that was still on her ring finger. She remembered when he'd received the ring from his father. He'd been thirteen. His father had told him that he was growing into a man and this was his future—his destiny.

She had been awed not only by the beautiful ring with the intricate crest, but also the fact that Luca had a destiny to fulfill. She didn't have any such thing. Her family was ordinary, and she'd always longed to be extraordinary. And she'd almost done it. She had been on her way to having one of the most famous faces in the world.

But now she was pregnant. Her future as a model was over. Sure, she could lose the weight. Maybe she could avoid stretch marks. But even if she could regain the same figure—and that was a big *if*—she would have lost her traction in the business. Her slot would be filled by younger, more glamorous girls. She would forever be playing catch-up, and in the process, her child would only get bits and pieces of her time.

"What has you so quiet?" Luca asked as he leaned back against the black leather upholstery.

"Just thinking how far we've come since you received this ring from your father."

"It seems like a lifetime ago."

"Will your father be happy about the baby?" She hoped so. She wanted her child to be surrounded by love.

"My father will be over the moon that I'm finally doing what he's always wanted—settling down with a family and taking over the business."

"Wait." She sat up straight and turned to him. "You're taking over the business? Since when? What about your job in Milan?"

"Things have changed since I've been here. Certain matters have come to light, but we don't need to get into all that now. We have a wedding to go to."

"You're sure you want to go through with this marriage?" Elena asked for about the fifth time that afternoon.

"Quit asking. The answer is always going to be the same. Yes, I want to marry you."

If only he meant that for all the right reasons. She had no illusions about this marriage lasting, and so she would have to guard her heart. Letting herself think this marriage was anything but a show would be a disaster for her and her child. She had to stay strong for her unborn baby.

He'd never imagined that he'd be doing this.

Luca stood at the front of the chapel in his new suit. While Elena had picked out a white dress for the ceremony, he'd decided that a new suit was in order. Luckily, they had one in his size.

He resisted the urge to tug at his collar as the pianist played the wedding march. This was it. He was doing the one thing he'd vowed never to do—getting married.

But if he had to marry anyone, he was thankful it was Elena. They were compatible. Or at least they used to be. They'd shared more than twenty years of friendship. Surely they could draw on that and find common ground.

And then she appeared at the end of the aisle. It didn't matter that there were no guests. They had asked the photographer and his assistant to bear witness, and that was all they needed. The only important people were standing right here in this historic chapel.

As she made her way up the aisle, the photographer took numerous pictures. Elena seemed surprised that there was a photographer present, but with the help of Luca's assistant, he'd tended to as many wedding details that he could think of. And he figured that with the lack of any family present, Elena could share these photos with family and friends.

But he wouldn't need any photos.

There was no way he would forget his beautiful bride. Her dress was white and tea length, falling just below her knees. The straps were off the shoulder and the bodice fit her snugly. It was as if the dress had been made for her. She took his breath away. Too bad this wasn't a real marriage—wait, had he really thought that?

Before he could delve further into his thoughts, Elena stepped up to his side. With one hand clasping a colorful bouquet of pink and white peonies, she slipped her free hand into his.

The older minister peered at them over his reading glasses. "Have you both come here of your own free will?"

Luca felt the initial tightening of Elena's hand. He willed her to stay calm. He knew she didn't want to marry him but that she would do it for the love of their child.

"I have," Elena said softly.

"I have, too."

And so the minister went through the ceremony. Luca didn't know what he expected to feel, but as the minister said, "Until death do us part," Luca felt the walls go up around him. He knew he shouldn't shut down, but he couldn't help it. The devastation of his mother's murder still had lingering effects.

He'd witnessed how his father had utterly withdrawn from their family after his mother died. His father had always been working and never had time for his children—children who were hurting, too, and left to find their way through the darkness alone.

Luca couldn't imagine giving his heart to Elena—if she even wanted it—and then losing her. It was better to keep a wall between them. It was safer. For both of them.

But above all, this marriage would allow Luca to claim his heir—the future of the DiSalvo name. Luca's father would have no choice but to recognize that Luca was now all grown up and responsible—responsible enough to take over the family business and turn it around. Where he'd once felt a family obligation to fix things when his father asked for help, Luca now felt driven to keep the business and the title viable. It was a new experience for him.

"I now pronounce you husband and wife. You may kiss the bride."

Elena looked at him with a wide-eyed stare. It wasn't exactly the passionate look that he'd expected to find on his bride's face. Still, it was up to them to convince people that the marriage was real—no matter how temporary.

His gaze dipped to her pink, glossy lips. Her mouth had tormented him each night in his dreams. Her sweet kisses had left him longing for more. And now he had the perfect excuse to kiss her once more.

But he hesitated. Common sense told him to make it a quick peck. He could feel the minister's expectant gaze on him.

Luca pulled Elena close. And for a moment, he stared into her eyes. They were the most beautiful shade of forget-me-nots. The name was most fitting, as her eyes were quite memorable. In fact, they were totally unforgettable. Every time he stared into her eyes, it was like she spun a spell over him. Just like now…

His head lowered and he claimed her lips. And then, forgetting about this being a quick peck, he drew her even closer. In that moment, nothing mattered but them. Forgetting that they were still in the church, he deepened the kiss. Elena opened her mouth, welcoming him inside. Her kiss was extraordinary, and he didn't think he would ever take it, or her, for granted.

He didn't want to let her go. Because once he released her, he knew that the wall dividing them would immediately come back up. And though it might be safe behind that wall, it was also cold and lonely. But with Elena in his arms, there was a warmth growing and spreading within his chest.

Just then Elena pressed her palms to his chest and pulled back from him. Reality came crashing back in, popping the bubble of happiness that had momentarily encapsulated them. Luca glanced away, not wanting her to realize how that kiss had moved him.

Luca realized that going forward he had to be careful around her. Happiness didn't last. He'd learned that lesson the hard way. First, with his mother dying. And finally with his father hiding within his work and ignoring his children.

Luca had done the only thing he knew how to do at the time—let loose and lived life to its fullest—even risking life and limb routinely. But now he knew how to curb those urges. He knew how to tuck his feelings into that little box in his chest.

He could do this—he could be the public husband Elena needed. And he could be the father to his child that his father had never been to him.

CHAPTER TWELVE

SO NOW WHAT?

Elena sat next to Luca as their chauffeured car made its way across the city. She stared at her bridal bouquet. She was now Mrs. DiSalvo.

With the shock of what they'd just done starting to wear off, reality was hitting her hard. A whole gamut of emotions warred within her, leaving her stomach in a knot.

Elena DiSalvo. Mrs. DiSalvo. Mrs. Luca DiSalvo.

And what was up with that kiss at the altar? If that had all been for show, it was quite convincing—too convincing. There was more to that kiss than Luca doing his husbandly duty. If he was hoping to change her mind about sharing a bed, it wasn't going to happen. No matter how many heart-fluttering kisses he plied on her.

She glanced over at Luca, but he appeared preoccupied with his phone. She wondered if this was what their future would be like if they were to stay together—awkward and quiet. The funny thing was, before they'd slept together, their relationship had flowed easily. Before that night, they'd been able to laugh and joke around. But now, post-sex, things were so different.

She gazed out the window at the passing cityscape. This definitely wasn't the way back to the palace. "Luca, where are we going?"

"You'll find out soon enough."

"But your sister will be wondering where we went."

"I'm certain my sister is well distracted by her new fiancé."

Elena couldn't argue with that statement. Annabelle had never looked happier than she had this week. She was practically glowing.

That was the way a woman should look when she was getting married. It wasn't how Elena had looked today. And she knew it was selfish, because they'd done what they needed to for their baby. But she couldn't help but feel as though she'd missed out on something very profound and moving.

Sadness crept over Elena. This wasn't how she'd envisioned her wedding day. When she was younger, she'd dreamed about her wedding being the happiest day of her life. Of rose petals lining her path, with her family looking on and her eager groom awaiting her at the end of the aisle.

She stared blindly out the window. Tears pricked the backs of her eyes, but she blinked repeatedly, willing them away. After all, those had been dreams of a gullible young girl. She was now a mature woman who knew that life rarely lived up to anyone's dreams.

This marriage was a means to an end. A business arrangement of sorts. Try as she might, none of those explanations soothed the throb in her chest.

The car slowed down and turned into an underground garage. Elena was jarred from her thoughts, but it was too late to look around to figure out where they were. She was certainly confused.

"Luca, what have you done?"

His brows scrunched together. "Why do you make it sound like I've done something wrong?"

"I don't know. Have you?"

"Certainly not. I just thought the occasion deserved something extra."

"Extra?" She had no idea what he meant by that comment.

And Luca wasn't offering any other clues.

When the car pulled to a stop, the driver opened the door for her. She stepped out into the garage next to a bank of elevators. Luca rounded the car and took her hand. He led her to the farthest elevator and pressed a button. Instantly the doors swept open. Inside he swiped a card and pressed another button labeled PH1.

"Luca, what are you up to?"

"It's a surprise."

"Don't you think we've had enough of those for one day?" The excitement of the day really had taken a lot out of her. Especially as she found herself getting tired easier than normal since she'd become pregnant.

"I promise, soon you can rest."

She sent him an I-don't-believe-you look. "Just tell me what you're up to."

He didn't say a word as he stared straight ahead.

The anticipation was getting to her. She had to admit that normally she loved surprises and Luca knew it. But today was far from normal. What in the world did he have planned?

The doors swished open to reveal an expansive suite decorated mostly in white with strategically placed wine-colored accents. One wall consisted of floor-to-ceiling windows that looked out over the beautiful city. The soft golden rays from the setting sun gave the place a warm, inviting glow.

She turned to Luca. "I don't understand."

And then, without warning, Luca lifted her into his arms.

"What are you doing? Put me down."

"Smile for the camera." Luca smiled and nodded toward the photographer and his assistant, who had been at the church.

She forced a smile while the photographer snapped one photo after the next.

"Could I have one of you two kissing before you put her down?" the photographer asked. He obviously wasn't in on the fact that their marriage was for show only.

"Of course," Luca said a little too eagerly. And then he looked at her as though begging her to just go with it.

Luca's hands gripped her tighter as he rolled her body closer to his. As his face drew closer, her pulse raced. This wasn't a good idea. And yet neither moved to stop it.

Their gazes met and held. In the background, the camera flashed. But for Elena, all she could see was the desire reflected in Luca's eyes. Was she looking at him the same way?

He didn't have to beg. The truth was that she enjoyed his kisses, a lot. A whole lot.

Just then he pressed his lips to hers. Was it wrong that she was grateful for this excuse to kiss him? And what would happen when their excuses for being intimate faded away?

She'd be left with these delicious memories. And so she took advantage of the moment. She wrapped her arms around his neck and deepened the kiss. He tasted minty and delicious. And his kiss was filled with passion and promises of more.

Elena couldn't write off the rush of desire as a little too much champagne, because she hadn't had any. Nor would she have any in her condition. So did that mean all these rising emotions were real?

Luca pulled back and gently lowered her feet to the ground. His gaze met hers. They stared at each other for a moment as though they were each trying to figure out what had just happened. But with the photographer walking them through various poses—from sipping nonalcoholic apple cider to cutting the cake—they didn't get a chance to discuss what had happened during that kiss. Maybe it was for the best. Emotions were running high today, and it was hard to tell what was real and what was an exaggeration.

And then there was their first dance as husband and wife. Luca knew she enjoyed jazz, and so he put on "It

Had to Be You" by Tony Bennett and Carrie Underwood. The volume was just right to wrap around them, cocooning them from the outside world and transporting them to a place where normal rules didn't apply.

She paused for a second, wondering if Luca had picked out this specific song on purpose. It wouldn't be unrealistic. She hadn't missed his detailed level of planning for this rushed wedding. If she wasn't careful, she'd start to get caught up in this fantasy and believe that this wedding was real in every aspect.

The rays of the setting sun on the distant horizon painted the penthouse a warm gold. The piano music played and Tony Bennett's soft voice filled the air about them. This whole scenario was amazingly romantic.

As Luca's arms wrapped around her, her thoughts went back in time. When they were kids and weren't permitted to attend the palace balls, she would put on her finest dress and Luca would be in his school uniform. They would dance in the grand foyer. They'd both ended up laughing as they pretended to be all grown up and used proper mannerisms.

But tonight there was no pretending. They were adults, and being proper didn't appear to be on the agenda this evening. Luca held her close—quite close. And it was taking all of her will not to rest her cheek against his shoulder.

When her body accidentally brushed against Luca, need flared within her. She wanted her husband with every fiber of her body. Her insides heated up as desire pooled in her core.

The breath caught in her throat. *This can't be happening.* She couldn't give in to her longings.

Luca leaned close and whispered, "Relax."

The way his breath tickled her ear sent goose bumps racing down her arms. All the while, she had to think about something else—anything but the way her body was responding to Luca's. She focused on the lyrics of the song playing in the background. It was a duet, and they were singing about finding that special someone and how fate played a role.

But Elena hadn't found that special someone. She wasn't even looking. She didn't want to be lied to again.

Not that Luca would lie. He'd tell her straight up that he didn't love her. He had a double-reinforced wall about his heart and there was no breaking through it. He made sure of it.

The thought made her sad.

This wedding—this whole day—was too realistic. And yet, it was all a show. She couldn't let herself get caught up in it. Even the song was surely just a coincidence.

The backs of her eyes burned with unshed tears. These darn hormones had her reacting to things that she would otherwise be able to shrug off.

Luca continued to twirl her around the floor. She attempted to put a respectable distance between them. Because if she wasn't careful, she was going to get swept up in this piece of fiction. In the end, she would have nothing but a broken heart. And that would forever ruin her relationship with Luca. How could they raise a child together if nothing existed between them but hostility?

Just then the music switched to a love song by Frank Sinatra. The beautiful lyrics made her think of everything they were both deprived of by this empty marriage. They were doomed to live a lie.

Oh, no! This is just too much.

Elena pulled herself out of Luca's arms. Her gaze sought out the hallway and then she ran. She didn't know where she was running to, but she just couldn't pretend to be the loving bride any longer. The photo session was over. The whole thing was over. This was a mistake. A big mistake.

She just needed a few minutes to gather herself. And for

those stupid love songs to stop playing. She didn't want to think about how things were supposed to be. She was having enough problems dealing with how things were.

Elena ran to the first bedroom she came across and threw the door shut with a resounding thud. She willed Luca not to follow. She didn't know what to say to make this situation all right for both of them.

CHAPTER THIRTEEN

ONE MOMENT SHE was in his arms…

The next she was gone.

Luca stood there, watching as his wife ran away from him.

What had happened? He thought he was doing a good thing. He knew that Elena never imagined this for her wedding, but he'd wanted to give her some nice memories. He'd tried to remember all her favorite things, from the chocolate cake with raspberry ganache to the jazz music.

It hadn't been easy to arrange this evening on the spur of the moment, but thankfully he had a well-connected assistant. He had every intention of bribing her to follow him to Halencia. He could well imagine his perfect assistant handling the business while he was spending time with his family.

That was, if he still had a family. Why had Elena run off?

Maybe he'd tried too hard.

The thought was driven home by the lyrics of love reverberating off the walls and enveloping him. That had definitely been a miscalculation. What did they say? That hindsight was crystal clear? In that moment, he knew exactly what that meant.

Luca strode over to the stereo system and switched off the music. And then he turned to the photographer and his assistant. After thanking them for making room for them in their schedule, Luca showed them to the door. He didn't give them any explanations—mainly because he didn't have any.

He wished he knew exactly what had upset his bride.

Was it the music? Was she that miserable being married to him? Or was it the pregnancy hormones?

Was it wrong that he hoped for the last option?

Luca rubbed the back of his neck and stared down the hallway. It seemed like a lifetime since he'd been able to talk to Elena casually. Before Paris, he'd known how to make her smile. He'd known which words to say to encourage her when one of her projects seemed insurmountable. He'd known how to make her laugh out loud until happy tears pooled in her eyes.

And yet, he realized it really wasn't that long ago that he'd had his best friend. If only he hadn't broken the cardinal rule of best friends—don't sleep together. Since that unforgettable night, he'd lost his ability to speak to Elena without upsetting her. And this evening was no exception.

With much trepidation, he stopped in front of the closed bedroom door. He still didn't have a clue what to say to her. *I'm sorry*? But he wasn't sure what he was sorry for.

He rapped his knuckles on the door. "Elena?"

No answer.

"Elena, please talk to me."

Again, there was no answer. Worry settled in.

He knocked again. "Elena, I'm coming in."

He tried the doorknob, but it was locked. Surely she didn't feel that she had to lock the door around him. What in the world was happening to them?

"Elena, you're worrying me. Please tell me you're all right."

"I'm fine."

He breathed a sigh of relief. "Will you let me in so we can talk?"

"No. I don't want to talk."

Now what? He wasn't just going to walk away. There had to be a way to fix things. He lowered himself to the floor. He leaned his back against the doorjamb.

"I'm not going anywhere," he said as a matter of fact. "I'm going to stay right here until we work this out."

No response.

He would keep talking and hopefully he would get through to her. It'd worked in the past. But that had been when they were kids, when Elena hadn't understood why he got to do things at the royal palace that she was not permitted to do. At the time, he hadn't understood, either. When you're a kid, social status doesn't mean anything, especially when the person in question is your best friend. But now that their circumstances had shifted dramatically, he didn't know how to deal with the changing landscape.

If he was this confused, he couldn't imagine that Elena was doing any better, considering she was pregnant. The thought of the baby—his baby, *their* baby—was still mind-blowing. And maybe the wedding celebration on top of it all had been a bad choice.

He leaned his head against the door. "I only meant to make you happy today. I heard you on the beach when you said you wanted to be able to tell people about your engagement. I thought that would extend to your wedding. I wanted to make it a special memory for you. I knew I couldn't give you the magical day you've always dreamed of, but I tried to make it not so depressing."

This was so much harder than he'd ever imagined. "I know ours isn't a marriage made of love, but it's one based on a lifetime of friendship. Maybe it will be stronger than others. Because whether you believe it or not, I'm still your friend. I know that you hate peas. That you're afraid of horror movies. And that your favorite color is purple. And I really, really miss my friend. Is there any chance I can have her back?"

The silence dragged on, and he didn't know what else to say.

Then the lock clicked, and the door snicked open. And

there stood Elena. He got to his feet. The sadness in her eyes ripped at his heart. Was he responsible for all this?

He didn't think about it; he just reacted. He reached out and pulled her into his arms. And to his surprise, she wrapped her arms around him. Her head rested on his shoulder.

This right here—it was right. He felt calm and centered when she was in his arms. Or maybe it was because she wasn't upset with him any longer. It didn't matter. He just had to keep the peace. It was good for them and it was good for the baby.

When they pulled apart, he noticed the tear marks that had smudged her makeup. He didn't say a word about it and pretended he didn't notice. He took her by the hand, which he immediately noticed was cold.

He guided her over to the bed, where they sat side by side. She picked up something. It looked like a slip of paper. The way she held it made it seem important.

"What do you have there?" he asked.

Her gaze moved to him and then back to the paper. "It's a picture of our baby."

That was the last thing he'd expected her to say. The thought of seeing their baby for the first time filled him with anxiety. It would make this so real—so binding.

Suddenly he felt trapped, and the walls were closing in on him. He got to his feet and started to pace. This wasn't how an expectant father was supposed to feel. What was wrong with him? He'd failed his family, and now he was about to fail his child.

"Don't you even want to see it?" Elena's voice interrupted his thoughts.

He stopped next to her.

She handed over the black-and-white photo. He stared at it. This was his baby?

He squinted, trying to make out more than a blob. Try as he might, he didn't see anything that resembled a baby.

"What's the matter?" Elena asked.

"Ah…what?" He wasn't sure what to say that wouldn't get him in more trouble.

"You were frowning when you looked at the sonogram. If you don't want anything to do with the baby, just say so."

Luca shook his head. He decided to leave his uncertainties about his parental abilities unspoken. "It's just that I can't make out the baby. It's just such a…"

"Go ahead. You can say it. It's a blob. I call it my little peanut. That's the gestational sac. It was too early to make out the baby."

"Oh." He sat down on the edge of the bed and gave her the photo. "I thought I was missing something."

"Just relax. We both have a lot to learn."

It was nice to know that he wasn't in this all alone. "I'm really sorry I made such a mess of things today with the wedding and the reception."

She looked at him. "You didn't. It…it was really nice. It just wasn't real."

"But it was real. We are married."

"But not for the right reason." When he went to protest, she pressed a finger to his lips. "Do you love me? Not like a friend, but like a lover with that I-can't-live-without-you passion?"

He wanted to tell her that he did, but he couldn't lie. He never allowed himself to love anyone. Maybe it was his parents' numerous fights behind closed doors—fights they didn't think anyone ever heard. But he had, and he distinctly remembered his mother saying that she wished she'd never married his father.

He'd only been ten, but that night he was certain the world he knew would never be the same. Because his mother did pack her things. She took him and his very young sister and they went to his uncle's. He'd never thought his parents would work it out. But somehow, some way, they did return to his father in Halencia. He never did learn if his mother had married his father out of love or duty.

Or maybe he'd dismissed the idea of love when his mother had been murdered. When he learned that life ended in a split second that you could never be prepared for. He watched his father—the strongest man he'd ever known—disappear within himself and become a shell of the man he'd once been.

If that was love, Luca was certain that he didn't want any part of it.

"No. I'm not in love with you." His voice was soft, as though that would ease the blow.

"Good." Elena blinked repeatedly and swallowed hard.

"Good? I didn't think you'd say that."

"Why not? I've already had one man lie to me. At least you're honest."

He was quiet for a moment as he digested her words. "So you're okay—I mean, you don't have any expectations about us?"

"I expect that we'll do whatever it takes to protect our child."

"Agreed. But earlier—"

"Was pregnancy hormones and exhaustion."

"You're sure?" When she nodded, he said, "Then we should get you home." He got to his feet. "Stay here. I'll be right back."

He strode out of the room. He grabbed his clothes from earlier and changed into them. This evening hadn't ended the way he'd planned—with a fancy dinner including all of Elena's favorite dishes. But he'd never been around a pregnant woman before. In the future, he'd see to it that she didn't overdo it.

Now dressed in shorts and a collared shirt, he returned

to Elena's bedroom. The evening had come to an end. He should feel relieved, but he didn't.

She looked at him, and her eyes momentarily widened. "What happened to your clothes?"

"What?" He glanced down at his outfit. "They look fine to me. And here are yours. Hurry and change. I'll have the car brought round."

Before she could protest, he closed the door and walked away. He strode back to the living room, where he blew out all the candles that adorned the room. This whole evening had gone astray. And now Luca had to face spending his wedding night without his bride.

And try as he might, he couldn't stop thinking of that kiss at the chapel and then the one here at the penthouse. He hadn't married Elena out of love, so what was up with the feelings that had bubbled up inside him when the minister pronounced them husband and wife?

CHAPTER FOURTEEN

WHY HAD HE suddenly gotten so quiet?

Elena sat in the back of the town car as it eased down the private lane to her parents' house. Luca sat beside her, staring out the window. Ever since he'd seen the sonogram, he hadn't said anything about the baby. Was it possible he was having second thoughts about being part of the baby's life?

She wanted to ask him then and there, but she couldn't. She didn't want the driver to overhear.

And then the car pulled to a stop in front of her parents' house. They got out and strolled up the walk. Before they made it to the stoop, Elena stopped and turned to Luca. "Don't forget your promise to keep the marriage and the baby a secret."

"I won't." In the moonlight, Luca looked so handsome. He'd worked so hard to make today memorable, but she'd gone and ruined it. The guilt weighed on her. She would make it up to him. She wasn't sure how just yet, but something would come to her.

Luca cleared his throat. "And now you and that little one need to get some rest."

This was the opening she needed. She swallowed hard as her stomach quivered with nerves. "Do you want the baby?"

His eyes widened in surprise. "I married you, didn't I?"

"Answering my question with a question isn't an answer."

"It's all you're going to get tonight. It's getting late and we're both tired."

"That's it?" Her voice started to rise. "You're dismissing me and my concerns."

Luca shushed her. "We don't want to make a scene. We'll talk later."

"Sometimes you can be the most frustrating man."

He smiled at her like she'd just paid him a compliment. Then Luca swiped aside a strand of her hair and tucked it behind her ear. He leaned toward her. Her heart lodged in her throat as she realized he was going to kiss her. She should turn away and rebuff his attempt to smooth things over. But she couldn't move.

Then his lips pressed to her forehead. Her forehead? Really?

His voice was deep when he said, "I'll see you tomorrow for Annabelle's party."

She didn't respond.

And then her husband retreated to the waiting car.

Elena stood there watching as the car pulled away and the taillights eventually faded into the night. Had today really happened? And then she glanced down. The light along her parents' cobblestone walk reflected off her brand-new diamond ring.

Wondering if Luca had forgotten about his ring, too, she pulled out her phone. She dashed off a quick text. Seconds later, he texted her back.

Thanks for the reminder.

"Elena, is that you?" Her mother's voice came from the doorway.

"Yes, it's me."

"Well, what are you doing lurking around in the dark? Come inside."

Elena slipped the rings from her finger and slid them in her purse. It felt wrong to be hiding them, but how could she explain this to her mother when she couldn't even explain all the conflicting emotions she was experiencing?

Not that her mother gave her much time to think about

the wedding as her mother launched into a series of questions. "Did you talk to the reporters today?"

"How did you know about them?"

"Everyone on the palace grounds knows. What they don't know is what they wanted with you. Lucky for you, the people who live around here aren't up on reading the tabloids. But my friends read them, and I've been fielding calls all day. I don't know what to tell them."

"Tell them the stories are all lies."

"Even the one about you being pregnant—"

"What?"

"Yes, they have photos of you visiting the doctor's office, and some unnamed source let it slip that you're carrying that man's baby."

She wanted to tell her mother the whole truth, but she'd promised Luca to keep this secret for a few more days. And her mother was known for her lack of discretion, which was why her father never talked about his work at home.

"That…that is another fabrication."

Her mother eyed her. "Are you sure?"

"I'm sure that I'm not carrying Steven's baby. It's not even a possibility. Now, I'm tired and I have a busy day tomorrow, so I think I'll turn in—"

"Are you going to Annabelle's party?"

Elena nodded.

"With Luca again?"

"We don't have any plans, but I'm sure we'll run into each other, since I'm a guest and he's the brother of the hostess."

"Have a good time."

"I will. Good night." She made her way to the steps, anxious to get to her room and be alone with her thoughts.

But sleep didn't come easily. She kept replaying the events of the day. She wondered if they had made the right choice to marry. She'd always believed that people should marry for love, and now she'd done the exact opposite.

Because there was definitely no love in the relationship— not the kind that should exist between husband and wife. And she wasn't about to put her scarred heart on the line, especially for a man who'd repeatedly rejected love from those around him. She wondered if he even knew how to love someone.

She knew his mother's death had left a scar on him. It had set him adrift and made him willing to take needless chances with his safety. In fact, she'd worried more than once that his daring stunts of cliff diving and bungee jumping would cost him his life, but he'd made it through that rebellious period with only a couple of broken bones and a bruised ego.

He'd worked so hard to distance himself from his family. She knew what he'd been doing—protecting himself. Because the family that he knew had crumbled.

Was that what he was doing now? Was he holding her at a distance because he was afraid that if he let her in and it didn't work out his life would crumble again? Or did he feel absolutely nothing but friendship for her?

He could do this.

He could pretend he hadn't just married the most beautiful woman in the world.

Thank goodness Elena had thought to text him the night before about his ring, because it had completely slipped his mind. He'd almost blown it, and just after he'd promised Elena that he would keep their marriage under wraps until Sunday, when Annabelle's engagement festivities were officially concluded.

But he had to admit to himself that spending his wedding night alone was a complete and utter downer. He'd never considered marrying, but that didn't mean he didn't understand that the wedding night was supposed to be quite memorable. Instead, he hadn't even gotten a good-night kiss. Was this the sort of future he'd doomed them to?

He recalled their conversation before they said their vows. Elena had made him agree that they wouldn't share a bed. At the time, he'd been so concerned about claiming his son or daughter that he'd have agreed to almost anything. It wasn't until now that he'd realized what this concession truly meant.

He never contemplated what it would be like having a platonic marriage with a woman as beautiful as Elena, both on the inside and out. After all, he was a man. He couldn't just not notice that she was stunning. He wasn't the only one who noticed her rare beauty. She couldn't even walk down the street without men whistling.

But what none of them knew was that she was now his legally and otherwise—although the *otherwise* had a bit of a hitch. His thoughts rolled back to the kiss they'd shared yesterday after the wedding. It had caught him off guard. He'd thought he could do this whole fake marriage thing, but now he was having serious doubts.

"Luca, what are you doing all the way over here?"

He blinked and realized that he'd been totally lost in his thoughts. And then somehow the object of his daydream appeared before him. Elena stood there giving him a strange look.

"What did you say?" he asked.

She waved away his words. "It doesn't matter. You look like you have something on your mind. What is it? Or do I already know?"

"You know?" And then he realized that his voice came out a bit off-key.

She sent him a strange look. "Yes, I know. My mother told me about the latest story in the tabloid. I'll give them this much—they sure don't waste any time in going after a person."

"I take it there was another story about you?"

She nodded. "I thought you knew."

"Um, no. Do you think they went digging up more information on you when you didn't appear at the gate yesterday to answer their questions?"

"Something like that. Apparently they have a photo of me visiting my doctor's office."

"So what does that mean? You can't be the only woman who visits her doctor."

"Apparently they've got an unnamed source in the office, and they told them I was pregnant."

"And your mother knows."

Elena nodded. "But I hedged around her questions. So she doesn't know what's real and what's lies. I hate this."

He took her hand in his and gave it a squeeze. "I know you do. But it's almost over. If you want, we can just tell everyone today."

"The idea is so tempting, but Annabelle is so happy. I don't want to ruin this once-in-a-lifetime experience. Your sister really went all out for this celebration, and I noticed that you two are getting closer."

He nodded. "She's a little less angry with me for being gone all these years."

"So then there's good coming out of this week?"

"I suppose you could say that."

"Then I will put off my mother for a bit longer. If only I could disconnect her internet for the rest of the week, it would certainly help."

"Would you like me to borrow a pair of wire cutters from the palace staff?"

"You have absolutely no idea just how tempting that idea is."

They both laughed. And he couldn't help but stare at her. Her face lit up with happiness. Her eyes twinkled. And once again he felt an odd sensation in his chest—a warmth.

CHAPTER FIFTEEN

EUROPEAN FOOTBALL.

Elena stood on the sidelines and smiled. Thankfully Annabelle had given them a heads-up about today's activities so she could dress appropriately in shorts and a yellow cotton top. It'd been more years than she wanted to count since she'd hit the field, but she did have to admit that she'd played pretty well in her day.

"Okay, everybody, gather round." Annabelle waved everyone over. "What should we do? Pick two captains and let them choose teams? Or should we play guys on girls?"

The second option definitely got more votes from the women. But the men were shockingly quiet.

"Well, it seems it's a draw." She turned back to Grayson, and they whispered back and forth for a minute. Then he handed her something. "Okay. Since it's a tie, we're going to toss for it. Heads we do coed. Tails we do boys versus girls."

Annabelle flipped the coin high in the air. It turned end over end, reflecting the sunlight in the process. She caught it and looked up with a smile. "Looks like it's coed. Now for captains. Let's see."

"You and Grayson should be captains, since it's your party," one guest interjected.

Elena liked the idea. "Yeah, go for it."

As more and more people cheered on the idea, Annabelle waved her hands, trying to silence everyone. "I hate to disappoint everyone, but I'm not playing. As most of you know, I'm not coordinated in the least. So I'm going to be the cheer squad." She rushed over to a chair a few feet behind her and grabbed two little white pom-poms. She shook them and smiled broadly. "I came prepared. In my place, I elect Elena."

Elena couldn't help but smile. She liked that after all these years, Luca's sister still thought so highly of her. And since they were now family, it would certainly help matters.

But Elena thought of her condition—she didn't think playing football with the guys was such a good idea. One misplaced ball could hit her abdomen. But how in the world did she gracefully back out without upsetting Annabelle?

Annabelle gestured for Elena to step up beside her. Maybe it'd be possible to coach from the sidelines. That sounded like a good plan. If anyone said anything, she'd blame her lack of activity on her job and not wanting to return with a black eye or broken nose.

Elena took her place next to Annabelle. It was then that she noticed Luca. He was staring directly at her with a distinct frown. What had she done now?

She glanced away, hoping no one would notice his odd behavior. If he didn't lighten up, people were going to start suspecting that something was up between them.

Annabelle took both Elena's and Grayson's hands and raised them above her head. "Okay, these are your captains. And just like when we were kids, they are going to take turns picking players. Good luck—"

"Wait a second," Luca said. "I don't think that's a good idea."

Annabelle's smile faded. "What? The game?"

"No," Luca said, approaching them. "I don't think Elena should play football."

Annabelle's forehead creased. "Is there something we don't know?"

Elena knew what he was up to, and she didn't like it. Her hands balled up at her sides. They might be married now, but she could take care of herself and their baby. Perhaps it was time they laid out some understandings about this nontraditional arrangement.

Not about to let Luca make a scene, Elena spoke up.

"What's the matter, Luca? Are you afraid that I'll beat you like when we were kids?"

"No, I was thinking that you might not want the ball hitting you. You know, to the stomach or, worse, the face. A broken nose probably won't help your career."

They might be thinking along the same lines, but that didn't mean she was going to let him tell her what to do. "And that's why I was planning to coach from the sidelines."

"Or you can keep me company." Annabelle gave her a hopeful look. "I'll share my pom-poms with you."

Before Elena could respond, Grayson spoke up. "Actually, this will work out. As it was, we were going to have an extra person. Now the teams will be equal."

"What do you say?" Annabelle asked.

"Looks like I'll be joining the cheering section." Elena refused to look at Luca.

Annabelle glanced around. "And now I need a replacement captain. Luca, since you caused the ruckus, you can be the captain. Get over here and start picking players. We have a game to play."

Elena joined Annabelle off to the side of the field that had been painted up with white lines just like a regulation field. Even nets stood at either end. And the part Elena liked best was the hot dog and refreshment cart. She was getting a little hungry…and since she was eating for two now, she had the perfect excuse to ditch her diet for the day.

"So what's up with you and my brother?" Annabelle took a seat in one of the fold-out chairs.

Elena sat next to her. She willed herself to act normal. "Not much."

"Sure seems like something to me. The looks you two were sending each other were rather stormy. I hope you two aren't fighting. You barely see each other anymore."

"Oh, we're not fighting. I promise." At least not yet—not until she was alone with Luca.

"You're sure? Because I could say something to him. Now that my brother has reemerged into our lives, he seems to think he knows what's best for everyone. Don't let him push you around."

"Trust me, I've known him long enough to know all his tricks."

"Good." Annabelle smiled. "Us girls, we have to stick together."

"Yes, we do."

Was it wrong that Elena was starting to feel like she would have an ally in Annabelle? Her friend didn't even know the truth yet. Would Annabelle be upset when she learned that her brother had eloped? Would everyone think that he had married beneath himself?

Elena lifted her chin a little higher. She was, after all, famous. That had to count for something. She would make sure people respected her, starting with her husband.

"What was that back there?"

The hiss in Elena's voice drew Luca up short.

He stopped on the beach and glanced around to make sure they were alone. They'd meandered toward the beach while everyone else headed back to the palace to get cleaned up before dinner. But right now, food was the last thing on Luca's mind.

He turned back to her. "What are you talking about?"

"That scene you made before the football game. You shouldn't have done it."

"Well, excuse me for worrying about my—" he caught himself before he said *wife* "—my child. I was just doing what I thought was best."

"That's not for you to do. I can take care of myself. I was about to back out of playing the game before you interrupted."

"I didn't know." He suddenly felt as though he'd done

something wrong when all he'd meant to do was make sure that everyone was safe. Being a husband and father was trickier than he'd imagined.

"I think the problem is that we rushed into this marriage and we didn't take time to figure out how it was going to work."

He had a distinct feeling he wasn't going to like what she said next. "And how do you think it should work?"

"Well, my life is in Paris. I plan to return there."

He didn't like the thought of her being so far away. "When do you plan to leave?"

"My flight is scheduled for next week."

He nodded, but he didn't speak right away. Time was running out for them. He took a moment before he spoke. He'd already learned the value of carefully considering his words where Elena was concerned. "You do realize the paparazzi is going to follow you around and dig up whatever dirt they can find?"

She shrugged it off, but he caught a glimpse of the worry in her eyes. She didn't like living her life in the spotlight. So why was she in such a rush to get back to that world? Was it truly her career? Or was she anxious to get away from him?

"How will you work? Soon you'll be showing."

She said something, but it was so soft that he couldn't quite catch it. "What did you say?"

"I was fired."

"I'm sorry. I didn't know." And then another thought came to him. "So this means you don't have to leave?"

"I've been hoping to work in another area of the fashion industry. Something behind the scenes. So my pregnancy won't be an issue."

His hopes were dashed. "And this work, it's that important to you?"

She nodded, but her gaze didn't quite meet his. "I'm

being mentored by Francois Lacroix, one of the greatest fashion designers in the world."

When she mentioned the name, Luca was surprised. Even he had heard of the man. As she talked about this new endeavor, she became animated. Her face lit up and it was obvious that she'd found something that brought her tremendous joy.

Luca could see why this was important to her. "He must see a lot of promise in you. I'd like to see your designs."

Elena's blue eyes widened. "You would?"

"Sure. I think it's great that you are doing something you're passionate about."

"I don't know why I was worried that you'd try to talk me out of it. You always supported me, even when everyone else washed their hands. Like when I wanted to test out of school early so I could move to Paris."

"How could I tell you to stay put when I didn't?"

"But it was more than that. You always told me that I could do whatever I put my mind to. Unlike my mother, who thought I should stay close to home and find a suitable husband. She never did understand my need to venture into the world and find my place."

"So you're really happy in Paris?" He braced himself for her answer.

"I am happy. I don't know if it's Paris or the fact that I'm chasing my dreams. Can you imagine, instead of me modeling someone else's clothes, one day it might be my name up there and someone else might be wearing my fashions?" A broad smile lit up her face.

He didn't want to stand between Elena and that happiness. But they did have a marriage and a baby to consider. That had to be their priority. Surely she'd agree.

"And what of the baby and our marriage?" he asked.

"I gave it some thought last night, and I think I have a compromise of sorts."

"I'm listening." He doubted he'd like this suggestion, because it probably had to do with Paris.

"I think you and I should stay married for the next year. By then the baby will be born, and we can decide whether to continue the marriage, or if either of us wants out, we can end it."

Well, that sounded good so far. "I think that's agreeable."

"As for the living arrangement, I'll be spending the bulk of my time in Paris, and I'm sure you'll be spending most of your time in Halencia."

"No."

"What do you mean, no? You won't be staying in Halencia?"

"No, we aren't going to live apart."

She frowned. "Of course we are. We can visit each other on holidays. This doesn't have to change things between us unless we let it."

His jaw tensed. It had already changed everything. As soon as he said, "I do," his whole world seemed to shift, and he had yet to regain his footing. "And the baby? Am I never supposed to see it, either?"

"You're impossible to talk to when you're angry." She turned and started to walk away.

He reached out, catching her wrist. "Elena, don't walk away. We need to get this all out there. What about the baby?"

She sighed and turned. "He or she will live with me in Paris. You can visit as much as you like."

"And that's it?" he ground out between clenched teeth. "I'm just going to be the absentee father?"

She moved the sand around with her foot. "I thought about it, and I just don't see any other alternative—at least not until the child is older."

"And by then I'll be a stranger to them." His voice was filled with anger. He hadn't even realized until this moment just how passionate he was about playing an important role in his child's life. "Is that what you want?"

"I…I don't know. What else can we do?"

At this point, he was the one to turn and walk away. He had to put distance between them, because he didn't trust himself to pick the right words in the heat of the moment.

Didn't Elena understand what she was asking of him?

Sure, maybe he'd never expected to be a father, but that choice had been taken out of his hands. And now, well, he was starting to imagine a little boy, inquisitive and daring, or a little girl with her mother's forget-me-not blue eyes and blond locks. He was starting to put images to the concept of Elena being pregnant. With each passing day, it was becoming more of a reality to him.

And he wanted to do more for his child than give them his name. But now Elena was blocking him from doing that. She'd essentially written him out of her life as well as the baby's. Now what was he going to do about it?

He'd really mucked things up.

Later that evening, Luca sat at the enormous wooden desk in the palace library. The remainder of the lemon grove's financial reports had shown up while he was out. Now it was his job to formulate a plan to salvage his legacy. He needed to turn things around. He just couldn't fail his family again.

But instead of figures and projections, all he could think about right now was Elena. After telling himself that he'd keep his cool and watch what he said, he'd blown it. He just couldn't stand the thought of not playing a vital role in his child's life. That fact should shock him after telling himself for years that he wouldn't have a family, but instead the decision to be an active part of his child's life came easily to him—as natural as breathing.

And for Elena to try to cut him out of that experience

was unthinkable. He'd thought he knew her, but perhaps he was mistaken. Could that be right? Was Elena really a stranger to him?

"How does it look?" his father asked as he strode into the room.

Torn from his thoughts, Luca glanced up. "Are you sure this is everything?"

"Of course. Why? What are you missing?"

"Profits. And your debt ratio is astronomical."

His father's face was pale and drawn. As he looked at his father, Luca could see the toll the years had taken on the duke. He didn't look good. Luca truly had been gone too long. It had been easier to be secluded from his family than to have to deal with all the problems and responsibilities family entailed—like the problems facing him now.

But those days were over. If he were honest with himself, that decision had been made when his sister invited him back to Mirraccino for this celebration. He hadn't fully realized it then, but where he normally avoided family gatherings, he was drawn to this one. Of course, that might have had something to do with the fact that his sister had also told him that Elena had been invited.

Luca just never imagined that he would arrive to find out that his father was in such deep financial trouble. It would be a miracle if they'd be able to keep their home.

His father pulled a wooden chair next to the desk and settled on it. "I tried. It just got away from me. I thought I could turn things around."

Luca focused on the summary spreadsheet that he'd created on his laptop. "I've done an overview of your debt, expenses and revenue. Without a major influx of cash, I don't see being able to turn things around." When he glanced over at his father, he caught him blinking repeatedly. This display of emotion from his stalwart father shook Luca to the core. "I'm sorry."

His father sniffed back the rush of emotions. "You have nothing to be sorry for. I am to blame."

"I should have come back sooner instead of letting you deal with it all on your own."

"What can we do?"

Luca leaned back in his chair and rubbed his jaw. "I'll be honest—it isn't good. If you were one of my clients, I'd tell you to sell everything, make settlements with your creditors and start over."

"But our home—I couldn't bear to lose it. It's full of memories…"

Of Luca's mother? Was it possible that his parents cared more for each other than he would ever know? Perhaps relationships were more complicated than he'd imagined. He was certainly learning that with Elena.

"Can I ask you something?" Luca uttered the words before he evaluated the ramifications of what he was about to ask.

"Sure. You know that you can talk to me about anything."

Luca had never felt that way about his father, but perhaps the years and loneliness had mellowed the man. "It's about Mother."

"What about her?"

"Did you ever love her?"

His father leaned back as though the question struck him physically. "Why would you ask such a thing?"

This was where it got difficult. Luca swallowed hard. "I heard you two. When I was little, you would fight, a lot. Annabelle was too young to remember, but I do. I remember Mother saying that she wished you two hadn't married."

His father's shoulders drooped. "I'm sorry you overheard us. We thought that we were being discreet." His father took a moment as though to sort through his memories. "Your mother and I were practically strangers when we married.

It was arranged to strengthen alliances between Halencia and Mirraccino and it took us a long time to find common ground. With each passing year, our respect for each other grew, as did our friendship. It was hard won, which I like to think made our relationship stronger."

"Why did I never know any of this?"

His father shrugged. "I guess you never asked and I never thought of it."

"But you two ended up loving each other?"

"How could I not love your mother? She was the most amazing woman I'd ever met. She was gracious and kind, not to mention a beauty. But she had a strong spirit and was quite determined to do things her way. There were numerous areas where we had different views, including her allegiance to her brother, the king. That's what most of our heated exchanges were about. But what you heard were words spoken in the heat of the moment. What you didn't hear were the apologies."

Luca couldn't quite digest all this information. He wasn't sure what to make of it. His parents' story certainly wasn't like the fairy tales. Theirs was complicated and messy.

And Luca didn't do messy.

"Thank you for telling me," Luca said.

"I hope it helps you."

Luca wondered if his father knew more than he was saying, but Luca wasn't going there. They had another matter to discuss.

"I've gone over these numbers for the past few hours, and at this point, I know that if something isn't done right away, you'll lose everything." He took a deep breath. "I have some money set aside, which, along with my trust fund, we can use to pay off some of the more pressing debts, but it still won't be enough to make the company solvent. However, it should give us some breathing room."

"You…you would do that?"

"Why do you sound surprised? This is my legacy and that of my children. I want to hold on to it as much as you."

"Children?" There was a hint of glee in his father's voice. "Does this mean you've decided to settle down with a family?"

Avoiding the question, Luca said, "It means I have a vested interest in making this work. And it means I need to step up my efforts to bring in a new revenue source, and I think I know of a way."

The answer was the king. He had connections far beyond the normal businessman. In fact, the Mirraccino palace in many instances acted as an agent for its citizens. Now, granted, the lemon grove was not part of Mirraccino, but they were family. Luca could only hope that the king did better by his extended family than Luca had done by his immediate family. Guilt weighed heavy on his shoulders for pushing away his family and ignoring his obligations after his mother's death.

Everything was now in jeopardy—his tenuous relationship with his father and his sister as well as the lemon grove. He had to hope that if he fixed the business then his relationships would continue to fall into place. But how could he get to the king when he was sequestered behind guarded doors?

Elena's image came to mind. Her father was the only person the king had been seeing since the truth of Luca's mother's murder had been revealed. The news had hit the king especially hard, since Luca's mother had been trying to protect him from one of his own trusted employees.

Luca dismissed the idea of involving Elena. It didn't feel right. Besides, with the way they'd left things, she wouldn't be in any frame of mind to help him. There had to be another way.

CHAPTER SIXTEEN

THERE WAS NO avoiding this evening's festivities.

As it was, Elena had pleaded a headache the day before and stayed home, missing out on the croquet and bocce ball tournaments. She had been looking forward to them, too, because they were activities she could do and not worry about the baby. She had to admit that she did have a bit of a competitive streak.

But she knew that Luca was upset with her. In fact, their last conversation had been the angriest she'd ever seen him. He was usually so laid-back and let things roll off his shoulders. But this thing with the baby—it really got to him.

Was it possible the self-proclaimed bachelor was more excited to be a father than he was willing to admit? If so, it would be the first sign that Luca was letting his guard down. Was it possible? Or was she only seeing what she wanted to see?

Elena rushed around her bedroom in her parents' home. Tonight was a dinner and dance that would wrap up the weeklong celebration. This morning Annabelle had phoned to check on her and make sure that Elena would be in attendance for the evening's festivities.

Knock. Knock.

"Dear, are you almost ready?" Her mother's voice echoed through the closed door.

"Almost."

"I just don't want you to be late. And the car is here—"

"What car?" Elena rushed to the window.

Was Luca out there waiting for her? Her stomach quivered with nerves. They'd left things in such an awkward spot that she wasn't sure what to say to him. She had no answers, just more questions.

"I assume Annabelle sent it for you."

Not Luca. Okay. "I'll be down in a jiff."

"Do you need any help?"

"No. Thanks. I've got it." She rushed back to the full-length mirror.

Tonight she was wearing another one of her own creations. It was a light blue material. The shade was similar to her eyes, or so she'd been told. It had a strapless beaded bustier and attached to it was a long chiffon skirt in the same shade. It wasn't one of her more daring designs, but this was, after all, an appearance at the palace. Traditional trumped experimental in this particular scenario.

She wondered if Luca would like it. He had no idea that she was going to wear an Elena Ricci original. But on second thought, her clothes would probably be the last thing on his mind tonight. She'd hoped that he would have calmed down enough to call her by now, but there was still no word from him.

She slipped on white sandals that strapped over her pink-painted toes and wrapped around her ankles. She pulled up the zipper in the back of each shoe. When she grabbed her clutch purse from the bed, it was time to put on a show.

With each step, her nerves became more taut. She had no idea what to say to Luca, and there was no avoiding him this evening. She truly wanted to make things better between them. Their marriage had barely made it twenty-four hours before they'd had their first major fight. If she believed in omens, this would be a worrisome one.

The clap of hands had her gazing at the bottom of the steps. There stood not only her mother but also her father.

"Father, what are you doing here? Shouldn't you be with the king?"

"Your mother told me you were getting all dressed up tonight and I couldn't miss it."

She rushed over and gave him a kiss on the cheek and a

hug. She loved her father. He might not have been around as much as she'd wanted, but when he was there, he was alert and attentive.

And then she turned to her mother, who now had tears in her eyes. They hugged. Her mother might be difficult, but her heart was always in the right place.

As Elena made her way out the door, she realized her child deserved a loving home just like that, not a home filled with heated words or, worse, stony silence because the parents were frustrated with having to give up their dreams. If she couldn't find a way to build a genuine marriage with Luca, she knew she'd have to end things. Otherwise, it wouldn't be fair to any of them.

This acknowledgment hit her in the chest, knocking the air from her lungs. What would happen to Luca if she walked away? In the end, would he be relieved?

She halted the disturbing thoughts. She was jumping too far ahead. First, they had to get through this evening, and considering where they'd left things, it would be a challenge.

The car ride to the palace was short, and in no time she was being ushered inside. The grand dining room was set for the party. The table was the longest Elena had ever seen in her life—it would easily accommodate fifty.

Elena had only been in this room once. She had been quite small, and she and Luca had been sneaking around the palace. The room had been opened up for cleaning, and she had been floored by its vastness. She knew instantly that she didn't belong there, but it didn't stop her from having a quick look around. She had been a curious kid, anxious to find out what she'd been missing out on.

Now as an adult, she was still awed by the room and its elegance. The room was decorated in red brocade wallpaper. On each wall were portraits of family ancestors. Crystal chandeliers lined the long table.

And once again, she didn't feel as though she belonged in this room with royalty, statesmen and dignitaries. Even if she had known them when they would play in the flower gardens and swim in the sea, she wasn't one of them. Even with her secret marriage to Luca, she didn't feel like a member of this prestigious group.

It looked like everyone had arrived. They were all standing off to the side of the table in small groups, enjoying wine and appetizers served by the staff. They were done reliving some of the highlights of their childhood. Tonight they were all elegantly dressed adults, here to honor Annabelle and her soon-to-be husband.

Elena was so relieved that she and Luca had kept the scandal, the elopement and the baby all under wraps. After tonight, they wouldn't have to keep choking down the truth. They could be themselves, and maybe once the pressure was off they could figure out what the future held for them.

She scanned the room, but Luca was nowhere to be found. How could that be? This was his sister's party. He wouldn't miss it, not now that he was trying to make up for the past.

"There you are." Annabelle rushed over. Her off-white gown was figure fitting and accentuated all her attributes. She looked stunning.

"Sorry. I didn't think I was late."

"You aren't. Everyone just wants to get an early start on the evening." Annabelle gave her a worried look. "Are you feeling better?"

"Yes." Elena felt the heat swirl in her chest and rush to her cheeks. "I'm really sorry about yesterday. I just wasn't up for a day in the sun."

"I understand. With headaches, the bright light is the worst." Annabelle took her by the arm and led her over toward a cluster of people. "Let's get you a drink."

"Actually, I was going to ask you if Luca is coming this evening."

Annabelle glanced around. "He should be here. I know that he had an important meeting earlier, but he promised that he would be here. I'll go find him."

"No, let me."

Annabelle nodded. "But don't you go and get lost, too."

"I won't. I promise."

Perhaps it was best she met up with Luca away from prying eyes. She had no idea how it would go, because she'd never been in such a serious situation with Luca before.

She hoped they could find a way to smile and get through the evening. Just tonight and they would have made Annabelle's celebration perfect.

She started for the door when Luca stepped inside. Elena stopped in her tracks. She observed the frown on his face and the way his eyes were full of turmoil.

Oh, no! This was not good. Not good at all.

The situation was dire.

More so than Luca first thought.

How in the world was he supposed to convince Elena to stay with him in Halencia now? There was no way he could provide her with the life she would expect and deserve, not unless there was a miracle. The only thing he did know was that the news could wait until tomorrow.

Luca tugged at the collar of his white dress shirt. This was the last place he wanted to be. He did not like tuxes. They were stuffy and uncomfortable. They had to have been created by a woman, because he couldn't imagine a man designing something so miserably uncomfortable.

He hadn't even worn a tux to his own wedding. So when his sister insisted that he wear one this evening, he'd almost blurted out about the wedding. But he caught himself in time. So the only reason he was wearing this monkey suit was to appease his sister and possibly Elena.

He'd really messed things up on the beach the other day.

He'd lost his cool, and she'd been avoiding him since then. He'd thought of calling her, but what they needed to say to each other was better said in person.

And then his gaze latched on to Elena. She was standing there in a beautiful dress, but it was the expression on her face that made the breath catch in the back of his throat. She was staring at him with a lost look on her face. She was looking at him like he was a stranger. The knowledge dug at him.

They approached each other, their gazes never wavering.

At the same time, they said, "We need to talk."

"There you are, brother. I was worried you got caught up in something and forgot the time." Annabelle rushed up to them.

"I could never forget you," he said and forced a smile.

"Good. It's time to sit down." Annabelle pointed to the table.

"So much for talking," Luca whispered in Elena's ear.

He knew his sister had done a formal seating chart, which meant he wouldn't be seated next to Elena. She would probably be at one end while he was seated at the other with a chatty woman next to him. Tonight he wasn't in the mood to make light conversation.

When Luca started searching out his seat, his sister said, "You're up here, next to me." And then before he could ask, Annabelle said, "And Elena is right next to you."

That was very unorthodox, and his sister always maintained formality at these occasions. She was up to something, but he was so off lately that he couldn't put his finger on exactly what his sister had planned.

Annabelle clinked her glass. "Everyone, please have a seat."

It took a few minutes until everyone was seated. It was then that Luca noticed there were three empty seats—all directly across from him. What was she doing?

Annabelle remained standing. "I have a few more guests."

Through a side door Elena's mother entered, followed by both of their fathers. Oh, no. They were so busted. He didn't dare look at Elena. He could already feel her gaze boring into the back of his head.

Annabelle started speaking with a very serious expression. "Ladies and gentlemen, thank you all for coming." As she kept talking, she gave him and Elena some strange looks. "I'm thankful that my big brother is home with his family. And if the news I've uncovered is any indication, I think he'll be spending more time here."

A murmur rippled around the table.

His father sent him a questioning look, but Luca pretended not to notice. This was not good. Not good at all. The parents hadn't even been clued in and here was his sister about to blow the whistle in front of the whole family and their closest friends.

It was like watching a crash in slow motion and being too stunned to act. His sister was standing there smiling and getting ready to reveal their secret marriage. How was everyone going to react?

CHAPTER SEVENTEEN

THIS WAS GOING to be a disaster.

Elena lowered her gaze as Annabelle continued to address the guests. Why was she doing this? Had Luca told her? Elena couldn't believe he would tell his sister without mentioning it to her, but obviously someone had told her about the marriage.

And then Elena wondered just how much Annabelle knew. Did she know about the baby? *Please don't let her blurt that out.* Elena really wanted to tell her parents when the time was right. They deserved to know first.

"It has come to my attention that my big brother has been keeping a rather large secret from us," Annabelle said.

All eyes trained on Luca, followed by the murmur of voices. Everyone was trying to guess the news. But they were never going to guess that they'd eloped.

Heat engulfed Elena's chest, neck and face. If Annabelle was trying to punish them for keeping this secret, she was doing a good job. If only Elena could fade into the woodwork, she would—in a heartbeat.

Luca glanced at her. Her gaze searched his to find out if he'd known his sister was going to do this. As though he could read her thoughts, his brows rose and he gave a slight shrug.

Great! Annabelle was running loose. And who knew what she was going to say. Elena reached out for Luca's hand. They were in this together. He squeezed her hand, but the reassuring gesture did nothing to settle her queasy stomach.

Annabelle continued, "And now for the news that has come to light." She paused as though for dramatic effect. "My brother and the lovely Elena have eloped."

Gasps ensued around the table.

Elena chanced a glance at her mother, who was all smiles. Thank goodness! At least one person was happy for them. Elena wasn't sure whether Annabelle was happy or angry. Not that she would blame Annabelle for being upset. This was supposed to be her time in the limelight.

Annabelle said, "Tonight's celebration has turned into a wedding supper and reception in the ballroom." She turned to them. "Come on now, stand up, you two. You surely didn't think you were going to get away with this, did you?"

Neither of them answered. They just held on to each other's hands.

"Ladies and gentlemen, please allow me to introduce my brother, the Earl of Halencia, and his wife, Elena."

Everyone clapped and smiled, including all the parents and most of all Annabelle, who rushed over to hug Luca.

And then she moved to stand in front of Elena. "I can't believe you kept this a secret."

What was she supposed to say to that? "I'm sorry."

"Don't be. If you're happy with my stubborn brother, then more power to you." Annabelle smiled broadly and held out her arms. "Welcome to the family, sis."

"Thank you."

Elena hugged her back. But she couldn't help wondering if this was all for real or if Annabelle was trying to make the best of an awkward situation. Maybe in the rush to the altar, they should have given more thought to their families. Suddenly Elena felt very guilty for leaving them all out of it.

There were hugs all around with the parents and words of congratulations exchanged. Everyone seemed to be taking the news well.

Before the rest of the guests could congratulate them, the staff arrived with trays of food. Everyone took their seats to make things easier for the waitstaff.

Luca leaned over to Elena. "Did you know about this?"

"I had no idea. So how did your sister find out?"

"I don't know, but I intend to find out." He leaned over to his sister. "So how exactly did you find out the news?"

Elena, curious to know the answer herself, leaned closer.

"You mean besides you two acting rather oddly?" When Luca frowned, his sister continued, "Well, there was a delivery for you from the courthouse. I happened to be in the foyer at the time. So I signed for it."

"You read my mail?" Luca asked.

"No. But I do have eyes, and I read the return address. It wasn't hard to put two and two together. With a little research, I had confirmation. It would have been nice if you'd told me."

"We were trying not to ruin your big week."

"You didn't ruin it. I couldn't be happier to know that you are settling down, and with the one person in the world I've always thought was made for you." Annabelle reached out and squeezed his arm.

"Thanks, sis."

Elena blinked repeatedly, hoping to keep her makeup from smearing. She had no idea that his sister's opinion of their marriage would hit her so emotionally. These pregnancy hormones were going to turn her into a crier if she wasn't careful.

When Annabelle's gaze met hers, Elena mouthed a big thank-you.

All the while Luca continued to hold her hand. And it was like a weight had been lifted from her shoulders. Now if only everyone was excited about the baby, but that would wait for another time.

His sister hadn't been kidding.

Luca was impressed. Somehow in such a short amount of time, she'd thrown together a beautiful reception. There was a receiving line, where he and Elena were given best wishes by everyone. Hugs abounded, including another from his father. Two hugs in one night was a record for sure. Maybe the years *had* mellowed his father.

Small tables with white tablecloths surrounded the dance floor. Each table had candles as well as pink, purple and white flower centerpieces. Purple, blue and pink spotlights added a fun vibe to the room. Luca wasn't much for decorations and weddings, but he was touched that his sister had gone to so much trouble for them.

There was only one thing missing from this impressive event—his uncle, the king. It saddened Luca to know that the king was so distraught over events that were not his fault. Still, it was the king's lord-in-waiting who had not only been a spy, but had also murdered the king's sister—Luca's mother.

The king had taken the responsibility for the horrific event personally. His dubious health had declined even further, and he remained sequestered, only dealing with his secretary—Elena's father. It was a sad state of affairs, but Luca refused to let it ruin this moment.

In the background, a live band played. His sister insisted that he and Elena have the first dance. With so many people watching them, it wasn't nearly as intimate as the dance on their wedding night.

He glanced down at Elena, who was suspiciously quiet as they moved around the dance floor. A frown pulled at her lips, but when she noticed that he was looking at her, it disappeared.

"Is everything all right?" he asked. "I mean, you are feeling all right, aren't you?"

"Yes. Why do you ask?"

"Just checking. I'm not used to being around a pregnant woman. So if there's anything you need or want, let me know."

"I will."

They continued dancing. He glanced around at the people and the decorations. "Can you believe my sister went to all this trouble?"

"It's beautiful. But I feel bad that we ruined the last night of her festivities."

"You have to admit that we did try our best to keep a lid on the news. And we almost pulled it off. Don't worry. She's really happy for us."

"I'm glad."

"Then why aren't you smiling?"

A smile blossomed on Elena's very kissable lips, but it didn't quite reach her eyes. Something was bothering her, but this wasn't the time to delve into it.

When the dance concluded, they were about to leave the dance floor when his sister started to chant, "Kiss. Kiss. Kiss."

It didn't take long until everyone joined in, cheering them on.

His gaze moved to Elena's. "Shall we?"

Elena's cheeks took on a rosy hue. Her gaze met and held his. She looked so beautiful, and she was his wife—a concept he was still getting used to. And then she nodded.

He pulled her close and claimed her lips. They were sweet like the berries they'd enjoyed at dinner. And though her kiss was reserved at first, it didn't take long until her arms slipped up around his neck and her lips met his move for move.

Oh, yeah, there are definitely some amazing perks to this fake marriage.

The whistles and applause brought him back to earth. With great reluctance, he released her. Elena's gaze met his once more, and he could see that the kiss had gotten to her as much as it had him. But where did that leave them?

Her life was in Paris. She'd made that abundantly clear.

And he had nothing to offer her—he was about to lose his legacy to creditors. The future looked dismal at best.

At that point, they moved off the dance area to make room for the other couples to take a spin around the floor. Elena's mother came over to speak with her daughter at the same time as his cousins, the twin princes, came over to congratulate him.

Soon the conversation turned to sports. Their group expanded with more men, all giving their thoughts about the upcoming European football season. As usual with this group, opinions were plenty and the conversation was heated. Some things hadn't changed, no matter how much time Luca had been away.

He had no idea how much time passed before he broke away to find his beautiful bride. He'd looked everywhere for Elena. He even asked his sister to check in the ladies' room, but there was no sign of her. Was it possible she'd left her own reception?

He was just about to give up when he noticed that the door to the balcony was slightly ajar. He moved to close it when he noticed a figure in the moonlight standing at the far end that overlooked the gardens.

He stepped outside to get a better look and then realized it was indeed his bride. She hadn't left him after all. A smile pulled at his lips.

He started across the balcony. When he got closer, he noticed that she was frowning again. It was the same look he'd caught on her face earlier when she didn't think anyone was looking. Something serious was on her mind, and he needed to know what it was so he could fix it. It just wasn't right that the bride wasn't having a good time at her own reception.

Even for tonight, he'd set aside his massive problems with the lemon grove and dealing with his father. There was no point in letting them ruin this evening, since there was nothing he could do tonight to change their situation. He just had to hope that tomorrow would bring him the answers he needed.

He made his way across the balcony to Elena's side. "What are you thinking?"

"Nothing."

He didn't believe her for one moment. "It is definitely something."

She turned to him. "Do you really want to know?"

He nodded, because he didn't have a clue why she was upset. Everything had gone so well tonight. Everyone was happy for them. They should be celebrating that their plan was working out.

"You. Me. Us. This phony marriage."

"What about it?" When she didn't immediately respond, he said, "If you don't talk to me, there's no way I can help."

She licked her lips. "I...I've been an outcast my whole life—"

"What are you talking about?"

"I'm talking about growing up here, on the royal grounds. I was never a real part of you and all your cousins. Sure, I got to live here and it was amazing, but I always felt like I was on the outside looking in."

"That's not how any of us saw it. You were always one of us."

"No, I wasn't. I was the daughter of the help."

"You were more than that and you know it." He reached out to her, but she backed away. "We included you in everything."

Elena shook her head. She clearly remembered all the formal events, dinners and parties she had been forbidden to attend. "Not everything."

"Those other occasions weren't important—"

"Maybe not to you, but they were to me. While you and

your sister and cousins were all getting dressed up for a fancy party, I was left alone. I was the only one not invited."

"I'm sorry. You know I would have included you if I could have." Luca frowned. "But I don't understand. That was all a very long time ago. What does any of this have to do with our marriage?"

"I'm getting to that. After feeling like an outsider my entire childhood, I will not be left on the outside of our marriage."

"What's that supposed to mean?"

"That if you can't open up and tell me how you feel about the baby, I can't do this."

What did she mean, she couldn't do this? He was too afraid to ask. He didn't even understand what had brought this on, but he refused to let his marriage fall apart at their reception. That just seemed epically wrong.

"Elena, I do open up to you, as much as I open up to anyone."

"But that's the thing—you don't. You play everything close to the vest. I don't even know if you're going to let down your guard and love our baby."

"Luca, is that you?" Annabelle called out. She came closer. "Oh, Elena, this is where you've been. Somebody we both know—" she nodded toward Luca "—got worried when he couldn't find you."

"Sorry," Elena said. "I just needed a little fresh air."

"No problem. But as soon as you two are ready, it's time to cut the cake."

"We'll be right there," Luca said. He waited until his sister walked away and then he said, "Elena, I know you want a lot from me, and I'm trying my best. Just give me a little time."

"What makes you think that time will help?"

"This does." He leaned forward and pressed his lips to hers.

When they kissed, everything seemed right in the world. There was no need for words. Problems got lost in the haze.

There was just him and her, lost in the moment.

Lip to lip. Heart to heart.

If only life could be so simple.

CHAPTER EIGHTEEN

WHAT ARE WE supposed to do now?

Elena looked at Luca, who was wearing a bewildered expression that must have matched hers. They stood just outside one of the elaborate guesthouses on the estate. They were secluded.

Just the two of them.

And now they would have to talk.

They stood there for a moment in the dark with the stars twinkling overhead. In any other scenario, this would be so romantic. But what their families didn't know was that Luca was not in love with her.

"Shall we go inside?" he asked.

She nodded. "It's late and I'm tired."

In the next moment, she was swept off her feet.

"Luca, you don't have to do this. There aren't any photographers around this time." And then she had second thoughts about her assumption. "Are there?"

"Why are you asking me? I didn't plan this."

And then Elena realized that Annabelle had planned this special evening. And that could only mean one thing— Annabelle approved of the marriage. At last Elena felt as though she'd been accepted. She was one of them—for however long it lasted.

Luca arched a brow. "And what has you smiling?"

Elena realized that she was indeed smiling. She shrugged and then went with the moment. She wrapped her arms around his neck as he carried her into their temporary home. They had been explicitly told that they were to stay put until Monday—or longer if they liked.

"What's up with you?" she asked.

"Me? Why does something have to be up?"

"Because you've been acting surprisingly happy tonight."

"And the problem with that is?"

"The last time I saw you, we'd argued and you'd walked away mad."

"Maybe I had time to cool off and regret walking away."

What was he saying? She wasn't quite sure. But as he carried her into the cozy cottage, she noticed the soft, jazzy tunes filling the air. Her gaze scanned the dimly lit room. Candles were scattered about, from the mantel of the fireplace to the coffee table. The French doors stood wide open with the gentle breeze off the sea rushing into the room.

Elena wasn't sure she wanted to ruin this moment with any serious conversation. Perhaps the reality of their situation could wait until tomorrow. After all the effort that had gone into this setup, it'd be a shame not to enjoy it.

She leaned close to his neck, brushing her lips gently across his skin. Mmm…he smelled like soap combined with his own manly scent. She breathed in deeper.

"What are you doing?" he asked.

"Smelling you."

"What?"

She couldn't help but smile at his startled tone. "You smell good." She leaned in close again. "Really good."

He lowered her feet to the ground. "It's probably best if you don't do that again."

But her arms were still looped around his neck, and she didn't feel like letting go. Maybe it was all the romantic songs that had filled the ballroom. Or maybe it was dancing with him most of the evening and staring into his eyes. Whatever it was, she was going with it.

"Loosen up. This is our wedding night do-over."

"We can't have a do-over." He loosened her arms from his neck and walked over to the open French doors.

"Sure we can—"

"A do-over implies that we had a first wedding night. And I distinctly recall spending that night alone. Remember?" He turned away from her and stared out at the star-studded sky. "It was one of your stipulations to our marriage."

"And a woman reserves the right to change her mind."

She walked up behind him. With his back to her, she leaned her cheek against his shoulder while slipping her arms around him. Her hand rested over his chest, where she felt the beat of his heart. It was strong and fast.

He cleared his throat, but when he spoke his voice was a bit raspy. "You were very serious that day."

"I'm sorry about that. It was a very emotional day and it crashed in on me."

"I think it's best we stick with the original agreement."

What was that supposed to mean? Her mind jumped to all the wrong conclusions. But then she stopped herself. In the past, jumping to conclusions had done nothing but get her in trouble.

With great trepidation, she asked, "Why is it for the best?"

"You know why."

She pulled back. "No, I don't. But I'd like you to explain it to me."

He shook his head. "Let's not get into this now. It was a nice evening. Let's leave it at that. I'll sleep on the couch. You can have the bed."

"No."

He turned to her. "No, what?"

"No, I'm not going to leave it at that. I want to know what you meant."

"Why do you always have to be so stubborn?"

"I guess I was born that way." She pressed her hands to her hips. "Now quit trying to change the subject."

He raked his fingers through his hair and sighed in defeat. "Because the one night we spent together, I awoke in the morning to find you crying. You regretted our night together. And I don't want a repeat of that experience."

He'd heard her? He'd never said a word about it. If he had, would it have changed things between them? She wasn't sure, but she wanted to clear the air now.

"I wasn't crying because I regretted that you and I had gotten closer. It was quite the opposite. I enjoyed it and that scared me."

"Scared you?"

"Yes. I knew you didn't want a serious relationship. And without us being able to move forward, I knew I would lose you—lose our friendship. I thought I'd once again made a huge mistake. What you saw was me being afraid of losing you."

His eyes searched hers. "Really? That's what you were upset about?"

She nodded. "After all, we've been through thick and thin. I couldn't imagine never speaking to you again."

"You never have to worry about that. I don't know how this whole thing with us is going to work out, but I will always be here for you. That I promise."

"I will be here for you, too. Always and forever."

His head lowered, and he claimed her lips. It seemed so natural, so right. Maybe that was because they were, in fact, newlyweds. Or more likely it was because they'd been made for each other, but one of them had just been too stubborn to see it until now.

But suddenly Luca pulled back. "We shouldn't be doing this."

"We just talked about this. Everything is okay now." She lifted up on her tiptoes to continue the kiss, but Luca leaned back.

"There are still things we need to talk about."

"It can wait. I promise, it'll be all right." She ran her hands up over the front of his shirt to his shoulders, where she slipped off his tux coat. It fell to the floor in a heap. "Tonight isn't for talking."

"It isn't?" His voice was deeper than normal.

"No." She pulled on his bow tie, loosening it. And then she undid the top button of his shirt. "I can think of other, more pressing matters."

"I think I'm getting the idea, but could you be a little clearer about what's on your mind?"

Her fingers undid another button. And then she lifted up on her tiptoes and pressed a trail of kisses along his neck. "Are you getting the idea?"

"Uh-huh." He moved just then and claimed her lips with his own.

This time his kiss wasn't tentative, but rather full of raw desire. As their kiss deepened, hope welled up inside Elena that this was the turning point in their relationship. That, at last, Luca was letting down the walls around his heart and allowing her in. There were still a lot of details to be sorted out, but as long as she knew Luca wanted this marriage for the right reasons, she would meet him halfway.

In the background, the Frank Sinatra love song that had played on their wedding day started up. She would never hear that song again without thinking of this moment. She leaned into Luca like she'd been wanting to do all week. She gave in to the passion that welled up within her, slipping her hands up over his shoulders and wrapping them around the back of his neck. Her fingers combed through his hair.

A kiss had never tasted so good. He tasted of sweet wine and chocolate. His touch was gentle yet needy. Joy filled her knowing that at last they were on the right page.

He pulled back ever so slightly and rested his forehead against hers. "Mrs. DiSalvo, shall we have our wedding night?"

Her heart fluttered. "Oh, yes."

And she sealed it with a kiss. Words were overrated in

this moment. They could communicate lip to lip, hand to hand and body to body.

In the next moment, he swept her up in his arms. With the warm sea breeze caressing them, he carried her over to the four-poster bed draped with a sheer white canopy.

He lowered her onto the fluffy white comforter and stared into her eyes. "It's as if I'm seeing you for the first time."

She smiled up at him. "I hope you like what you see."

"Oh, definitely." But then a worrisome look came over his face.

"What is it?"

"I just don't want to do anything to hurt you."

"You won't." She was trusting him with her heart. "Not unless you don't come closer and kiss me some more."

"That I can do."

He leaned down and pressed his lips to hers.

CHAPTER NINETEEN

THAT HAD BEEN a mistake.

A big one.

Luca slipped out of bed, dressed and went out to stand on the deck overlooking the sea. He shouldn't have let things go so far last night. Sure, he'd wanted Elena more than he'd ever wanted any woman he'd ever known. And yes, they were married, so it was expected.

But what he hadn't done was be totally up front with Elena.

Ever since they'd said their wedding vows, he'd been seeing her in a different light. He'd always thought she was pretty, but now when he looked at her, she took his breath away. And with the pregnancy, she wasn't as thin as she was for the catwalks. He liked those emerging curves a lot—a whole lot.

But he had to tell her that his situation had changed—and not for the better. He was not the man she thought she'd married—

"Hey, what are you doing up so early?" Elena's sleepy voice came from behind him.

He turned around to find her wearing his white dress shirt from last night. The shirt stopped halfway down her thighs. Her long blond hair was tousled. And she'd never looked sweeter.

She reached him and wrapped her arms around his neck before lifting up and pressing a kiss to his lips. Memories of their steamy night together sprang to mind. His body was immediately ready for a repeat.

No. He steeled himself. He was not about to cave again. He had to settle things between them.

Elena pulled away. "Can I get you some coffee?"

"I didn't think you were allowed that now that you're pregnant."

"I'm not. But that doesn't mean I can't get you some. I'll just have some juice or whatever I find in the fridge."

"Oh. Okay. That sounds good." Maybe some caffeine would help straighten his thoughts.

"You know, I've been doing some thinking about our situation," Elena called out from the kitchen. "I'll tell you in a few minutes."

There was a knock at the door.

"I wonder who that can be," Elena said. "I'll get it."

Luca leaned his arms on the railing surrounding the balcony. He stared off in the distance. He couldn't believe that he finally knew what he wanted, but it was just out of his reach.

It was like having an angel on one shoulder and the devil on the other. One prompted him to use his relationship with Elena to gain an audience with the king. It was the only viable way he could get a quick resolution to the lemon grove's troubles.

But the other prompted him to put Elena first. It was a tremendous favor to ask her to get an audience with the king while he was sequestered. The only way to do it would be for her to sneak him in. And that would leave her in a very awkward position with her father.

"These arrived for you." She handed over a newspaper and a big manila envelope.

"Thank you." He glanced at the return address on the envelope. He knew the significance of both items and set them aside.

"Aren't you even going to look at the package? It might be important."

"The envelope contains our wedding photos. I thought you might want them, so I had the photographer rush over the proofs."

"Oh. Okay. And is there any significance to the newspaper?"

He nodded. "We're in it."

"What?" She rushed over, grabbed it and found their photo on the front page. "But how did they get this? The picture is from our wedding at the church."

"I leaked it to the press."

"But why?"

"Because I was tired of their lies. I wanted them to have the truth. Now the world knows we're married."

Her gaze searched his. "You don't care if everyone knows that you married a…" Using air quotes, she said, "'Home wrecker'?"

"You are anything but. In fact, I should make that Steven guy come clean to the world—"

"No! Don't." When he sent her a puzzled look, she added, "It'll just dredge up that mess all over again."

He sighed. "I guess you do have a point. I just hate the thought of him getting away with lying to you."

"He's not. Not exactly. His soon-to-be ex-wife is making sure he's miserable."

"Nothing like a scorned woman."

Elena smiled. "Exactly. I'm sure she can make him squirm in ways you can't even imagine."

"Hmm… I'll have to make sure I don't get on your bad side."

"True." She smiled broadly. "But you don't have anything to worry about after last night. Right now, I feel like anything is possible—"

"Elena, don't go getting too excited."

"Don't worry. I know that we still have steep hurdles to cross. But if you give a little and I give a little, maybe we can meet somewhere in the middle. And our child will win by having both parents in their life."

Guilt assailed Luca. He'd been so caught up in the surprise reception last night and then being alone with Elena that he hadn't been thinking clearly. She'd been so different—so bold. And he was weak when it came to her kisses.

He took a big gulp of coffee. He swallowed, and his stomach churned. Maybe coffee on top of guilt was not a good combination for this morning. He set aside the coffee.

"Elena, come here." He guided her over to the wicker chairs. "There's something I need to tell you."

She looked at him. "I know."

"You do?"

"Yes. Your sister told me last night that you are going to be working with your father in Halencia. So you'll want to spend most of your time there. And that's why I've been thinking—"

"Wait." He waved his hands to gain her attention. "Is that all my sister told you?"

Elena's forehead creased. "What else should she have told me?"

"Nothing. Because she doesn't know this yet."

"Know what? You're worrying me."

He blew out a long breath and leaned forward, placing his elbows on his knees. "There's a problem with the estate. Huge problems."

"What kind of problem?"

"Financial. My father—he ran the estate into debt."

"Oh, no." She reached out and placed her hand on his shoulder. "I'm so sorry to hear this."

Luca's worried gaze met hers. "It isn't like my father to fall behind on his credit payments. He's used the estate, our home, to secure loans—loans that he doesn't have a prayer of paying off."

When Luca chanced a glance at her face, it was pale. She was getting the drift of the severity of the situation.

He didn't want to, but he had to go on. "I've had to use

my savings to stave off the creditors. And now I have nothing to offer you."

"Of course you do. I didn't marry you for your title or your money—"

"But you have a right to expect those things. And I can't give them to you. Well, I still have the title, but at this point it isn't worth much."

"It's okay," she said confidently. "I've got enough money to support both of us and the baby."

"No!" He jumped to his feet and moved to stand by the wall. "I'm not having you do that."

"You mean you're too proud to take money from a woman?"

"No, what I mean is that for a long time I shirked my responsibilities, and I won't do that again. I have to make this right and not take the easy way out. If I did that, if I counted on you to pull me out of this mess, how would our child ever respect me?"

He couldn't just stand there. He knew that Elena must now think less of him for letting things get to this point. If he was a proper son, he would have been there for his father before the business hit this critical juncture.

Luca took off down the steps of the decking bordering the cottage. He didn't have a particular destination in mind. He just needed space to figure out his next step.

"Luca, wait!"

He couldn't face her, not after he'd let her down. He kept going—kept moving down the beach.

"Luca, stop!" Elena cried. "There has to be a way to fix this. We just have to think about it."

Luca begrudgingly stopped and turned to the deck. "I did. And… Oh, never mind."

"No, you were going to say something. I want to know what it is." When she reached him, she placed a finger beneath his chin and lifted until they were eye to eye. "Speak to me."

"The only way to save the estate and the business is to find an immediate influx of cash." Maybe he'd been wrong. Maybe it was his pride and not some do-gooder notion that had him refusing to ask for her help. "I suggested that my father take on a partner with deep pockets, but he outright rejected the idea. He said that this was our legacy and only a DiSalvo would ever own the lemon grove."

"Even if it means losing his business and his home?"

Luca sighed. "Yes. He's a very stubborn man."

"Maybe he sees this as his chance to reconnect with his son."

The same thing had crossed Luca's mind. "I shouldn't have let things get to this point."

When Elena didn't interrupt, he was inclined to expand on his statement. The truth of the matter was that he hadn't opened up to anyone about this part of his life. By not talking about it, sometimes it was easier to pretend that his mother hadn't been stolen away and his family hadn't fractured under the weight of grief.

"It wasn't always this way," he said aloud as a way of convincing himself. "After my mother's death, I needed my father's assurance that everything would be all right—that we would be all right."

Luca drew an unsteady breath as his thoughts rolled back in time. He didn't want to go there and experience the too-familiar pain. Still, he needed Elena to understand how important his endeavor to save the lemon grove was to him. It was his plan to undo some of the damage that had been done to his family.

"My father withdrew from my sister and me. He was cold. He didn't cry. He didn't speak of my mother. I was convinced he didn't love her."

Elena sat down on the beach and patted a spot next to

her. When he joined her, she said, "Maybe he was in shock.
I don't know. But anytime I saw your parents together, there
was obvious affection."

"I'm starting to think you're right. But back then I was
an angry, confused kid. When my sister couldn't get love
and assurances from my father, she turned to me, and I
failed her."

"You can't blame yourself." Elena reached out and
placed her hand over his. "You were so young. It was just
too much."

"But I was the oldest. I should have been there for Annabelle. I should have been her rock."

"And because you couldn't be there for your family after
your mother's death, you're trying to make up for it now?"

He shrugged and then nodded. Finding warmth and
strength in her touch, he laced his fingers with hers. "Do
you think it's too late?"

"No. I think saving your family's business is heroic."

"But I haven't accomplished it yet. The only option I
can think of is to gain one of Mirraccino's contracts. They
are lucrative and far-reaching with their export business.
I talked with Demetrius, but he said that they are experiencing a full audit after what the king's lord-in-waiting did
to my mother. There's fear that he was embezzling from
the crown. Demetrius said he couldn't do anything for me
now, but that we could revisit it in the future. The problem
is that will take too long. The creditors will call in their
loans before then. The only way to get around Demetrius's
decision is to go directly to the king, but I can't get to him."

"And you need my help to get access to him."

Luca nodded.

Now it was up to Elena. And he had no idea how she
would feel about pulling strings with her father in order to
help him. He hated to put her in this position, but at that
moment, he just couldn't think of any other plan.

CHAPTER TWENTY

TALK ABOUT STRESSFUL.

Luca had been in a lot of tense business meetings, but this one was the worst.

He sat on a wing-back chair in the king's suite of rooms. He hadn't been in here since he was a little kid, and to be honest, it was still a bit intimidating as an adult. The room was regally decorated, mostly in maroon, with cream-colored walls. The furniture was all antique and he couldn't even begin to guess their ages, but every item was well maintained.

The king was up and dressed, but he looked to be a shell of the man that Luca once knew. Luca couldn't decide if it was age or stress or a little of both.

Luca had given his uncle an overview of the challenges facing the DiSalvo family. He had brought some projections with him, but he knew not to present them unless invited. As of yet, no invitation had been extended. The king had merely listened and nodded at the appropriate moments. And now that Luca had said everything that he'd come here to say, silence filled the room.

After a few moments, the king said, "Luca, I am sorry I haven't been around, especially as I hear that you and Elena have married. I want to offer you my best wishes."

"Thank you, sir. We appreciate it."

"I hadn't realized that you two were seeing each other. But then again, I haven't exactly been accessible recently. But I thought that Elena's father would have mentioned it."

Luca swallowed hard. "Actually, it was a bit of a whirlwind relationship, and we sort of kept it to ourselves."

"I can understand. Once upon a time I was a young man. Things can happen quickly." The king stared off into the distance as though he was caught up in memories. "I've watched Elena grow up, and there's something very special about her. She'll make you a good wife. You take care of that girl."

"I will, sir." This was his chance to get the conversation back on track. *Please let him agree.* "That's why I'm trying to secure a deal for the lemon grove."

"About that, I am sorry. But my son is right. We cannot grant new contracts right now. The kingdom's records and finances are all under review. Everything is on hold at the moment."

"I understand." He might understand, but that didn't make his situation any better.

"Once every file and account has been audited to make sure that criminal didn't embezzle or sell any national secrets, our security will return to normal and new business will commence. If you could just wait, we will give your proposal due consideration."

Luca couldn't just walk away. Even though the king couldn't help him now, he wanted to do or say something to help his uncle, or to just let him know that he wasn't alone. "Sir, you know that what happened with my mother wasn't your fault. And no one blames you."

The king's tired eyes widened. "How can people not blame me? That murderer worked for me. He was right here in this palace." A sorrowful expression filled his face. "I am so sorry this happened to your mother. I can't express enough my sorrow and regret that this happened."

How exactly did he respond to that? Luca never blamed him. "I appreciate your words, but you don't need to apologize."

"I should have known something was wrong." His fist pounded on the arm of his chair. "What kind of ruler am I if I can miss something so important?"

"You are human like the rest of us. Please believe me that

no one in my family—or in the palace or, for that matter, the nation—blames you. But people do miss you."

"Thank you. I will take that under consideration."

After thanking the king again for seeing him, Luca made his exit. He was in no better position than when he'd arrived. But he was in no worse shape, either.

And yet, he could feel everything he'd strived for slipping away. His childhood home, his legacy—it all now hung in a very precarious position. And should he fail to save it, he imagined that he would lose contact with his father and sister once more. This was why he kept people at a distance. Letting them in just set him up for more pain.

Most important, he would lose all of his savings on this venture and have no way to support Elena and the baby. He raked his fingers through his hair. If this was the best he could do, then perhaps he didn't deserve this family.

As he made his way out of the palace, he knew he would find a way to make this all work. He had to. Everyone was counting on him.

The deed was done.

Elena couldn't believe she'd begged her father to let Luca speak with the king. She knew her father didn't want to do it, but she'd pleaded with him and told him that her entire future was on the line. He'd asked if it was really that important, and she'd promised that it was. She knew that if Luca didn't save his legacy, their marriage didn't stand a chance of surviving—if it ever had.

She sure hoped Luca knew what he was doing. He seemed so certain the king would help that she wondered what would happen if the king's hands were tied just as his son's were. Elena didn't know a lot about how the government worked, but something told her the king would not override the crown prince's decision, not when the king was positioning his son to take over the kingdom—at least, that was what her father had led her to believe.

After stopping by to check on her mother, Elena retrieved her sketch pad and colored pencils. If nothing else, she could get some work done. Now that her modeling contract with Lauren Renard had been dissolved, Elena needed to focus on her new career path—designing her own fashions.

When she arrived back at the cottage, it was empty. Luca still hadn't returned. She'd taken that as a good sign—the king was hearing him out. And though Luca didn't go on and on about his family's business being in danger and what that would mean to his father, she knew it had Luca tied up in knots. If it was possible to get the lemon grove on level financial ground, would Luca be more open about his feelings toward the baby? And her?

But Elena foresaw a problem with his plan. Luca was trying to take on this enormous problem all by himself. Granted, she wasn't that familiar with the business world, but to her it seemed like the more people you had brainstorming ways to solve a problem, the quicker and easier the solution would be derived.

She grabbed her phone and selected Annabelle's number. Elena hesitated before she pressed Send. Sure, Annabelle had invited her to her engagement festivities, but how would she feel about Elena inserting herself into family business? Would she be willing to talk to Elena about something so intrinsic to her family?

There was only one way to find out. Elena pressed the button. The phone rang once, twice...

"Hey, Elena, I was just thinking about you." Annabelle's cheerful voice came over the line.

"You were?"

"Uh-huh. I was wondering how the impromptu honeymoon is going."

Elena paused, not sure what to say.

"Elena, is something wrong?"

This was her opening. She just had to take it. "That's the thing—the honeymoon, it's not going so well."

"I'm so sorry. Is there anything I can do?"

"Actually, there is. I need to talk to you about Luca—"

"Elena, who are you talking to?" Luca's voice boomed across the room.

Elena jumped. She hadn't even heard him enter the cottage. She turned to find a dark look on his face. She wondered just how much he'd overheard.

She held up a finger to get him to wait and then she spoke into the phone. "I've got to go."

"I'm here whenever you need to talk."

"Thanks. I appreciate that." Elena disconnected the call. She turned to Luca. "I didn't hear you come in."

"Obviously." His tone rumbled with agitation. "What exactly were you planning to say before I interrupted?"

Elena felt bad that he'd misinterpreted what he'd overheard. "It was nothing bad."

He crossed his arms and waited.

"I was talking with your sister and I was going to see if she had some ideas of what to do about the lemon grove."

"Why would she have any ideas?" His brows drew together in a formidable line. "This isn't her problem."

"The last time I checked, she was part of your family, and the lemon grove does belong to your family."

"But this is my problem, not hers...and not yours."

His last words stabbed at her heart. Even though they'd gotten married, made mad, passionate love and she was carrying his child, Luca still refused to let her in. What was his problem? When was he going to learn that people weren't out to hurt him?

In this moment, she felt as though she was fighting for the future of her marriage. "This *is* my problem. I'm your wife, remember. And it's your sister and your father's problem. What is wrong with you? Why can't you let people in?"

"I don't need to let people in. I do fine on my own."

She lifted her chin. "If you're so fine, why do you look so miserable?"

"Because I came home to find my wife doesn't believe that I can take care of our family."

"And so you're going to stand on your pride instead of reaching out for help."

"I don't need help. Just leave me alone."

Really? This was how he was going to play it? He'd been pushing her away for too long now. And she wasn't going to put up with it anymore.

"Luca, I love you. I want to help you. What is so wrong with that?"

He shook his head, and his gaze didn't meet hers. "I didn't ask for anyone to take pity on me."

"It's not pity. It's what people do when they love each other." And then she realized that the night they'd spent together might have meant something totally different to him than it had to her. "Luca, do you love me?"

He didn't say anything. And then he walked toward the balcony. If he thought he was getting away and avoiding this, he was wrong. She followed him.

"Luca." When he didn't even acknowledge that he'd heard her, she tried again. "Luca, answer me."

He turned to her. "I can't tell you what you want to hear. I can't be the man you want me to be."

Tears pricked the backs of her eyes, but she refused to give in to her pregnancy hormones. She blinked back the moisture. She refused to let Luca see how much his words hurt her.

"You might not love me, but you can't say the same about your family."

"I don't need them, either. Why do you think I can't be happy alone?"

"Because I believe that everyone needs somebody. I have to believe that, otherwise…" She stopped as her emotions threatened to overtake her.

"Otherwise what?" His intent gaze studied her as though trying to ferret out the truth.

She swallowed hard. "Otherwise you won't be able to love our child."

He didn't say a word. Not one syllable. Instead he turned to stare out at the sea.

That's it! She had tried to be understanding, but she'd had enough of his stubborn attitude. If he couldn't meet her halfway, she was done.

"You know, you don't have to face the world alone." She held back from saying that she would stand by his side through anything. "Your family would rally around you if you'd let them in. That's what families do."

He turned to her. His eyes were dark, and his stance was rigid. "And what makes you think I need their help?"

"A better question is how are you supposed to be a loving parent to our baby if you never let anyone in?"

"Stop saying that." He stared at her as though shocked that she would say these things to him. "I do let people in."

"No, you don't." She didn't know why she bothered. He'd counted on himself for so long now that he didn't know any other way to be. "I give up. I love you, but obviously that's never going to penetrate the wall around your heart."

He looked at her, but he didn't say anything. This was where he should profess his love for her, too. And yet there was nothing but a stony silence.

Though it was breaking her heart, she just couldn't imprison him or herself in a one-sided marriage. She knew he would stay out of obligation, and if she didn't walk out that door right now, he would be miserable for the rest of his life. And she loved him too much to do that to him.

"I can't do this anymore." She turned for the door.

"Where are you going?"

"At last, you speak. If you must know, I'm going to my parents' for dinner. They invited us both, but I can't imagine that you would want to go. I'll give them your regrets." She continued to the door. And then she paused and turned. "I guess this is goodbye."

"Goodbye?"

"Yes. Tomorrow I'm returning to Paris. I'll email you with any important information about the baby. Goodbye, Luca."

She turned and headed out the door while she could still maintain a dignified expression. Because that had been the hardest thing she'd ever done in her life. Her heart felt as though it had been ripped from her chest.

CHAPTER TWENTY-ONE

WHAT HAD JUST HAPPENED?

Luca stared at the closed door as he gathered his thoughts. In the heat of the moment, he decided Elena leaving was for the best.

He paced back and forth in the cottage, feeling like a caged animal. Why did everyone in his life keep telling him that he was doing things the wrong way? All he was trying to do was stand on his own two legs. Was that such a bad thing?

Of course not.

He contemplated walking out the door and not stopping. He needed away from the palace and Mirraccino—away from Elena. But for the first time ever, he couldn't imagine being on his own again. Every time he thought of the future, he saw Elena in it.

The voices of Elena, his father, the king and others echoed in his head. He had to get out of there. He headed for the beach. The sounds of the water, the birds and the breeze were calming. Now he had to unravel this tangled mess, because so much was at stake.

Never before had he had this many people foisting their opinions and advice upon him. All of them wanted him to do this or that, but none asked what he wanted to do.

The last time—the only time—he'd done what he was told, it had been with his mother. He didn't let himself think of her very often, but her memory filled his mind now. He reached for the chain that hung around his neck, a constant reminder of her—a source of comfort in times of trouble. He removed the chain from his neck and clutched the St. Christopher medal in his palm.

When he was a child, his mother was the only one to

guide him—to tell him what needed to be done. His sister had been too little, his father too busy and Elena too awe-struck by the fact that he was a part of the royal family.

In the years since his mother's murder, he'd been doing his best to navigate life on his own. Was it possible that in his efforts to avoid another loss that he'd built these walls around himself that Elena mentioned?

He supposed it was true. He'd never really stopped to think about it. But it was the only way he knew how to be. He didn't even know how to change.

But if he didn't do something, he was going to lose the woman he loved. It was the first time he'd allowed himself to admit his intense feelings for Elena to himself. And in-stead of it being scary, it was freeing. It was like stepping out of the shadows and into the sunlight.

He knew she still had the ability to hurt him, but by de-nying his feelings, he was hurting himself more. But was it too late? Would she give him a second chance?

He had to prove to her that he'd changed—that he was willing to let people into his life. And he knew how to do it. He would start with his father and sister.

He had an idea of how to save the lemon grove, but he couldn't do it by himself. Finally, he was hearing what Elena had been telling him. He wasn't in this battle alone. There were people around who wanted to help, if he'd let them.

First, he would speak to his father, Annabelle and the newest member of the family, Grayson. When Luca went to Elena, he was going to show her that family meant ev-erything to him.

Elena and the baby were his everything.

CHAPTER TWENTY-TWO

ELENA HAD ARRIVED home early for dinner.

She had nowhere else to go and nothing she wanted to do. And since she was leaving in the morning, she thought she would spend the extra time with her mother.

"Dear, you really don't have to help with dinner. I can manage," her mother insisted as she tried to prepare food while balancing on her crutches.

"Mother, why don't you sit at the table and I'll bring you whatever you need?"

"Well, that probably would be easier. Thanks." She moved to the table. "But something tells me you have more on your mind than worrying about me. For a newlywed, you've been spending a lot of time at home. What's going on?"

Elena didn't know how to respond. She just wasn't willing to admit to anyone that her brief marriage was a bust. Every time she thought of vocalizing the words, the backs of her eyes started to sting. She couldn't avoid the subject forever, but for just this moment, she wanted to pretend that her heart wasn't breaking in two.

Elena started slicing cheese. "Can I ask you something?"

"Sure. Does it have to do with sex?"

The knife slipped, barely missing Elena's finger. "Mother!"

"Okay. I was just kidding." Her mother sat at the table cutting orange wedges for the fruit and cheese tray.

Elena kept her gaze on the task at hand, not wanting her mother to read too much in her gaze. "When you first got married, did you— Well, was Father a little distant?"

"Your father? No. He's always been romantic and passionate—"

"Mother, I thought we said we weren't going there."

Her mother laughed. "Passionate about his feelings, daughter. I've always known where I stood with him."

Which just reinforced her decision to end things with Luca. She never knew where she stood with him, and she couldn't live like that.

"I take it you and Luca are having some problems adjusting."

"Something like that." Maybe if she opened up a little more, her mother would be able to give her some helpful advice. After all, her mother knew how to maintain a successful marriage. "It's just that he won't open up and let me in. And now that I'm—"

She stopped. How could she just go and almost blurt out that she was pregnant? Now wasn't the time for that news.

"You really are pregnant, aren't you?" The glee was obvious in her mother's voice. She got to her feet in record time and rushed over to put an arm around Elena. "I'm so happy for you."

When they pulled apart, Elena said, "No one knows."

"Haven't you told your husband?"

"He knows." Since she'd already said more than she intended, she might as well finish confessing. "It's the only reason he married me."

"What?" Her mother sounded shocked. "Surely you don't believe that."

"How can I not believe it? I asked him once if he loved me, and he said no."

"But that can't be right. I've watched you two over the years. It's as plain to me as the nose on my face that you two belong together. I just wondered how long it would take you to figure it out."

Elena sniffled. "I figured it out, but he didn't. And I can't live with someone who doesn't love me back. It's not right for me, and it's not right for our baby."

"Oh, Elena, think hard before you do anything drastic. Sometimes we only get one chance at love."

The sound of footsteps had them both turning. There in the entrance to the kitchen stood Luca. He looked awful. His face was pale and drawn. Elena's first instinct was to go to him, but she held herself back. If this was going to work, he had to make the first move.

"I knocked," he said, "but I don't think anyone heard, so I let myself in. I hope that's all right."

"Of course it is," her mother said, as though there wasn't a thing wrong. "You're family now. You are welcome here anytime."

"Thank you." His gaze met Elena's. "That means a lot."

Her mother smiled. "I hope you brought your appetite. Elena and I have been cooking up a storm. We can eat as soon as my husband arrives."

Elena stood by quietly, wondering what his real reason was for being there. Part of her was frustrated and she didn't want to have the same argument with him again. But another part of her wondered if maybe her words had finally gotten through to him.

"Actually," Luca said, "I was wondering if I could borrow your daughter for a little bit."

"Certainly. She's all done here."

When Elena didn't make any movement to go to him, Luca said, "Elena, there are things I need to say to you. It's important."

He deserved to wait a minute. She wanted him to know that she wasn't going to jump every time he called. Most of all, he had to know that he'd truly hurt her.

"Please," he pleaded.

That was what she needed. She turned to her mother. "Are you sure you've got everything?"

"Positive. Thank you for your help. I appreciate it and our chat. Now go." She shooed them from the kitchen. As they were going out the door, her mother hollered, "And if you don't make it back this evening, we'll have leftovers tomorrow."

Oh, her mother, ever the optimistic one.

Elena wasn't as hopeful. Maybe she was building up her own walls now. But she just couldn't get her hopes up and let her heart get broken all over again.

CHAPTER TWENTY-THREE

LUCA HAD NEVER been more nervous in his life.

Neither said a word as they walked. He didn't have a destination in mind. He just needed time alone with Elena. And now that he was with her, the words inside him twisted up in a knot and clogged his throat.

Their meandering led them to the cliff overlooking the sea. The sun hovered on the horizon, sending magnificent shades of pink and purple streaking through the sky. But nothing could hold a candle to his wife's beauty.

And if he didn't say the right things now, he knew he was going to lose her for good. His chance at having a family would be gone. And he didn't know how he would live with the knowledge that he'd ruined it all.

He swallowed hard. "Elena, please don't do this. Don't leave."

She maintained a considerable distance between them. Her gaze was cool and distant. "I want you to know that I really appreciate all you've done for me. Not many men would have stepped up and proposed marriage to protect their unborn baby from a scandal."

"I did what I needed to do. And I'd do it again."

"But that's the thing—you don't need to do anything else. The crisis has been averted. We can now go back to our lives."

"Elena, please don't do this."

"I can't continue to live a lie. If we can't fully and honestly communicate with each other, we can't have a healthy marriage."

"Listen, I'm sorry about not telling you about my family's financial crisis as soon as I learned about it. But thanks to you, we have a plan in place to get us through this rough patch. I just came from talking to my father, Annabelle and Grayson. We are going to contract with Fo Shizzle Cafés for as much produce as they can take. And we spoke with Demetrius, who was able to give us a date for when the royal family will start taking on new contracts again. He said ours would be the first they considered."

Elena shook her head. "You're still not hearing me. I'm not talking about business."

"But I reached out to my family for help. Isn't that what you wanted?"

"Partly. But you still won't let anyone know how you feel."

He raked his fingers through his hair. "And how do you want me to resolve that?"

"I don't know. I'm not sure it can be resolved. That's why I'm going back to Paris in the morning."

"You mean alone?"

"Yes. It's best for everyone."

Again, there was a coolness to her words. Her voice was almost monotone, and he noticed how her gaze didn't quite meet his. He felt like she was blocking him out—like he was suddenly a stranger to her. And he didn't like it. Not one little bit.

He wanted his Elena back—the person who made him laugh, who was full of emotion and tenderness. This aloofness wasn't like her.

And then it dawned on him that this was how it must have been for Elena to deal with him all this time. It was as if he suddenly truly understood what his efforts to protect himself had done to those around him.

"Elena, I am sorry for blocking you out. I was afraid. Afraid of losing you from my life, whether it be an unexpected death or indifference or something else. I'm not afraid to love you anymore."

She stood there much like a statue. She didn't say anything. In fact, she didn't react at all. Hadn't she heard him? "Elena, I love you."

CHAPTER TWENTY-FOUR

SHE'D HEARD HIM.

She'd tried not to, but his words penetrated her heart.

She didn't react right away, because she was still processing this information. It was a lot to take in. And they had to get this right.

Elena lifted her chin. "Are you saying all this because you now feel that you have something to offer?"

"What?"

"The deal with the lemon grove. Are you willing to take a risk on us because you want your child to grow up on the DiSalvo estate?"

"No. No. No. Didn't you hear me? I love you. I know it took a long time for me to get it all straight, but I'm here now, asking you to forgive me. I've made a lot of mistakes, but I never meant to hurt you."

Her heart fluttered. These were the words she'd been longing to hear for so very long. A tear splashed onto her cheek. She swiped it away.

Luca got down on one knee and took her hand in his. "I did this once and I meant it, but I didn't get it exactly right, so I'd like a do-over. Is that all right?"

She nodded as a smile pulled at her lips. At last, the wall around his heart had crumbled. Her heart pounded with love and joy.

"Elena, I love you. If I am honest with myself, I've always loved you. When something good happens, you're the first person I think of to tell. If something bad happens, you're the one I want to share my troubles. Yours is the last face I want to see at night and the first in the morning. I want to spend the rest of my days showing you just how much I love you. Will you spend the rest of your life with me?"

"Yes. Yes. Yes." She drew him up to his feet. "I love you with all my heart." And then she took his hand and pressed it to her abdomen. "We both do."

Luca stared deep into her eyes. "I'm the luckiest man in the world."

"And I am the luckiest woman. I get to spend the rest of my life with my best friend."

She lifted up on her tiptoes and pressed her lips to his.

EPILOGUE

Eleven months later

ELENA STOOD IN the gardens of the royal palace. Annabelle and Grayson had just been married. Elena and Luca had stood up for them. And the king had attended, now that he was back to being himself.

It was so nice to be back in Mirraccino. She said that every time she and Luca visited, which was often. As much as she loved Halencia, it would never have that special something that Mirraccino did. Maybe it was because this was her childhood home…or maybe it was because it was here that she'd met the man of her dreams, who at that point had been a little boy who didn't mind getting his formal clothes dirty playing with a girl. Elena smiled at the memories. They seemed so long ago now.

While Luca talked with one of his many cousins, Elena excused herself. European football was something that still didn't interest her—no matter how much Luca tried to sway her. Although she had enjoyed playing football with Luca as a kid, it didn't hold her attention in the same way. Now the only thing she recognized about the game was which jersey matched which team. What could she say? Fashion was in her blood. Only in a different way now.

She moved around the vast gardens. The walkways were lit up with torches that gave a soft glow to the fragrant foliage. Their garden in Halencia was just as beautiful, but not nearly as vast. It was where Elena spent a lot of time now that their son, Marco, had been born. Instead of modeling glamorous fashions, she was now doing something she loved—designing. Her debut fashion show was planned for this fall. She couldn't wait.

When fingers wrapped around her shoulders, she jumped.

"Hey, relax. It's just me," Luca murmured very close to her ear. Then he leaned over and pressed his lips to the nape of her neck. "What had you so deep in thought?"

"I was just thinking about the path we took to get here. It's hard to believe that we once played hide-and-seek in these gardens and now your sister is having her wedding reception here."

"I was beginning to wonder if she was ever going to get married—"

"Luca, really. Just because you rushed me down the aisle doesn't mean everyone wants to elope."

"Are you saying you regret our rush to the altar?"

"Of course not." She lifted up on her tiptoes and pressed her lips to his. "I love you, Luca. With all my heart."

"I love you, too." He kissed her again. "Are you sure you don't want a wedding do-over?"

"I'm positive. But I must admit that if I was going to have a wedding, I'd want it to be like this one, even if it took your sister a year to plan."

Luca glanced around. "I guess it isn't too bad."

Elena lightly punched him on the shoulder. "It's gorgeous. I'm so happy for your sister."

"I'm thinking I might have to hire her."

"For what?"

"I want to throw a party."

Elena frowned at her husband. "I told you I don't want to get married again. We got it right the first time, even if it took us a little bit to figure it out."

"Who said anything about getting married again?" He arched a dark brow. "I'm thinking that we have our first anniversary coming up and it deserves a party."

"You really want to go to all that trouble?"

Luca drew her close in his arms. "Mrs. DiSalvo, haven't

you figured out that I would go to the moon and back for you?"

She tilted her chin up. "I wouldn't let you get that far away."

Between his sweet words and the way he stared deeply into her eyes, her heart tap-danced in her chest and her knees became rubbery. She loved the way he could still make her feel as giddy as she had when this whole love affair began.

"Why's that?" he asked.

"Because I couldn't bear to be separated from you for that long."

"Don't worry. I'll always be right here." He pressed his hand to her heart.

She lifted up on her tiptoes and pressed her lips to his. Her heart swelled with love. She didn't know it was possible to love someone this much.

A lifetime together would never be enough.

* * * * *

If you loved this novel, you won't want to miss
THE MILLIONAIRE'S ROYAL RESCUE,
the first book in Jennifer Faye's
MIRRACCINO MARRIAGES *duet.*
Available now!

If you want another marriage of convenience
romance, make sure to watch out for
BOUND TO THE GREEK BILLIONAIRE by Rebecca
Winters, the second book in her
THE BILLIONAIRE'S CLUB *trilogy.*

"Ellie? Ellie Owens?" he asked.

"I just go by Elle now, but yes. Nice to see you."

Nice, but a total shock. Racking her brain, she remembered the last time she'd seen him—graduation. At twenty-two, Cam had not only been the older brother of the love of her life but he'd already been to college and had returned with a full beard.

The truth was that Cameron Dumont had always sort of intimidated her. Hell, he'd intimidated the whole town. He was a loner, always off in some corner. Not brooding, but watching, observing, with a self-assured confidence that no other adolescent possessed. With long hair and dark looks, he'd always seemed... dangerous, she decided. He was full of muscles and well over six feet tall.

Looking at him now, it was evident that he was still built and dangerous-looking, if not cleaned up a bit from ten years ago. Elle felt a little flutter of some kind of awareness as she took in his now beardless, square jawline, broad shoulders and arms rippling with muscles.

"Welcome home, Elle," he said. "You look... great."

* * *

Saved By The Blog:
This matchmaking gossip columnist
won't stop until true love wins!

FALLING FOR THE RIGHT BROTHER

BY
KERRI CARPENTER

First Published in Great Britain 2017
By Mills & Boon, an imprint of HarperCollins*Publishers*
1 London Bridge Street, London, SE1 9GF

© 2017 Kerri Carpenter

ISBN: 978-0-263-92306-3

23-0617

Our policy is to use papers that are natural, renewable and recyclable products and made from wood grown in sustainable forests. The logging and manufacturing processes conform to the legal environmental regulations of the country of origin.

Printed and bound in Spain
by CPI, Barcelona

Award-winning romance author **Kerri Carpenter** writes contemporary romances that are sweet, sexy and sparkly. When she's not writing, Kerri enjoys reading, cooking, watching movies, taking Zumba classes, rooting for Pittsburgh sports teams and anything sparkly. Kerri lives in Northern Virginia with her adorable (and mischievous) rescued poodle mix, Harry. Visit Kerri at her website, www.kerricarpenter.com, on Facebook (Facebook.com/AuthorKerri,) Twitter and Instagram (@authorkerri) or subscribe to her newsletter.

For My Dad

If only everyone had a dad like mine,
the world would be a much better (and funnier) place.

Chapter One

Good morning, avid readers! Who's ready to be saved by the blog? Boy, do I have some juicy gossip that will help you escape the day-to-day life of our very small town.

Rumor has it one of Bayside's most infamous residents is returning today after a ten-year absence. You may remember this gal as lover of all things Jasper Dumont. Who can forget the time she declared her love for him by, ahem, making that little video? Haven't seen it? I'm sure someone saved a copy. *Smirk*

Personally, I'm thrilled that she's back. So with that, let me, your fabulous Bayside Blogger, be the first to say... Welcome back to Bayside, Ellie Owens.

Elle stepped off the airport tram, thanked the driver and retrieved her luggage. Inhaling a deep whiff of air, she caught the familiar salty scent she associated with home.

As the tram drove away, she stood on the stone sidewalk in the center of town, taking a moment to reacquaint herself with Bayside, Virginia. Still pleasant to look at with its town square full of eclectic shop fronts and its flower-lined streets. Tucked behind one side of the square was the bay, the heart and soul of the town. The water looked calm today as fishing boats returned to their docks after their early-morning fishing trips.

Elle knew if she squinted her eyes just right she would be able to see the small, two-bedroom bungalow she'd shared with her father until she'd turned eighteen and went off to college, and then directly on to Italy after that. One of the many things she'd missed from home was her brightly painted yellow house with its rickety deck and even more dilapidated dock that stretched out into the water. It wasn't unlike the other houses on that side of the bay.

She also knew that if she stood out on the dock, she would be able to take in the much larger and more impressive houses—mansions, really—on the other side of the water. That's where the Dumont house sat, surrounded by tactfully placed trees and discreet fences.

How many nights had she sneaked out after she was supposed to be asleep to take in the lights and music coming from that magical house? It seemed the Dumonts threw parties with the same frequency that other people went to the grocery store.

Apparently there was nothing like a Dumont party. Everyone in town had heard about the expensive champagne, live music and occasional fireworks. Although that wasn't surprising for a family who had made more money than God in real estate.

She'd heard that one time the Dumonts had hired ballroom dancers to entertain their guests. Another time they'd flown in a top chef from Japan to make fresh sushi for Mrs. Dumont. Once they'd even hired a troupe of Cirque du Soleil performers for a birthday celebration.

But out of all those special occurrences that came and went, one thing was always present. One person, actually. The person who'd taken on the role of prince of the castle in her childhood fantasies.

Jasper Dumont.

Even a shy bookworm like Elle had known of Jasper. In fact, everyone in town knew Jasper. Well liked, crazy hot, an incredible athlete in multiple sports and the most popular kid in school. No wonder Elle had harbored a huge crush on him.

When his parents had thrown their parties, she used to pretend that Jasper was dancing in a tuxedo and drinking champagne. In reality, he was probably at one of the parties in the local park drinking cheap beer with the rest of the cool kids.

She'd certainly never been invited to those parties. But Elle's dad had always said she was an old soul. And maybe she was. Maybe she wanted to be kissed on the dance floor, like they did in the old black-and-white movies as twinkly lights illuminated the scene. Maybe she'd promised herself that one day she would go to this fictional party at the Dumonts'.

The funny thing was that Elle had attended tons of parties like that when she'd moved to Italy. She'd drunk amazing sparkling wine in centuries-old piazzas. She'd danced around local vineyards and listened to phenomenal musicians while sitting on the Spanish Steps. She'd even made out in the Blue Grotto when she visited Capri. Didn't get much more romantic than that.

But that dream—that silly childhood dream—would always persist. Who forgot about their first love? Even if that first love was the exact reason why she'd had to leave her home.

The sound of a honking horn drew her attention. A tall, attractive man dressed in jeans and a T-shirt stepped out of a silver truck and walked toward her. Elle felt her eyes go wide as she realized who it was.

No way, she thought.

"Cam?" she called out with a small wave as she pushed her large sunglasses on top of her head.

He stopped midstride, smack-dab in the center of the street. She thought his mouth fell open but couldn't quite see from her angle. Cocking his head, he pushed his hands into the pockets of his worn jeans and took her in. Not until a car horn blasted did he move. Shaking his head, he waved to the driver to pass and continued toward her.

"Ellie? Ellie Owens?" he asked.

"I prefer Elle now, but yes. Nice to see you."

Nice, but a total shock. Racking her brain, she remembered the last time she'd seen him—graduation. At twenty-two, Cameron Dumont had not only been the older brother of her biggest crush, but he'd already been to college and had returned with a full beard.

The truth was that Cam had always sort of intimidated her. Hell, he'd intimidated the whole town. He was a loner, always off in some corner, watching, observing, with a self-assured confidence no other adolescent possessed. With long hair and dark looks, he'd always seemed… dangerous, she decided. He was full of muscles and well over six feet tall.

Looking at him now, it was evident that he was still tall, built and dangerous looking, if not cleaned up a bit from ten years ago. Elle felt a little flutter of some kind of awareness as she took in his square jawline, broad shoulders and arms rippling with muscles.

"Welcome home, Elle," he said. "You look…great."

The disbelief in his voice didn't surprise her. After all, the last time she'd stood in Bayside, she'd been, well, less than glamorous, that was for sure. She'd never worn makeup—her father never allowed it. And when your dad was the chief of police, you tended to listen. Her wardrobe choices hadn't been the most flattering, either—lots of jeans, flannels and sweatshirts. Total tomboy clothes. And maybe she'd carried around a little extra weight. But she'd been more into academics than athletics.

Somewhere between college and moving to Italy she'd dropped the weight, figured out how to apply makeup and let her straight brown hair grow out of the unfortunate cut she'd gotten at her dad's barbershop at the end of high school.

"Thanks," she said with a smile.

"Have you always had those dimples?"

"What?" she asked with a surprised laugh.

"Nothing. Sorry."

Searching the square, she tried to find her father's car before she realized that she had no idea what kind of vehicle he drove now.

"I just got in from the airport. I'm waiting for my dad to pick me up," she explained to Cam.

He shook his head. "Sorry, I should have said right away. Your dad called me this morning and asked if I could bring you home. Something came up." He looked away.

The reminder of why she'd returned from Italy came crashing back into her mind. "Is he at the doctor's?"

Cam nodded and quickly changed the subject. "Let me help with your bags." He grabbed all three of her bags with an exaggerated groan. "How many bodies do you have in here?"

"Just a few." Elle picked up her carry-on and purse, then followed him to his truck. She noticed that *Bayside Builders* was emblazoned on the side in black block lettering. After securing her luggage in the back, Cam surprised her by opening the passenger-side door. She slid into the truck as he skirted the hood and climbed into the driver's seat.

After starting the engine, he turned to her again. "It's been a while, Elle."

She could feel the heat flooding her cheeks. Was he referring to the night she wished she could forget? There was one particular bad memory she'd give anything to erase. "That was a long time ago, Cam," she said defensively.

Frowning, he turned in his seat to face her. "What was a long time ago?"

She rolled her eyes. "You know exactly what I'm talking about." Seeing his blank expression, she paused, then decided to get it all out in the open. "The video...about Jasper," she whispered, even though they were alone in the truck.

If she closed her eyes, she could see her dad's disappointed face as he watched his only daughter hiccup and slur as she drunkenly professed her love for Jasper Dumont.

How could she think making that video would get Jasper to notice her? Maybe because the alcohol hadn't allowed her to think at all. It definitely didn't help when her oversize T-shirt had slipped off her shoulder, giving way to a wardrobe malfunction that would have made any reality-TV star blush.

To be honest, it wasn't as though Elle had obsessed over the video every day for the last decade. Certainly not while she'd lived in Italy, the most beautiful place in the world. Why was it, then, that as soon as she stepped onto the sidewalk of her hometown the memory of the one bad thing she'd ever done came slamming back in crystal clear vision?

To her shock, Cam started laughing, his deep voice filling the truck. "Oh, my God, I forgot all about that."

What the hell? How could he act so blasé about the fateful event that almost got her suspended and laughed right out of town? Even now the thought of it could produce an embarrassed blush on her face the color of a ripe Italian tomato.

He must have noticed her doing her best blend-in-with-the-seat impression because his own expression softened. "Don't tell me that stupid little video is why you've stayed away all these years?"

Stupid? Little? No way. It had been the single most humiliating experience of her life. And while it might not have been the reason her dad had shipped her off to college in a galaxy far, far away, it hadn't helped matters.

In the end, her dad had, as usual, been right. She'd needed to get far away from Bayside—to forget, and to become her own person, without all the baggage weighing her down. Besides, she'd loved college, especially when she took a year to study abroad. Her love affair with Italy began then, and concluded after her graduation, when she'd moved to Florence for grad school. Staying in Italy for an art history major was a no-brainer. She'd been able to work in the most amazing museums and galleries. Every second she spent at the Uffizi, San Marco Museum, the Accademia or the Palazzo Vecchio had been among the most amazing moments in her life, and did help her forget. A little.

Still, she'd missed home.

"Happy to be back?" Cam asked as if he'd read her mind, before pulling out into the light traffic.

"I missed…certain things."

"Your dad," he supplied softly.

She smiled for a moment before it faded. The worry that had nestled inside her belly began to spread, causing her to roll down her window.

"How is he really?" she asked quietly.

Elle still couldn't believe her dad had kept the cancer diagnosis from her. When he'd finally told her, he'd been so flippant about it. "Oh, it's only bladder cancer. That's one of the easy ones."

There was nothing easy about cancer.

Cam followed suit and rolled his own window down. "He had some rough moments toward the end of the treatment period. But I think overall he's doing really well. Except for a couple days off here and there, he never stopped working."

For twenty-four years her dad had been the chief of

police in Bayside. After her mom had died, they'd moved back to her father's hometown for a fresh start. While he'd retired a couple years ago, no one could keep a man who'd been working since the age of ten at home. He'd been volunteering as security at the local high school ever since.

"Really?" she asked.

Cam nodded. "Sure. Heard he broke up a minor fight last week."

"A fight? Is he okay? Should he even be doing that right now?"

He slanted a steady glance in her direction. "He's fine. Don't worry. The whole town's looking out for him."

Yeah, the way they'd looked out for him ten years ago? Elle shook her head and willed the memories away. It hadn't been the town's fault he didn't get voted in as county sheriff. That had been her doing. Her and that damn video. She wiped her sweaty palms on her khaki linen pants.

Cam turned the truck onto Bay View Road, heading away from the center of town. They passed the fork in the road, the one that would take them to either the east side, known as the nice, wealthy portion of town, or to the west side, where she lived.

"Really," he added with another sidelong glance as she raised an eyebrow.

"Please tell me the truth." She could hear the urgency in her voice.

"The truth is he has cancer."

She gulped. "I gathered that part already." Typical. The very few conversations she'd ever had with Cam had been pretty similar. He hadn't been known for his words. Or his demeanor. Really, he'd been a loner. A tall, somewhat scary kind of recluse.

Elle didn't know what she was expecting now. To be honest, the fact that he was giving her a ride home was a huge step toward the socialization of the Cameron Dumont she knew.

Then he did something that surprised her. Cam reached over and squeezed her hand.

Her eyes grew wide and she inhaled sharply. If anyone ever asked, she would claim it was nothing short of shock at him being nice. The reality of the situation was that the touch of Cam's callused hand on hers made her feel…something.

"He's going to be fine," he said.

She didn't know why, but the statement made her feel better for the moment. "So," she began, searching for something to say as she reclaimed her hand and clasped it with the other one. "You're still in Bayside."

"Yep."

"Working for your parents' company?"

His hands tightened on the steering wheel. "Nah. I started my own business."

"Really?" That was a surprise. Cam was the oldest son in a four-generation family business. Naturally, he was supposed to take over the reins. "Also doing real estate?"

"Construction. I'm a contractor."

"Bayside Builders," she said, putting it together. He looked over. "I saw the name on the side of the truck."

"That's my company."

She wanted to ask more questions, but they'd reached 14 Bay View Road. Cam threw the truck into Park and slid out of his door. But Elle didn't move. Instead, she let her homesick eyes drink in the sight of the one level house she'd lived in for most of her life. It looked exactly the same, even though she could tell it wasn't. Her dad had put a fresh coat of paint on. There were new shutters and the landscaping was different.

But it was home and therefore would always be exactly what she needed to see.

"Traditionally, you leave the car when you reach your destination."

She glanced up at Cam standing in her window, watching her. Rolling her eyes, she offered him a small smile. "Good thing you're here to help me with these super hard ways of the world."

His mouth twitched before he opened her door and reached across her to unbuckle her seat belt. Elle caught a whiff of a very masculine scent. Something musky, but clean. Like a really fresh soap laced with wood.

"When did you get rid of the beard?" she couldn't help asking.

Confusion passed his face. Then he ran a hand over some appealing-looking stubble. "Years ago. Had to back when I worked for my father."

Now that she was allowing herself a really good look, Elle acknowledged that Cam and Jasper barely resembled each other. Jasper was all light hair and crystal-blue eyes, tall but lanky, while Cam was dark and large. Both brothers were attractive—beyond attractive, really—but in very different ways.

"Do you even have a key to get in?" Cam's question burst her bubble and she finally exited the truck.

"No worries." After she walked to the small front porch, she bent over and smiled as her fingers touched the key in its usual place under the decorative ceramic frog that held watch at the front door.

Cam dragged her bags into the house and stepped back onto the porch. She turned to thank him for the ride, but before she could get the words out, he put his hand on the top of the door frame. Even though she could—and should—take a step backward into the open living room, she didn't move. His eyes raked over her entire body until she squirmed.

"I'm glad you're back, Elle." Then he abruptly turned and walked back to his waiting truck.

With that, she nodded, wondering why she suddenly felt light-headed.

Cam considered himself to be a rational, sane man, but something happened to him when he saw Ellie Owens again. And that reaction defied reasoning.

"Damn," he said aloud as he drove away from her house and made his way back down Bay View Road. When he reached the fork, he started veering toward town before he remembered that he'd left his favorite cordless drill at his parents' house the night before.

Yanking the steering wheel to the left just in time, he made his way toward the east side of the bay. He'd been called by his mother to fix a shelf. Funny how when he'd arrived, tools in tow, there was nothing to fix. Instead—surprise, surprise—an attractive woman had been seated in one of the living rooms. His mother's interior designer this time.

Cam loved his mom, but her attempts at fixing him up had been increasing at a fast pace over the last two years—ever since he'd turned thirty. Even if he'd been onboard with her efforts, she clearly didn't know his tastes. Cam preferred a certain kind of woman. When his thoughts turned back to Elle, he swerved again before righting the truck.

Little Ellie Owens, who used to keep her head in a book, or in a sketch pad, while wearing jeans with patches over the knees. She'd never stepped a toe out of line until that idiotic video surfaced. Cam remembered how embarrassed Jasper had been seeing her announce her undying love for him. In Cam's opinion, it never seemed like much of a burden to have a woman show you some love. Especially a woman as grounded as Elle. Of course, Jasper had been in a pretty serious relationship back then.

Regardless, somewhere along the line, she'd grown up into a gorgeous, stunning woman. Gone was the plain-Jane scholar. In her place was an accomplished, interesting person.

Cam turned into the gates of the mansion at 1954 Bay View Road and offered a wave to Stan, the head gardener. Then he parked his truck, and ran in the back door to retrieve his drill. He was about to climb back into the truck when he noticed that not only were his parents' cars in the driveway, but so was his brother's. Cam climbed the steps to the front porch and pushed his way inside the large and impressive house he'd been lucky enough to grow up in.

He heard the shouting before he even entered the solarium.

"It's not that big of a deal."

"You think you can come in here and start making changes like you own the place?" his father asked.

"I kind of do own the place."

"Not yet," his mother's voice rang out. "Not while your father and I are still in charge."

Cam didn't have to be in the room to know that Jasper would be rolling his eyes the same way he was doing himself at the usual argument. His parents and brother butted heads on a daily basis.

"If you'd only let me implement a few small changes. Tweaks," he added quickly. "We need a better social media plan. Our communications department is currently living in the stone age figuring out how to make fire."

"It's like you don't even want to be part of this company, the way you keep trying to change everything." Cam could hear the frustration in his father's voice.

His own stomach clenched at the comment.

"Of course I want to be part of the company. Why else

would I be here?" Jasper replied. "I'm simply trying to bring us into this century."

Feeling a thickness in his throat, Cam decided to save his baby brother. Giving a quick cough to announce his presence, he stepped into the room.

"There's my handsome son." Lilah Dumont rose and patted him on the cheek before pulling him into a hug.

"Hey," Jasper called out. "I thought I was your handsome son."

She turned back to him. "Oh, you are. But only when you aren't irritating me with new proposals involving hashtags."

Cam hoped that Jasper saw the look of adoring, unaffected love their mother shot in his direction. But by the way Jasper had turned toward the window, he suspected not.

"Hey, Pops," Cam said to his dad.

"Why aren't you at work?" his dad asked as a reply and a welcome.

"Why aren't any of you?" he countered.

"We are working." His mother poured a glass of lemonade and handed it to him. "We're discussing your brother's latest idea." She used air quotes and Cam was fairly certain he could hear Jasper grind his teeth. "Then we were going to talk about the next fund-raiser."

Cam lifted an eyebrow. "Fund-raiser?"

"Yes."

"Ah. A party," he stated. His mother could justify giving a party more easily than some people could drink a glass of water. Although Lilah Dumont was so much more than a party-loving socialite. She could make just as many deals as his father simply by schmoozing during a black-tie event. Where Collin Dumont was old-school business etiquette, Lilah was about face-to-face interaction. Underestimating either her intelligence or business savvy had been the web that caught more than one misjudging fly.

"Social media is an inexpensive way to throw a party," Jasper contributed from the corner. "A virtual party. Keeps costs in check, connects you with the right people."

"Why not be personal? Why does everything have to be over the computer or smartphone or Instagram?" his mother asked. "People like personal interactions. That still means something."

Cam thought he would try and back his brother up. "Jasper does have a point. Perhaps we need to cut down on the amount of parties?"

His mother looked indignant. "Everyone loves our parties. You know that."

"Isn't less more in this situation?"

Lilah rolled her eyes. "Less is never more. I despise that saying."

On this one topic, his mother and father were in agreement. Cam had to suppress a groan. If another Dumont party was on the horizon, that meant he would have to take out his tux—again—and put on a happy face—again. Two things he hated almost as much as his mother's parties.

Jasper appeared to have forgotten his earlier hurt and turned to Cam. "Why aren't you working your butt off somewhere? Aren't you usually covered in dirt and sweat by this hour?"

"I had a meeting with a client earlier this morning." He grabbed an apple from a large display of fruit placed in the middle of a marble table. "You'll never guess who I picked up after that."

"It's bad enough that you drive that thing instead of a real car," Jasper began.

"Hey, I like my truck. I'd like you to know that Lamborghinis are not the only car available. Anyway, I did a favor for Ted Owens this morning."

"His doctor's appointment," his dad said from his chair. "I need to give him a call later and see how that went."

There were a lot of things that could be said about Collin Dumont, but one area Cam thought his dad did right. He respected his staff, his friends and the other citizens of Bayside. He'd been friends with Ted for years, and Cam heard the note of concern in his voice.

"Right. He had an appointment, so I had to pick up his daughter."

"Ellie?" his mother asked. "She's back from Italy?"

"Who's Ellie?" Jasper wondered.

Sometimes Cam didn't know if he should be appalled by or jealous of his brother's ignorance.

"You've gotta be kidding me, right?" Cam said. "Ellie Owens, the daughter of Ted, former chief of police." At Jasper's blank stare, he continued. "You were in the same class in school."

"Did we date?"

Their mother let out a loud chuckle. "Oh, most certainly not."

"She was in love with you," Cam said loudly and slowly, to get through to Jasper.

"Didn't she make some video about you that got played at your prom?" their father asked from behind the iPad he was now reading.

Cam tensed. He'd never understood why Elle had made that video in the first place. The whole thing was out of character. Feeling oddly protective, Cam decided to steer the conversation away from the video talk. "She's back. I'm not sure for how long, but she's here now for her dad. She looks amazing, by the way. All grown up."

"No kidding?" Jasper's tune changed quicker than he could get his Lamborghini from zero to sixty.

"Apparently Europe agreed with her."

"Good for her," Mrs. Dumont put in as she poured more

lemonade into her glass. "I always thought she was sweet. And everyone knew how smart she was. Top of her and Jasper's class. Or she would have been…"

"Didn't she throw herself in the bay after that prom?" Collin asked.

Another aspect of that story that had never made sense to Cam. Supposedly, she'd been so upset after the video aired that she'd pitched herself off the dock into the bay. Some called it a last-ditch effort to get Jasper's attention.

"Oh, yeah," Jasper replied.

The thing about attempting to drown yourself was that people who did so usually couldn't swim, Cam thought. Elle had been a great swimmer. He shook his head. A mystery for another time.

"Invite her to the party on Friday," Collin contributed, still reading his iPad, no doubt having pulled up the *Wall Street Journal*.

"Great idea," Lilah added.

"Um, I don't know if that's…"

"I'm willing to extend the olive branch to a hot girl," Jasper said.

Cam ignored his brother's wink. "Did you say Friday? The party is happening this Friday? It's Wednesday."

"Invitations went out two days ago. What is life without a little surprise and excitement?" His mother's eyes sparkled.

"I didn't get an invitation," Cam said.

"That's because I didn't want to give you a chance to RSVP no." Lilah beamed at him.

Cam clenched his teeth. He'd had plans to quit work early on Friday and take a couple of his employees golfing. "What's the reason for this party?" he asked.

They all looked at each other for a split second before his mother said "April," with a definite nod.

At the same moment his father said, "Flag Day."

Cam rolled his eyes, not sure where to start.

"Oh, who cares why," his mother called out. "It's a party, not a funeral, so get that stick out of your a—"

"Ah, that's enough," Collin said, as Cam tucked his tongue in the side of this mouth.

"But you are expected to be there," Lilah said, using her I-raised-two-boys-so-don't-even-think-about-messing-with-me tone.

"Seriously, Mom." Cam put his glass down on the table a little harder than he'd meant to and returned the uneaten apple, as well. The sound of heavy crystal hitting marble echoed throughout the room. For a moment, no one spoke. Then Collin looked up from his iPad.

"Just because you didn't want to work for the family doesn't mean you're not part of it."

Cam hated the hurt that flashed in his father's eyes. He knew he'd put it there by one selfish decision. He began to speak to his dad, but Jasper stopped him.

"Don't be so hard on him. I stepped up. I work for the family."

Cam knew Jasper wasn't saying that out of spite. He was only trying to help.

"And what an employee you turned out to be. Always wanting to change every damn little thing."

That same painful look flashed in Jasper's eyes now and Cam wanted to kick himself. He hadn't planned to come in here today to upset everyone. Nor had he intended to cause so much ill will when he stopped working for his parents and started his own company.

But it didn't take a soured afternoon to see the results of his decision. He carried around the guilt on a daily basis.

Cam used to go to every construction site of every building, shopping mall, apartment complex or whatever else his dad had been working on. Collin had proudly introduced him as the future head of Dumont Industries to anyone who would listen. That included Rick, the foreman on one of his job sites.

Rick had been the first person to really talk to Cam about construction. He'd patiently answered question after question. Walking around wearing a hard hat, looking at foundations and I beams made Cam feel excited. Not once had he ever felt that way in the office with his dad.

One summer Cam had announced that he would be working with Rick on the construction of a new multiplex. His dad still hadn't realized that Cam liked working with his hands, enjoyed building things. Instead, Collin had bragged that his son wanted to learn the business from the ground up, and wasn't that just great.

But even as a sixteen-year-old, Cam knew he'd found his calling. His dad never forgave him for it.

Cam pulled himself back to the present when his father let out an awkward and forced cough.

"I need to take this." He waved his phone and made a quick exit from the room, hurt trailing in his wake.

Cam didn't look at his mother when she rose from her seat, nor did he say goodbye as he left the solarium and headed back through the sprawling house toward the front door. He turned only when he heard his brother's voice.

"Cam, wait." Jasper bounded toward him, his expression concerned.

"Don't worry about it," Cam said. "And don't listen to the old man. You're doing a great job."

Jasper's face fell. "Yeah, I can't get my own father to listen to my ideas, let alone the rest of the board. Quick, someone get me on the cover of *Forbes*."

Cam didn't know what to say and he couldn't stand seeing the frustration in his brother's eyes. "Listen, I'll stop by your place later and fix that balcony door."

Jasper shook his head.

"What?" Cam asked. "It's been hanging off the hinges

for weeks. And while I'm there I can measure for those shelves you were talking about."

"Stop," Jasper said. "You don't owe me anything, Cam."

But he did. Cam was in debt to his little brother and fixing a few things around his condo didn't even come close to making up for it.

"I'll be by around seven," he said, his voice offering no room for argument. With his hand on the brass doorknob of the opulent front door, he asked his baby brother, "Are you happy?"

"What?"

"Answer the damn question, Jasp."

Jasper let out a long exhalation. "I'm fine. Stop worrying about me. Things are going fine."

But he did worry about him. More than his brother realized. Because Jasper had stepped up for him and Cam would spend the rest of his life making it right.

"Hey, bro. Answer me this." Cam waited for Jasper to meet his eyes. "Do you really not remember Elle Owens?"

Jasper shrugged. "Kind of. But if you say she's gorgeous now…"

Unbelievable. Because to Cam's way of thinking, the woman he'd picked up this morning was pretty damn unforgettable.

"I never said *gorgeous*." But he very easily could have. Suddenly, Cam felt incredibly uncomfortable.

His brother grinned as Cam flipped him off and left the house, thoughts of just how gorgeous Elle had become following him out the door.

Chapter Two

"Cancer free as of today."

The breath she let out was full of relief. Elle had been holding her jaw so tight that her face actually ached.

"Seriously?" she asked tentatively. She knew better than anyone that her dad had a habit of downplaying. The fact that he hadn't shared his diagnosis—even during their recent Christmas visit—until a couple weeks ago still had her seeing red.

"Cross my heart." Her dad kissed her on the head before engulfing her in a long, hard hug. Nothing could have felt better. "I'm sorry I wasn't there to pick you up this morning."

"Oh, don't worry about that." She waved a hand in the air as she took in her father. He looked mostly the same, a little thinner maybe, and a bit pale. But that was to be expected. "Tell me everything the doctor said, and start from the beginning."

Even though he rolled his eyes, Elle held firm. She would get the truth of the situation even if that meant calling the doctor herself.

"Our food is going to get cold," he said, gesturing to the spread on the table.

"It won't if you hurry up and tell me."

"You've always been the most stubborn little thing," he said with a laugh.

She returned with a chuckle of her own. "Wonder where I get that trait from."

"Fine, fine. The treatment seemed to work. When I went back in today, doc said the scope we did last week didn't detect any cancerous cells."

He was beaming and Elle wanted to share in his joy, but she'd done a fair amount of research on bladder cancer. They would need to stay on top of this to ensure it didn't return. Her dad would have to get scopes often and probably for the rest of his life.

A small concession for keeping him in her life. With her mother already passed, Elle would do anything to protect her only remaining parent. Even though she barely remembered her mom, she wanted to think that her returning from Italy would have made her proud.

But for the moment, she'd try and enjoy the victory with him. She reached for a pair of wineglasses when an invitation on the counter caught her eye.

Her father followed her gaze. "Mrs. Dumont is having another party on Friday and the theme is *Printemps*." He rolled his eyes as he took the wineglasses from her hands.

"Springtime," Elle murmured. "Well, that's a fitting theme." She leaned back against the counter. "Are you going to attend?"

He let out a loud chuckle. "That'll be the day. Don't know why they even invite me to those damn dreaded things."

Elle smiled and they sat down at the table and toasted with a bottle of wine she'd brought back from Italy.

"To your health," she announced, her glass held in the air.

"To my baby girl being home."

"Cin cin." With that, they clinked glasses.

To celebrate her return, they were enjoying a huge bowl of spaghetti and meatballs. Her father had insisted on cooking "his specialty." Elle had to laugh. She couldn't even begin to count the number of times they'd feasted on this exact meal when she'd been growing up.

Not to mention that she'd lived in Italy for the last six years, plus one year of study abroad in college. She'd been spoiled by the outstanding culinary pleasures of Italy. But watching her father slurp up his spaghetti, with sauce dotting his chin, seeing the pride when he announced that he'd heated up the frozen meatballs and garlic bread, made this the best pasta she'd ever tasted.

As they ate, Elle filled her dad in on her flight and he told her some of the local Bayside gossip. A nice breeze came off the bay and filled the house with the awakening scents of early spring.

"I have a friend in Florence who would go nuts over this," Elle said, referring to the chocolate éclair her father had bought at the local bakery.

"Speaking of people you know in Italy…"

Oh, jeez. Her dad was anything but subtle.

"What about that nice fellow I met at Christmas when I was visiting?" he asked.

"Marco," she said.

"Yeah, him. He seemed nice."

Marco was great. Sexy and sweet. They'd dated for the last year. "I didn't know how long I would be here and neither of us wanted a long-distance relationship."

"You don't have to have one. Why did you come back to Bayside, Ellie?"

His question stung. Did he not want his only child here with him? *For you. Because I was worried about you, of course.* "I guess I just needed a change of scenery."

"You guess, huh? Well, I just hope somebody wasn't worried that their aging dad needed a chaperone…"

Biting back a smile, she shook her head. "Never."

"Ellie…"

"Elle, Dad. I go by Elle now."

"Right, sorry." He patted her cheek. "You know you'll always be my little Ellie." The uncharacteristic sentimentality came and went before she could blink. Quickly, her dad returned to his usual pragmatic ex-cop self. "I'm worried. What are you going to do here? There aren't any galleries or museums in the area."

She chewed on her lip before rising to close the window. The truth was she had no idea what she would do for work. She'd contacted every museum within an hour's drive of Bayside—not many—and come up empty-handed. Italy might have the most fantastic jobs for her, but Bayside had her family. A family that she had been desperately worried about.

Financially, she would be okay for a couple months, especially with her father refusing her offer of paying rent. Still, she'd need to find some kind of job.

Returning to her seat, she looked at her father. "I'm working on it. Don't worry."

He pinned her with one of his cop stares. "'Don't worry.' When you have a kid someday you'll realize how stupid that little statement is."

Elle followed her dad when he rose from the table, taking their plates into the kitchen. "Daddy…"

Dropping a plate, he spun back to face her. "I will always worry about you."

Sighing, she did the only thing she could think of. She wrapped her arms around her dad until he relented and returned the embrace. "I know you will, and that's why I love you."

Finally, he let out a deep sigh. "I guess that will have to be enough for now."

They finished clearing and cleaning the dishes. Then her dad did something she'd greatly missed while she'd been away. He turned on the radio to an oldies station, the music wafted throughout the house. Happily, she sat down with him in the living room as he perused the daily paper and she pretended to do the crossword puzzle.

"So, Cam Dumont picked me up today." She surprised herself with the comment, unsure what made Cam spring into her mind. But now that she was thinking about him, there wasn't any harm in remembering the way his worn jeans had fit him so perfectly. Or how the masculine, dark stubble on his face had produced butterflies in her stomach. How would it feel against her cheeks?

"Cam's a good guy."

"Yeah, he seemed…great." She eyed her dad who wasn't taking her bait for more info.

"What are your plans for tomorrow?"

Elle sat back considering. She had no idea. With no job and no friends, she didn't have many options.

As if reading her mind, her dad said, "Why don't you go check out The Brewside? It's a coffee shop that opened about two years ago," he explained. "It's right in the town square."

"I could do that. Maybe I could bring my sketch pad, too."

Before she'd moved over to the administrative side of the art world, she'd dreamed of becoming an artist in her own right. Then she'd become so immersed in her career, not to mention all the other amazing opportunities afforded her living in Italy, that her favorite hobby had been pushed to the back burner.

Energized by the idea of taking time for her own art, she grinned.

"You look more and more beautiful every time I see you." The compliment, not to mention the change in conversation, took her by surprise, but the soft tone of her dad's voice almost undid her.

"Oh, Daddy. You saw me three months ago. I haven't changed since then."

He picked up a silver-framed picture from the end table. Without seeing it, Elle knew it was a shot of her at fifteen, after she'd climbed a tree. She was wearing cutoff jeans and an unfortunate maroon sweatshirt, her hair in pigtails displaying her makeup-free face, which had been going through an adolescent breakout phase. She'd been so clueless.

Her dad turned the photo around. "You've changed a lot since this. The time goes so fast," he said, more to himself than to her.

"I think it's time for you to go to bed. A weepy daddy is a tired daddy."

"You might be right about that. It's been a long day, but a good one. Welcome home, princess." He kissed her forehead and made his way toward his bedroom.

Feeling antsy, Elle put down the crossword puzzle, grabbed an afghan from the couch and made her way out onto the deck. The water was calm tonight, and as usual for this time of year, the temperature was dropping rapidly. She wrapped the blanket around herself as the sounds of the water lapping soothed her.

Looking up, she gazed at the sky, full of glittery stars. It was strange to think that last night she'd seen the same stars from across the ocean. Now she was back in her hometown, not quite sure how that fact made her feel.

For the second time that night, Cam entered her mind. She wasn't sure how she felt about that either.

Why in the world was she thinking about a man she hadn't seen in a decade and spent a whopping thirty minutes with? It didn't make sense. And yet, she couldn't seem to stop.

She shook her head. Most likely, she was overly tired from a long day of travel and an emotional reunion with her father. That had to be the only reason she couldn't stop thinking about Cam's enticing smile, his mysterious eyes, his amazing body.

Obviously, being with her dad was her number one priority. Just eating dinner with him and seeing with her own two eyes that he was okay made her feel better. But her dad and this tiny house were only a small part of Bayside. Tomorrow she had to face the rest of the town.

Elle knew she'd come a long way since that picture her father had looked at earlier. Undoubtedly, she'd changed. Now she just had to figure out to how convince everyone else.

After seeing her dad off to work the next morning, Elle set off to check out The Brewside, sketch pad in tow.

As she walked along the path next to the bay, the cool morning air hit her face. It felt great after a restless night's sleep. She'd finally fallen to sleep in the wee hours only to wake up around four thirty. Stupid jet lag.

And perhaps Cam Dumont kept her tossing and turning, too.

But she was not going to dwell on that little detail. Even if she was wondering where he lived. And where he'd set up his business. And what he did for fun.

She stopped in her tracks. "Stop thinking about Cameron Dumont," she whispered. With a nod, she continued on her way.

She found The Brewside Café easily enough. Nestled between a shoe store that had been in the square forever and a newer, expensive-looking clothing shop, it was painted the same crisp white, accented with blue shutters, as the other establishments. Pots of flowers flanked the entrance. She pushed open the door to the sound of bells chiming and was hit with the welcoming aroma of rich coffee beans.

Inhaling, Elle stood there for a moment, soaking in the

caffeine goodness. Once she had her fill, she stepped inside and took in the quaint decor. The raised ceiling was supported by exposed beams, and the dark wood floors gave the place a rustic feel. The tables were made up of wooden barrels with either glass plates or old doors on top. Copper pots and old kitchen utensils adorned the walls, as did a variety of vinyl records and framed black-and-white photographs. A display case with pastries dominated one wall and a large bar with coffee machines and an antique brass cash register stretched along the back.

After studying the menu, Elle stepped forward and ordered an espresso and a wheat bagel. As one of the workers began filling her order, a tall man with a beard and friendly blue eyes stopped wiping the counter and studied her.

"Hi, I'm Tony. I own this place," he finally said.

Elle shook his hand. "Oh, nice to meet you. I'm—"

"Ellie Owens. I know."

"How do you know?" She couldn't place him and was pretty sure they hadn't gone to high school together.

"Offering a legal, addictive stimulant every morning makes me the best friend of pretty much everyone in town. I have a knack for remembering faces and I've never seen yours before." He picked up a copy of the local paper and handed it to her. "Plus, you've been outed."

"Excuse me?"

"By the Bayside Blogger. You made both the online and print versions of the paper."

She stared at the front page of the newspaper. "Who's the Bayside Blogger?"

"Only the most popular columnist in the whole *Bayside Bugle*." A woman wearing a flurry of bright colors planted herself by Elle's side. "Riley Hudson," she announced. "We graduated in the same class."

Right. Riley Hudson of the Hudson family that had lived in Bayside for so many generations many people thought they'd probably discovered it. If Elle remembered correctly, Riley had been the most outgoing person in their class, popular, pretty and always dressed like she'd just stepped out of a fashion magazine. Basically, she'd been Elle's polar opposite in high school. Given how she looked now, her fashion sense hadn't changed. She was wearing a chartreuse A-line dress, a cute little fuchsia scarf and matching sunglasses perched atop a head of thick, wavy red hair.

"Hi, Riley. Nice to see you again."

"You, too. Welcome back."

While Riley said hello to Tony and put in an order for a nonfat latte, Elle quickly scanned the paper. The headline Lovesick Ellie Owens Returns to Bayside, splashed across the front page of section C, almost made her choke on her drink. The article following went on to sum up her brief, yet crazy history with Jasper, with an even quicker mention of her time in Italy.

Did people really read this? Did her dad? Biting her lip, Elle pushed down an uneasy feeling. She'd embarrassed her father beyond belief back in high school, and the last thing she wanted to do was repeat the past.

Elle turned her attention back to Riley as the other woman said, "If you want to know anything about the Bayside Blogger, just ask me. I read her column religiously. It's like the *New York Post*'s Page Six, only here in Bayside. Want to sit together?"

Elle found her energy infectious. She nodded and followed Riley to a table. "So it's like a gossip column?"

"It's annoying." This came from the guy behind the counter who had filled Elle's order. "Damn Blogger got me in trouble with my girlfriend when she reported that I had been out with my buddies at the Beer Bash."

"You were at the Beer Bash, Brody. I saw you," Riley stated.

"But maybe I told Elizabeth that I would be watching a game over at Alan's that night."

Riley rolled her big emerald green eyes. "That's your fault then. The Blogger was simply reporting the truth."

He moved away, mumbling something under his breath that sounded a lot like "damn busybody." Riley smiled and turned her attention back to Elle. "Are you excited to be back?"

"I guess." She couldn't hold in a long yawn. "Sorry. I'm jet-lagged."

"Living in Europe for six years. That's so glamorous. What did you do there?" Riley added a couple packets of sweetener to her latte and then sat back with a moony look on her face. "I imagine you lounging at cafés for hours with hot Italian men hanging on to your every word. I see plates of sinful pasta and caprese salads and you drinking amazing wine while tourists rush into the Duomo behind you."

Elle laughed at the imagery. "The wine part's true enough." She leaned across the table and lowered her voice. "But you forgot about the shoes. Oh, the amazing designer shoes."

An appreciative sigh escaped Riley's lips. "You're killing me. Hashtag, jealous."

After sampling her bagel, Elle took another sip of coffee. "I wish I could tell you it was all play and no work, but truthfully, I did have to make a living. Even in a country as laid-back as Italy, they tend to expect payment for things like housing and food."

"Sticklers." Riley shook her head. "What did you do?"

"My last job was at an up-and-coming gallery right around the corner from the Duomo. But I've worked in a ton of museums there."

Riley looked down. Noticing Elle's sketch pad, she pointed at it. "Are you an artist, Ellie Owens?"

There was a certain awe in the question that filled her with pride. "It's a hobby, and actually, I go by Elle now."

"No more Ellie?" Riley cocked her head.

"Let's just say I retired her a long time ago. So, what do you do now?"

Riley ran a hand along her plaid computer bag. "I'm a writer."

Elle smiled. "That would explain the colorful descriptions. What do you write?"

"I'd like to write the next great American novel. Or at least a really juicy romance novel devoured by women at every beach in the country. But for the moment I'm a reporter with the *Bayside Bugle*. I write for the Style & Entertainment section."

Something from earlier niggled at her brain. "Wait a minute." Elle put her bagel down. "If you write for the *Bugle*, you must know who this Bayside Blogger is."

"I wish. I have friends that have offered me big money to reveal her identity. Sadly, the only person who knows is our editor in chief, Sawyer. He's also received offers of money, concert tickets, home-cooked meals, you name it. But he won't budge."

"Sawyer Wallace? Wasn't he a couple years older than us in school?"

"Two," Riley confirmed.

"Didn't he drill a hole between the boys' and girls' locker rooms once so he could get an eyeful?"

Tony chuckled from behind the bar.

"Annoying then and annoying now. He hasn't changed."

But Riley's face did. Elle couldn't help but notice her cheeks redden. Interesting. As interesting as the fact that she'd just spoken more to Riley Hudson in the last ten minutes than all of high school. Not that Riley had ever been mean to her. But they'd run in very different circles.

The bells above the door jingled and in walked none

other than Cam Dumont. Elle looked up as Riley waved a hot-pink nail-polished hand and called, "Hey, good-looking."

"If it isn't the girl trying to turn Bayside into her own version of sophisticated Manhattan," he replied.

"One small step at a time. Speaking of elegance and style, I got the invite to your mother's *Printemps* soiree. You know I'll be there."

"You and the rest of the planet." Cam rolled his eyes and turned toward Elle. "Morning, Elle."

"Hi, Cam. Nice to see you again."

He moved to the counter and placed an order for an extra-large coffee to go. While he talked with Tony, Elle couldn't help but notice once again the way Cam's worn jeans clung to certain places in a really awesome way. In fact, now that she was observing, she had to admit that with his tall, muscular body, slight stubble on his chiseled face and too-long dark hair, Cam Dumont was a nice healthy dose of man candy. No wonder she kept thinking about him last night. And this morning.

She could only imagine that when he got to work and slung a tool belt around his waist he would become even more appealing. And maybe if it was a hot day and he needed to take off his shirt...

"So, Elle, have you seen Jasper yet?"

Elle sloshed the remainder of her espresso onto the newspaper. She accepted the napkins Riley offered, even as she became aware that Cam, Tony, Brody and the table of older men sitting on the other side of the room all turned in her direction at the question. She felt she should have some grand, detailed story to tell Riley in answer, when really the truth was simple. "Nope," she said softly.

"Well, you'll definitely see him at the *Printemps* party tomorrow night."

"Actually, I'm not going to the party," Elle said.

Riley appeared taken aback, as if Elle had just reached across the table and slapped her. "Excuse me? Hold the presses. Why in the world are you not coming tomorrow?" Her hands gestured wildly and her mouth went into a pout.

Elle laughed. "For one thing, I wasn't invited."

"But your dad probably was. Oh, by the way, I'm so sorry to hear about his cancer. How's he doing? You have to come tomorrow," she continued, without taking a breath. "I'll introduce you to the new faces of Bayside. Not that there's many."

Blame it on the jet lag, but Elle didn't know if she could keep up with Riley.

"Oh, my God, there's this guy I should totally set you up with. I mean, unless you're still stuck on Jasper."

Cam cleared his throat, calling both women's attention to him. "Uh, yeah. I'm supposed to invite you to the party tomorrow." He didn't meet her eyes. Instead, he looked into his cup of coffee as if it held all the answers of the universe.

Jeez, Elle thought. Could he be less excited? He made it sound like he was inviting her to a mass murder.

"Aww, Cam, are you inviting Elle? That's sweet."

"I'm not. My mom wanted me to."

Even better. And why did it bother her that he wasn't the one inviting her to the party? "I probably shouldn't go," she began.

Eyes shining, Cam let out a huge breath. Then he took a long swig of coffee. "Yeah, probably better."

Hold on, did Cam not want her to go? Why the hell not? Because of the video?

Buoyed by a sudden stubbornness, she said, "You know, on second thought, maybe I *should* stop by. I mean, since your mom extended the invitation to me and all."

Riley clapped her hands together in quick succession. "Yeah."

Cam's face fell. "Are you sure? It's, ah, a formal, black-tie kind of party."

"Not a problem. I recently bought a gown when I was visiting Milan. It'll be just perfect for the occasion."

Did he think she couldn't afford a gown or something? That she'd never been to a formal party? She may not have a bank account like his but, hell, who did? Besides, Elle couldn't figure out why he wouldn't want her there. But she'd show him. Not only would she go to that party, but she'd look better than she ever had in her entire life.

"A gown from Milan? Oh, my God, you are like the coolest person I know. I must raid your closet immediately."

Elle smiled at Riley even as she watched Cam seething.

"My mother's parties are overrated. Trust me," he said through clenched teeth.

Enough was enough. She was tired, a little overwhelmed and greatly annoyed. She stood and turned to Cam. Trying to get up in his face proved difficult, considering her five feet six inches didn't come close to his height. Still, she tilted her chin up and pegged him with her most intimidating stare.

"Maybe I should come to that conclusion myself."

Riley stayed silent as she watched the two of them from the table with an interested look on her face.

"It's not going to go the way you want," Cam said quietly, so only she could hear.

"What way is that, exactly?"

He looked as if he wanted to say something. His mouth even opened slightly, but no words came out. Elle could practically see the wheels churning in his brain.

"Jasper," he whispered, his eyes glued to hers.

Just as she'd suspected. Even Cam thought she would still make a fool out of herself over his brother.

It hadn't even been a full twenty-four hours since she'd

returned and she already felt like a total outcast. Stupidly, she'd thought a full decade away would have given everyone ample time to forget about that one little moment when she'd lost her mind.

Her cheeks felt warm as she tried to hold the embarrassment at bay. She wanted to yell at Cam, tell him she wasn't some girl obsessed with her high school crush. Truthfully, she didn't know how she'd feel seeing Jasper again. Her stomach tightened at the thought of it. But she was back in Bayside, so she knew it would happen eventually. What did Cam think? She would see his brother and throw herself at his feet?

How many other people would assume the same?

Beyond frustrated with Cam and his presumptions, she gathered her things and nodded to Riley. Then she narrowed her eyes at Cam. "I wouldn't miss this party for anything in the world, Cameron Dumont."

With that, she pushed open the door with all the dignity she could muster.

Chapter Three

Bayside Blogger @BSBlogger
First nugget of the day. Ellie Owens in @TheBrewside,
a certain yummy recluse antagonizing her until she fled
the scene…

"Elle, wait up!" Cam called as he rushed out of The
Brewside. It had taken him one whole second to realize
he'd really hurt her feelings.

It wasn't that he didn't want Elle to come tomorrow
night. It was more that he didn't want her to become upset
at the party when the local gossips would no doubt descend
on her like a scene from Hitchcock's *The Birds*.

And dammit, he knew she'd changed. Jasper had
changed, too. But the rest of Bayside? Still the same. *That*
was the problem.

Bayside was his home and he loved it. But that didn't
mean he was oblivious to the inherent small-town quirks—
like gossip, clinging to the past and more gossip.

Elle and Jasper in the same room with the entire town
watching was a recipe for disaster.

But at the moment, Cam needed to find Elle and explain. Or at the very least, apologize. He spotted her light
brown hair blowing in the soft breeze coming off the water.
She was halfway across the square. He rushed in that direction.

"Elle, hang on."

"I'm done talking to you." She kept walking.

Finally close enough to stop her, Cam reached for her arm. He grabbed hold for a second before she shook him off and turned around to face him. "What is your problem?"

"I only wanted to say…"

"What?" she snapped.

"I'm sorry."

"Well—oh."

By the way she blinked multiple times in rapid succession without any words coming out of her mouth, he'd obviously taken her by surprise. She started biting her lip, and then squinted up at him.

"I think you got the wrong impression back there," he said. "My parents' parties…" He threw his hands up in the air. "They are… I mean, it's just that the people that go… I really don't…"

Her face fell and she shrugged. "I get it. You don't want me there. You think I'll make a scene and ruin the event. Is that what you're trying to say?"

"No."

"Then *what*?" she asked.

"I hate those parties."

There, he'd said it out loud. He'd never really told anyone that before, although he was sure many people assumed as much. After all, a surly guy hanging out in the corner, downing beer instead of expensive, imported champagne, and talking to as few people as possible, might give off the impression he wasn't the party-loving animal the rest of the Dumonts were. He felt almost guilty admitting that. Like he was betraying his family, and hadn't he already done that when he'd shirked his birthright and started his own company?

"You hate the parties? Really?" She emitted a little laugh.

"Why are you laughing?"

"It's funny. Unless they've drastically changed, your parents' parties are supposed to rival…" she tapped a finger against her lips, pausing in thought "…Oscar parties, inaugural balls, royal weddings."

His turn to laugh. "Can't say I know about any of those things. Listen, I don't think you'd make a scene tomorrow, although to be honest, it would be a hell of a lot more fun if you did."

"Cam." She rolled her eyes, but was smiling as she did so.

She had a nice smile. Really nice, he noticed. It brightened up her face and brought out those adorable dimples in her cheeks.

And the sun was catching her hair, casting a golden hue on the brown tresses.

"Cam," she repeated. "Tell me the real reason you don't want me to come to the party."

He looked around the square, at the stores that hadn't yet opened for the day. Some wouldn't open at all, their owners here only for the busy summer tourist season. In the distance, he could hear the squawking of gulls as a fishing boat no doubt returned to the bay.

Bayside was home. It always would be. There was something comforting about that.

"You know," he said, gesturing vaguely. "Some things have changed around here since you left. But others, not so much."

Elle nodded even as she narrowed her eyes. "That's kind of the way of the world."

"One of the things that changed… I mean, you really should know something." He wasn't doing this right.

"What is it?"

He studied her face for a long moment before running a hand through his hair. "Nothing. Never mind."

"You sure?"

He decided to avoid her question and change the subject instead. "So, do you really have some fancy dress from Milan?"

Elle smiled. "I don't know about fancy. I was going more for sophisticated. But yes, I have a dress from Milan."

"Did you go there often?"

She bit her lip, considering. "I went every so often. What I really loved was taking weekend trips to Southern Italy. Naples has the best food."

Cam found himself genuinely interested. How could he not be when she became so animated talking about a country that she clearly loved. Her eyes were practically sparkling.

"I thought all of the food in Italy was amazing," he offered.

She licked her lips, an enticing gesture that drew his gaze right to her.

"Oh, it is. Trust me. There's no salt in the food in Tuscany, which takes some getting used to. But once you do..." She kissed her fingers. *"Molto bene. Delizioso."*

There was something really appealing about this woman. It went beyond her looks, which were obviously stunning. But something else drew him to her.

"Of course, the wine is insane. Chianti was a personal favorite. And don't even get me started on the gelato." She winked at him. "I'm really going to miss that."

"I've seen gelato here," Cam said.

Her face fell. "It won't be the same."

"Hey," he said, reaching out and touching her arm. "You sure you're okay being back here?"

She glanced around the square, a million thoughts crossing her face. She let out a long sigh.

"Elle?" he prompted.

"I will be fine. I know it. I've missed it here."

"But you're going to miss Italy, too." He said it rather

than asked it because it was so clear she was struggling with this move.

Cam rolled back on his heels as he studied her. She had really beautiful eyes. They were so expressive, yet inquisitive. He bet she didn't miss much. Including her father's recent health scare. Cam had to hand it to her. She could have come back for a short visit. Instead, she'd dropped her life, all the things she adored, to return to Bayside.

She gave up her life for her dad. It caused a pit to form in his stomach. She'd run toward her family while he'd run from his and everything they offered.

"Hey, you okay?" she asked. Cam had been right. She was perceptive.

Without overthinking it, he said, "You're pretty amazing, Elle."

Those fabulous eyes widened. "Thank you…Jasper."

Momentarily confused, Cam realized that Elle was looking over his shoulder. Turning, he saw his brother strolling from his car toward The Brewside.

Jasper turned in their direction and gave a small wave to Cam, before he took in Elle.

Could he be more obvious about giving her a long once-over?

Once he'd assessed Elle, he quickly switched courses and headed their way.

"Good morning," he called.

"Hey, Jasp, what are you doing in town? Shouldn't you be at the office already?"

Cam really didn't care about the answer to that question. He was too busy watching Elle for her reaction. She was smiling as she noted his brother approaching.

"I have an off-site meeting first. Cam, why don't you introduce me to your lovely friend." Jasper didn't so much as look toward him as he said this. Instead, he sidled up to Elle and offered her a hand.

Cam shoved his own hands in his pockets. "You already know her."

But Jasper was shaking her hand, anyway. "I'm only kidding. How could I ever forget someone as beautiful as Ellie Owens?"

Elle pulled her hand out of Jasper's grasp. "Wow, so early for such a cheesy line."

Score one for her.

Undeterred and offering Elle what Cam liked to call "Jasper's megawatt smile," his brother leaned closer and put a hand over his heart as if it was breaking. "Ouch. But you are beautiful."

Elle leaned in as well and winked at him. "But I didn't used to be. In fact, the last time you saw me I probably looked quite different. That can only mean that someone told you I'd returned."

A crease formed on Jasper's brow. "Maybe I just remember you."

"Hmm, perhaps," Elle said with a coy smile. "Although I think you've taken me in longer this morning than you did in all our years of high school."

It wasn't often a female addled Jasper's brain, and Cam was enjoying it.

"I was an idiot in high school," his brother said, stepping forward again. Taking her hand once more, he added, "Forgive me?" with another Jasper smile.

Elle tilted her head before removing her hand yet again. "It's fine."

Shifting uncomfortably, Cam eventually elbowed his brother in the ribs.

"Ow." Shaking him off, Jasper returned his attention to Elle. "How long are you back in town?"

"I'm not sure, actually." She chewed on her lip. "I just got back from Florence yesterday."

"Did you come back with your boyfriend? Husband?"

Cam snorted, unable to hold it in. Elle shot him a look.

"Actually I just broke up with the man I was seeing. I'm single now."

"I'm sorry to hear that." Jasper snapped his fingers. "We should grab dinner some night. Catch up."

Elle studied him, appearing amused at their meeting. Besides that, Cam couldn't tell what else she was thinking. Did seeing his brother remind her of her adolescent crush? Personally, he thought Jasper was laying it on a bit thick, but he'd seen plenty of women succumb when his brother wasn't being half as charming.

"Maybe. We'll see."

Score two points for Elle. A team, Cam decided, he was firmly rooting for.

Jasper seemed confused at her reluctance. "Here," he said, pulling a business card out of his jacket pocket. "Give me a call if you change your mind." His megawatt smile appeared once more. "In the meantime, you should come to a party tomorrow."

"The *Printemps* do at your parents' house?" she asked innocently.

Jasper's face lit up. "Yes. Please come as my guest."

"Actually," Elle said, "your brother already invited me."

"My brother…" Jasper turned to him and his left eyebrow arched dramatically. "Oh, really?" He darted his gaze between the two of them, waiting for some obvious sign of understanding. "So are you going…together?" He gestured from one to the other, then leaned toward Cam and whispered, "That's faster than you usually move."

Before Cam could counter that, Elle spoke up. "No, we're not," she stated quickly.

Too quickly, Cam thought. And why should that bug him?

Jasper took a step closer. "Good to hear." He offered Elle a wink.

"Well, I really should be going. I wanted to get some sketching in today and the light is just right at the moment. But I'll see both of you tomorrow."

She began to walk away, a feminine sway to her hips that Cam knew both his and his brother's gazes were drawn to.

"Ellie Owens?" Jasper said out loud, after running a hand over his mouth.

"She goes by Elle now," Cam said, still watching her walk off.

"Little Ellie Owens?" The surprise in Jasper's voice was comical.

"The one and only," Cam said drily, slapping a hand on his brother's back as they watched Elle's retreating form.

Jasper scrubbed both hands over his face. "When you said she'd changed, you weren't kidding. She's gorgeous."

Yes, she is. "She's okay."

"Cam, come on. Too bad she didn't look like that in high school." Jasper wiggled an eyebrow for emphasis.

Shaking his head, Cam resisted the urge to sigh.

As he rubbed his hands together, Jasper's smile grew wide and playful. "Seems like the two of you have gotten cozy pretty fast. Definitely can't wait for tomorrow's party now."

Not for the first time in his life—hell, not for the first time today—Cam had to remind himself that he did in fact love his little brother. No matter how irritating he could be.

"Jasp." He snapped his fingers in front of Jasper's face. "What about Mindy?"

"Who?" he asked dreamily.

Cam groaned. "Mindy. Your girlfriend."

To his credit, Jasper bowed his head as his face reddened. Then his usual playful grin returned. "I'm kidding. She's out of town. And I wasn't hitting on Elle, so stop with the reproachful look."

"Could have fooled me."

"I was flirting. Flirting is not the same as full-on hitting on a woman. And why should it bother you, anyway? Thought you gave up dating after Spacy Stacy."

Cam's own grin came fast and wide. "Spacy Stacy was harmless." True, she became easily confused over minor details and anything involving numbers, sports or current events. But she'd been fun for a while.

"Harmless but hot. Some of my favorite traits." Jasper chuckled, but Cam knew he was only kidding.

His brother clapped him on the back. "I just want to see you happy."

"Who said I'm not happy?" Cam countered.

Jasper nodded in the direction Elle had taken. "I think maybe you could be even happier. You just have to let yourself accept it."

Cam rolled his eyes. "You sound like one of those stupid daily affirmations podcasts that Mom listens to."

Jasper pointed toward The Brewside. "I'm going to get some coffee. And don't knock the podcasts. Maybe you should listen to one before the party tomorrow. Maybe it will help you find your mojo with Elle."

Cam tried to reach out and slap him on the arm, but his brother was too fast. "I'm over dating," he yelled, but Jasper ignored him. Cam watched him walk away.

Their mother always promised fireworks at every party she threw. Between Jasper, Elle and the busybodies of Bayside, Cam feared there might be more than one kind of fireworks tomorrow night.

Chapter Four

There's nothing like a Dumont party! I'd never miss an opportunity to mingle with my faithful followers. Anonymously, of course.

Rumor has it that little Ellie Owens got invited by both Dumont brothers. Hmm, that's an interesting twist. Who do you think she'll dance with first? Check back tomorrow for the answer...

Elle's fantasies about attending a Dumont party had always been just that. A fantasy. Tonight, though, the fantasy had become reality and she was now standing outside the sprawling mansion on Bay View Road feeling very, very apprehensive.

Of course, her dad hadn't helped matters. He'd made it known that he was less than pleased she'd decided to go to the party. That only added to her nerves.

At least she was confident about her outfit. She loved the floor-length scarlet dress outlined with a thin layer of sparkly silver beading. The minute she'd seen it in the window of the boutique in Milan she'd known it was special. The dress came up around her neck but left her shoulders bare. Her figure was on full display as the sinfully silky material clung to her curves, and the slit in the skirt came up high, showing off her toned legs and the glittery heels she wore. Because of the high neckline she'd scooped her hair up into an intricate style that had taken way too much time and way too many bobby pins to secure. But with her dangly silver earrings and bright red lips, she knew the look was complete.

Drawing on that assurance, she entered the Dumont estate. She smiled at the waitstaff flanking the entrance with trays of champagne. Deciding a little liquid courage might be just the thing to calm her, she happily took a glass before giving her wrap to yet another staff member.

Since she'd never been inside the Dumont house, she took a moment to look around. Elegant staircases on either side of the foyer led up to a balcony, accented by a large crystal chandelier. As she walked across the marble floor, her heels made a *click clack* sound that echoed off walls adorned with priceless paintings. She'd like more time to get a better look at them.

Stopping at a large mirror set in an ornate gold frame, she checked her makeup and hair one last time. Satisfied, Elle took a large gulp of champagne, put the glass down and proceeded along the hallway to a set of glass doors that were immediately opened by gloved servants.

It was like an old black-and-white movie. The only thing missing was Cary Grant walking around the corner.

Elle paused a moment before stepping onto a large terrace. Steps cascaded down to a second and then a third terrace, all of which were bordered by sprawling lawns and gorgeous flower beds. The water stretched out below, with multiple docks extending into the bay.

Slowly, she took three steps and froze. The large orchestra decided just then to take a break, and it provided the exact right moment for every pair of eyes at the party to turn in her direction.

Oh. My. God.

Embarrassment coursed through her as her pulse picked up into a fast rhythm. Whispers carried up to her, causing her to consider running for the exit.

"Is that Ellie Owens?"

"Remember how she was in love with Jasper?"

"That's not Ellie. Ellie never looked like that."

"Remember that video she made?"

"Didn't she throw herself in the bay that night?"

She'd definitely wanted to make an impression. But Elle had been hoping that people would be dazzled by her dress as she talked to them one-on-one throughout the night. She had not planned to be the center of freaking attention. And where the hell was the orchestra?

As if on cue, Mrs. Dumont flicked a hand toward the conductor and he immediately began a new tune. Slowly, people returned to their drinks, food and conversations as Lilah Dumont, decked out in an elegant green gown glistening with gold beading, made her way toward Elle with open arms.

Elle allowed herself to be embraced as her hostess exclaimed, "Ellie, it's so good to see you. Welcome back!"

"Thank you for inviting me, Mrs. Dumont. Everything looks amazing."

"As do you." The older woman gave her a quick assessment. "You've certainly changed, Ellie."

"Oh, I go by Elle now."

With a soft pat to her cheek, Mrs. Dumont said, "Elle it is then. I'm sorry about what brought you home. Your dad is looking much better, though. He said he's in remission." A genuine smile touched the woman's lips.

Elle nodded. "Yes, his last doctor's appointment went well. But we'll have to make sure he stays on top of the situation. From everything I've read, this type of cancer can come back quickly. I'd like to meet his doctor," she added.

"He's the best oncologist in the state."

Realization dawned as she met Mrs. Dumont's gaze. "You helped, didn't you?"

Waving a hand in the air, Lilah winked at her. "It was

only a matter of a quick phone call. It also helps that a wing in that particular hospital is named after us."

What must it be like to have that kind of money? Elle wondered. She would be forever grateful. "Thank you so much. I don't know how to repay—"

"It was nothing. Now, if you'd really like to repay me you can do so by mingling and having fun."

Smiling, Elle nodded. Then she took a deep breath and made her way toward the other guests. As she walked across the patio, she spotted familiar faces—former classmates, teachers, local shop owners. Searching the crowd, she noticed her favorite art teacher and was about to say hi when a tall man wearing a tailored tux approached her.

"Ellie Owens?" he asked.

"Guilty," she replied. Taking a moment to place him, she finally remembered. "Tyler Briggitt! How are you?" They'd been in the same class in high school. Tyler had also been one of Jasper's closest friends.

"Great, no complaints. I'm working at the bank now. Welcome back. So," he began, "have you seen Jasp yet?"

She snagged a champagne flute from a passing waiter and took a fortifying sip. "Um, yeah. I ran into him yesterday, actually."

"That must have been awkward." Tyler leaned toward her, glanced to the right and then the left. Finally, he lowered his voice. "Remember that video?"

"Like it was yesterday," she said under her breath.

"That was some crazy stuff. Really bad."

"It certainly wasn't my finest moment." She tried to answer nonchalantly as Tyler turned to snag an appetizer off a nearby table. Maybe Cam had been onto something yesterday. After all, he'd tried to warn her that people didn't always forget the past.

"Man, I remember when they showed it at our senior prom—" Tyler began.

"It's so nice to see you again." Elle cut him off quickly. "But I see Riley Hudson over there and I'd really like to say hello. Have a great night."

Tyler didn't seem taken aback as Elle walked briskly toward Riley.

"Elle, hey." Riley waved when she spotted her.

"You look beautiful," she told the reporter. And she did. Riley was wearing a lavender chiffon gown with a low back. Long amethyst earrings dangled from her lobes and she'd accentuated her eyes with a soft lilac shadow.

"Thanks," Riley said brightly. "And you, wow. You look amazing. Red's a good color for you." She tipped her glass against Elle's in a toast. "Here's to two hot chicks and an incredible party." Elle took a huge sip as Riley added, "Are you having fun?"

"Um…" she began.

"Uh-oh, what's wrong?" True concern flashed in Riley's eyes.

How to explain? Elle knew she'd messed up senior year. But she'd thought that people would have enough class not to bring it up. Especially not the first person she talked to. Stupidly, she'd assumed that after ten years people would be interested in her life today as a sane, normal adult.

"I guess I was just hoping to blend in a bit more," she admitted quietly.

"Then, honey, you shouldn't have worn that dress." Riley's face softened. "Your return is the talk of the town. It'll die down."

God, she hoped that was true.

"But in the meantime…" Riley nudged her in the ribs with her elbow and Elle followed her stare across the terrace "…Jasper's right over there."

Now it was going to get weird. The whispers started up before she could even decide if she should walk over to greet him. Did no one remember anything else about her? What about her art? Or how she'd drawn that comic strip for the school newspaper? How she'd made the honor roll every single semester and eventually became valedictorian?

Well, she would have been valedictorian if the video had never come out. She could hear the principal's voice as if it had been yesterday.

"Ellie, your grades place you at the top of your class academically. But after that video... It just wouldn't be right."

Back in the present, her fate was decided when Jasper spotted her. He whispered something to the man he'd been chatting with, then headed toward her.

"I'll just let you two talk," Riley said, putting her champagne glass down on a table.

"No, Riley, wait," she said. But her old classmate was already walking away, waving at Jasper as she did.

Heat permeated every inch of Elle's skin as she felt all eyes on her and Jasper. Why had she wanted to come to this party? Her goal in being back in Bayside was to blend in, not stand out. And certainly to not make a fool out of herself or embarrass her father. Again.

"Ellie," he said, reaching for her wrist. "It's awesome you're here."

She couldn't help but notice that everyone around them was unabashedly watching her every move.

"Hi, Jasper," she said, squirming.

"Having fun?"

Not particularly. "It's great. Quite the turnout. Looks like the whole town is here." *Watching me. Judging me.*

"My parents' parties are always like this."

Something shifted and Elle reminded herself that she was an accomplished grown-up, not some shy bookworm who'd drunk too much one—and only one—night and paid a price for her bad choice. Let people watch the two of them talking. Nothing was going to happen. She'd make sure of that.

"I understand you took over your parents' company," she said, pushing her shoulders back and holding her head high.

A grin, fast and real, lit up his face. But quickly, interestingly, it faded. "Not yet. They're both still working pretty hard. But I'm in line to take over."

"I have to say I'm surprised."

His gaze dropped to the ground. "You and everyone else."

Feeling bad, she reached for his arm. "No, not like that. I only meant that I assumed Cam would take over, since he's older."

The statement appeared to placate Jasper and he reached for her fingers, squeezed then held on. Elle realized too late that she shouldn't have touched him. Nearby guests seemed to collectively hold their breath, and she could have sworn a flash went off.

She untangled her hand from his as he said, "Thanks, Elle. Yeah, my brother wanted to start his own company— much to our parents' disdain, especially Dad's. But there it is."

She wondered if Cam was here yet. Surely he would arrive soon. She wanted to hear more about his business and how he'd transitioned from Dumont golden boy to entrepreneur in his own right.

Jasper studied her for a moment, and she didn't know why, but she had the overwhelming urge to fidget.

"What?" she asked.

He shook his head. "Nothing. Sorry. It's just really nice to have you here."

For years she'd watched these parties from across the bay, desperately hoping to someday be in the very position she was in right now.

Yet it didn't feel like a dream come true. Jasper was nice enough, and of course he was beyond handsome. Still, something was missing. Or maybe someone…

Normally, Cam waited as long as possible before heading over to his parents' house for one of their dreaded parties. But tonight was different. He still hated putting on a tux and he really hated the mindless conversations he was about to endure, but there was a spring in his step that was usually absent.

"Someone got here nice and early. For a change," his mother called as he stepped onto the upper terrace. He gave her a quick hug, and when she pulled back, she smoothed a hand down his lapel. "You look dashing, Cameron."

Cam quirked an eyebrow. "Cameron, huh? Are we being formal tonight?"

Lilah Dumont chuckled. "Yes, you know our parties are always formal. Have you said hi to your father yet?"

"No need." Collin Dumont sauntered over, wrapped an arm around his wife and nodded briskly. "You're here early," he offered.

"So I've been told. What do I have to look forward to? Fireworks? A Ferris wheel? Dragons?"

"No, smart-ass," his mother said. She gestured toward a tray of champagne flutes, but Cam shook his head. He'd grab a beer later. "The most interesting thing tonight has been the arrival of Elle Owens."

Of course, Cam thought. "Where is she?" He found himself searching what felt like the population of the entire town to spot her. Poor girl probably needed someone to talk to. His gaze finally landed on the bottom terrace, where Elle stood in a dark red gown, her brown hair piled on top of her head. Even at a distance, her skin glowed, her dimples winked and that dress fitted her like a glove.

In a word, she looked stunning. His breath caught as she smiled.

Suddenly his stupid tie felt way too tight.

"They've been talking for the last twenty minutes or so," his mother added.

Cam shook his head and took a closer look at the situation. Elle was talking to none other than Jasper.

The man she'd been head over heels in love with back in high school. The guy who always got the girl. The brother Cam owed a huge debt of gratitude to.

"Nice for her to have a friend," he mumbled, and then quickly scanned the rest of the crowd. The usual suspects all seemed accounted for. But no matter how many times he tried to force his eyes away from her, he couldn't stop returning his gaze to Elle.

She laughed at something Jasper said and Cam could see that everyone around them was trying very ineffectively not to stare. Like goldfish being ogled in their bowl.

And did they have to stand so close to have a damn conversation? He shifted his weight and struggled with his tie again.

Jasper chose that moment to throw his head back and laugh. When he recovered, he stepped even closer. Gritting his teeth, Cam let out a gruff cough at the same time about ten flashes went off.

"Damn," he grumbled, as Elle and Jasper jumped apart. He could tell his brother tried to say something calming. But Elle ducked her head and retreated from the scene, leaving Jasper frowning into his champagne glass.

Cam's jaw ticked and he felt his hands curling into fists even as his mother was going on about something.

And why should Elle and Jasper bother him, anyway? It wasn't his problem. She wasn't his responsibility to watch over, and she certainly wasn't his girlfriend.

Yet he suddenly had an overwhelming desire to make

sure she was okay. Without another word to his mother, Cam took off.

It didn't take long to find her. He simply went in the opposite direction of the crowd, who were still talking in hushed tones about the reemergence of Ellie Owens.

"Elle?" he asked quietly.

She was standing under the gazebo at the edge of one of the gardens, looking out toward the bay. The twinkly lights illuminated her hair and accentuated the sparkles on her dress. When she turned toward him, Cam practically fell over.

She was absolutely breathtaking.

"Hi." The shy smile on her face fell the moment Cam neared.

"Not having the best night?" he guessed.

She didn't answer for a long moment. Finally, she sighed, a long, frustrated release of breath. "Not really."

From behind his back, he pulled out two bottles of beer. Her eyes lit up with interest. When he cocked his head, she nodded, and he proceeded to open them with the bottle opener he'd slipped into his pocket.

After a silent toast and clink of the bottles, she took a long pull then closed her eyes, looking content. Tentatively, he stepped closer. "May I?" he asked.

At her nod, he leaned on the railing and took in the view as he indulged in his own long pull of beer. They were quiet for a few minutes, enjoying the music of the band behind them and the gentle sound of water lapping in the nearby bay.

"You can barely see my house from here," she said, breaking the silence, her eyes trained out into the darkness. "I've been looking at your house from across the water most of my life."

"I was always jealous of your side of the bay. Really," he said at her skeptical glance. "You have neighbors and there were always picnics and barbecues happening over there. Our closest neighbor is acres away."

"Are you kidding? You have these lavish parties all the time. That's nothing compared to our lame barbecues."

"I'd much rather be flipping a burger than pretending to like caviar in front of my parents' clients."

"You don't like caviar?"

Cam was about to answer her when he realized she was joking. He leaned on the railing.

She brought the bottle to her lips and downed a good portion of the amber liquid. "What are you doing out here, anyway?"

"I came…" Why had he come after her? "I only wanted to…" What? What did he want?

She tilted her head, searched his face and waited.

"I figured you might need a friend."

Her eyes softened.

Cam threw back more beer. "And I like to hide during these things."

She laughed, and he decided he liked the way it made her face light up.

"I've never had any desire to be on a stage before," she told him. "Now I know why. I felt like everyone at this party was staring at me. I guess you were right to warn me yesterday."

Cam ran a hand over his face. He hadn't done a good job shaving on purpose. It drove his mother nuts when he didn't shave for one of her social functions. "For what it's worth, I would have rather been wrong. Besides, I've never liked people looking at me, either." He wasn't sure why he decided to tell Elle that.

She offered a half laugh. "I was under the impression you didn't like most things."

He grinned. "Not true. I just don't freely share my interests."

"What are your interests?"

He turned, leaned his back against the railing, swigged more beer. "Lots of things. Baseball, my truck, a cold beer on a hot day." He saluted her with his bottle. "I like working with my hands, always have. I like dogs and I'd like to get a puppy one of these days. I like a good book."

"What genre?" she asked.

"Thrillers mostly."

Mirroring his pose, she met his gaze as he told her about the last book he'd read. The next fifteen minutes passed as they talked about books, movies and television shows.

They finished their beers as a nice breeze filtered off the bay. It helped cool him down. When had he gotten so warm, anyway? But then he noticed her dainty shiver. Immediately, he removed his suit jacket and draped it around her shoulders without her asking.

Surprise flashed in her eyes. "Thanks," she said.

He shrugged. "You're cold. I gave you my jacket. That's how it works."

Tapping one of those sparkly fingers against her red lips, she admitted, "You were always kinda mysterious. No one knew much about you. You kept to yourself and drove a truck and had a beard."

"I didn't always have a beard."

"Felt like you did. During high school, you looked older than you were."

A fact that he'd used to his benefit whenever his friends wanted some cheap beer, he thought with a silent laugh.

Gazing at her now, with moonlight washing over, her eyes alight with amusement, her slender body swimming in his jacket, he thought he'd never seen any woman look so beautiful. He took a step closer. "So you really didn't know me at all."

Staying in place, she angled her head to look up at him. "Apparently not."

"How do you feel now that you are learning a little about me?" Was he flirting with her? Some part of his brain screamed for him to stop, but standing this close felt too damn good.

"I feel like I might be interested in hearing more."

And she was flirting back. Double damn. Elle Owens had been in love with his brother her entire life. Maybe Jasper hadn't been into her back in high school, but if what Cam witnessed earlier tonight was any indication, he was interested now. Cam would not, could not, interfere with his brother. Not after what his brother had done for him.

So he took a step back. And hated the way it made him feel.

"Jasper," he blurted out. She narrowed her eyes. "You and Jasper must have had a lot to talk about earlier."

He didn't miss her questioning look. Hell, he didn't blame her. He was running hot and cold.

"I don't really want to talk about Jasper."

"What do you want to talk about?"

She shrugged at first, but then she launched into what was really bothering her. "How is it that I've been gone for an entire decade, but tonight it felt like I'd been in Europe for ten days? People don't seem interested in learning who I am today."

"I don't know if that's true. You need to give it a little time. Your return is a big deal in this small town."

"I don't know how many more nights like this I can endure."

"If it makes you feel better, I liked who you were back then. And so far, I like who you are today."

Her mouth opened and closed. "You aren't like everyone else."

"Yeah, I've gotten that my whole life."

She giggled.

"Listen, you've changed a lot since you were eighteen.

You're beautiful, smart—hell, you've lived in Europe. But you've been gone for ten years. People are interested."

"You think I'm beautiful?"

The amazement he heard in her voice pissed him off. How could she not know she was stunning? Wasn't it obvious? It seemed so to him. Even if she hadn't been wearing that hot red dress… His mind went to a very dark, but very happy place at the idea of her not wearing a dress.

He stepped toward her once again, invading her personal space. "You don't think so?" It was a challenge, but he didn't know why. Only that he needed her to get it.

"I happen to think I'm very pretty. But I also know I haven't always been."

To her credit, she didn't back off. Impressive, since Cam knew he was physically intimidating.

"So what?"

"So people in this town only see the drunk girl in that video professing her love for someone who was way out of her league."

Cam slapped his hands down on the railing on either side of her, boxing her in. "The people of this town are idiots."

She continued to hold her ground, tilting her head up to meet his gaze. "But you're not."

"I don't generally call myself an idiot, no."

"You're telling me that you look at me now and you don't see young, sweet, if misguided, Ellie Owens?"

"I'm looking at you right now and what I see is a smoking-hot, stubborn woman with thick hair and shining eyes and smooth, silky skin." He emphasized this by running a hand up and down her arm. Despite still wearing his jacket, she shivered, and he moved even closer.

His eyes locked on to her red lips. When her tongue slipped out to moisten them, he almost groaned. He raised his other hand to the side of her face. Wanting to kiss her more than he wanted to breathe, Cam began to lean down. His lips hovered a hairbreadth from hers.

Then a loud explosion sounded, followed by a round of applause and cheers. Jumping back, he ran a hand through his hair, as Elle looked up at the fireworks lighting the sky above them.

The moment was ruined, but Cam knew they'd been saved from making what would have clearly been a horrible mistake.

He usually felt grateful at such times. Weird thing was, tonight he felt nothing but disappointment.

Chapter Five

Am I the only one who saw a gorgeous Ellie Owens enter the *Printemps* party like a princess? The really exciting part was when Ellie and everyone's favorite hunk, Jasper, finally rendezvoused on the terrace for over twenty minutes, if my calculations were correct. (A watch didn't fit with my outfit.)

New-couple alert? Not quite yet. Our Cinderella left Prince Charming holding his imported champagne, and disappeared for the rest of the night. Of course, yours truly has an idea as to where she went. Didn't anyone else notice the other major player who was missing from the party…?

The following evening, Elle walked into the Boat House, one of Bayside's nicer restaurants, located on the water. Riley had texted her early that morning, stating they needed a postparty recap.

Wearing a chic black jumpsuit with large emerald jewelry, Riley was already seated at a high table in the bar area, furiously scribbling away in a reporter's notebook.

They made quick work of ordering their drinks. Elle got a glass of pinot noir and Riley decided on a pomegranate martini.

"What are you working on?" Elle asked, nodding toward Riley's notes.

"This article that's been plaguing me. My stupid boss wants more articles on the food scene." Riley made air quotes at the idea. "We live in Bayside, not New York. There's not really a food scene here."

Elle sat back and studied her friend. Riley dressed like she was on a trendy television show and talked about New York constantly. "You seem to really love big cities."

Riley nodded. "I did. I do," she said, quickly correcting herself.

"So why didn't you move to one after school?"

She chuckled. "Are you trying to get rid of me already? We just became friends."

Elle blushed. "I didn't mean it that way."

Waving a hand in the air, Riley didn't look the least bit affected. "I'm kidding." The drinks arrived and she took a sip of her martini. "I went to NYU and stayed in Manhattan after college."

"Really?" Interested, Elle took a sip of her wine. Good, but not quite like a glass in Florence. Table wine in Italy was better than expensive bottles in the United States. "Why did you come back?"

Riley's clear green eyes clouded at the question. Her entire demeanor changed and she quickly looked down at the table. "Let's just say that I went to New York with a goal to conquer the city." She twisted the cocktail napkin that had come with her drink. "In the end, the city conquered me."

Nodding as if she understood, even though she definitely wanted to hear more, Elle decided to change the subject. "So, did you have a good time last night?"

Riley smiled. "I did. Didn't see much of you, though. After you talked to Jasper, that is."

Sitting up straight, Elle said, "Oh, I didn't do anything with Jasper, if that's what you mean."

"I didn't think you had." Riley took another sip of her drink.

She knew Riley was probing, and ordinarily she wasn't into gossip. But it was so refreshing to have a friend to gossip with, Elle let her guard down. "I was talking to Cam for a long time, actually."

Riley's eyebrows shot up. "Cam Dumont? Seriously?"

It dawned on Elle that she'd spoken more to Cam in the last three days than she had in her first eighteen years. Just as she'd told him last night, he was mysterious. Always had been. But now that she was older, that ambiguity intrigued rather than intimidated her. When she spoke with him, it felt like he was really listening to her, absorbing her words, adding his own thoughts. She'd stayed with him for an hour and the time seemed to fly by. When he'd stepped closer to her, she'd reveled in his nearness, become excited about what might happen.

Shrugging at Riley's question, Elle took a long gulp of her drink. "Is that so surprising?"

"Well, yeah. Cam's a nice guy, but he isn't the, um, biggest conversationalist in Bayside." Riley sat back and tapped a manicured finger against her lips. "That must be who the Bayside Blogger was talking about in her post this morning."

"You're kidding, right?" Elle took a quick glance around the room. Was that blogger here now, hidden among the patrons?

"You made the top of her article today. She said you had disappeared from the party, but so had someone else, although she didn't say who it was. I didn't even think about Cam."

Narrowing her eyes, Elle leaned forward. "What do you know about him?"

"Oh, jeez, not much. Cam keeps to himself. He's friendly enough, always says hi to me. Wait a minute…" Riley copied Elle's posture. "Do you like Cam?"

Elle rolled her eyes. "Check yes, no or maybe?"

"Okay, let me rephrase. Are you interested in Cam?"

"I just got back to town. I'm still jet-lagged." Riley

nailed her with a pointed gaze, but Elle tried to hold firm. "Besides, I'm not interested in anyone, most certainly not a Dumont brother."

The truth was, she wanted to know more about Cam. But what she emphatically didn't want to do was cause more gossip to come her way by switching from one brother to the other. Of course, that would imply she'd actually been with one brother before, which she obviously had not.

Luckily, Riley forgot about the Dumont brothers and the two of them moved on to discussing the different gowns at the party. After that, they talked about Florence, and Elle filled Riley in on the last art gallery she'd worked at before coming home.

"What are you thinking for work now that you're home?" Riley asked, as they enjoyed their second drinks of the night.

Elle blew a wayward hair out of her eye. "That's the big question. The types of jobs I'm qualified for, like gallery work, don't really exist here."

Riley looked pensive for a moment before snapping her fingers. "Maybe you can teach art in a school?"

She'd thought of that herself. "I would probably enjoy that, but unfortunately, I don't have my teaching certification, so I'd have to go back to school for it. And I'll need some source of income soon. I'm not opposed to waitressing."

"You can't come back from your glamorous life in Italy only to waitress in Bayside. There has to be something else we can find for you."

"Well, this looks like trouble."

They both glanced up to see Jasper, wearing khaki pants and a mint-green polo, a light-colored jacket thrown over his arm, strolling over to them. He leaned against the table, acknowledged Riley, then turned his attention completely to Elle. Once again, she felt every pair of eyes in the place swivel in her direction.

"What are the two most beautiful women in Bayside talking so intensely about?"

Elle couldn't miss the interested way Riley watched them.

"We were discussing what kind of job Elle should go after," Riley informed him.

"You can always come work for me," he said quickly.

Elle's cheeks were heating up under the intense stare from Jasper, the attention of the whole bar, or both. "That's a really nice offer," she said, scooting her chair away from the table. "But I'm not suited to real estate."

"My parents think I'm not, either."

It was a small comment, fast in delivery, and said with a smile. Yet Elle perked up at it, her heart going out to him and the way that smile didn't quite meet his eyes.

"I'm sorry." Lame as far as responses went, but it was all she could think to say.

"Why don't the two of you have dinner with me?" Jasper suggested hopefully.

"Oh, um… I'm not really dressed for dinner." Elle motioned to the tight black pants and plum top she wore.

"Are you kidding? You look great. Riley, you in?" Jasper's eyes lit up.

"Let's do it." Riley popped up off her chair and followed Jasper to the hostess station.

What would her dad think of Elle having dinner with Jasper? Would he even find out? Would the Bayside Blogger? Was the mysterious writer here right now?

Elle shook her head. She was being ridiculous and paranoid. Dinner with Jasper and Riley would be fun. Plus, with Riley there, how much gossip could come out of the evening? Would the Bayside Blogger care if she ordered the scallops or the crab cake? Unlikely.

She took the seat Jasper held out for her at a table near the window overlooking the bay. They ordered drinks and Jasper asked Riley how things were going at the paper. As she filled him in, Elle did a quick check of the restaurant. No one seemed to be paying them any attention at the moment.

Thank God. Elle finally sat back and took a long drink of water. Just as she'd hoped, with Riley at the table, chattering away, everyone must have understood that this dinner was nothing more than three friends—well, sort of—having dinner together.

Riley's phone let out a little chirp and she reached for it. "Oh, sorry, it's Sawyer."

"Her boss," Jasper explained.

"Oh, right, she mentioned him the other day."

Riley's eyebrows pulled together and her mouth puckered as she read the text.

"Everything okay?" Elle asked, finally relaxing enough to sit back comfortably in her seat.

Shaking her head, Riley let out a huff. "No. I swear, Sawyer Wallace is driving me nuts. One of these days I'm going to throw him right in the bay."

Jasper let out a laugh. "That will be interesting. Make sure and give me advanced warning so I can be there with my camera."

"Oh, I will." She put her cell phone in her purse and turned to Elle with pleading eyes. "I'm so sorry, but I have to go back to the office."

Nooo! Elle sat up straight. "Are you sure? Is everything okay?"

"Sawyer has an issue with one of my stories. It's set to run tomorrow and we're on deadline. The man can't do anything over the phone or email. I'm sorry," she repeated to Jasper.

"That's a bummer," he said. "Tell Sawyer I said he owes you a full dinner and drinks."

"Don't worry, I won't let him forget he ruined my plans." Riley rose and turned to Elle again. "I really am sorry, but please try to have fun."

Elle smothered the large frustrated sigh she wanted to let out. "Of course. And if everything gets worked out quickly, come on back."

"Yeah, we'll save you dessert," Jasper offered.

"Thanks, guys." With that, Riley took her exit and Elle and Jasper were alone.

As they mulled over the menu, Elle couldn't help but glance around the room, constantly noticing person after person turning to watch them.

Once his scotch arrived, they gave their orders to the waiter and Elle settled back in her chair. Jasper immediately started chatting about some of the recent happenings around town.

She watched him as he talked. He was so handsome, she couldn't help thinking. His looks were reminiscent of an old-Hollywood actor. Golden hair and light eyes, tall and lean. Not to mention he was wealthy, well educated and came from a great family.

And yet she didn't feel that little pull. That tingling feeling of awareness she usually got when she was attracted to someone. That feeling she used to get when she was around him back in high school.

That feeling she'd experienced last night as she stood under the gazebo with his brother.

Now, there was something to think about. But luckily, Jasper unknowingly saved her from having to deal with that acknowledgment when he began asking her questions about her time in Florence.

A short while later, she was digging into the stuffed flounder dish she'd ordered.

"Did you ever study abroad?" she asked as he finished questioning her about Italy. She still didn't feel any kind of spark, but she had to admit he was a good conversationalist.

He shook his head. "Unfortunately, I never had time."

Cocking her head, she asked, "What do you mean?"

"Let's just say that I went off to college and was very focused." He stretched both hands out in front of him. "I had a goal and nothing was going to deter me from reaching it."

Interesting, she thought. Elle would have imagined his college days would be filled with frat parties and road trips. After all, he'd been the most popular kid in school.

"What did you major in?"

"Business. What else?" He grinned. "Then I got my MBA."

He went on to describe some of the jobs he'd held both during and after earning his MBA. Impressed, Elle had to admit there was more to Jasper than she'd thought.

"And now you're being groomed to take over the family business." She said it with a smile, but when she saw the shadows pass over Jasper's face, her smile faltered. "You okay?" she asked.

He shrugged. "I'm fine. I wouldn't say I'm being groomed so much as being used for a placeholder."

"What does that mean?"

"My parents are still hoping Cam will come back."

She opened her mouth to protest, but Jasper held up a hand to stop her.

"I love my parents and they have a lot of amazing traits. But one thing I'll never get is how much stock they put into these antiquated ideas. Martinis before dinner, no social media, oldest son takes over the company."

Elle bit her lip. "I'm sure most of it's generational."

"Maybe. But if they want Dumont Incorporated to have

a fighting chance in this generation, they need to start evolving."

"Have you talked to them about it?"

"I've talked. They've yelled. I've tried again. They've rolled their eyes." He reached for his scotch, then realized his glass was empty. Looking up, he didn't quite meet her eyes. "But enough about that." He grinned. "First-world problems, right?"

"Maybe," she agreed. "But they're still important problems to you."

Now he did meet her eyes. "Thanks, Elle. You know, if I wasn't da—"

A flash went off and they both turned in that direction, to find a table of women unabashedly watching them. All three held cell phones in their hands. Elle looked to the left and noticed two more tables of people observing them.

She sat back and shook her head. Jasper raised an eyebrow.

"Doesn't it bother you?" she asked.

"What?" he said with a blank stare. "People assuming we're on a date?"

"Exactly. I don't want to be the center of attention."

She'd been a quiet, serious teenager. Except for her stupid crush on Jasper. A crush, she'd learned tonight, that had been based on nothing concrete. Because the Jasper she'd just finished having dinner with was nice and sweet and very smart. But he wasn't her soul mate. She didn't feel attracted to him at all. In fact, what she felt was sorry that he was going through a rough time with his parents.

After the party last night and dinner now, Elle could truly say that she really never knew the real Jasper Dumont, and she had to wonder if anyone else did, either.

At this realization, she sat up straighter, then folded her napkin and placed it on the table. "I know we haven't ordered dessert yet, but would you mind if we got out of here?"

His face softened. "Absolutely." He signaled the waiter for their check. "And, Ellie?"

She looked up.

"I meant Elle," he said with a grin. "Thanks for listening tonight."

"Anytime. And I mean that."

Once the bill was paid and they were outside the restaurant, Jasper turned to her. "How did you get here?" he asked.

"My dad dropped me off, actually. Kind of like high school." She smiled. "I don't have my own car yet."

"Let me drive you home," he offered.

"Actually, it's nice to be in the fresh air. I think I'll walk off that yummy dinner. But thank you."

Jasper replaced his keys in his pocket and zipped up his jacket. "Then you have to let me walk you. Maybe you'll even let me in on what happened back there." He nudged his shoulder against hers.

They began heading toward the path that led around the bay.

"I don't want to make a mistake, I guess. And certainly not while everyone's watching me."

He exhaled and then stopped at one of the overlooks that offered a great view of the water and harbor. "That's how I feel every single day at work."

She raised an eyebrow. "Come on. You're a Dumont. Your name is on the stationery," she teased. But he didn't smile.

"It's kind of a lot of pressure to have your name everywhere."

Turning her head, she took in his expression. It was strange to see this serious side of Bayside's golden boy. Unsure what to say to make him feel better, she leaned against the railing while she considered. The metal barrier squeaked and rocked. It was loose. Elle took a step back.

She could see the wheels turning in his head, even as he grabbed her fingers and squeezed. "Anyway, don't let me ruin our night. We had a great dinner."

"Excuse me? Dinner?" This came from a voice that happened to sound both high-pitched and unhappy.

Elle and Jasper turned around. A pretty woman, petite, with blond hair and well-tailored clothes, approached them.

"Never mind the dinner, what in the hell are you doing holding hands with a beautiful woman?" she asked, her eyes trained on Jasper.

He edged away from Elle and held up his hands in front of him in surrender. "What are you doing home?"

The woman took a step closer. "I came home a day early to surprise you. Looks like I did more than that."

Feeling beyond awkward, Elle coughed lightly. "I think you have the wrong impression." The other woman crossed her arms over her chest and shot her an oh-really-please-tell-me expression. "We went to high school together and we were only catching up. I'm Elle," she said. "Elle Owens."

"Mindy Peterson. Jasper's girlfriend."

Oh, crap. A myriad of emotions filtered through Elle and she had no idea which one to hone in on. Jasper had a girlfriend? As she continued standing there like an idiot, head bobbing back and forth as she looked from Jasper to Mindy, she felt dumber than ever, and that made the anger come.

"You have a girlfriend?" she said, her voice coming out louder than she'd intended.

"Unbelievable." Mindy shook her own head, her perfect blond hair cascading around her like she was in a shampoo commercial. "He didn't tell you about me? What the hell, Jasp?"

Mindy took another step toward Jasper and Elle figured that was her cue to leave. She mumbled something about heading home, but neither seemed to hear her. So she turned to go, remembering too late that her back had been to the water and the rickety railing.

Before she could stop the inevitable, or even let out a scream, Elle was falling into the bay.

Chapter Six

Who was spotted at the Boat House this evening? None other than little Ellie Owens and Jasper Dumont, at the most romantic table at the restaurant. Wanna know more deets? Come chat with me on Twitter…

Elle could definitely swim, but while she was under the still-cold-from-the-winter water, she considered staying under the surface indefinitely. There was no way she wanted to face Jasper and Mindy after falling into the bay.

Or anyone.

Ever again.

As she began making her way to the top, she realized that her clothes were weighing her down. Panic overtook her and she started to flail her arms and legs. But no sooner had she started squirming than she felt a pair of strong arms encircle her middle securely and propel her upward.

Surfacing, she spit water out of her mouth, gave a couple coughs and pushed her hair from her face. Twisting, she came face-to-face with a handsome chin covered with dark stubble and glistening drops of water.

Cam Dumont had come to her rescue.

"Are you okay?" he asked, trying to grab hold of her again. She remained quiet, more out of embarrassment than anything else. But he must have taken her silence for shock or injury. "Elle? Talk to me. Are you okay?" he repeated, as they bobbed up and down in the frigid bay.

"Cam, do you have her? Is she okay?" Jasper's voice filtered down from the overlook above them.

"Elle?" Cam tried again. He ran a hand over her face before grabbing her to him, pressing her wet body against his rock-hard abs and pecs. She couldn't help but think if she was about to die of embarrassment, being smothered against Cam's body wasn't the worst way to go.

"I'm fine," she finally mumbled against his chest.

"What was that?" His worried voice washed over her.

"I'm okay," she said loudly, out of breath from treading water.

"No, you're not okay. Why did you do that?"

Huh? Do what?

Cam's lips were starting to turn blue. She could imagine how hers looked.

He fisted his hands in her shirt, bringing her to him. "I love him, but trust me, Jasper's not worth it."

What a weird statement.

She pushed away from him. "I can swim. Let's get out of here." With a couple big kicks, she began to make her way to the edge of the water. Cam helped her up and over the supporting wall and then hoisted himself over, as well.

He reached for her again, his eyes searching, looking over every inch of her. Then he pulled her into a tight hug. "Jesus, you made my heart stop."

Wow, he really seemed worried. Falling into the frigid water of the bay at night wasn't exactly her idea of a good time, but it was as if she'd done it on purp...

That's when it dawned on her. Cam thought she'd thrown herself in the water on purpose. "Oh, no," she said quickly. "I fell in accidentally."

Elle's pulse started pounding a mile a minute. Flashbacks to the night of her dreaded senior prom slammed into her brain. As if that stupid video hadn't been bad enough, she'd fled the gym and run home. Only someone had called her name, and when she'd turned, her foot had slipped and into the bay she went. That had been an accident, as well, only no one had believed her. They all thought she'd been so upset over Jasper that she'd thrown herself in.

Ridiculous. She would never attempt to get attention that way. Only a crazy person would. But as she began to see the crowd forming on the overlook, she quickly realized that she was close to being labeled a crazy person once more.

She pushed back from Cam and met his gaze. "I swear. I turned to leave and didn't realize where I was standing, and the railing over there is loose. Someone should fix that. You're in construction. Maybe you can do it." She was fully aware that she was rambling but his expression hadn't changed. If nothing else, she didn't want anyone to think she'd thrown herself in on purpose. And most definitely not Cam Dumont.

"This was an accident?" he asked, disbelief clouding his voice.

"I swear."

She wanted to say more, but at that moment Jasper, Mindy and a whole bunch of other people came running down the embankment.

"Is she okay?" Mindy asked.

"Elle, are you okay?" Jasper asked, reaching them. "You're shivering." He ran his hands up and down her arms. "Jesus, you're freezing."

Mindy slapped his arm. "Give her your coat."

Jasper looked down at his expensive jacket and then took in her soaking-wet body. Before he had to decide if her possible hypothermia was worth it, a soft jacket was being draped around her shoulders. Cam pulled his flannel coat around her tightly, zipping up the front. He must have shed the jacket before he jumped in the water. He rubbed his hands up and down her arms, even as the crowd around them continued to grow.

"I'm sorry, Elle," Mindy said. "I got the wrong impression back there."

"'S 'kay." She ground out the reply through teeth that were now chattering.

Elle wanted to melt into the ground, and only half of it had to do with the heat Cam's capable hands were generating. Hearing the hushed, but excited whispers in the crowd, Elle knew without a doubt that everyone was assuming she'd done yet another foolish thing to win over Jasper.

Humiliation flushed her cheeks even as her teeth rattled together.

"Elle, what happened?" Riley asked, elbowing her way through the crowd.

"I'm…fine…nothing…to…worry…about…"

"I saw everything," someone in the ever-growing crowd said. "She fought with Jasper and then went overboard."

"No, Jasper's girlfriend pushed her over," someone else offered.

"Jasper Dumont has a girlfriend?" another person asked incredulously.

Elle sneezed once, twice, three times in rapid succession.

"Enough," Cam called out. "I'm getting her home. Now."

With that, he picked her up. If she wasn't so busy dying of mortification, she would totally swoon at the ease with which he lifted her. Instead, she snuggled into his chest and closed her eyes.

Next thing she knew, Cam had set her in his truck, turned the key in the ignition and was blasting the cab with heat. Then he walked to the driver's-side door and stripped. Just tore his top off right there in the community parking lot. His pants went next.

Wow. Don't need a heater anymore.

Cam got into the car wearing nothing but a pair of wet boxer briefs. Wet and very snug black boxer briefs.

After closing his door, he leaned over and framed her face in his hands. He looked deeply into her eyes. "Do I need to take you to a hospital?"

Elle froze. Cam was touching her and he wasn't wearing any clothes.

And he looked good. Damn good.

"You're naked," she squeaked. As soon as the words left her mouth she wanted to get out of the car and throw herself back in the bay.

A cocky grin appeared, lighting up his eyes with mischief for a second. One second. Then his usual serious expression returned. "I'll take that as a no."

"Why did you take your clothes off?"

"You seem to be distracted by my nakedness. That means you're not thinking about how you just pitched yourself over the railing and into the freezing water." He turned one of the vents in his direction and the blast of air made his wet, curly hair blow.

"Excuse me? I did not." She pointed over her shoulder in the general direction of the dock. "Tell me you don't think I did that for attention."

He shrugged and stayed silent.

Huffing out a breath, she pulled his jacket around her tighter. "The railing is loose and when Mindy showed up, I figured she and Jasper probably needed some alone time, so I turned to leave. I guess I'd lost track of how close to the railing I was standing and… Why am I defending myself to you?"

He quirked an eyebrow.

"Seriously, Cam. You are so annoying."

He threw his head back and laughed. The movement

did interesting things to his solid body. "Put some damn clothes on already," she yelled.

The laughing stopped but the smile remained. More like a smirk, but still… "I don't have any extra clothes and I'm not putting on those wet ones and dying of pneumonia."

"Fine." She turned to the window as he put the truck into Drive. "What were you doing down there, anyway?"

"It's Saturday night. I was going to have a beer with a friend of mine. Saw you, ahem, meet Mindy, and then go into the water."

She whipped around. "That's another thing. You could have given me a heads-up about Jasper's girlfriend."

Elle felt Cam stiffen next to her. Maybe it had been a passing headlight, but she also noticed that a shadow fell over his face. "Must have been awkward."

"A bit. I mean, I wouldn't have had dinner with him—"

The car swerved. "You had dinner with my brother?"

"It's not like it was a date. Riley was with us until she got called back to work. It was just one little dinner."

"Probably wasn't so little to Mindy."

Elle felt awful. She would never, ever, ever go out with someone else's boyfriend. Ever.

"The whole town saw that go down. Didn't they?" she asked quietly.

He turned and gave her a long once-over before returning his gaze to the road in front of him. "Yep."

"Well, isn't that just peachy. Looks like I stepped off the plane from Italy and walked right back into the past."

"Elle…" he began. But he didn't say anything else.

Leaning her head against the seat rest, she closed her eyes and willed the entire last couple days to be a dream. From the *Printemps* party with all the looks, stares and whispers, to dinner with Jasper and meeting his girlfriend, to the damn Bayside Blogger, Elle wanted a do-over in a big way.

"I've said it before but I'm going to say it again. I'm glad you're back," Cam said in his rough, yet massively appealing voice.

His words struck her deeply. Because the only thing she wouldn't change from the last couple days was sitting right next to her.

"Hey, Cam." She kept her eyes closed. "Not that I needed it, but thanks for saving me tonight."

Sunday was Cam's one day off. As such, it was typically spent sleeping in, being lazy, watching whatever sporting event was in season and generally relaxing.

So why, then, could he not seem to chill out and decompress like every other Sunday?

Maybe because he didn't usually spend his Saturday nights jumping into the cold-as-hell bay rescuing gorgeous women.

Or maybe it had to do with the memory of said gorgeous woman's wet body plastered against his.

During the car ride to Elle's house, he'd caught her eyeing him. Her interest had made his body react in ways that were completely inappropriate for confined spaces. And pantless men.

"Damn, Elle," he mumbled as he flicked through the channels on his big screen. He'd been through all two million channel options only a total of ten times already. There was nothing he wanted to see, except maybe Elle's face when he'd removed his clothes.

Yeah. That hadn't been so bad.

He rose and circled the room, trying to figure out what would make him feel less restless. The fact that Elle's face kept popping into his mind only served to irritate him more.

Like the rest of the town, he'd been quick to assume

that she'd pitched herself into the inky, black water. And he could tell how much his assumption had cost her.

But was she still into Jasper? Cam shook his head. Hell if he could figure out what she was thinking. All he knew was that he was having a bunch of inappropriate thoughts about a woman who had once been seriously into his baby brother.

But Elle truly didn't seem as interested as everyone thought. And neither did Jasper. Which meant…maybe Cam could step into the ring.

He ran a hand over his hair. Damn if he didn't want to see her again. Would that be so wrong?

Guilt coiled in his chest, but that guilt went to war with the desire curling in other areas. Even if he knew how to get in her good graces…

Actually, he knew just the thing.

Picking up his cell, he punched in a number, a grin spreading on his face. Not long after that phone call, Cam made the short drive to Elle's father's house. He'd spent a lot of time at this house when Ted was sick, fixing odd things here and there and planting some flowers and stuff around the porch.

Those flowers currently looked like they were blooming, and he mentally patted himself on the back. Hopping up on the porch, he was about to knock when he heard raised voices coming from the back of the small house. Elle and her dad must be in the kitchen. Silently, he pulled open the screen door and walked inside.

"I swear, Dad. For the hundredth time, I did not purposely throw myself into the water." Ted must have said something in reply but Cam didn't catch it. Then Elle retorted, "I didn't do it in high school, either. I promise you the railing was wobbly."

Ted Owens coughed. "The Bayside Blogger reported—"

A low groan sounded from Elle. "Please don't tell me

you read that crap, too. Come on, Daddy. You know me. Don't you?" she asked after a pause.

Deciding to save her, Cam revealed himself. "She's not lying." Two sets of very similar green eyes turned in his direction. "The railing was loose."

Was being the operative word. After he'd delivered Elle to her worried and obviously upset father, a nearly naked Cam took a hot shower, redressed and then returned to the scene of the crime, where he'd quickly secured the railing with the help of the large lantern he kept in his truck for night jobs.

After he'd seen the evidence for himself, he realized she'd been telling the truth all along.

"Cam," Elle said in surprise. "What are you doing here?"

"I… Hey, it smells really good." That's when he noticed the pots on the stove, the plates, napkins and silverware set on the table, and the apron tied tightly around Elle's narrow waist.

"Ellie's cooking dinner tonight." Cam spotted the quick look of pride Ted shot toward his daughter before he set his features into a hard expression again. "And you," he started, pointing a finger at Cam.

Even with many inches in height and considerably more muscle than the guy, Cam backed up. There was nothing like a father protecting his daughter. His beautiful, vulnerable daughter, whose head was currently tilted as she watched him with interest.

"What did I do?" Cam asked from the corner.

Elle bit down on a smile and mixed something in a pot.

"You dropped my daughter off wearing nothing but your underwear."

"He was cold, Daddy," Elle unhelpfully offered with a grin as she placed large hunks of mozzarella cheese and thick slices of tomato on a plate with some green leafy thing.

"Then you'd think some clothes would help out."

Cam cringed. Being naked in the truck with Elle probably hadn't given off the best message. Still, he had pulled her out of the water. "I am not the villain here. I'm the good guy."

"That's up for debate," Elle said under her breath.

"I saved her."

"I don't need saving," she said, looking indignant as she wielded a bottle of balsamic vinegar. "And if I ever do need saving, I can do it myself."

"Oh, yeah," Cam said, walking around Ted and aiming a disbelieving look at her. "Like you did last night. Hmm, was that before or after you fell into the damn water?"

Ted took a seat at the table and crossed one leg over the other. Not attempting to hide an amused look, he sat back and observed the two of them.

"That. Was. An. Accident." Her face was dewy from the steam coming off the pots on the stove. Cam thought she looked appealing as all get-out. She drained water from a pot and then quickly threw the contents into another pan, mixing everything together.

"We're only looking out for you, princess."

"Yeah," Cam added. And when had that started? he wondered.

"Excuse me." Elle hip-bumped Cam—hard—and continued assembling the meal. She lifted the pan, her muscles straining as she dished the contents onto a large platter. "I didn't realize I had two dads now," she said to Cam, mirroring his thoughts. "When did you start monitoring every little thing I do?"

"I, uh…"

"Daddy," Elle said, with a nod to the platter. Dutifully, Ted put the food on the table. "Cameron, make yourself useful," she said, handing him a large bowl of salad and a basket of bread to put there, as well.

A moment later, she had untied her apron and both Elle and Ted were sitting at the table. "Are you going to sit down or what?" she asked.

"Ellie," Ted warned. "Manners."

"Sorry." She looked up at Cam. "Oh, hero extraordinaire, would you like to join us for dinner? It would truly be our honor."

Cam was taken aback. He hadn't come over for a free dinner, although it smelled so good, he definitely didn't want to pass on it. "I, uh, didn't even bring anything."

"You've done plenty," Ted said. Then he turned to his daughter, who had perked up at the statement. "Cam came by almost every day while I was going through treatment. He really helped out around here."

Elle studied Cam, her eyes softening. "Thank you. That means a lot to me."

Touched at the sudden emotion pouring from her, he quickly made a joke. "Hey, if I knew I would get some home-cooked meals out of the deal, I would have done a lot more."

Comfortable conversation passed between them as they ate. There was no further mention of the bay, Jasper or what had transpired the night before.

"I didn't know you could cook." Cam took his last bite. "This was really delicious." He meant it. Elle *was* a good cook. Another point for her.

When had he started keeping track?

"There's a lot you don't know about me, and thanks." She tried to cover up a proud smile, but he'd caught it.

"So I guess now that you've fed me I should come clean and tell you the real reason I came by."

Elle tilted her head in a way identical to her father. Cam stifled a grin.

"Not to see if I was okay?" she asked.

"I can see that you are. Actually, I have a job offer for you."

Ted put down his fork, an attentive expression on his face. Folding her hands together, Elle rested her chin on them. "What kind of job?"

"Nothing permanent, unfortunately. I'm doing a renovation for an old high school friend. She's pregnant with twins and wants a real fancy nursery with the works. She's been looking for someone to paint a floor-to-ceiling mural in the designated room, but hasn't found anyone she likes." He took a sip of the wine Elle had put out for dinner. "I said you were into that kind of stuff."

"And she just hired me based on you telling her about me?" Elle's eyes were huge.

"I vouched for you."

"I can't believe you thought about helping me find a job," she said, awe lacing her voice.

"You mentioned you didn't know what you were going to do for work."

A huge smile blossomed on her face and made Cam smile in return. "I can't even begin to thank you enough."

Embarrassed, he shrugged. "It was nothing."

Ted got up, patted Cam on the back. "It's something. I'll let you two talk over the details." With that, he walked toward the living room, carrying his glass of wine.

"It's short notice. But you start tomorrow morning. I can pick you up on my way over. Carson, my friend, does want to see some samples of your work, so I hope you have something you can show her."

Elle nodded. "Seriously, this is so awesome of you."

She covered his hand with her own and Cam felt a jolt all the way down to his toes. All he could do was stare into her eyes. Those deep, fascinating eyes.

Instinctively, he laced their fingers together. He couldn't

remember the last time he'd held hands with a female. Never much cared for it. But it felt good with Elle. It felt… different.

"What color are your eyes?"

She'd been eyeing their joined hands, but looked back up at his question. "What?" She laughed. "Um, green."

"No." He shook his head. "They're too pretty to be just green."

A blush tinted her cheeks. "Thanks."

"Ellie," her father called from the other room. Like two teenagers making out, they both pushed back from the table, yanking their hands apart. "Do we have any more of this wine?"

Laughing lightly, she stood up. "You don't need any more." She turned from the table and froze. "How pretty. Look." She pointed out the window.

Cam didn't need to look to know what she was talking about. The sunset over the bay was amazing most nights. Tonight, however, it was extraordinary. Blurring shades of orange, red, yellow and pink were reflecting off the water, making it seem like there were two sunsets instead of just one. The changing light highlighted Elle's hair, casting a glow around her.

"The dishes can wait. Come here." She slipped out the sliding doors that led to their tiny deck.

Following, he shoved his hands in his pockets as she leaned on the railing. "Careful," he teased. "Railings tend to fall around here."

"Aren't you clever," she answered in a dry voice.

Holding in a chuckle, he focused on the peaceful sunset instead. Minutes passed as they stood together in comfortable silence, watching the sky change colors.

He liked being around Elle. Most women wanted to talk about their feelings. Not that there was anything wrong with that when it was needed. But there was a lot to be said for enjoying a quiet moment.

Plus, she could hold her own with him.

And she could cook.

And she was gorgeous.

Sneaking a glance at her, he felt his heart practically stop. She'd let her hair out of its ponytail. Now the wind was moving through it, light brown strands flying around her face. The setting sun cast an aura over her that highlighted her smooth skin. Awash in light, with a dreamy expression on her face, she looked serene, calm. Exquisite.

Exquisite? Ah, hell. He liked her.

"Damn."

She turned her head at his oath. "What was that?" she asked, an amused expression on her face.

He couldn't like her. Not if she had any feelings for his brother. That wouldn't be right.

All he wanted to do was kiss her. With his body tensed and primed at her nearness, he desperately wanted to draw her to him. He wanted those lips on his, those arms around him.

"Cam?"

He met her curious gaze. Why couldn't she be weird or crazy or just not his type?

"What are you thinking?" she wondered aloud.

"Do you still have feelings for my brother?" he blurted. Idiot. Her face fell and then he cursed himself for that. "Sorry, it's none of my business."

"It's okay," she said, waving her hand. "Jasper... I never really knew Jasper."

"You were in the same class." It sounded like an accusation.

"That doesn't mean anything," she said slowly, taking a step toward him. "Dinner last night was the longest we've ever talked."

It hit Cam then, crystal clear. Jealousy over that dinner was what had been bothering him all day. What had kept him awake the night before.

Feeling irritated even now, he wanted to pace. But she was standing so close. He could smell her perfume, a flowery scent that mixed with the aromas from the kitchen. Shouldn't go together, but to him, it was intoxicating.

"Look, Elle, just tell me, once and for all, do you have feelings for my brother?"

"No," she practically screamed. "And for the record, I would never go after someone who was taken."

"Great. I don't want you to do that."

"Then what do you want, Cam?"

"I want to kiss you."

"So kiss me."

She didn't even register her own words until his lips were on hers.

This was no ordinary kiss. Cam practically devoured her. Greedy, ravenous, moving over her lips so expertly that she forgot to be offended, appalled or even surprised. Instead, she fisted her hands in his shirt and pulled him closer.

Cam's response was a low guttural growl that made her feel insanely feminine, wanted, desired. When he yanked her up onto her toes, she went willingly.

They feasted on each other for minutes. Or maybe seconds. She wasn't sure. The only thing she could be sure of was that this was the most passionate kiss of her life.

When Cam pulled back, she wanted to protest. Instead, she looked into his eyes as they searched her face. His arms were wrapped around her tightly, possessively, as he kissed the tip of her nose, with such sweetness she almost cried. Then he took a step back and they stared at each other.

"Feel better?" she asked to break the silence.

"I definitely feel…something." He offered her a cocky, yet endearing, grin. His eyes raked over her from head to toe and back up again. Then he shoved his hands in his pockets. "Good night, Elle. See you tomorrow."

In a daze, Elle walked back into the kitchen. Holy crap. Cam Dumont could kiss. Pausing in the dim light, she pressed a finger to her swollen lips. They felt like they were on fire.

Funny how the last time she was in this house, all her thoughts of romance and passion were centered around Jasper. Now Cam dominated her mind.

Stopping suddenly, she clapped a hand to her mouth. *Oh, no. I can't like Cam.*

Dashing into her bedroom, she closed the door and leaned back against it. What was she doing? She couldn't kiss Cam. Not after liking his brother for most of her adolescent life. The entire town—not to mention that damn Bayside Blogger—would have a field day.

And that kind of attention was the last thing she wanted. Her dad would be beyond embarrassed.

There was only one thing to do. She would make sure she didn't kiss Cameron Dumont ever again.

Chapter Seven

Elle slammed the lid of the laptop down. "Damn Blogger," she muttered through clenched teeth.

How in the hell had she found out that Cam had been to her house the night before? After finishing the last gulp of coffee, Elle put her mug in the dishwasher.

"His truck," she said into the silence of the house. Her dad was still sleeping. Of course, anyone in town could have driven by and seen Cam's truck parked in front of her house. She grabbed her purse, sketch pad and notebook, and went on the porch to wait for Cam.

Glancing at the houses to the left and right, she wondered if one of her neighbors had been the little birdie who told on her. Maybe one of her neighbors was the Bayside Blogger.

Maybe they were watching now.

Paranoid. She needed to get a grip.

Cam's truck rounded the corner and pulled to a stop in front of the house. She rushed over and yanked the door open, even as Cam was getting out to open it for her.

She pointed to the road. "Drive."

His lips twitched. "Yes, ma'am."

The truck lurched into a U-turn and she scrunched down in her seat, trying to keep out of sight. Noticing her peeking over the edge of the window, Cam threw the truck into Park, turned toward her and placed his arm over the seat back. He leveled her with a questioning stare. "What gives?"

Scrunching down in her seat, she whispered, "I don't want her to see me."

"Who?" he asked, eyes darting around.

"The Bayside Blogger," Elle said through clenched teeth. "She's everywhere."

He chuckled. "Oh, is that all?"

"Cam, this is serious," she hissed. "Keep going and get off this block before more people see you on my street."

He obeyed, but she didn't miss his eye roll. "You're kidding, right?"

Once they'd cleared Bay View Road, she sat up straighter and smoothed her hair down. "The Bayside Blogger tweeted that you were at my house last night."

"So?"

Why were men so clueless? she wondered not for the first time in her life.

"I *was* at your house last night," he said.

"I know that. But now everyone else does, too."

He sneaked a glance at her before returning his attention to the road. "I don't see what the problem is." Flicking his signal on, he made a left turn toward the other side of the bay. "I had a good time last night."

The husky tone of his voice made her heart rate speed up as the memory of his lips on hers slammed into her mind. Even with his window down and the cool morning air filtering into the cab, she could feel her cheeks heating.

"This is traditionally where you say you also had a good time," he offered.

She wanted to. Even before that, she'd enjoyed watching him with her dad during dinner, and appreciated having a verbal sparring partner.

But there could be no more kissing. She'd decided that last night, and she needed to stick to her decision.

"I…" She didn't know how to finish that sentence. It didn't matter anyway, because Cam stopped the truck, gave her a long once-over and then announced that they'd arrived.

"Nice house," she commented, taking in the large brick home, circular driveway and tasteful landscaping.

"Tell me about it. I've done a lot of work on it since it was built two years ago."

They got out of the cab and walked toward the door together. "If it was only built two years ago, why have you done so much work? What could it possibly need?"

"Shoddy workmanship from the start," he said, knocking on the front door. "They hired an idiot contractor and the list of issues could wrap around Bayside three times over."

"But we're getting them all taken care of now." The statement was made by a pretty woman of about thirty years old, with a very pregnant belly, who appeared in the doorway.

Elle stepped into an impressive foyer with marble floors and a grand staircase leading up to the second level. A grand mirror on one wall enlarged the room, while framed photos and a few paintings on another wall gave it a homey feeling.

She turned to the woman, who was studying her closely. Cam made the introductions.

"Elle, this is Carson Rothchild. Carson, as I mentioned, Elle may be able to help with the mural you want for the nursery. She's an artist and just returned from Italy."

Carson's eyebrows shot up. "Italy? Really? That's impressive."

"Thanks," she replied. "I mostly worked in museums and galleries, but I do paint and may be able to help."

Seeming antsy, Cam switched from one foot to the other. Carson laughed. "Oh, go back, already. I know you're dying to see the shipment."

"It arrived okay?"

"Early this morning. Too early. You need to talk to your subcontractors about the importance of beauty sleep."

"Noted." Cam turned to Elle. "I'll just leave you guys to it then. Holler if you need me." With that, he walked back through the house like he owned it.

"New quartz countertops in the kitchen," Carson explained as she rubbed her belly.

"The things that excite some people," Elle said, rolling her eyes, and Carson laughed.

"Exactly." She steered them toward the staircase. "Come on up and I'll show you the nursery."

"When are you due?" Elle asked.

"Three months. Twins. Surprise," she said with a huge smile. They stopped outside a room. "This is it."

Elle walked in and struggled not to ooh and aah. The room was so sweet, with light colors on the walls, a plush carpet, two large bay windows and two cribs against one wall. "What an adorable room."

Carson walked a little circle before settling in a rocking chair. "I think so, too. We're having two girls, hence the pink-and-purple color scheme. But I'd really like that wall over there—" she pointed to it "—to have a floor-to-ceiling mural."

Elle examined the room and took into account the existing color palette, the decorations and toys already bought. Making a few notes, she also took the lighting into account.

"This is a really great space and there are so many fun directions you can take a mural. If you decide to go with me, I'd like to talk to you and get a feel for your interests, ideas and what kind of things you're thinking about already."

Leaning her head back on the rocking chair, Carson offered a wry smile. "If I hire you? Honey, you are hired."

Pleased, Elle felt extreme happiness at the idea of having a job. Even if it was only a short-time thing. "Thank you so much," she said.

"No, thank *you*. Once I set my mind on something, there's no going back. For whatever reason, I decided I had to have a mural. But you," she said, pointing at Elle, "are the first person to come in here and ask what I would like."

"Really?"

"Everyone else with the ability to do this kind of painting told me what I needed."

Elle laughed lightly. "Artists are crazy people."

"Crazy or not, I want you to do this."

"In that case, I'd like to take some measurements."

For the next two hours, the two of them chatted and got to know each other. Elle got the specs she needed and more. After talking to Carson she had a clear vision of what would work for the mural.

"When can you start?" Carson asked as she poured a cup of coffee for Elle. They'd moved down to the kitchen.

"I'm going to work on sketches tonight and should be ready to show them to you tomorrow. I can start as soon as you decide on the design you like best."

She passed sugar and a little white pitcher of cream to Elle. "You are a godsend." She took a sip of the tea she was having. "Now that all that work and art stuff is out of the way, I have to ask you something."

Smiling, Elle put her mug back on the table as she helped herself to one of the shortbread cookies Carson had set out. "Shoot."

"Well…I've been reading about you."

The bite of cookie she'd just taken sank like a ten-pound weight to the bottom of her stomach. "The Bayside Blogger?" she asked, already dreading the answer.

Nodding, Carson pushed her tea away. "I have to say that I'm curious. Are the things she's reporting true?"

Elle placed the other half of her cookie back on the plate. "No. Kind of. I guess." She let out a little half laugh as she tried to think what she should say.

Carson leaned forward. "I didn't mean to embarrass you."

She waved a hand. "You didn't. I embarrassed myself years ago."

"I'd rather have the truth from you than read it online."

Grateful for this refreshing viewpoint, Elle relaxed again. "Thank you. Some of the things are true. I did have a crush on Jasper in high school. And I did make a video declaring that love. And that video was played in front of the entire school at our senior prom. After prom I did fall into the bay, but that was an accident, trust me."

Saying all that out loud had her stomach churning and she shuddered a bit. She added, "But that was a long time ago. I don't have feelings for him anymore."

"Do you have them for anyone else? Come on, indulge a super pregnant woman."

"I haven't even thought about dating, to be honest."

Carson tilted her head, studied Elle. "I think someone has thought about dating you."

Curious, Elle met her eyes. "Really?"

"I saw the way Cam looked at you this morning."

Elle shook her head violently. "Oh, no, no, no. He didn't look at me any way."

Carson laughed. "That's not a bad thing. Cam's hot. And successful."

"He's great. But I really don't—"

"And when he's not being so broody, he's very sweet. You should think about it. Heck, if I was single, I would."

"You would what?" The man of the hour strolled into the room. Seeming comfortable in this house, he leaned over and snagged a cookie. As he bit into the shortbread, Elle's eyes were drawn to his lips. The lips that had been on hers less than twenty-four hours earlier.

Elle squirmed in her seat. "Nothing. We weren't talking about anything important."

The way her eyes darted between the two of them, Carson must have felt bad for Elle. "How are things in the bathroom?"

Cam shook his head and let out a long, low whistle. "That contractor really screwed you."

"If I had a nickel for every time he says that I'd be able to build this entire house from scratch again," she said to Elle.

"You're practically doing that already. How's it going here?" Cam asked.

"You finally brought me the right person for the job," Carson said.

Cam looked pleased. "That's good to hear." He turned to Elle. "I can run you home if you want to work on sketches. Or we can set up an area for you here."

"I think home would be good. My supplies are there." Honestly, she wanted to get away from Cam, because the more she was around him, the more she thought about that kiss, and the more she couldn't squash the thought that she wanted to do it again.

Carson walked them to the door. "I'll see you after lunch, Cam. Elle, so nice to meet you. I can't wait to see the designs you come up with."

As they walked to the truck, Cam reached for her arm, but Elle quickly evaded him. They could not touch. Not in public. Not anywhere.

Cam must have caught on to her mood because instead of opening her door, he kept his hand over the handle. "What gives?"

"Nothing gives. I'm anxious to get to work."

He studied her for another moment, his dark eyes roaming her face, searching for the cause of her behavior. Finally, he backed up, opened the door and watched her slide in. But instead of closing the door, he leaned in, planting one palm on the center console and the other on her headrest, boxing her in. With their faces a mere hairbreadth apart, he said, "Good. Because I would hope that kiss last night didn't scare you off."

Turned on beyond belief, Elle couldn't speak. So she shook her head instead.

"Great. Because I plan on doing it again soon."

The next week and a half was fairly uneventful. Unless Cam counted the fact that, due to working with a certain brunette artist every day, he tossed and turned at night and was losing sleep at an alarming rate.

Elle was a hard worker. There was no denying that. If he let her, she'd put in even longer hours that he did. In fact, she would get so engrossed doing her drawing and painting that he'd taken to giving her a thirty-minute warning at the end of the day.

He headed upstairs now for that very reason. But when he reached the nursery, he stopped right outside.

Once again, Elle was in the zone. She was wearing what Cam had come to think of as her working outfit. Every day she showed up in an old pair of overalls with a different color T-shirt underneath and a matching bandanna keeping the hair off her face.

Today, she had a smudge of paint on her cheek, and Cam twitched with the urge to cross the room and wipe it away. While he was there, he could take her in his arms again.

A noise drew him out of his lustful thoughts. He realized she'd begun humming. He wondered if she was aware that when she was in her element like this she wore a contented smile.

Cam was fascinated by her. Every day he found himself standing in the doorway for longer periods of time, watching her. He couldn't help himself—she was just so damn appealing, the way she became entranced in her art. She'd use large, exaggerated strokes sometimes; the brush swishing across the canvas. Other times, like today, she'd work on more intricate details. Her eyes would narrow and she'd steady her hand as she added different colors to the mural.

In a move he'd come to love, she'd step back, tap the handle of her paintbrush to her pursed lips and study her work. Her head would tilt this way and that as she considered.

This was a different side of Elle. An amazing side. He wished the entire town could see what he got to witness every day.

A small, sweet sound escaped her lips. She was pleased with her work today. Cam backed up. Maybe he could let her have a little more time today. Just this once…

A week later, Cam was still feeling pretty frustrated.

The work on the house was slightly ahead of schedule. He'd also just won a bid he'd been working on for a couple months.

But it didn't take a genius to figure out his irritation was rooted in the hot artist currently housed on the second floor.

He'd meant what he'd said to her in the truck. He did plan on kissing her again. But so far, he'd given her some time and space.

Ah, hell. Maybe he was the one who'd needed the time and space.

Damn woman had gotten under his skin. And when was the last time that had happened? Maybe his first crush back when he'd been what? Thirteen? Fourteen?

Women didn't usually get to him. He led a simple life

filled with hard work, a cold beer at night and lazy Sundays. Women had a way of complicating even the most basic plans.

Then why was it that all he could do lately was think about Elle? Wonder what Elle was doing when she wasn't working on the mural?

"Hey, boss," Tom, one of the younger guys on his crew, yelled. "That Ellie Owens chick wants to see you."

At the sound of her name, he whacked his thumb with the hammer he was wielding. "Dammit," he shouted.

Tom chuckled. "Ouch. You know, I typically aim for the wood. Not my finger."

Cam flicked a different finger up at Tom's smart remark. Then he descended the ladder and went off in the direction of the nursery.

Once he got there, he saw that he wasn't the only one. Carson, along with some friends, her sister who was visiting and the fancy interior decorator she'd hired were all standing in the hallway outside the nursery. Cam noticed a big pink bow was tacked to either side of the door and Elle stood next to it with a nervous smile on her face.

"What's going on?" he asked in a gruff voice.

"Oh, good, Cam's here," Carson said, excitement in her voice. "We're all here now so we can finally see." She was practically dancing in a little circle.

"Careful," Cam said. "Those babies might make an early appearance."

The women all laughed, but Cam didn't see what was so funny. He was serious.

When she let out a delicate cough, all eyes focused on Elle. "If I may have everyone's attention…" she said. "I want to thank Carson for giving me this opportunity. The mural is finished and I really hope you like it. So without further ado…" She gestured to the door.

Cam watched as Carson removed the pink bow and

slowly entered the nursery. He didn't need to be inside the room to hear her gasp of pleasure.

When he finally did poke his head in, he saw that Carson's hand was over her mouth and her eyes were filled with tears. Elle was standing to the side, hand to her own mouth, chewing on a nail. The other women were also staring at the wall, huge smiles on their faces as a chorus of oohs and aahs and "how sweet" and "so precious" filled the room.

Cam took another step in and his eyes roamed over the mural. He wasn't about to cry and sigh like the women, but he was impressed as hell.

"Oh, Elle," Carson said, grabbing her hand. "It's…it's so beautiful. I can't believe it."

"You like it then?" she asked shyly.

"Oh, my God, of course. It's beyond my wildest expectations. I mean, I know I approved the design, but this is just…to see it in real life… I can't believe how wonderful it is." Carson turned to him. "What do you think, Cam?"

He walked closer and took in the wall, painted in soft pastels. It depicted stars in the sky and a slender moon overlooking a grassy meadow with a stream running through it. There were two cherubs playing among the trees, as fairies watched them from the branches. Somehow Elle had managed to add touches of some kind of glitter that made it seem like fairy dust was being sprinkled over the babies.

"It's stunning," Cam said, stepping back from the wall. His breath caught at the sight of Elle's huge smile. He loved when she smiled like that and wished she'd do it more often. "Great work, Elle."

"Great?" Carson said. "This goes way beyond *great*. I can't wait to show all of my friends." She pointed at Elle. "I'm telling you, you are going to have so many people clamoring for your artistic skills, you're never going to have time to sleep again. This is the most perfect, wonderful, amazing nursery ever."

"Speaking of needing an amazing nursery…" Carson's friend Polly spoke up.

All the other women started squealing and Cam jumped back. Looking from one to the other, he had no idea what he'd just missed.

"You're pregnant?" Carson said in a high-pitched voice. "Oh, my God."

Beaming, Polly rubbed her belly. "A boy," she said with a huge grin.

More screaming ensued and Cam took another step toward the door and sanity.

"Elle," Polly said. "I'd like to be your first referral. Would you please consider doing something like this in my nursery?" She gestured to the mural. "Would you be able to do something for a boy?"

Nodding emphatically, Elle stepped forward, and the women started talking a mile a minute as ideas about murals for boys flew around the room.

Cam backed out of the room quietly, although with the level of noise inside, they wouldn't have noticed him, anyway. He made his way downstairs with a big smile on his face. Elle did good work and he was thrilled he was able to help her.

At the same time, disappointment settled into the pit of his stomach. Her job completed, Elle wouldn't be in the same place as him anymore. He'd come to look forward to eating lunch together, taking coffee breaks and driving her home at the end of each day.

But now she would move on. He knew he should do the same. The problem was, he didn't know if he could.

Chapter Eight

I've been receiving a lot of mail, tweets and Facebook messages asking about Ellie Owens. Sadly, our gal has been hiding. Would I lie to all of you? Nope, not a chance. But who knows? Maybe she'll pop up at the Bayside Spring Festival today...

"Do you really, really want to go to this?"

At her dad's stoic expression, Elle relented. But not without a silent sigh.

"I go to the Bayside Spring Festival every year. Why would this year be any different?" he asked.

"But do you really need me to go, too?"

Elle had been back in Bayside for almost a month now. Since she'd finished the mural for Carson Rothchild last week, she'd been in talks to not only do a mural for Carson's friend Polly, but to paint and design the entire room. As much as she was looking forward to that, the actual work wouldn't take place for another month.

Since none of the work had begun yet, though, she'd mostly been hiding out. Except for meeting Riley for coffee a couple times. In the meantime, Elle had decided the best way to stay off the dreaded Bayside Blogger site was to hide out at her dad's house. Even though she'd told her father she'd been busy job hunting—which she had—she was mostly trying to not do anything worth talking about.

"You have to get out of this house," he said, reaching for his hat and jacket.

This time, she couldn't hold in the sigh.

He looked over at her. "I mean, I'm still sick. And weak," he added with a big frown.

She wasn't buying it. Elle knew when she was being taken. After all, her dad had been outside planting flowers earlier. And the other day, he'd been at an all-day poker game with his old friends from the force. Not to mention his coloring looked much better and he was starting to gain a little weight back.

No, her dad wasn't frail and incapable of driving himself into town for the annual festival. There would be a couple different bands, lots of food and some boat races. Nothing strenuous whatsoever. In fact, it even sounded fun.

While the town hosted lots of different events in the busy summer tourist season, this festival was only for residents. A sort of early kickoff to summer and farewell to winter party.

But with everyone in town in attendance, Elle's chances of drawing attention to herself grew exponentially. Although…there was one person she'd kind of like to see.

Hating to admit it, Elle missed Cam's company. It was interesting how a man of so few words could make her smile and feel at ease.

But even the thought of bumping into Cam didn't have her running to the car.

"Remember, I have cancer," her dad said.

"Somehow, I don't think I'll forget that," she replied with a resigned sigh. Knowing she'd lost the battle, she grabbed her jacket and took the keys her father offered.

Ten minutes later, Elle had dropped her dad off near the center of town and circled around until she found a parking spot. Instead of getting out of the car, she stayed put. Maybe she could hide out here for the entire festival. Would her dad really notice if she didn't load up on funnel cake and overly sweet lemonade?

Tilting the rearview mirror, she checked her makeup and hair. Completely normal. Then she glanced down at her clothes. She'd put on a pair of dark jeans and a light pink top. Nothing flashy to draw attention.

She was completely average.

Still, her fingers bent around the steering wheel and held on tight. Breathing in and out, she centered herself, quiet and calm permeating the car. Until a tap on the window almost made her jump out of her skin.

"Cam," she said, as she rolled the window down.

Leaning in close, he gave a wry smile. "You know, I thought it was a one-time thing, but now I see you really don't understand the basic concept of getting out of a parked car. I'm willing to offer a class."

She rolled her eyes, pulled the key from the ignition and got out. "Ha-ha, aren't you hysterical."

After she locked the door, she took her first good look at him. He wore a pair of old jeans and a fitted blue jersey with his flannel jacket over it, and she noticed he hadn't shaved today. The stubble did something to her. Made her breath catch as she imagined kissing him again, having that stubble rub against her cheeks.

His dark eyes were watching her, flicking over her face. How bad would it be to just go up on tiptoe and press her lips to his, only for a second?

"Cam…" she began. Elle moved toward him, not believing what she was about to do. What she'd wanted to do for the last couple days.

Then a horn sounded and a group of teenagers came running by, ruining the moment.

Was that look on his face disappointment? she wondered. She hoped so. It would mirror her own feelings.

At least the interruption forced her to remember that she was in public and she did not want to draw any attention to herself today. So she offered Cam a small smile and began to walk toward the festival.

"How are things going at the Rothchild house?" she asked.

"No complaints. We're finally nearing the end." He fell into step alongside her.

"What will you do after this project? Do you have something else lined up?"

He nodded. "There's always more. I've been working on something with my brother, actually. That will need some attention soon."

"I miss seeing Carson every day."

"She's planning some kind of baby party thing."

Elle chuckled. "That's called a baby shower, and I got my invitation."

"So you'll be going?"

She slid him an odd look. "Of course. She wants people to meet the artist who did the mural. Could mean more business for me."

"I was starting to think you've been hiding out."

Shocked that he would figure that out, she stumbled on a rock. Cam reached for her arm before she could topple over. At his touch, her breath hitched.

"You okay?" he asked, his deep voice husky and thick with emotion. He didn't let go of her arm. Instead, he used the leverage to pull her closer.

"Yeah," she said, eyes plastered on his mouth. On lips that were within reach.

"Elle?"

She jumped, then turned to see Riley hustling toward them.

"You decided to come, after all! I'm so happy you stopped hiding away in your house." Riley looked back and forth from her to Cam, then raised an eyebrow.

"I haven't been hiding. I've been job hunting and it's kept me busy."

"Uh-huh," Riley said with a smirk. Sliding her arm through Elle's, she steered her toward the festival, with Cam following. "You have got to tell me what's going on with you two," she murmured.

Elle felt the heat on her face and was happy that Cam was walking behind them at the moment. "Shh," she whispered.

Riley laughed. "Come on, both of you. There's a decent band playing already and Mr. Healey is making some really good shrimp quesadillas."

The three of them entered the festival, and Elle took in the event that covered the entire town square, along with the marina and the surrounding docks. Seemed like every local business was participating. Tents and tables were set up in front of the storefronts, displaying various clothing, jewelry, accessories and more. Elle couldn't wait to do a lap.

She noticed The Brewside was handing out small samples of coffee, drinks and baked goods. Most of the restaurants had followed suit, giving away their various specialties and offering coupons and discounts. The mixture of yummy smells was better than any welcome mat.

Bayside hadn't forgotten about the kids either. Elle saw the middle of the square was dedicated to games with prizes of stuffed animals and small toys.

The festival was packed and everyone appeared to be having an amazing time. Laughter carried on the breeze and the sound warmed her heart. She'd really missed this festival while she was away.

On the far end of the square, they'd set up a stage and Elle, Cam and Riley listened to the band for about twenty minutes. While Riley and Cam headed off to get food, Elle sneaked away to check on her dad. Once again she realized she had no reason to worry, when she saw him holding court with a bunch of his buddies, laughter and curse words flying as they no doubt relived tales from their days as cops.

Meeting back up with Riley, she took the quesadilla her friend offered and they found seats on a nearby wall that overlooked the marina, where they could listen to the band and people watch at the same time.

After they finished their food, which was delicious, Elle asked, "Where's Cam?" She realized asking the question had been a mistake when she saw Riley's eye light up.

"He ran into someone from work. Okay, spill," her friend said emphatically.

"What?" Elle asked.

Riley's eyes grew huge. "What? Oh, my God, are you seriously playing coy?"

Elle took a sip of lemonade and shrugged her shoulders.

"I'm going to call you Ellie, which I know you hate, until you tell me what is going on between you and Cam Dumont."

Sputtering on her drink, Elle put the glass down and met Riley's smug expression. "Nothing is going on. I ran into him when I was parking and we walked over together. That's all."

Shaking her head, Riley tsked. "I don't believe you, Ellie. There's been something between the two of you since you got back. I mean, the way he looks at you—"

"How does he look at me?" Elle asked too quickly.

"See? I knew it. Do you have a thing for Cam?"

Elle dodged the question. "For the foreseeable future I'm going to be settled here in Bayside. I just want to find some work and keep a low profile. You know what I mean?"

Riley looked thoughtful for a moment. "The Bayside

Blogger? You don't want her to know about your crush on Cam?"

"I don't want to be the object of her column. I just need some time to settle back in. I've been gone a long time and coming home… Well, it's been harder than I thought it would be."

Once again, her thoughts turned to the video she'd made in high school. Truth was, she hadn't even known she was being filmed.

But she did know how disappointed her dad had been. She'd never forget the expression on his face when she'd gotten home from the prom.

Not until she'd been much older did she find out the full truth. She'd known that her dad had wanted to run for county sheriff, and she'd always wondered why he hadn't won the election. After all, he had the best qualifications of anyone on the force. He'd started off in New York City, and he'd been in the military before that.

Then she did some digging and found an old article from the *Bayside Bugle*. There it was in black-and-white— an op-ed piece talking about Ted Owens and his lack of control of his child.

That article had helped Elle to get her priorities straight. It had also been a jarring reminder that her dad had sent her away. But that had been her own fault. She'd been taking Italian classes since high school and decided that going to Italy—and staying there—would help her dad even more. The farther she got from Bayside, the better off her dad would be. Without his daughter to humiliate him.

Shaking her head, she tuned back to Riley, who was watching her intently. Reaching over, her friend squeezed her hand. "Don't worry, Elle. Everything is going to work out. You'll see."

A big splash sounded and they both turned in the direction of the bay. "Are people jumping in? Seriously?"

Riley asked. "The temperature may be starting to warm up, but that water is still freezing."

"Don't remind me," Elle said, making her friend laugh.

Elle noticed a group of people gathering at the dock. The hairs on the back of her neck stood in high alert. "What's going on?"

"Probably just some teenagers being teenagers," Riley suggested.

Elle started walking toward the dock—the same one she'd fallen from not too long ago—with Riley close behind. But a bad feeling niggled at her, even as Cam started running toward her, a worried look on his face.

"Hey, Elle," he called. "Come this way."

He tried to reach for her arm to steer her away from the crowd, but she sidestepped him and kept going.

But as she approached the dock, her heart nearly stopped. A huge sign erected right where she'd gone over the railing declared Jump for Love.

"There she is!" someone shouted.

Everyone present turned in her direction. Mortified, she heard the familiar whispers start up, saw Bayside residents all pointing at her as she walked forward, even while Cam and Riley called her back.

But wanting the full picture, she went all the way up to the dock, amid the sneers and whistles.

"Here she is, our little Ellie Owens." This was said by a guy she recognized from high school, but whose name she couldn't remember. "Come on up here, Ellie."

She planted her feet and stayed right where she was. Unfazed, the announcer continued with his spiel. "Ellie Owens jumped overboard for the love of Jasper Dumont. You, too, can take a turn, for only ten dollars. All proceeds go to the high school drama club."

Embarrassed beyond belief, she watched with wide eyes as a couple younger guys handed over some cash, gave

Elle a salute and jumped into the freezing water. A roar rose from the crowd.

"That idiot," Riley said through clenched teeth. "I'll never write a good review of a high school play again."

Appreciating the loyalty, Elle shook her head. "Don't take this out on the kids. They don't deserve it."

"What they deserve is a better example." Cam pushed through the crowd and starting walking toward the guy. Elle noticed his fingers curl into fists and jumped forward.

"No, no, no. Please, Cam. Let it be."

The crowd turned its attention in their direction, and for the second time that day she felt her cheeks heat up. But she managed to pull Cam back. As she did, Elle spotted her dad at the side of the crowd, his face ashen.

"My dad. I have to go talk to him." But even as she started to make her way in that direction, she watched him shake his head and walk away with one of his friends.

She'd done it again. Humiliated her father.

That left only one thing to do. Head held high, she pushed her shoulders back and made her way up to the dock. She reached into her purse, pulled out a ten dollar bill and shoved it into the guy's hand.

His face changed quickly. Even as some of the people in the crowd gasped and others laughed, the guy hosting this "event" lost his smile and his eyes went wide. Guilt practically poured out of him, but that wasn't her concern.

She'd begun walking away when the guy called out to her. "Wait, you, um, want to jump in?"

Elle paused, but didn't look back. Instead, she said loud enough for him to hear, "I've already had my turn." And she didn't stop walking this time until she'd reached her car and driven away.

Chapter Nine

My, my, the annual spring festival certainly provided the gossip this year. If anyone thought they were going to get away with making fun of little Ellie Owens and her high school shenanigans again, they might want to think twice! This hometown heroine left us all speechless yesterday with her act of charity in the face of adversity. Looks like the joke's on you, Dan Chumsky, for trying to embarrass her.

Sitting in his truck later that evening, Cam watched Elle's house for any sign of life. What he really wanted to do was go beat the living crap out of that thoughtless moron Dan Chumsky. He'd been a jerk in high school and clearly, not much had changed since then.

Watching Elle's face as she'd realized she was being ridiculed was one of the most painful things Cam had experienced in a good long time. Making the situation even worse was how heartbreaking it had been to watch her seek out her dad—only to have Ted turn away.

What the hell had that been about? Cam tightened his fingers around the steering wheel. *Poor kid*, he thought. He'd had a feeling she'd been hiding out for the last couple weeks. Now he knew he'd been right.

Well, the hiding was over, he thought as he pushed away from the steering wheel. Flicking his seat belt buckle, he growled. Elle was a good person. So she'd made one bad decision in high school. Hadn't they all done things back then they regretted?

The night was quiet. But then he heard what sounded like a door opening and closing, and he decided to take a chance.

Walking around the small house, he saw her on the deck. "Elle, listen here," he said, taking a step onto the deck. Her head snapped to the side and he froze.

It didn't look like she'd been crying, but there was definitely hurt and pain on her face. Her lips were pinched together and frown lines surrounded her eyes.

"Ah, hell." He bounded across the small space.

"Cam, what are you—"

Cutting off her question, he grabbed her and pulled her to his chest. That damn floral scent of hers infiltrated his senses as he held her close. She stood stiff in his arms for a few moments, before finally softening and letting out a long sigh.

I'm sorry about what happened today, Elle. But he couldn't quite get the words out. Instead, he tightened his grip on her.

When she pulled away after a couple minutes, he felt the loss. His body ached to be near hers again. Elle walked to the railing, hopped up and sat on it, facing him.

He propped an elbow beside her.

There was a certain sadness in her eyes. Even in the dark, Cam couldn't miss it and he hated it. "Listen, Elle," he began.

She held up a hand. "Stop. I know what you're going to say." She jumped down and turned to face the water. "It wasn't my fault. That guy's a jerk. I shouldn't let it bother me. Blah, blah, blah."

Pretty darn close to what he was going to say. Except for the blah, blah, blah.

She turned those pretty green eyes on him. Why did

she have the ability to make him want to melt with a simple stare?

"Well?" she asked. "Wasn't that what you were going to say?"

He threw an arm over her, boxing her in against the railing. "Not even close." With that, he brought his mouth to hers, taking her lips roughly, selfishly.

As fast as the kiss happened, he stopped it, pulling back, hoping he hadn't crossed any lines. But meeting her now-hazy eyes, he realized that Elle had enjoyed it as much as he did. So he leaned back in and brushed his lips over hers once, twice, three times, as gently as he could. Framing her face in his hands, he took her lips softly this time with small, tender kisses.

Elle sighed and folded into him. His palms left her face to circle her as she ran her own hands up his back, over his shoulders, and finally, into his hair.

Again he pulled back. This time, she smiled shyly and then tugged him toward her. With a not-so-gentle nibble, she sucked his bottom lip into her mouth, a sensation that had him inhaling sharply out of sheer pleasure. Then she plunged her tongue inside his mouth, and he didn't have the brain cells left to understand what was going on. Only that he'd never had a kiss that felt this damn good.

Cam had no idea how long they stood there, making out on the deck, as the water gently lapped and the moon shone down on them. But when they finally looked up at each other, he saw that her lips were swollen, the skin around her mouth was reddened from his stubble and her eyes were glazed.

It made him want to yell out in triumph.

Instead, he ran a finger over the soft, silky skin of her cheek. She shivered.

"You're a man of your word," she said, her voice husky.

"Excuse me?"

"The second kiss you promised me. It was good."

"Damn good," he agreed, grinning at her like an idiot.

She watched him for a long moment. Then her smile faded and her eyes cleared up. "But we can't keep doing that."

"Why the hell not?" he demanded.

Trying to push away from him, she furrowed her brow when she realized he was holding her tight, with no plans to let go. "Because," she continued. "I didn't come home for a love affair. And I certainly didn't return so I could keep humiliating myself."

"Does kissing me humiliate you?"

She winced. "No, I didn't mean that."

"Why'd you come home then?" he asked simply.

"For my dad. I should have been here the day after he was diagnosed. Would have been if he'd told me," she stated. "Cam, I embarrassed him today."

"You think kissing me would embarrass Ted?"

"That's not what I mean." She swung her head back and forth. "I can't keep kissing the brother of the guy I was in love with in high school. People will—"

"Talk," he finished for her. "They'll always talk. They'll always gossip. So what? Your business is *your* business. Who cares what these people think?"

She laughed at that and Cam enjoyed seeing her face light up.

"You need to get away for a day," he blurted. She tilted her head and he figured why stop now. "I have a cabin, about an hour from here. It's nothing special, but going there always helps me clear my mind. Tomorrow's Sunday, and I thought I might go fishing. Why don't you bring your notebook and paints and stuff? Keep me company." Had he really just gone on and on like a bumbling preteen?

Elle kept her mouth closed and didn't say a word. He could see the wheels of her brain turning. Clearly, she was trying to figure out all the reasons—probably valid reasons—why she shouldn't go with him.

Then, she surprised him.

"What time should I be ready?"

The next morning, Cam practically jumped out of bed. Truth be told, he hadn't planned on going to the cabin today, and he certainly hadn't planned on inviting Elle.

He'd bought and remodeled the cabin three years ago, and tried to get up there as often as he could. He didn't need to be anyone special there. He didn't need to be a Dumont. He could relax and forget about the world, while wearing a pair of ratty sweats and not combing his hair.

Which was why it didn't make any sense that Cam showered, slapped on some aftershave, ran a comb through his hair and picked out a pair of recently washed jeans and a black shirt.

"Where you going so early?"

He spun around at the sound of his brother's voice. Jasper strolled over from his car to where Cam was hoisting his fishing equipment into the bed of the truck.

"Thought I'd get in some fishing today," he explained, not quite meeting his brother's eye.

"Want some company?"

Something in Jasper's voice sounded off. He stood before Cam wearing clothes that were more than likely the same from last night.

"Been home yet?" Cam asked.

"Nah. I was at Mindy's."

Hope rose in Cam's chest. If Jasper spent the night with Mindy, that meant they were still together, which implied Jasper wasn't interested in Elle and therefore Cam wouldn't have to back off.

He shook his head and threw a six-pack of beer in the back. "Things are good between the two of you then?"

Jasper looked to the side.

"Jasp?" he prompted. Leaning against the bed of the truck, he waited. When it became clear Jasper wasn't going to say anything more, Cam demanded. "What the hell's going on?"

His brother shrugged. "Got into it with Dad last night. Couldn't sleep."

Cam jutted his chin forward in question.

"Same old," Jasper offered as explanation. "I had an idea—a good idea—and Dad rejected it. Immediately. Without even hearing me out." He began pacing back and forth in the driveway. "How am I supposed to accomplish anything if he won't loosen the reins?"

Cam knew that Jasper's gripe wasn't a one-time thing. Butting heads with their parents was becoming a daily occurrence. And that was all Cam's fault. If Jasper hadn't done him the favor of stepping into his shoes so Cam could go off and start his own company, his little brother wouldn't be so damn miserable all the time.

"Listen, Jasp…" Cam ran a hand over his face while he tried to figure out what to say. "I'm sorry. If you want to ditch this job, you know you can always come work for me."

Jasper's lips twitched. "Work for you? As what, exactly?"

"Well," Cam said. Then his own lips broke into a grin. Jasper didn't exactly know how to use his hands, he didn't like to get dirty and he pretty much hated everything about construction except the final product. "I'd make up something for you." And then he could stop feeling guilty over his brother.

Jasper's eyes softened. "I know you would. But I think all those degrees I've acquired might help me in securing a position somewhere less…rustic." He stuffed his hands in his pockets. "So, I repeat. Want any company?"

Clearly, this fight had been rougher than usual, because in the three years Cam had owned the cabin, Jasper had been there maybe twice. Jasper claimed he wasn't an "outdoor kind of guy" even though the cabin boasted every amenity Cam had in his regular house.

"Actually…" Cam began. Damn, he felt like such a jerk. His brother was obviously hurting, but what Cam really wanted was to spend the day with Elle. Alone.

"It's okay," Jasper blurted out, saving him from making a tough decision. "You know I don't really like that woodsman life."

"I have a huge plasma TV, cable, a hot tub and a wine fridge for my 'woodsman life.'"

"Whatever. There are trees and bunnies and stuff up there."

Cam chuckled, silently relieved. Though, man, his brother looked rough today. "But seriously, everything good with Mindy?"

Jasper looked away again. Then he quickly launched into it. "She's mostly fine. Still kind of weirded out about me having dinner with Elle. Doesn't help matters that Elle is so freaking hot."

In the middle of hoisting a bin of fishing supplies, Cam fumbled and the box landed with a loud crash in his truck.

"Careful, dude," Jasper said. "Anyway, I heard about what happened to Elle at the festival yesterday. That's messed up."

"It was definitely messed up."

"She okay?"

"I think she's going to be fine."

"Maybe I'll stop by her house today."

"No," Cam blurted out, before silently cursing himself. Jasper's head snapped up. "I mean, I think you showing up at her house after what happened yesterday would probably embarrass her."

"Makes sense." Jasper tucked his tongue in his cheek and handed Cam a small bag he'd put some essentials in. Cam tossed it in the truck. "You're acting weird, Cam."

He didn't know why he didn't come clean and tell his brother about Elle, only that he wanted to keep that little secret to himself. "Didn't sleep well myself. Anyway, I should be getting on the road."

Jasper studied him for a long time. So long that Cam had to suppress the urge to shuffle his feet and duck his head.

"Sure." Jasper slapped a hand on the truck and started walking back to his car. "Whatever you say." He got in his vehicle, clearly not buying any of it. He rolled down the window and shot Cam an unreadable look. "Well, have a good time. By yourself." He threw the car in Drive, but didn't pull away from the curb.

"Will do," Cam answered.

"Oh, and Cam?"

"Yeah?"

"Tell Elle I said hi." With that, Jasper grinned, peeled out and sped around the corner.

Cam stood at the bottom of the driveway, shaking his head. His brother could be right. Their parents truly didn't give Jasper enough credit. Apparently, Cam didn't, either.

Chapter Ten

A little over an hour later, Cam put the truck in Park and climbed out. After helping Elle from the vehicle, he grabbed a couple grocery bags and walked up to the front door. He found the right key on his key ring and let them inside.

Elle's intake of breath gave him a feeling of pride.

Shoving past him, she looked around the cabin, soaking in every detail, from the pictures on the walls to every piece of furniture. She made her way to the living room, studying everything as if there would be a quiz on it later.

For his part, Cam stayed in the entryway, trying to acclimate to seeing her in his space. He'd never brought a woman here before. Would the cabin retain the scent of her delicious floral perfume after she left? Would he think about her now every time he crossed the threshold?

"Cam, this is way beyond what I thought it would be."

He put the bags down. "What'd you think it would be like?"

"I don't know." She spun in a circle. "A one-room serial-killer type of place with an outhouse and no running water, maybe." She walked farther into the cabin as he chuckled. "Clearly, I'm an idiot. This is stunning."

So was she, and he liked the way she was reverently touching the wooden panels along the wall.

He gestured at the open concept, complete with vaulted ceilings, old wooden beams and skylights. "Kitchen is right there. This is the living area. Three bedrooms upstairs."

He tapped on a door around the corner from the living room. "This is a powder room. Two full baths upstairs."

"This is great. And look at these views." She wandered to the wall of windows that overlooked the large deck. Beyond it were trees, with mountains in the distance. Plus the lake below, with his own personal dock extending into it.

"Hot tub is out there, and access down to the water." He felt shy all of a sudden. "Gonna get this stuff inside. I brought some food for lunch and dinner. Want to come down to the dock while I fish?"

She nodded, but kept running around the house, looking at each room and space. Stopping at every window, she would glance outside, let out an appreciative sound and move on to the next. It was like watching a little kid in a toy store.

"It's official," she announced, when she returned from exploring the upstairs. "I'm in love with this place. I don't know why you don't just live here permanently."

Cam threw the last item from the cooler into the fridge. "Believe me, it's tempting. But since the majority of my work is in, or near, Bayside, the commute wouldn't be fun. It is peaceful, though." With a proud glance around the room, he took a moment to admire his own handiwork. His eyes flicked up to find Elle watching him with a smile.

Embarrassed, he reached for the mini cooler he kept at the cabin. "So, sandwiches okay for fishing?"

Her eyes lit up. Cam would even go so far as to say they sparkled. If he used a word like *sparkle*, that is, which he clearly did not.

"Cam, you have a lot to be proud of." She moved to the door that led out to the deck. With her hand on the knob, she stopped. "And sandwiches are fine."

Two hours later, they were seated at the end of the dock. Sandwiches had been consumed, Cam had drunk a beer, while Elle had stuck to diet soda. He had already caught one fish and was feeling pretty good about his chances for more.

Next to him, perched on a wooden bench he'd built as part of the dock, Elle was scribbling away on her large drawing pad. She'd look up occasionally, or violently flip a page, but for the most part, she'd been quiet and keeping to herself.

Good thing he didn't need to concentrate after his line was in the water, though. While Elle sat silently, he kept stealing glances at her. She looked pretty in the early-afternoon light. The warm spring sun beat down on her, illuminating her shiny hair and smooth skin. She looked at home here. She was wearing a dark purple top with a plaid blouse over it and a pair of jeans. Cam couldn't help but notice how those jeans fitted her just right as they'd walked from the cabin down to the lake. Her hair was tied back in some kind of intricate braid and he liked how it was away from her face. He really liked her face.

"What are you thinking?" Elle asked. Her voice startled him from his very nonmasculine train of thoughts.

Obviously, he wouldn't let her know what he'd really been considering, so he improvised by reaching over and tapping her sketch pad. "I enjoy watching you work and I'm wondering what is keeping you so preoccupied."

"Do you want to see?"

She bit her lip for a split second. But it was enough to let Cam know that showing her work made her nervous. And also highlighted that oh-so-tempting mouth.

"I'd like that very much."

Taking a moment, she looked down at the page before handing her pad over to him.

Cam shifted in his seat as his eyes raked over the drawing. It was damn good. He already knew she had a natural flair for art after the mural she'd done. But this was different. It was great, too, but less busy, with simple, clean lines.

"You know what I find interesting?" he asked. "You wanted to get away from Bayside and yet you're drawing it." He nodded at the rendition she'd done of the town square.

A slight blush reddened her cheeks. Sitting back, she studied her drawing as Cam handed it back. "Huh. I hadn't realized," she said, more to herself than him.

Cam propped his legs on the cooler. "What's your deal with Bayside, anyway? Why all the angst?"

Huffing out a breath, she offered him a look that should have made him feel like an idiot. "Oh, I don't know. Maybe because I massively embarrassed myself and my dad by making a drunken video about your brother?"

"Oh, is that all," he teased. "I hold firm that you give way too much credence to the opinions of our beloved townsfolk."

"Easy for you to say from way over there. They won't let me forget about it."

"You don't have to acknowledge it. You know," he began, deciding to switch tactics, "I kind of liked that you declared your love for Jasp. No, really," he said, in response to her rolling eyes. "You were passionate and there's nothing wrong with being vocal about your passions. Although, to be honest, I never did understand what you saw in him back then."

Her mouth fell open. "Cameron Dumont, he's your brother."

"So the doctors claim. But I have my own suspicions." She smiled.

He shifted in his seat. "If I remember correctly, you were a really good student. Bright, smart, but shy, too."

She nodded. "Unlike most teenagers, I liked learning.

I was top of my class." Her eyes lost focus. "Or I was supposed to be."

"The video?" he asked.

"The video," she confirmed with a sigh. "And you're right. I was shy, too."

He sat back, studied her. "I've never understood that, either. You had a lot going for you."

She shrugged and then took a sip of her soda. "I think part of it is just how I am. But the other part had to do with losing my mom so young. My dad was great. He did an amazing job, but…"

"I get it. Must have been tough on both of you. Alpha-male cop like your dad trying to raise a little girl."

"Exactly. I've never really craved attention. I'm content to sit on the sidelines and watch."

"So here's my question."

"Ah, we finally get to the question." She tilted her head toward him.

"How does the smart, shy, never-step-a-toe-out-of-line girl end up getting wasted and making a video about my brother?"

"It was a mistake."

Mulling that over, he knew there was more to the story. "An out-of-character mistake. I never bought it. What really happened back then?"

She fidgeted on the bench. "I had been drinking that night," she said in a soft voice. "Only I didn't know it."

Now they were getting to the truth of the matter. And a truth that Cam had suspected for a long time. "Someone spiked your drink?"

"Two someones. I don't know if you remember them, but there were these girls in my class, Samantha and Parker."

Cam dug back and could vaguely picture them, sort of remembered their names. "The popular girls?"

"Understatement of the year. The thing is, I knew who they were, the kind of girls they were. The night before senior prom, they invited me for a sleepover. The same girls who had never spoken to me before. You'd think I would have figured it out."

She walked to the edge of the dock, crossed her arms in front of her, then turned back to face him. "Why would two of the most popular girls in our class invite a person they'd ignored since elementary school to a sleepover at the end of senior year?" He shrugged. "They'd found out about my feelings for Jasper."

She stepped closer, but didn't sit down. "They said we were drinking lemonade. It tasted like lemonade, only I remember feeling woozy and loose almost immediately. And then they told me they'd always wanted to be friends with me, but were afraid they weren't smart enough. I was so touched." She shook her head. "Stupid."

Cam really started feeling for her. "You were young. Naive."

"Sheltered. Don't tell my dad I said that." She offered a small smile. "After the enhanced lemonade, we started talking about boys. They went right to Jasper."

"How did they know about your crush on my brother?"

"They found my journal. I'd left it in the art room one day. God, Cam, that journal was so embarrassing. It was filled with all of my adolescent feelings for your brother. With illustrations and really bad poetry."

"So they found the journal, read it, used it against you, got you drunk and then made a video of you?"

Sitting back down, she concentrated on her old sneakers. "That pretty much sums it up. When they played it at prom, I just stood there, shocked. I'll never forget that feeling in my stomach. It was so awful. Everyone laughing, staring, pointing."

She shivered, even though it wasn't cold with the late

afternoon sun beating down on the dock. "In the video, I was wearing this really oversize shirt I used to sleep in. It had slipped off my shoulder and exposed my bra. And maybe a little more than that." She covered her face with her hands. Then she peeked through her fingers. "The principal thought I did it on purpose."

Cam stood abruptly and Elle's head snapped up, her hands falling to her lap. "Speaking of Principal Baker, why the hell didn't he go after those girls?"

A red blush tinted her cheeks. "Because I never told on them."

"Why not?" He sat next to her and grabbed her hands. "What they did was *not* okay. They got you drunk, stole your property, embarrassed you. In fact, the whole thing could have been a lot worse."

She tried to pull her hands from his, but Cam held on tight. He wanted to shake her. Why didn't she see how wrong this was? All these years the entire town had thought she'd done this inappropriate little thing. But in reality, she'd been the victim of two very mean bullies.

Finally, she freed her hands and stood. "Despite it all, they were still the popular girls. And I wanted to impress them. I was very inexperienced with…everything."

"You didn't get to be valedictorian." He rose now, as well.

"That doesn't matter. I had already been accepted into college."

"It does matter, Elle." He grabbed her upper arms. "It matters."

As her lips turned up in a sad smile, she met his eyes. "When my dad came to pick me up that night, I realized not being valedictorian didn't mean anything. Having the entire school laugh in my face wasn't a big deal. Because the completely silent ride home in our car gave me the time to think about it. Really think about it. The look on my dad's face was the worst thing in the entire world. That's what mattered."

She took a deep breath. "My dad couldn't get me packed up fast enough. He enrolled me in a presemester program that summer. Dropped me off in June. Because I'd disappointed him. That's the worst part of the story. The only person who ever loved me."

Cam's heart hurt for her. Did she really believe that? Ted Owens was a lot of things, but disappointed in his only child was not one of them.

"Being back here is so hard. I've missed the place. Before that incident, I loved Bayside. I felt safe here, you know? How ironic." She waited a beat. "When I was in Italy, I really missed my dad. But the stares and the whispers and that damn blog... Well, it's just difficult."

Cam wasn't good with words. Never had been. So he used action instead, and wrapped her in his arms.

When she pulled back, Elle framed his face with her hands. "Thanks for listening. It's really nice to have a friend."

His libido, nearly ready to charge out of the gate just being so close to her, feeling her body in his embrace, slammed on the brakes at the *f* word. His eyebrow shot up. "Is that what we are, Elle? Friends?"

She pressed her lips to his, softly at first. But then she poured herself into the kiss and Cam reaped the benefits of her passion.

"Special friends," she whispered against his mouth.

Taking in her swollen lips and hazy eyes, he had to agree. "*Special* sounds pretty damn good."

Chapter Eleven

Later that afternoon, Cam carried three fish back to the cabin. Elle wasn't usually into fish guts, but she had to admit it was kind of swoony to watch a super hot, totally alpha male clean and gut food that he'd caught with his own two hands. If only he'd done it shirtless...

Elle bit her lip at the thought and got to work herself while Cam grilled the fish out on the back deck. She set the table and threw together a salad with ingredients he had brought from home. She found premade potato salad and a bottle of red wine in the kitchen, as well.

When Cam returned with the cooked fish, she was sipping a glass. Nodding to the counter, she said, "I poured you some."

Now that she looked around at the food he'd brought and saw all the effort he put into their one-day trip, she realized that Cam Dumont was a really considerate guy. Even as she thought it, he pulled out a chair for her to sit down. Then he grabbed two candles, placed them in the center of the table and lit them. When he turned the overhead light low, the ambience became dreamy and romantic, and a little flutter started in her belly.

Despite the setting, they got through dinner with the conversation flowing smoothly from one topic to another. The fish was beyond delicious. But more than feeling satisfied over the food, she felt calm after the entire day. Elle hadn't realized how tightly wound she'd been.

"So," she said. She folded her napkin and placed it on the table. "Tell me about your job."

"Not much to tell."

She shook her head. "Of course there's something to tell. Besides, I've been yammering on and on about myself all day long." She pointed at him. "Your turn."

"You want to hear about my latest construction bid?"

He truly looked puzzled and it made her giggle. "No, silly, I want to hear about what made you start the company. I was surprised you weren't working for your parents."

"So were they."

His mouth was set in a grim line and his eyes had narrowed.

She stood and held out a hand. After a moment, he took it and let her lead him to the couch. "Tell me about it," she said softly, as she settled back into the comfy plaid cushions.

Cam sat, but wasn't able to get comfortable. "Are you cold? Want me to start a fire?" he asked, pointing at the fireplace.

She cocked an eyebrow. "Cameron Dumont, stop stalling. I'm not a reporter. I'm your special friend, remember?"

His grin came fast. "That's what we should get back to talking about. Actually, maybe not talk…"

"Cameron."

"Fine. I started my company about five years ago." He leaned back against the cushions. "I love construction. Love working with my hands, building things from the bottom up. I like the hours. I like working outdoors.

"I used to go to construction sites with my dad back in the day. It was my favorite thing to do with him. Only, he didn't realize how much it drew me… I started working some construction in the summers, on weekends."

"He thought you were studying the business, I bet," she

said, as Cam took a long gulp from a bottle of water. "Did you ever tell him how much you liked it?"

"Nope. Probably would have been easier on all of us if I had." He tilted the bottle to his lips again and this time finished the whole thing. "My entire life I was being groomed to take over the family business. Every party, every holiday, every bit of time I spent with my parents was about the damn business.

"Somewhere along the line, I came to a realization. I didn't want to be part of it, at least not in the traditional way. I wanted to start a construction department, head it up. I wanted it to be part of Dumont Industries. And about five and a half years ago, after endless hours of hating my job and being bored beyond belief sitting behind a desk in a suit and tie, I presented my idea to my parents."

"I didn't realize your company was tied to Dumont Incorporated," she said.

"It's not."

He said this with zero inflection or emotion, and Elle met his eyes. She could see the pain there. She would have to be blind to miss it.

"Putting it together now?" he asked. A muscle in his jaw ticked. "They acted like I'd deserted them. All I wanted was to do something that would make me happy."

Cam got up and walked to the mantel, propped an arm on it and stared into the unlit fireplace. "That was a rough time. We fought constantly. It was worse with my dad. He really didn't understand." He turned back to face her. "Acted like I was throwing my life away."

"You wanted to start a business. Most parents would be beyond thrilled if their kid showed that kind of initiative. I mean, I get that they were upset. But it seems kind of old-fashioned for them to be so upset about you not wanting to take over the company. You, the oldest child, shunning his birthright and all that."

"I agree. But I get where they were coming from, too. My dad and my granddad worked really hard to get that company where it is today. They have a lot of pride about it."

"But Jasper stepped up."

Cam remained quiet.

"Wasn't that a good thing?" she prodded.

He returned to sit next to her on the couch. "Jasper only stepped up to help me. I'm his big brother and I always tried to protect him, shield him from stuff. But one night we went out to a bar. I had one too many drinks and just let go and told him everything that was on my mind. The next morning he offered to take my place. My parents were less than thrilled. Jasper had done really well in school, but he hadn't been groomed the way I had. He'd never worked for the company. He always found internships and jobs with other real estate companies. Drove my dad nuts."

"So what happened? Because I already know that you did form your company and Jasper does work for your parents. What made them change their minds?"

"Lack of options, I suppose. They cut me off. I mean, I still have my inheritance, but they wouldn't help with my business at all. That's fine with me, actually. I'd been saving for a long time and was able to get a great loan."

His eyes shone with pride and it made her smile. Elle could only hope she would find some kind of work that made her feel the same sense of satisfaction.

"Every day I'm thankful for what I have and what I built. But even as I take a moment to enjoy it, I'm reminded that my little brother is across town fighting with my parents. They're all miserable and it's all because I wanted to work with my hands."

She leaned close and rapped him on the chest. "Passion."

"Huh?"

"Earlier, out on the dock, you said there's nothing wrong with being passionate."

"Yeah, so?"

"You were—you are—passionate about your company. I imagine you would have to be passionate to start a business from the ground up."

He blew out a long breath of frustration. "It hasn't been the same. Since I stopped working for my parents, it hasn't been the same between us."

"Of course it hasn't." His gaze flicked up to meet hers and she almost laughed at his perplexed expression. "Things change, Cam. Relationships evolve. That's how life is. Your relationship may have transformed no matter what you'd chosen to do." She rubbed a hand over his arm. "Have you ever talked to them about how you feel?"

The look he gave her made Elle want to laugh in his face. She may as well have asked him to eat mud-covered liver.

"You want me to talk about my feelings?" he asked, with zero emotion in his voice.

"It's not about what I want. It's about what you need. And from everything you've told me, it sounds like you need to talk with your folks."

"Maybe," he grumbled.

She decided to let it go for now. He'd probably had enough talking for a lifetime, although Elle was glad she knew the whole story now. But if she had to guess, his parents probably had no idea he felt this way. Not to mention his brother. When she'd had dinner with Jasper a few weeks back, he'd all but admitted his own angsty situation. Did Cam know anything about how Jasper felt? It probably wasn't her place to interfere.

"Hey, your turn." His gruff voice brought her back to reality. "What are you thinking?"

"Well," she began, studying him from her end of the

couch. "I was thinking that if you'd told me back in high school that I would be sitting here with Cameron Dumont, I would have thought you were crazy."

This statement appeared to shock him. "Really? Why?"

"Because you were Cam Dumont, older guy with a beard."

"I wasn't that much older. Just four years."

"Four years is a lot in high school," she said.

He scooted closer. "How about now?"

Glancing at him, she cocked her head. "No, four years seems great right about now."

She emphasized her statement by closing the remaining distance between them and planting her lips against his.

Cam met Elle's mouth with enthusiasm. Everything about today had been awesome. Normally, he considered this cabin his sanctuary. But the funny thing about Elle was that she seemed to fit right in and take everything in stride.

She'd sat with him while he fished, helped get dinner together and had been pleasant company. He'd honestly enjoyed his time with her. Even the talking part. Still, he couldn't deny that kissing her had been in the forefront of his mind the entire day.

Now it was happening. She inched closer, pressing her body against his. A guttural growl escaped his lips at the feel of her, soft and smooth and sexy as hell. His arms came around her protectively as he pushed his tongue into her mouth.

Somewhere in the back of his mind a voice was telling him to slow down or stop altogether. But that voice was dim to begin with and Cam had zero trouble completely dousing the sound.

Instead, he pulled her even closer as he pressed his lips against her neck. She made a little sound that he enjoyed, so he continued to run his mouth up and down the column of her neck as she grabbed his shirt, bunching it between her fingers.

She smelled so freaking good. As he made his way up to nip right behind her ear, he got a whiff of that floral scent again and it drove him crazy. He knew his breathing had become erratic and his pulse was off the charts, but he tried to stay in control.

Then she did something that surprised the hell out of him. Without warning, she leaned back, offered up a coy smile and then pushed him back against the pillows.

"There," she said and straddled him.

"Happy, are you?"

"Shut up and put your mouth on me again." But she didn't wait around, instead plastering her lips against his as her hands became very busy wiggling their way under his shirt.

As her silky fingertips glided over his skin and entwined in the hair on his chest, he became helpless to do anything remotely suave. Elle was in total control, and hell if that didn't turn him on even more.

Of course, she noticed. How could she not, when her jean-clad bottom was sitting right on top of that need? On cue, she began circling her hips against his erection while she continued to assault his lips. Her hands stayed busy, too. When they reached the top of his pants, he let out a whoosh of breath. Her fingers running over that very sensitive spot cleared every thought out of his mind.

He clamped his hands on her hips, dug his fingers in and flipped her onto her back. Letting out a little laugh, she drew her bottom lip into her mouth, and Cam knew for certain right then and there that she was going to be the death of him.

And what a great way to go.

"Gonna stare at me all night?"

"No, ma'am," he growled in a gruff voice. She reached

for the hem of his shirt and yanked it up and over his head. Then he covered her body with his, loving the way they fit together. In fact, he was so happy that he heard that ringing again. Only this time Elle stopped kissing him.

Their confused eyes met, and after a brief moment, they both smiled.

"My phone," she said, her voice breathy and light. Her cheeks flushed with color. "Ignore it."

"You got it." And he happily returned to running his hands from her waist up her sides and circling her breasts. She had the best body and he wanted to explore every inch of it. He didn't care if…

Ring, ring.

Okay, so he would destroy her phone and then explore every inch of her.

Ring, ring.

She murmured against his lips, the sound conveying pleasure, need and want. He understood the feeling. He unbuttoned her blouse and then hastily pushed it off her, along with her T-shirt. All Cam wanted at the moment was to feel her skin against his.

But first he had to take a second to soak her in. Her breasts were pushed up against a lacy pink bra, inviting and sexy as hell. He leaned down to get a better taste.

Ring, ring.

While he was enjoying running kisses along the enticing curve of her breasts, as her breath came out in short little spurts, that damn voice that he'd extinguished earlier roared back to life. Her phone had gone off multiple times. Something nagged at him to sit up and pay attention.

"Hey," she protested, as he pushed himself up to his knees.

"Your phone." His voice came out in a croak and he had to take a second to steady his racing heartbeat. He'd had more game as a pimply high school kid.

But as he got some distance from her, he realized why they had to break apart. Her dad might need her. Who else would call multiple times?

"Your dad," he said.

"Is definitely not someone I want to think about while we're shirtless together." But then her playful smile faded and she must have realized the same thing. "Where's my phone?" she asked, a worried expression on her face as she scooched up into a sitting position.

"Here," he said, finding it under her discarded shirt.

Her eyebrows drew together and her lips pursed as she studied the screen. "I don't know this number, but it's a Bayside area code."

Pressing a couple buttons and then holding the phone to her ear, she listened until her face fell and her eyes widened.

"What's wrong?"

She put the phone down even as her bottom lip began to tremble. "It's my dad. He's in the hospital."

Chapter Twelve

Elle stood in the sterile hallway of Bayside Memorial Hospital, unmoving and unblinking. That distinctive smell of antiseptic and bleach infiltrated her nose as a doctor's name echoed over the loudspeaker.

Finally, she shook her head and tried to concentrate on the doctor standing in front of her. Wearing his white coat, a stethoscope slung around his neck, he scanned the clipboard in his hands.

Elle took a deep breath. "So you're telling me that nothing is wrong with my dad?" Still in a state of shock and disbelief, she ran her hands through her hair.

Again the doctor searched his chart, checked something off with his pen and then looked up. "We've run a series of tests since his friends brought him in. Everything's coming up negative—which is good in this case," he quickly added.

"But he collapsed. His friends said he was out of breath." She clamped down on the urge to scream. She and Cam had broken all speed records getting back to Bayside, only to find her dad lounging in his hospital bed with a bowl of pudding in one hand and the remote to the wall-mounted television in the other.

Elle leaned forward and whispered, "My dad has cancer."

To his credit, the doctor offered a genuine smile. "Since I happen to be his oncologist, I am aware of that." Reaching in his pocket, he produced a business card. "Here is all of my information. Your father's one of my favorite patients. He's also one of my orneriest."

"Thank you. And you're sure that his collapse had nothing to do with the cancer…? What?" she asked, seeing the grin that appeared on the doctor's face.

"You should talk to your dad. I think you'll get a better picture of what really happened today. In the meantime, he's going to be just fine. We'll keep him overnight and run a couple more tests. More than likely he'll be released first thing tomorrow morning."

"Thank you." As the doctor walked away, Elle narrowed her eyes and tried to process the events of the day. Even though she was still worried about her father's sudden collapse, now that she could see that he was okay her adrenaline was falling and exhaustion was taking over.

She pressed her shoulders back and pushed through the door to his room.

"Hey, sweetie," he said. "Doc said I have to stay overnight. At least the game's on." He pointed the remote at the TV.

"Right," Elle said wearily. "Do you want me to stay here with you tonight?"

"Of course not. All I'm going to be doing is sleeping. And hopefully eating more pudding."

She rolled her eyes. "Are you sure? Because I don't mind."

"No, I'll be just fine."

"Speaking of being fine, the doctor said your collapse had nothing to do with the cancer." When he didn't say anything, Elle pushed. "What do you think it had to do with?" Still nothing. She snatched the remote from his hand and turned off the game.

"Hey!"

"What did you do today?"

"Nothing."

She cocked an eyebrow and crossed her arms over her chest.

"Honestly, sweetheart. I just hung out with the guys. A typical Sunday."

Not buying it, she began tapping her foot in an irritated rhythm.

"Okay, we might've overdone it a little bit."

"Overdone it? What exactly were you doing with your friends?"

"Don't get upset. There's this thing I've always wanted to do, and Herb thought it would be fun. He also went through a bout with cancer last year."

Uncrossing her arms, Elle pinned her dad with a stare. "What was the thing?"

"Just this little activity that's been on my bucket list."

"Care to share?"

"Skyd—" He coughed loudly into his fist.

Elle's heart dropped. "Excuse me? What did you just say?"

With a long, drawn-out sigh, Ted looked toward her. Although his eyes settled on something over her left shoulder. "Skydiving. We decided to go skydiving."

Rapidly blinking as her brain tried to process this latest information, Elle opened her mouth, only no words came out.

"It was amazing," he continued. "Nothing like it. What a rush. Of course, once I landed, I got a little winded. No big deal."

"No big deal?" Her voice came out loud and harsh.

At that moment, the door opened behind her and she heard Cam's voice before she saw him. "Everything okay in here?"

"No, no, everything is not okay. In fact, it's pretty far from okay. Do you know what he did today?" She pointed at her father as her voice continued to rise. "Do you know how he ended up in the hospital? He jumped out of a plane with his friends."

Cam's eyebrows shot up and he let out an amused sound. "No kidding? That's awesome."

"Right!" Ted agreed. "I don't know why she's so worked up."

"Worked up?" Elle paced to the window and back. She stabbed a finger in her dad's direction before swinging it at Cam. "Don't encourage him. He is in the hospital."

"And he's fine."

"He shouldn't be doing anything to put him in the position of not being fine," she said.

"The man just dealt with cancer," Cam said.

"Exactly my point." She threw her hands in the air.

"In my opinion, he should get to live a little."

"Oh, really? Well, in my opinion, this is none of your business."

Cam rocked back on his heels. "I think you need to calm down. Look at him. He's fine."

Elle gestured with both hands. Wildly. "We're in a hospital. Does that seem fine to you?" She took a step closer to Cam.

Following suit, he closed the distance between them so that they were nose to nose. "I think he had a little incident and will be home tomorrow."

"Wanna know what I think?" her dad piped up from the bed.

"No," they answered in tandem. Finally, an agreement.

"You need to back off," Cam suggested.

"Back off? I only just found out about the cancer. I've been back a matter of weeks and he's throwing himself out of moving planes. Do you know how worried I've been?" Her voice cracked, but she kept her gaze locked on Cam's.

His smug expression softened. "I do." He ran a hand up her arm. "I'm sorry."

Elle peered into Cam's eyes and saw such kindness there. She wanted to fold herself into his arms and stay that way for a long time. She wished they could beam themselves back to his cabin and return to that couch.

The strangest thing was that she'd experienced sensitivity and understanding with a guy before. And she'd definitely felt her share of lust and longing. But she'd never found one guy who made her feel both.

At that moment, it was a good thing they were in a hospital, because her own heart gave a little flutter.

"So that's settled," her dad called from the bed. Elle jumped back a foot. Yikes, her dad was in the room. "Everybody okay now?"

With her eyes still trained on Cam, she considered the question. Given her recent realization, she was anything but okay. Luckily, a nurse entered the room and asked to see her.

After following her outside the room to the nurses' station, Elle was given a series of forms to fill out. When she was done, the nurse offered an understanding smile.

"Visiting hours are just about over. Please say your goodbyes for the night."

Elle walked back toward her father's room. When she looked inside the window in the door, she saw that her dad had fallen asleep. She watched as Cam covered him with a blanket and turned off the television.

"How are you doing?" he asked when he'd exited the room.

She didn't say anything, because the truth was she wasn't doing all that well. What kind of daughter was never around when the important stuff happened?

"Elle?" Cam pressed. "How are you feeling?"

"Embarrassed." What was it about this man that broke down her usual walls and made her reveal each and every thought in her head? "I'm never here when he needs me," she admitted in a quiet voice. "When he was diagnosed I was a million miles away in Italy. I wasn't here for his first round of treatment."

"He didn't tell you about his illness. You can't blame yourself for that."

Standing up straighter, she shook her head. "If I had lived here I would have known. He could hide the diagnosis from me because I didn't have any way of finding out over in Europe. And today…"

"Was a good day," Cam finished. "You weren't in Italy. You were a little more than an hour away."

"But—"

"And now you're here with him." He pushed a stray hair back from her forehead. "You are allowed to leave for a day. You're a good daughter. Stop feeling guilty."

Something about his tone of voice—or maybe the stubborn look in his eyes—had the sides of her mouth twitching. "You're so bossy."

He winked at her. "Only when I need to be. Now, stop feeling sorry for yourself and let me take you home."

She peeked in the window of her dad's room once more. He was out for the night and she could come back first thing tomorrow morning. After all, he'd said he didn't want her to sleep in the hospital. But if something happened…

"The nurses will call you if anything goes down," Cam said, reading her thoughts.

Nodding silently, she gathered her things and walked down the hallway with him. When they got outside, she took a moment to breathe in the clean, non-hospital-smelling air. Looking up, she saw a sky full of stars twinkling down on them.

She used to look at those same stars in Florence and wonder what was happening in Bayside. She'd wonder if anyone from home missed her or if she'd ever return.

"What are you thinking about?" Cam's voice pulled her out of her thoughts.

"How I keep running away," she said truthfully.

"There's a solution to that, you know."

Even though she was still looking up, she knew he'd turned. She could sense those penetrating eyes on her. Goose pimples spread over her skin. "What's that?"

With a gentle hand, he brought her head down so she had to face him. "Stop running."

It sounded so simple and Elle desperately wished it was. But she knew better. She knew the way this town was.

"I know it's been hard for you. And yesterday was a real pisser of a day. But if you stop fleeing, exist here in Bayside without the threat of leaving again, you might give the town a chance to learn who you are now. They only know the Ellie Owens who ended her time in Bayside with a crazy incident."

"I thought you said that 'incident' was passionate," she teased.

"I said *you* were passionate. Besides, I was trying to get into your pants."

She blushed. "Thanks."

"And I'm still trying." He pulled her against him, encompassing her in his strong arms. She loved when he did that.

Still, she shoved back slightly. "Cam, someone will see."

He didn't respond. Only watched her with a smile on his lips. "I'm going to kiss you now. And you're right, someone might see."

Then his lips were on hers and thinking about someone catching them melted away. The only thought was Cam. She gave herself over to the kiss. Over to him. Elle let herself get carried away in that parking lot because the idea of not kissing Cam seemed equivalent to not breathing.

When he lifted his head, she noticed that his eyes were

cloudy. Dark and stormy and full of passion. They had to mirror her own, if her accelerated heartbeat was any indication.

"I should take you home," he said, his voice gruff.

"Yes, you should." She stared at him, searching his face for the sign she needed. When his eyes dipped to take in her lips, she had her answer. "But..."

"But what?" he quickly asked.

"But it might be better if you take me to your home instead."

Cam studied her for a full second. His grin started slow and ended up being fully delicious. "Yes, ma'am."

Hand in hand, they dashed to his truck. She didn't consider the fact that people could probably see them. She didn't contemplate if this was right or wrong. She didn't even care if the Bayside Blogger reported on this.

The only thought in Elle's head was how fast they could get to Cam's house.

Cam didn't particularly remember driving back to his bungalow after the hospital. He wouldn't be able to tell anyone what he and Elle talked about as they drove through town. And he didn't recall taking Elle's hand and heading up the walkway to his front porch.

But he would never forget the way she looked standing in his living room with the full moon beaming through the window, casting a glow on her beautiful face.

Did she have any idea how gorgeous she was? Cam racked his brain, but honestly couldn't recall meeting a more exquisite woman in his life. And the fact that she was fun to talk to, that she listened attentively and that she could go with the flow only added to her appeal.

He dropped his keys on the table by the front door. Or hell, maybe they missed and fell on the floor. He had no idea. All he knew was that Elle Owens was inside his house, watching him with a knowing smile and a twinkle in her eyes.

Cam considered himself to be a confident man. He felt comfortable in his own skin. But ever since she'd told him to take her to his house, it was as if he was a fumbling teenager again.

It wasn't as if he'd never been with a woman before. Still, something held him in place. He dragged a hand through his hair, at a loss for what to do or what to say.

"You gonna stand way over there all night?" she asked with laughter in her voice.

"Can I get you something to drink? Are you hungry? Do you want a tour of the house?"

Her lips curved, spreading slowly into a devastating smile. Then she crooked her finger at him. "Come here, Cam."

As if on autopilot, he glided across the room, closing the distance between them. Elle wound her arms around his neck. Tilting her head back, she pinned him with a perceptive stare.

"Are you nervous, Cameron?" Before he could answer, she continued. "Because if anyone should be nervous, it should be me."

Her statement snapped him out of his stupor. Wrapping his arms around her tiny waist, he drew her closer to him. "And why would you be nervous?"

She bit her bottom lip briefly before saying, "Because you're Cameron Dumont, old and mysterious loner."

He felt his eyebrow quirk at the description. "Old?"

She grinned. "Yep. That's what I said."

He leaned down and nipped her earlobe. "Nothing wrong with being old." He pressed his lips to the column of her neck. Her throat was sensitive, he'd found. But he kissed it again. She smelled so good there. "Old goes hand in hand with experience."

Her head fell back as he moved his lips up to her jaw-line and around to the other ear. He sucked her earlobe into his mouth. "Experience is good," she said with a ragged breath.

"Then get ready. Because you're about to get a taste of it."

With that, he reached down and scooped her up in his arms. He liked her quick inhalation. Even in the dark, he could see that her face was flushed and he liked the way that looked on her.

Cam quickly made his way down the hallway to his bedroom. But once there, he didn't release her. Instead, he took a moment to relish the feel of Elle in his arms. As he placed a kiss on her forehead, he indulged himself in feeling her silky hair against his skin. Despite driving to and from the cabin, spending a couple hours in an antiseptic-filled hospital and fishing in the lake, she still managed to smell amazing—as if she bathed in flowers.

Bathed in flowers? Oh, man. He was falling hard for Elle Owens. If that thought didn't scare the crap out of him, he would actually laugh at himself. In fact, he couldn't stop a chuckle from escaping now.

"What is it?" she asked, squirming in his arms.

He took one long look into those dreamy green eyes and any anxiety simply melted away. So did his laughter.

"Nothing," he told her.

"Seems like something," she countered.

He answered her with a kiss. A long, intoxicating kiss as he gently set her on the floor. Running his hands through her hair, he pulled her to him so he could deepen the kiss. When she opened her mouth and he slipped his tongue inside, he was surprised to hear a moan. Was even more shocked that it came from him.

When Elle moved her lips to the side of his neck, he let out another groan, but stayed busy by reaching for her shirt. He made quick work of the buttons and pushed the plaid material off her shoulders. Even as she continued her clever work on his neck and jaw, he reached for the bottom of her T-shirt. He pulled it up and over her head.

She stood before him in her lacy pink bra and snug-fitting jeans. It might possibly be the hottest sight he'd ever seen.

She nodded down at her half-clothed body. "You gonna stop there?" Her voice was husky and full of need. He knew the feeling.

Suddenly overtaken by his own want, he felt as if something snapped inside him, and he crushed his mouth to hers. The next few minutes were a blur of undressing each other, with clothes flying around the room as they attempted to continue kissing and touching.

Her bra was nice, but removing it was even better. Ample breasts filled his hands while she yanked at his jeans, finally dropping them to pool around his ankles.

With a laugh, Elle fell backward onto his bed, her hair splaying across his dark blue bedspread. Cam took that as an invitation and covered her with his body. He was down to his boxer briefs.

She pointed a slender finger toward his underwear and the erection that was pulsing to be let free. "Cam?" she asked.

Her eyes had turned a dark forest green. He could see it by the light of the moon shining in through the bedroom window. Her chest was rising and falling. "Yeah?" he groaned out.

She pushed up on her elbows, showcasing her luscious breasts, and gestured to his boxer briefs. "Lose the pants."

Elle couldn't believe this was happening. She was about to see Cam. All of Cam.

Who would have thought?

She shook her head. If she was honest—utterly and brutally honest—this night wasn't a surprise. Her feelings for him had been growing rapidly every day since she'd returned. Even in that first moment when he'd met her in the town square, she'd known. There had been...something. Something that shifted inside her.

She wanted him naked, but decided to help out by going first. Trying to be as seductive as possible, she removed her panties.

His eyes darkened as they swept over her entire body. Slowly, greedily. His breathing picked up, too.

As if in slow motion, she watched as he hooked his thumbs in the waistband of his sexy-as-hell black boxer briefs. Why all guys didn't wear boxer briefs was beyond her.

Her mouth went dry. She wanted to make some kind of nonchalant comment, but there was no way her brain could form words at the moment. Not at the sight of Cam's incredibly impressive erection.

Looking up, she saw that he was watching her—taking in her every movement in that quiet, steady way he had.

"Elle, are you sure?"

It melted her heart that he asked. A safe bet would be that she'd never been surer of anything in her life.

"Cam..." she began. There were so many things she wanted to say, yet at the same time, all she truly wanted was to feel his body on top of hers. She wanted to revel in the sensation of skin on skin and bodies fused together. "Kiss me," she whispered.

Not wasting any time, Cam placed one hand behind her head as he lowered both of them onto the soft mattress. He covered her lips with his as his hands ran over her body. Hands that were rough and callused from work. And that hardness felt amazing. Everywhere they touched tingled.

He had a long day's growth of stubble on his face and

she could feel it rubbing against her skin as he moved his head down her throat and over her collarbone to the swell of her breast. She sucked in an uneven breath as his skillful tongue found her nipple. Arching her back, she pushed herself up to give him better access. After he finished with one breast he moved to the next, and Elle was helpless to do anything but enjoy the sensations as she dug her nails into his back and hung on for dear life.

When he was done with his exploration, he lifted his head and met her eyes. She saw something there. Something she hadn't expected. Something much stronger than simple lust. And whatever that something was, it both exhilarated and scared her.

"Cam, let me—"

He touched a finger to her lips. "No, tonight is for you."

"Oh, well—" Her words cut off when he pressed his lips to her stomach and began a slow descent even lower.

Cam used his lips, his tongue to pleasure her, with each movement he made increasing the need building inside her. When he slipped one finger inside her, she called out his name. But he was relentless, urging her to go higher and higher as he found a sweet rhythm with his mouth.

Just as he touched his thumb to her most sensitive nub, she tensed before crying out again. Then she was falling, and he moved back to nuzzle her neck. The moon seemed to be right outside his bedroom window and was like a spotlight illuminating them as if they were the stars of the entire night.

She reached for his head and brought his lips to hers. The kiss was deep and had her revving up all over again. Cam began to move his erection against her and Elle opened her legs to accommodate him.

"Wait," he said.

Her head flew up. "What?"

With a wry grin, he tapped her nose and sprung off the

bed. He hunched over as he fumbled through the bedside table. Elle quickly realized he was getting a condom. She had been so involved with him that she hadn't thought of it herself.

Protected, Cam positioned himself at the end of the bed. He wrapped his arms around her legs and pulled her to him. He pressed against her opening and slowly, so incredibly slowly, entered her.

She moaned, long and low, at the feel of him inside her, even as her body shifted to accommodate his size. Cam brushed a strand of hair off her face and locked eyes with her.

"Are you okay?"

Biting her lip, she nodded. "Are you?" she asked.

"Yes." His voice was gruff and insanely sexy. "Oh, yes."

And then he began to move. Slowly at first, like silk gliding on top of satin. As they continued to move together, finding a rhythm that worked for both of them, he released her legs and brought his body over hers fully. With hands braced on either side of her head, he increased the tempo.

"Yes, Cam," she called, along with a thousand other incomprehensible words. He answered with moans and grunts as she tightened her grip around his shoulders.

She didn't know how long they moved together as one, but only wished this exquisite feeling could continue forever. She urged him forward by wrapping her legs around his waist, and Cam took advantage of the position by driving into her harder and faster.

Elle could feel the climax building. Just as she was on the ultimate verge, Cam covered her lips with his and pumped into her once, twice, before finally letting go. He was perfectly in tune with her.

And then together they fell from the high, wrapped in each other's arms as the moon shone down on them.

* * *

Well, that had been…really freaking amazing, Cam thought as he snuggled into Elle's warm, soft body.

They'd just finished round two of their night together, and Elle had fallen fast asleep in his arms. He was spooning her now even as her chest rose and fell in a slow rhythm.

He ran a hand over her arm. Her skin was so silky and fresh. Frowning, he noticed the red marks along her face, chin, chest. Probably in other places, as well. More intimate places. It was from his stubble. *Should have shaved*, he thought. Although there was something damn appealing about seeing her body marked by his.

His woman.

Whoa. Cam almost shot up in bed at the notion. But he didn't want to disturb Elle.

What would she do if she heard him call her his woman? Cam didn't need to think hard, because he knew exactly how she'd react. She'd fly out of his life faster than his new chain saw could cut through a tree.

Since she was asleep at the moment, though, he indulged himself by pulling her even closer. He draped an arm over her waist and splayed his fingers over her stomach.

Elle had been back in Bayside a short time, yet she'd been through so much. Not to mention what she'd gone through back in high school.

Cam's temper flared when he thought about those idiotic, mean girls and how they'd gotten her drunk. And yet Elle had never told on them. She'd kept that secret and let herself be ridiculed. That entire night could have ended a lot worse.

Cam wanted her to speak up for herself. He wanted her to give a big middle finger to the entire town. He wanted her to write an op-ed for that stupid blogger she was always worried about.

She murmured in her sleep, a cute sound that had his heart clutching.

He liked being with her. Not just the sex although that had obviously been phenomenal. Just being around her. And he wanted to do it more. Usually, Cam was pretty secretive in relationships. Not because he had anything to hide, but more because he didn't feel the need to put himself out there. What he did behind closed doors was his business only.

For the first time in his life, he actually wanted to stroll down Main Street, hand in hand with his woman. It wouldn't be so bad to go out to eat and attend the different festivals Bayside held throughout the year.

Cam knew Elle wouldn't stick up for herself. At least, not yet. Until she did, any hope of "going public" as a couple was out of the question.

He groaned and Elle stirred. He tightened his hold on her.

Cam would just have to take matters into his own hands. If she wasn't ready to accept him as her boyfriend in public, then he would show her in private what she was missing.

He would make her realize how great it could be between them. And surely she would come around.

Elle woke up to the sound of birds chirping. The window was open and she could feel the morning breeze dancing along her arm. A slice of sunlight entered through that same window, warming her face even as she squinted her eyes at the intrusion of light.

She'd been dreaming. A wonderful, comforting dream that had filled her with happiness and contentment. A dream that had featured Cameron Dumont in a repeat performance of last night.

She couldn't stop the smile from spreading.

Cam.

She quickly cataloged the previous evening. Every touch, every kiss, every moan flashed through her thoughts the way sports shows did those postgame montages.

She bit her lip and timidly rolled over to face him. But to her dismay—and disappointment—the other side of the bed was empty. Strange, she remembered falling asleep in his arms, as his fingers brushed up and down her arm and his warm breath tickled her neck. Normally, Elle was a light sleeper, but she must have really been tired to sleep through him rising.

Of course, she had a pretty good reason for being tired. Her smile grew and she had to hold a laugh back from bubbling up in her throat. Instead, she stretched, her arms going overhead and her legs stiffening as she pointed and flexed her toes.

But where was the source of her morning-after happiness? She glanced at the clock on the end table. She knew that he had multiple jobs going at the same time. She wondered which one he was working on today and how early he had to leave.

Just then, she heard a noise and sat up in bed. Quickly realizing she wasn't wearing any clothes, she pulled the sheet up to cover herself. Before the door opened, she tried to run a hand through her hair, although she knew that was useless. She could feel the knots and tangles.

And then Cam entered the room and she instantly forgot whatever she'd just been obsessing over.

He'd pulled on a pair of sweatpants that hung loosely around his waist. Her mouth watered at the sight of his bare chest and the dark hair that trailed down into the waistband. She'd been running her lips over that trail only hours earlier.

Cam paused in the doorway and even from across the room she could see his eyes darken. He ran his gaze over her and she tightened her hold on the sheet, which was barely covering her chest.

"Good morning," she said, surprised to hear her voice sound husky.

"You're a sight," he said.

"So are you," she countered, and offered a smile. It was only then that she noticed he wasn't empty-handed. He was holding a tray piled with food. Elle couldn't believe she hadn't honed in on the coffee aroma. Normally, caffeine was the first thing on her mind when she woke.

"What's all that?" she asked.

"Breakfast." He walked toward the bed and set the tray down next to her. "I realize it's early, but I get up at this time for work. And I didn't want you to leave hungry."

Touched, Elle took in the spread. Fluffy scrambled eggs, toast, butter, jelly and coffee. Cam had even thought to bring the newspaper inside.

"Cam...wow."

He shrugged as if his effort was nothing.

She reached over and covered his hand with hers. Elle didn't want to make him uncomfortable, but she did want him to realize she appreciated it. "Thank you."

He answered by covering her mouth with his. She wasn't sure if he'd meant for the kiss to be light and airy, but as soon as their lips touched, Elle's entire body woke up and began to tingle with awareness. With need.

She moaned as his lips roamed over hers and his arms encircled her, pulling her in close. He ran light kisses down the column of her neck. The sensation felt amazing. Greedy, Elle tightened her grip on his arms and pulled him down to her.

Buzzzz...

Their heads snapped up at the sound. Cam touched his forehead to hers. "Sorry," he muttered against her mouth. He reached behind her and the buzzing sound stopped. "My alarm."

Elle stole another glance at the clock on the table. It was at that moment that she realized Cam had woken up earlier than he usually did just to make breakfast for her.

"I can't believe you did all this. God, you must have only slept a couple hours."

Again he shrugged. Then he planted a chaste kiss on her lips. "It was worth it to see the smile on your face."

Damn. It was a good thing she was already sitting down because there was no way she would have been able to stand after that comment.

"Listen, I've gotta get to the site. But stay as long as you want. Enjoy breakfast, go back to sleep, whatever you need."

"A girl could get used to this kind of treatment."

He didn't answer her, but Elle thought she saw something in his eyes. A glint of amusement? Awareness? Cockiness? She wasn't sure.

But as Cam gave her one last smoldering glance over his shoulder and exited the room, Elle had the distinct impression that he had somehow gained the upper hand.

Chapter Thirteen

Happy Monday, Bayside! Rumor has it that former Chief of Police Ted Owens was admitted to Bayside Memorial last night. My sources tell me he is going to be just fine. How is his prodigal daughter handling this latest setback? Maybe someone wants to offer her a shoulder to cry on? Oh, wait, seems as if someone already has...

The next night, Elle strolled into Max's Bar and Grill, which sat right off the town square. The decor was rustic, with dark wood, open rafters and a long bar in the middle of the room. There were high tables in the bar area and dozens of tables in the dining area. There were also dartboards on one wall and an old pool table on the other side of the bar.

She'd brought her father home from the hospital that morning and quickly learned that dads made the worst patients. He wanted a vanilla milkshake. She forced him to drink herbal tea. He wanted to watch ESPN. Elle convinced him to take a nap instead. Needless to say, she was thrilled when Riley texted her, asking after her dad and suggesting they grab drinks at Max's.

Elle bit her lip. Maybe she was even more glad, because Riley's invitation came right on the heels of one from Cam. After reading the Bayside Blogger's column earlier in the day, Elle wasn't quite ready to go public with him. Riley gave her the out she needed. Now she was feeling massively guilty.

Needing to do something while she waited for her friend, she pulled up her email on her phone. To her surprise, she saw a message from someone with a Smithsonian handle. Her heart rate picked up as she clicked on the message.

After reviewing your résumé and qualifications, we would love to have you come in for an interview for the position of assistant curator of our European collection.

Elle froze. This position had been at the very top of her wish list. But anything at the Smithsonian was ultra-competitive, so she'd assumed she didn't stand a chance.

Grinning, she reread the email and quickly shot back a note acknowledging that she'd received it and was more than happy to come in for an interview. She even did a little happy dance in her seat after she hit Send. Then her smile suddenly faded.

The job was in Washington, DC, a couple hours from Bayside. A couple hours from the father she'd just re-united with. From Riley and all the new business Elle had drummed up, thanks to her work at Carson's house.

But most important, it was a couple hours from Cam.

Tapping her fingers on the table, she stared at the front door intently. She was ready to burst and desperately needed someone to talk to.

Twenty minutes later, Riley flew inside, spotted Elle and rushed in her direction, even while waving to someone at the bar. Today she wore an adorable turquoise wrap dress and nude heels. Her hair was pulled back in a low ponytail, which accentuated her long neck and a killer statement necklace made up of an array of multicolored stones.

"Sorry, sorry, I know I'm late. But I have a really good excuse." Riley hung her purse on the back of the tall bar stool and hopped up on the seat. "Crazy day. Stupid Mondays. It should have been quiet in the office, but then there was this whole thing that happened in Marketing and Sasha called out sick, and of course Sawyer was all over me to pick up the slack. I mean, it's not like I don't do enough. Trust me, I do plenty. And besides, just because Sawyer is technically my boss doesn't mean that he has to be all uppity with me all the time."

"I had sex with Cam!" Elle blurted out, and then quickly covered her face with her hands. After a moment of complete silence, she peeked through her fingers and saw that Riley's mouth was hanging open.

"Do we need some drinks here?" a chipper waitress asked.

"Hell, yeah," Riley said, waking up from her shock. "Two glasses of pinot and keep 'em coming."

Once the waitress was out of earshot, Riley leaned toward Elle. "I like surprises as much as the next girl, but you gotta give me a little heads-up. I think I just had a heart attack."

"You? How about me? I'm the one who had sex."

"Yes, and I would have thought that act would have mellowed you considerably."

"Sorry," Elle sighed. "I just had to get that out."

Both of them remained quiet as the waitress delivered their wine and offered menus. She said something about a Monday night burger special, but Elle couldn't concentrate on food. In fact, she couldn't even remember if she'd eaten anything since her breakfast in bed, courtesy of Cam.

Cam…

She wondered what he was doing right now. It had been wrong—so freaking wrong—to blow him off tonight. But she'd just…what?

Riley was watching her closely, her emerald-green

eyes offering a knowing sparkle as she tilted her head and pointed a finger at Elle. "You're freaking out, aren't you?"

"Oh, my God." Elle dropped her head onto the table, but could hear Riley chuckle.

"I have a couple questions for you. Please answer all of them, but in no particular order."

Elle straightened and took in her friend as Riley began to tick them off on her fingers.

"How did this happen? Where did it happen? Why aren't you with him right now? And the most important question…" she paused for dramatic effect "…was it good?" She wiggled her eyebrows.

Elle exhaled a long breath that did nothing to relax her. Then she tackled each question in rapid succession. "I have no idea. His place. I'm a chicken. And OMG, stars exploded throughout the universe."

The waitress chose that moment to show up again. "Is there anything else I can get you ladies right now?"

"A cold shower," Riley muttered under her breath.

Elle stifled a laugh. "We're fine. Thanks."

"Okay, let's divide and conquer. I thought your dad went to the hospital last night."

Elle took a long swig of her wine. Then she told Riley everything that had happened the day before.

"Wow, just wow. Okay, first of all, how sweet is Cam for taking you to that cabin? You know, he's never taken a woman there before."

Elle sat up. "How do you know that?"

"How else? The Bayside Blogger reported it once." Riley sat back in her chair and fiddled with her necklace. "He must really like you."

She could feel her cheeks heating up. "Well, I…"

"It was also adorable that he waited at the hospital for you. And then breakfast in bed, when he already has to get up so early for work. Jeez, Elle, you should be on cloud nine today."

"I know, but—"

"And that brings me to the chicken answer. Don't get me wrong, I can always go for some good old-fashioned girl talk."

"But?" Elle arched a brow.

"Seriously, girl. Men like Cam Dumont don't just fall from trees. Trust me, I've been back in Bayside for a couple years and have stood under my fair share of branches." Riley held up her ring finger. "I have nothing to show for it."

Elle giggled. But she quickly grew serious. "It's complicated, Riley."

"So let's talk about it."

"I'm not ashamed of what Cam and I did. Not by a long shot. I just don't want this information to get out there."

Riley frowned. "You mean, out there on a certain blog?"

Elle nodded. "I feel like I have so many eyes on me as it is. I don't want any more attention. Especially when I don't know where this thing with Cam will go. Or if it will go anywhere."

"Why wouldn't it go somewhere?" Riley asked, and gestured to the waitress for two more glasses of wine. "Cam isn't exactly the love-'em-and-leave-'em type."

"But I might be," Elle admitted.

Riley's eyebrows shot so far up her forehead that they were practically on top of her adorable sparkly headband. "What are you talking about? I don't want to slut shame you or anything, but you can't just sleep with Cam and disappear."

"I don't plan on doing that." Elle paused. "Slut shaming?"

"It means…never mind, doesn't matter. The point is, you can't abandon Cam."

"I received an email today. I got a job interview. A really great job."

"Hi, conversation change." Riley laughed.

"Now you know how I feel when I'm with you," Elle teased. "The job is at one of the Smithsonian museums in DC."

"But what about your dad? Isn't he the reason you came back to Bayside?"

"Yeah, he is. But being only a couple hours away is a lot better than living an entire ocean away. Besides, the person in the position now is retiring and that won't happen for a couple months. So I'd still have some time here before I had to move up there."

Riley's face filled with understanding. And if Elle wasn't mistaken, disappointment. "So you slept with Cam last night and now you have an interview for a really great job that just happens to be a couple hours away?"

"That sums it up."

"It's a pickle." Riley accepted her second glass of wine from the waitress and took a long sip as Elle filled her in on the specifics of the position. "The job sounds perfect for you," she offered supportively.

Elle couldn't miss the wistfulness in Riley's voice. She was pretty sure people outside on the street couldn't miss it. "Riley, what gives?"

"I like having you around. It's nice having a friend."

Elle's eyes widened at the statement. "What are you talking about? You have tons of friends." Didn't she? "You know everyone in town."

"True. I am the social butterfly of Bayside." She did a little diva pose with one hand behind her head and her lips puckered into a cute pout. It made Elle laugh. Then her face fell. "I know a lot of people. I have a ton of acquaintances. But you're the only person who really listens to me. And I love hearing about you, too. I'm so glad you came back to town."

Tears prickled behind Elle's eyes. The truth was that Elle loved having a friend, too. She supposed they could still keep in touch if she left, but it wouldn't be the same.

An idea came to her suddenly. It wouldn't solve any problems, but it would make for a fun distraction. A diversion from the possibility of leaving her new friend, from being the main gossip item and, most important, from having to deal with Cam.

"Can you get a day or two off work this week?"

"I don't know. Maybe. Why, what's up?"

"Well, my interview is on Wednesday. Why don't we road trip up to DC, be tourists on Wednesday and stay overnight? An impromptu girls trip. What do you think?"

Riley smiled. "I think I love everything about this idea."

"Great. I'll make all the arrangements." She reached for her cell phone to make some notes. Riley put her hand over Elle's, getting her attention.

"Just do me a favor," her friend began. "Talk to Cam before we leave. Let him know how you're feeling."

"I…" She trailed off because she didn't know what to say.

"He deserves that much, at least," Riley said quietly.

No, he deserved a hell of a lot more than that, which was exactly what Elle was afraid of. Because she wasn't sure she was ready to give.

Elle returned home to find her father asleep and the rest of the house quiet. Yet she couldn't seem to settle. She stretched out on her old childhood bed and thought about what Riley had said earlier.

Cam deserved to know how she was feeling.

But what if he didn't understand? What if he didn't

agree? What if…he was standing at her bedroom window his hand poised to knock?

Elle let out a little yelp at seeing Cam's grinning face reflected through her half-open window. "Cam!" She quickly glanced back at the door, hoping her dad hadn't woken up.

Cam chuckled as she walked toward the window and opened it all the way. "What are you doing here?"

Her stomach instantly became a mass of nerves at the rugged stubble on his face. At the casual jeans and T-shirt he wore. At the sight of his handsome eyes sweeping over her body.

Her body was currently covered in an old Bayside High T-shirt and decade-old boxer shorts. Not to mention her hair was piled haphazardly on top of her head and she'd scrubbed all the makeup from her face.

In defense mode, she grabbed her light blue curtain and twisted it around her, hiding in the cocoon.

He chuckled. "What are you doing?"

"You can't see me like this," she uttered from behind her thin layer of protection.

Before she could react, his arm snapped out and grabbed her waist. He used that big palm to push her body until she spun in a circle and unwound herself from the curtain.

Elle bowed her head, but Cam's finger went under her chin, forcing her to meet his gaze.

"You look beautiful."

Funny how three little words could have the butterflies start up in her belly. She felt like a teenager again. "Do you want to come in or do you want to continue to gawk at me through the window?"

"I'm fine here." He pulled her hand to his lips and brushed a kiss over her knuckles. Her toes curled and she sucked in a sharp breath. "I missed you today." With that, he kissed her, and all those nerves simply dissipated as if they'd never been there to begin with.

He smiled. "I liked last night. I liked it a lot. I want to do it again."

It was her turn to smile. "Right here? Right now?"

He sat on the windowsill and gave a little nod toward her bedroom door. "I don't think your dad would appreciate finding me on top of his daughter in her childhood bedroom. Do you?"

"Who said you'd get to be on top?"

Cam's eyes darkened and he let out a very masculine growl.

"Cam," she began.

After giving her a quick once-over, he asked, "Are you having second thoughts about last night?"

His expression was serious and his dark eyes hesitant. But he continued to hold her hand, his fingers steady and sure as they wrapped around hers. His skin was rough and callused and she instantly remembered what it had felt like when it ran over her body last night. With her palm engulfed in his grip, she felt safe and protected.

Leaning forward, she pressed her lips to his. "No, I'm not having second thoughts," she told him. "Last night was amazing and I'm glad it happened, too."

His shoulders relaxed, as did his face. "Good." He leaned back against the frame of the window. "So what's this I hear about you and Riley leaving town?" He raised an eyebrow.

"Riley and… But how did you…"

He nodded, an amused expression on his face.

"The Bayside Blogger knows that Riley and I are going to DC this week?"

Cam frowned. "This week?"

"Oh. Well, it's just…" Cam straightened and a lump

formed in Elle's throat. She'd upset him. "We're only going for a day and a half."

He studied her. "You didn't mention it."

"We only just decided tonight at dinner."

She could smell him. Even with the distance he'd just put between them, his earthy, woodsy aroma wafted over to her, like clean, fresh laundry on top of recently chopped pine.

This would be the time to tell him the real reason she and Riley were heading up to DC. She needed to come clean about the job interview. She opened her mouth, but no words came out.

"There's something else, isn't there?" Cam asked.

It felt like he was reading her every thought. She didn't quite understand it, but Elle didn't want to tell him about the interview yet. Her earlier conversation with Riley played through her mind and she knew her friend was right. Cam deserved to know everything. Especially after last night.

Of course, she might not get the job. In that case, she would have possibly upset him for nothing. And yet she knew that was a cop-out, as well.

So she told him something else that was true instead. "I'm worried about the Bayside Blogger," she blurted.

"Elle," Cam said, sounding exasperated. "No one cares about that loony tune."

"Plenty of people care. You care." She pointed at him. "You knew that Riley and I are going to DC."

"First of all, I do not read her column or her tweets or twits or whatever. My mom, on the other hand, does follow her, and she told me about the trip to DC. And second, so what? You don't want people to know that the two of us are together? You're embarrassed to be associated with the likes of a mere contractor?"

What? No, of course she didn't feel that way. She felt

awful that he even had to say that. But then she saw the twinkle in his eyes. "Cameron Dumont," she said.

"Elle Owens," he replied.

"Of course I'm not embarrassed to be around you. It's just that I don't want any undue gossip filtering around town about me."

He held up his hand. "I understand, Elle."

She tilted her head. "You do?"

"I get that it's been rough for you since you got back. And hell, we don't know where this thing between us is going to go. So if it will make you more comfortable, let's keep it quiet for a while."

It seemed too good to be true. "Seriously?"

"Yeah. But only for a short time. I won't be your dirty little secret forever."

She laughed right before she nipped his bottom lip. "Ohh…" she purred into his ear, before biting there, as well. "Dirty little secrets are the best kind."

His arms wrapped around her and his lips were fused to hers instantly. The kiss took her breath away.

"I should probably be going," he said, when they broke apart.

"Mmm, probably." She licked her lips, reveling in the taste that was purely Cam. When she met his gaze, his eyes had clouded over.

"Keep doing that and I'm definitely staying. Definitely getting you in trouble with your dad."

She laughed, and he reached out and tucked a lock of hair behind her ear. Then he said, "Now that our dirty little secret has been taken care of, why don't we try dinner tomorrow? I know a place about twenty miles from here that you'll love."

"Sounds great," she said, and meant it.

Only the look on Cam's face said otherwise. Apparently, it didn't sound great to him. Peering closer, she saw a dark shadow there. She cast her eyes downward, but when she looked up again, Cam's normal stoic expression was firmly back in place.

He kissed her soundly on the lips and whispered, "See you tomorrow," before retreating into the night, leaving Elle feeling the same way she had at the beginning of the evening.

Very, very guilty.

Chapter Fourteen

Guess what, Bayside! We just got our favorite little gossip item back and it seems Ellie Owens might be leaving us for greener pastures in the nation's capital. *Gasp* Say it ain't so, Ellie! Even more interesting is the person who will be really upset by the departure of little Ellie. And it ain't her father...

Cam was having a real pisser of a day. One of those mornings where every little thing seemed to go wrong, from waking up late to bringing the wrong blueprints to forgetting his lunch.

That said nothing of his bad attitude and foul mood. His crew had been either tiptoeing around him or avoiding him completely.

Fine by Cam. He didn't feel like chatting.

Stepping back to study a particularly pesky piece of wood that needed a very specific measurement, he sighed. The truth was there actually was someone he'd like to chat with.

He'd like to do a hell of a lot more with her, too.

Damn, it had been only two days and he missed her. No, he thought, shaking his head. He craved her.

There was no doubt he'd been attracted to Elle since the day she stepped off that airport shuttle. But each day, everything about her, from her gorgeous looks to her amazing personality, infiltrated his usually well-guarded control more and more. Now all he could do was wait around for her to return from DC.

Since this was the first time Cam Dumont had ever waited for any female to do anything, he didn't know how to handle the feeling. So he indulged his sour mood and whacked a piece of scrap wood with his hammer.

"What did that wood ever do to you?"

"Shut up," he answered his little brother.

Unlike his crew, Jasper was undeterred at Cam's biting words. He hopped down into the pit where Cam was working.

"Rough morning, cupcake?"

Cam glared at him. "What are you even doing here?"

"Come on," Jasper cooed, as if Cam were some cranky toddler. "What's wrong? You can tell me."

With a quick once-over, Cam took in Jasper's gray suit, purple shirt and complementing purple tie, black Ray-Ban sunglasses and shoes that probably cost more than Cam was making on this job. His brother should, by all accounts, seem completely out of place among the tools and equipment, the mounds of dirt and scrap material. Yet Jasper had that way of fitting in everywhere.

"I've heard you've been a real peach this morning," he said conversationally.

"Who the hell said that?" Cam asked.

Jasper sauntered over to Cam's workspace and glanced at it, as if he knew what he was looking at. "You've managed to piss off the majority of your crew. What gives?"

Cam answered by shrugging.

Jasper sighed. "This delightful mood wouldn't have anything to do with Ellie Owens, would it?"

Cam made a rude gesture at his brother, then pushed his safety goggles on top of his head.

Laughing, Jasper held his hands up in a show of surrender. "Okay, okay. I'll stop messing around. Besides, I did stop by to see if you wanted to grab lunch. I have something to discuss about our project and you're not going to be happy."

"Super."

Cam and Jasper were renovating some storefront commercial properties in the center of town near the water. It was a bit of a passion project for both of them, but had come with many hiccups.

After Cam cleaned up his space—and himself—Jasper led him toward his car and they both hopped in. After a short ride, they pulled up in front of Max's Bar and Grill.

Once they were seated, burgers ordered and Cam had taken his first long gulp of cold, refreshing water, he noticed his brother lean back and assess him. "What?" Cam asked.

"Nothing. Just making sure you're really okay."

"Why wouldn't I be? Just in a bad mood today. Nothing to write home about."

"So Elle…" Jasper trailed off, fiddling with his paper napkin.

"Was only gone for two days. In fact, she should be back already."

Jasper gave him a quizzical look. "You haven't heard?"

"About?" Cam asked, as the waitress refilled his water glass.

He noticed that Jasper waited until she was out of earshot, then leaned forward. "Her job interview."

Cam grinned. "Elle got an interview? That's great." He couldn't wait to see her and congratulate her in person. But Jasper's face remained serious.

"Cam, the job is in DC."

The waitress showed up again and placed plates with large loaded burgers and a mountain of fries in front of them. "Hope you guys are hungry."

With the sudden twisting going on in his stomach, Cam could safely say he was categorically not hungry.

"You didn't know," Jasper observed.

He shook his head. "How did you find out?"

His brother reached over to the table next to them and grabbed a copy of the *Bayside Bugle* someone had left. He rifled through the pages and finally folded one back and slapped it in front of Cam.

Cam gritted his teeth. "That freaking Blogger."

"Yep," Jasper agreed. "That freaking Blogger says Elle is up for some position at the Smithsonian in DC."

Scanning the article, Cam shoved a fry in his mouth, but it tasted like sawdust. He didn't even flinch at the fact that it was way too hot.

"Well, good for her. That job sounds like it's right up her alley."

"Cam," Jasper began.

"What the hell is there to say? Elle and I aren't anything to each other. Just because we've slept together..."

"Excuse me, what?"

But he ignored his brother. "I thought I was doing the right thing."

"By sleeping with her?" Jasper asked, blowing on one his fries before popping it into his mouth. "Nothing wrong with that as long as she was willing."

Cam pegged him with a seriously-stop-messing-with-me look. "Of course she was willing." The mere thought of how willing Elle had been as he'd moved over her, under her, inside her, had Cam readjusting the way he was sitting. "That's not what I'm talking about."

Jasper lifted a brow and waited.

"She doesn't want our relationship getting out there because of this damn Blogger person." He flicked the newspaper.

Jasper chortled. "Sounds perfect for you. I don't remember the last time you openly dated someone."

Cam jutted a finger toward his brother. "Exactly. I usually like flying under the radar. But with Elle…"

Jasper nodded, understanding flooding his face. "You like her, Cam. Really like her. It's refreshing to see."

"Yeah, well, hell of a lot of good that does me if she's interviewing for a job hours away."

Jasper added ketchup to his fries. "It was only an interview. She might not get the job."

"Of course she'll get it. You should see this mural she did for one of my clients. Un-freaking-believable."

After taking a large bite of his burger and washing it down with a swig of Coke, Jasper sat back and seemed to consider something. "You don't want Elle to leave Bayside, right?"

His first instinct was to brush off the question. But the truth was Cam desperately wanted Elle to stick around. He wanted to spend more time with her—in and out of bed.

"Yeah," he answered.

"Then you need to give her a reason to stay."

Cam dropped the burger he'd finally picked up. "What are you saying?"

Jasper took another bite and then wiped his mouth before continuing. "Elle needs a job. But she had to go all the way to DC to find one. Make that easier on her." To emphasize his point, he tapped the briefcase he'd carted into the bar.

It was as if a lightbulb went on. Cam knew exactly what his brother had in mind and he felt like an idiot for not thinking of it himself.

"You follow?" Jasper asked.

He nodded emphatically and finally took a hearty bite of his burger, savoring the taste. "I do. Not a bad idea. You know, sometimes you're kinda smart."

"I thought I was annoying?" Jasper said with a grin.

"That, too. Although the level of annoyance will depend on what you have to tell me about our project. How bad is it?"

Jasper grimaced.

"Am I gonna need a beer to hear this?"

"You're gonna need a beer and a shot."

Cam sat back and steeled himself, ready to talk shop. But in the back of his mind, he couldn't help but relax. Jasper had come up with a great idea. It would entice Elle to stick around and had the added bonus of clearing up Cam's bad mood.

It should have been an amazing time.

Elle grabbed her cappuccino from The Brewside and went to one of the tables that had recently been placed outside. The weather had gotten warmer and the sun was reflecting off the bay.

She looked that way now. It had rained last night and the water was still a bit choppy. Birds were diving into the waves in search of food. A boat was in the process of docking.

She'd liked visiting the nation's capital. But the crazy traffic, the inherent commotion of urban living and the crowds of people were so different than Bayside.

She and Riley had gone to the National Gallery, walked along the Mall and watched the sun set over the monuments. They'd visited Georgetown and ate an amazing dinner on M Street. Not to mention the shopping.

At night they'd found a fun piano bar and sung loudly as they drank gin and tonics. Riley seemed in her element amid the hustle and bustle of city life. She'd kept pointing out different aspects of DC that Elle would get to enjoy if she landed the job and moved there.

The interview had gone incredibly well. She met with Will Mitchum, the curator of the Hirshhorn Museum and

Sculpture Garden, one of the seventeen Smithsonian Museums. They wanted to expand their European collection and Mr. Mitchum told her that the Smithsonian would be lucky to hire someone with her experience in the art world.

And yet Elle sat outside The Brewside now, with her drink untouched and her stomach in knots.

Riley had noticed her unease on the drive back home. But she'd said only one quick comment.

"You don't have to take the job if they offer it."

But Elle knew she would be an idiot not to accept such a perfect position. The job combined everything she loved about the art world.

Elle thought about her dad, who looked much better after his brief stint in the hospital. He was excited for her. And she'd be able to get back to Bayside on the weekends. If something really bad happened she could drive home in a matter of hours.

But I won't be here every day.

That was the real concern. Elle couldn't help but feel selfish. She should be thinking predominantly about her dad—and she was—but there was someone else who had managed to worm his way into her thoughts.

Cam.

Right on cue, she saw him entering the square and walking in the opposite direction of The Brewside. His long legs ate up the distance in quick strides. He was on a mission.

Coffee completely forgotten now, Elle stood up so fast that the table wobbled as she headed off to catch up with him. There were a few storefronts on this end of the square that weren't currently occupied. It looked like they'd been newly renovated, Elle thought. She could smell the distinctive aromas of fresh paint and recently cut wood.

Cam stopped in front of one of the stores and let out an oath.

"Hey," Elle called.

He spun around, a sour look on his face, and his fingers clenched into tight fists. She put her hands up in front of her in a show of surrender.

"Sorry." He shook his head.

"Rough day?" she asked.

"Annoying day." But his face softened as he took her in. He reached out, then let his hand fall. "Sorry, wanted to…"

He wanted to what? She glanced around the square, but no one was paying attention to them. Elle took advantage by throwing her arms around him and pressing her face into his neck. He smelled like Cam, and she quickly realized that in only two short days she'd come to miss that smell.

After a swift kiss, she stepped back. He watched her, an incredulous look on his face. "I thought you weren't going to do that in public."

She waved her hand nonchalantly, even though her eyes darted around the square again. "I just wanted to."

"You just wanted to," he repeated. "How was DC? Did you and Riley have a good time?"

Elle smiled. "We did." She twisted her hands together in an effort to keep them from fidgeting. "Actually, I should tell you something."

Cam leaned back against the building. "Oh, yeah? What's that?"

"I went to DC for another reason. I had a job interview at the Smithsonian. I'm sorry. I should have told you about it before I left."

"You're telling me about it now." He reached out and stroked her cheek.

"You're not mad?" Even she could hear the surprise in her voice.

Cam opened his mouth, but quickly closed it. Instead, he studied her from the top of her head down to her casual sneakers. "You look beautiful."

Flustered, she ran a hand over her hair and blushed. She was wearing a pair of tight jeans and a pink flowy blouse. She had on the minimum amount of makeup, although she was happy she'd remembered to apply her favorite shimmering pink lip gloss. In any case, Elle knew she didn't look spectacular in any way.

"You're funny," she said in way of a reply. "What were you swearing about when I came up just now?"

His eyebrows drew together again and he let out a loud groan. "My brother and I have a pet project." He gestured behind him to four of the shops. "This end of the square has sat unoccupied for a couple years now."

Elle glanced around. The stores in question were in a great location, overlooking the bay yet right in the middle of town. "I would have thought people would be lined up to have their businesses here."

"That's what Jasper thought, too. He looked into it. He found two interesting items. First of all, the guy who owned all of these commercial spaces raised the rent every single year. And I'm not talking a small amount. But the other issue was far more worrying. This building in particular hadn't been updated in decades. The place was falling apart."

"Again, I'm shocked that no one in town knew this," Elle offered.

"Turns out the guy had a friend on the town council. That friend is no longer serving good ole Bayside. Jasper bought this area."

Elle's mouth fell open. "Your family owns the town square?"

"Well, my brother and I own these buildings. A major point of contention between Jasper and my parents. But I think it was a great business decision. Besides, his heart was in the right place."

"Where do you fit into all of this?"

"Jasper hired me to bring everything up to code. With these four properties, we had to do some major renovations. Which brings me to my bad mood. The owner for this store—" he pointed at the building directly behind him "—pulled out."

"What do you mean? They're not going to open their business?"

"Apparently not. Paying the penalty and everything. We're going to hold a big grand opening for the new and improved square. I really wanted the whole area to be occupied when we did that, even if the individual stores weren't ready to open. Damn jewelry shop." Cam kicked at a stone on the ground.

They turned toward the building now. Elle could feel the tension coming off him. "I like this space," she said, peering inside. "There's so much natural light."

He nodded and pulled out a key chain with about thirty different keys hanging off it. "Come on, I'll show you around."

They entered the store and Elle took in the dark wooden floors and pristine walls. There were large windows that had clearly been installed recently.

"You mentioned natural light," Cam said. "The whole place is designed for that feature. In the evening, it will overlook the sunset across the bay." He pointed.

She glanced in that direction now. It was close to sunset and the sky had already begun to change colors. Elle's trained artistic eye took in the hues and shading. "Wow, that's going to be spectacular."

"Looks like it's going to be nothing at the moment."

"That's really too bad. I can totally envision it. Displays could hang over there." She pointed toward the right side of the large room.

"Oh, yeah?" Cam sounded amused.

"Well, if I were setting it up, I would use this entire wall for artwork, give the place some color and life."

Elle noticed that Cam was watching her intensely as she walked around the space. "What?" she asked, feeling self-conscious.

"You should set up this space."

Not understanding, she stayed quiet and walked toward the built-in counter, no doubt the cashier station. Running a hand along the sanded wood painted a fresh, crisp shade of white, she couldn't help but admire the workmanship.

"Elle, you should open a gallery here."

She did a double take. "What?"

"Isn't that what you did in Italy? You ran a gallery. Why not do that here? You've been looking for work."

"I can't afford to open my own business."

"That's what business loans are for. I can walk you through the whole process. I've been through it myself," he added eagerly.

It was a ridiculous idea, she thought as she turned away from Cam and walked farther into the space. Although she'd be lying if she claimed it wasn't an interesting idea to entertain.

The front room was perfect for displaying art. She could even dedicate a section to local artists. The back room was huge, but could probably be split into two. One side for packaging and mailing, and the other for a studio. Wouldn't it be interesting to rent it out to artists and have a glass wall so customers could watch them work?

Of course, she would probably have to portion off another section, too. After all, she'd need an office.

She groaned. What was she doing? She couldn't open a gallery here. Or anywhere.

Could she?

"You're intrigued."

She turned at the sound of Cam's voice, surprised that

she was standing in the far corner. How long had she been back here?

"I'm… I don't know what I am."

"You're second-guessing yourself, that's what you're doing." He walked over and took her hand. "Stop thinking of all the reasons you shouldn't or couldn't do this. Start thinking about the possibilities."

She clamped her lips shut, because she wanted to tell him to forget about it. This was a crazy idea. A really stupid, insane, irrational idea. Elle wasn't in the habit of making unreasonable decisions, especially when the rate of failure was so high.

So why did it feel really, really right?

Gnawing on her lower lip, she spun in a circle. Everywhere she looked, she could so clearly imagine a transformed space.

But she'd just had that interview in Washington, DC. For a really amazing job. Her dream job.

A dream job that didn't include her dad, or her hometown…or Cam.

"It feels damn good to run your own business."

She looked up when he spoke again. He'd shoved his hands into the front pockets of his well-worn jeans. For the first time since she'd met him—or returned from Italy and remet him—Cam seemed unsure.

"You put all of yourself into building it, maintaining it, fostering it. Your blood, sweat and tears keep you going through the rough times," he continued. "But no matter what happens, you know that you've built something special."

Something that didn't have anything to do with Jasper or that damn video. Something that would be all hers. And Bayside would finally see that she was a normal human being. Elle would finally be able to shed the image of little Ellie Owens and her crazy behavior.

Cam ran a hand along his jaw. "Look, I know you just had an interview for some great job. DC has a lot to offer. I'm not going to downplay that."

She stepped toward him. "What are you doing, then?"

He closed the distance and framed her face with his big, strong hands. "I'm pleading with you to consider an alternate idea. DC is not the only option." He nipped her lip before brushing his mouth over hers.

A shiver went through her and she wound her arms around his neck. His mouth was on hers again. She parted her lips and let him take what he needed.

Why are you pushing this idea?

She didn't ask it because she thought she already knew the answer. Cam wanted her to stay in Bayside.

Elle didn't know how she felt about that. The only thing she knew right now was that she was wrapped around his hard body and she could feel his erection against her stomach.

She knew that they were making out in a semipublic place.

She knew that she wanted to do more than merely "think" about his idea to open a gallery.

But more than anything, she knew that she wanted him.

She rose on tiptoe, playfully bit his earlobe and whispered, "Take me home, Cameron."

Cam had never driven so fast in his entire life.

But how else was he supposed to get Elle home and out of those clothes? A speeding ticket would be well worth it.

He wasn't sure how they went from talking business to not talking at all. But when he pulled up in front of Elle's house and she bolted from the car, he realized it didn't matter in the slightest. This was what he'd been waiting for since before she'd left for DC.

He ran after her, and as soon as he'd crossed the threshold and shut the door, her mouth was on his.

"Ted," he said against her lips.

Elle shifted back, an amused expression on her face. "Calling out my dad's name while kissing me! That's definitely a first."

He grinned. "Just making sure we're alone."

"Ah. He's at his weekly poker game." Her gaze drifted to the table, where a laptop sat open, some social media site queued up. Elle tiptoed closer and read something on the screen. Her face fell.

"What is it?" Cam asked.

She threw her hand in the air. "Bayside Blogger. Again. I don't even know why I'm surprised."

Cam peered at the screen but wasn't quite sure what he was looking at.

"How does she find out this stuff so fast?" Elle met his gaze. "She reported that I'm in talks to go into business with you. Dammit!" She kicked the leg of the table.

"Calm down, Elle," he said.

"Don't tell me what to do or how to feel. You don't understand."

He held a hand up. "The Bayside Blogger saw us go into the storefront. So what?"

"I don't want my personal business broadcast around the town. Don't you understand that? Don't you know what it reminds me of?"

He softened, if only for a second. What she'd gone through in high school sucked big-time. Cam got that. But what he didn't understand was how she didn't see that experience hadn't been her fault. And how no one really cared anymore. Cam knew one thing. He didn't like seeing Elle upset. And he would do anything to ease her pain.

"You got wasted and said some nonsense on a video. Kids do a lot worse than that. Get over it."

"Stop yelling at me." She spun and headed for her room.

Cam caught up to her easily. "Stop pretending to be some wounded little victim. Guess what? You're not."

"I never said I was. It's not my fault that everyone in this town sees me as nothing more than that crazy kid who was obsessed beyond reason with Jasper."

"Then make them see. You're better than this." Cam eyed her still-unpacked suitcase in the corner of the room. A stark reminder that she could leave at any time. That sobering thought made something inside him snap. "They aren't going to stop talking about you until you shut them up. You need to address what happened back then. If you act like it's not a big deal, it won't be."

Red tinged her cheeks. She pointed at him. "You're just saying this because you don't want me to take that job in DC."

"Damn straight I don't. I want you right here."

"Well, we don't always get what we want." She crossed her arms over her chest.

Outrage looked good on her, he couldn't help thinking. "Stick up for yourself, Elle."

Her lip trembled, but only for a moment. She regained her fighting stance and jutted her chin out. "Why do you even care?"

"Because."

"Because why?" she demanded.

"Because I've gotten to know you. Because you're more than what this town thinks you are. Because you're beautiful and smart. Because you're funny and sweet and kind. Because you have passion." He closed the space between them and crushed his mouth to hers. "Because I like you."

She was panting from his kiss, and fisted her hands in the front of his shirt and drew him closer. "You like me," she stated.

"I do." He kissed her again. Hard. But then something

changed, something shifted, and Cam felt himself calming down. His lips moved over hers softly, slowly. When he lifted his head, he looked into those gorgeous green eyes. "Elle, I'm falling in love with you."

Her mouth dropped open and her eyes widened. Because he was holding her, Cam could feel her heart pounding rapidly.

When she opened her mouth to speak, Cam abruptly put a finger against her lips. "No, don't." He shook his head. "I was ready. You're not."

"But, Cam," she protested. "You just said—"

"I know what I said. It's the truth." With that, he scooped her up in his arms. She let out a little sound of pleasure at being lifted, and then pressed her lips to the side of his neck.

When he went to lay her on the bed, he paused at her giggle. "What?"

"I have a twin bed. And you're so, um…"

"What?" he repeated.

"Big."

That one word ignited something purely masculine inside him. "I'm big, huh?" With a growl, he covered her body on the small twin bed so she could feel just how big he was.

Elle let out a sigh of pleasure and simply hung on as Cam feasted on her mouth. Clinging to his shirt, she tried to keep up with him as he captured her lips, her tongue, and took and took and took.

The sensations were so heady she didn't know how long she could last like this. Nor did she know what had just happened. They'd gone from arguing to full-on making out in the blink of an eye.

But when he anchored her head with his hands and

changed the angle of the kiss, she no longer cared. All she wanted was Cam.

He said he was falling in love with her. Not only like. Love.

What was more, he hadn't needed her to say it back. He was perfectly fine to express it himself.

She loved how sure of himself and his feelings he was. She loved the way he'd challenged her tonight, both with the idea of opening a gallery and with the Bayside Blogger. She loved the way he didn't let her sulk. She loved the feel of his hands on her skin and the way his mouth roamed over hers.

Oh, my God! I love Cam.

Elle gasped and he immediately backed off her. "What's wrong?" he asked.

She looked into his brown eyes, made even darker when filled with lust. "Nothing's wrong," she told him. Because she couldn't admit that she loved him without knowing if she'd take the job in DC. It didn't seem fair to him otherwise.

She might not be ready to express her feelings out loud to him, but she could show him.

For the next few hours, that's exactly what she did.

Chapter Fifteen

I have to admit that I was quite put out to learn that Jasper Dumont, the most eligible bachelor in Bayside, had a girlfriend. However, I will forgive all of my little gossip birdies this once because I've discovered that Jasper and Mindy are on the outs. Yikes! Although, if that's the case, perhaps a new girlfriend would be the perfect present for his upcoming birthday party. Too bad Ellie Owens is already taken…

It took Cam what felt like an hour to get his breath back and his heart rate to return to normal. Each time he was with Elle, it got better and better.

Turning his head, he slanted a glance at her now. She wore a satisfied grin and nothing else. To Cam, it was the hottest ensemble he'd ever seen. He leaned over and brushed a kiss across her lips.

"You okay?" he asked.

"Mmm," she replied. She ran a hand down his side, causing him to suck in a breath. "This room is now sacred."

He met her gaze. "You mean, you've never? Here?"

Laughing, she shook her head. "Nope. I was shy in high school."

He reached for his pants and began to dress. Elle watched with an amused expression. "I see how it is. You come over here, have your way with me and disappear into the night."

"Trust me, I'd much rather stay here with you all night.

But brotherly duty calls." She raised an eyebrow. "Jasper's birthday is tomorrow. He's having a party at our parents' house. Told him I'd help set up."

"Ah." Elle rose and snagged a robe from the back of the door. As she belted the short wrap, all coherent thoughts flew out of Cam's mind. The material skimmed her thighs and the cinched belt accentuated her tiny waist. With her messy hair, flushed face, swollen lips and bare feet, she looked good enough to eat.

He made a move toward her, but Elle slapped a hand against his chest. "Oh, no, I know that look now. Come one step closer and you will definitely not make it to Jasper."

"That's okay. The kid needs to experience some disappointment now and then."

"Cam," she said with a laugh, and threw his shirt at him. "Come on, I'll walk you out."

"You did get an invite to the party, right?" he asked as he finished dressing.

"I think the entire town got an invite. Meet you there at eight?"

He nodded and they left the room. But Cam didn't want to meet her there. He wanted to come pick her up and bring her as his official date.

He wanted to hang out with her all night, talking to his friends and enjoying a beer or two. He wanted them to go back out on that gazebo where they'd spent time getting to know each other during the last party. He'd steal more kisses before returning to admire whatever over-the-top surprise his mother had planned.

He wanted to drive Elle back to his house at the end of the night and peel her out of what he was sure would be a beautiful dress. He wanted to sleep with her wrapped in his arms.

"Cam?" Elle's voice pulled him out of the dream scenario he'd just escaped to.

"Sorry." Only he wasn't sorry. Wanting to be with Elle like a normal couple wasn't some crazy, off-the-wall idea.

He pushed her up against the living room wall and took her lips in a passionate, all-consuming kiss. Eventually, Cam pulled back and muttered, "I better get going. I don't think your dad would be too thrilled to find me wrapped around his half-naked daughter."

A deep, insistent cough followed his statement, along with "You got that right."

Elle froze. Cam turned to find Ted Owens standing in the doorway, arms crossed over his chest, face beet red. He jumped back from Elle, whose face matched her father's coloring.

The robe that had seemed so sexy only a moment ago now stuck out like a flashing neon sign that read Recent Sex Romp with Your Daughter. Cam shuddered, clenched his jaw and ran a hand through his hair.

The seconds dragged. Since neither Elle nor her dad were saying anything, he tried to think of something that could break the tension. But the look on Ted's face stopped that from happening. Even though Cam probably had a good half a foot and forty pounds on Ted, he was under no presumption that the ex-cop couldn't beat the crap out of him right now if he wanted.

Everyone knew you never messed with a father when it came to his daughter.

Still, he didn't want Elle to go through what would no doubt be a very awkward conversation alone. He opened his mouth but Ted threw up a hand.

"Nope. I don't want to hear it," Ted said sternly.

"Daddy," Elle began.

"I think it's past time for Cam to leave."

Cam wasn't budging. He straightened his shoulders and reached for Elle's hand.

He caught her brief smile at the gesture.

"It's okay Cam. I got this. Really," she emphasized.

Cam swiveled his head back and forth between Elle and Ted. They wore matching resolute expressions. Had the circumstances been different, he would have laughed.

With a final squeeze to Elle's hand, he took his leave. But he felt like a coward as he went.

Elle steeled herself as the front door closed and she heard Cam's truck rev to life before heading down the street. If only she could have been so lucky.

But she wasn't, and now she was standing in the middle of unchartered waters with her father. It would really help matters if he would say something. But as of right now, he'd turned to stone, holding his position of "pissed-off daddy" while nailing her with a rigid stare.

Could he just say something? Begin the conversation? It would almost be better if he started yelling. But this silent treatment was beyond uncomfortable. Where did parents learn that, anyway?

"Daddy," she finally murmured.

Ted held up a hand. "Are you and Cameron dating?"

She made sure her robe was still securely belted. "Well, we're, um…"

"Because the only reason to find your daughter looking like that—" he pointed at her "—and coming out of there with a man—" he gestured toward her bedroom "—is if she is in a serious, committed, monogamous relationship." He cocked an eyebrow and waited.

Elle sank into the nearest chair. "It's complicated."

Ted nodded. His cheeks were still red, but she could tell the fight had gone out of him. He walked to the kitchen, came back with his favorite whiskey and poured a glass for each of them. Then he downed his in about half a second.

"It's complicated?" He repeated her words. "Let's un-complicate it."

Elle wanted nothing more. But first, she needed to change into something that was a little less revealing. She ran to her room and threw on a pair of yoga pants and a sweatshirt. Then she returned to the living room and tossed back her shot of whiskey, the fiery liquid coating her throat and causing her to cough. "I can't talk to you about this."

"Why not? I'm your father."

Elle held on to her glass, turning it around and around. "That's kind of why I can't."

"Well, I don't see a line of people ready to listen. Looks like right now I'm all you got."

Something softened in Elle's heart. She took in her father, the first man to ever love her. "You've always been all I've got."

"Come here, princess."

She joined him on the couch.

"Tell me what's going on."

So she did. He already knew about her interview and job offer in DC, but Elle filled him in on Cam's idea for the gallery.

Ted appeared to be deep in thought. "Your options are to either take a job that you are well qualified for and you would probably love, in a city that is exciting and interesting and not too far from here."

"Right," she said.

"Or you can take a huge risk and do something new. Something that you would probably be good at, but will take a lot of hard work and would be very scary. And would have you staying in Bayside."

Again, she nodded. Then she gnawed on her lip and looked away.

"There's more, isn't there?" her dad asked.

Elle took a deep breath. "The Bayside Blogger has already reported that I had an interview and that Cam showed me the property for the gallery."

Her dad narrowed his eyes. "What in the hell does that Blogger have to do with any of this? More important, what does it have to do with deciding between the job in DC and opening a gallery here—which, by the way, I think you should do."

She wanted to scream. Her dad wanted her to stay in Bayside?

"Ellie?" He looked at her imploringly.

"Every time I see my name on that damn blog or in her column or on her Twitter account, I get this feeling in my stomach."

Concern filled his eyes. "But why, sweetheart?"

With a deep, shuddering breath, Elle let it all out. "Because I'm so worried that I embarrass you. That every time something about me goes public, you are humiliated, just like you were back when I was in high school." She stalked to the window. "I want to stay here, Daddy. I want to open a gallery. But I'm afraid that you don't want me to be here." She turned to look at him.

Elle didn't think it was possible, but her dad's face turned even redder than when he'd caught her and Cam together. Only this time he was angry.

"Don't want you here? Of course I want you here. Do you have any idea how much I've missed you these past ten years?"

"But you always encouraged me to stay in Italy."

"Because you love art. You always have. Where else were you going to get experience like that? I wanted the best for my child. That's what good parents do."

Elle sank into the soft cushions, feeling completely depleted. "But you sent me away to college. After, well, you know, after that thing in high school."

Ted nodded. "Ellie, you had already been accepted to that school. I suggested you do the prefreshman courses because I saw how embarrassed you were over that video. I thought it would be good for you to get away. You thought I sent you away?" He lowered his gaze. "If you'd spoken up and told me you didn't want to go, I would have never pressed the issue."

"But weren't you mad about that video?"

His gaze snapped up to meet hers. "Of course I was mad. Those girls got you drunk and filmed you."

A strangled sound escaped her throat. "You knew? All this time you knew it wasn't my fault?"

"Of course I knew. You were a good girl, Ellie. Why, all of sudden and right before you were set to graduate, would you decide to rebel? It didn't make sense. I knew you'd had a sleepover with those girls. You didn't get in more trouble at school because I spoke to that idiot principal."

"You did?"

"I also spoke to the parents of those girls. Unfortunately, I didn't have any concrete proof. As a cop, I understood I could only take the issue so far."

"You stuck up for me?"

Ted grabbed her hand and squeezed hard. "Always."

"But I thought that video contributed to you losing the county sheriff election."

Ted shrugged. "Maybe. But there was more to that election than one little teenage prank. There was a group of men who didn't want me as sheriff. I knew some of them were doing some shady things. I'll spare you the details," he said, in response to Elle's questioning gaze. "Look, honey. I might've lost, but I still had a good, long career that I'm proud of."

Elle sat back against the cushions and let out the longest breath she'd ever held. In fact, she may have been keeping it in for the last ten years. All this time she'd carried around guilt and shame. And now her dad was telling her that she'd misinterpreted everything? She would laugh if she wasn't feeling so exhausted.

"Wait a minute." Elle realized something. "At the spring festival, when they were doing that awful stunt at the water, I saw you in the crowd. You turned away from me."

Her dad appeared truly confused. "Was I wearing my glasses that day?"

Elle couldn't remember. More than likely, he wasn't. Ted forgot his glasses more than anyone she knew. "I guess you weren't."

Ted deflated. "The truth is, I did see you that day. And I saw what that moron Chumsky was doing. I was about to lose my mind when Ernie and the guys called me back."

"What?" Elle asked, shocked.

"I had a mind to slash that fool's car tires."

Elle's mouth dropped open. "Daddy!"

Ted shrugged. "Don't worry, I didn't do it. But no one's going to mess with my baby." He leaned over and cuddled her against him for a long-overdue hug. Then he kissed the top of her head and said the words she'd needed to hear for years. "The truth is, I want nothing more than for you to come live in Bayside again."

Her eyes filled and she hiccuped, trying to hold the tears at bay.

"Shh, none of that." He shifted, reaching in his pocket for his cloth handkerchief. "Now that that's all settled, let's get back to discussing this complicated thing with Cam."

Elle groaned. "I think I preferred talking about my adolescent traumas."

"I could tell that boy had a thing for you from the moment you got home. And he'd be a damn fool not to act on it now."

"He's not a fool. But I think I've been one. I'm the one who needs to act on it."

Ted kissed her head again. "Then get to it. Now that you're staying in Bayside, a couple grandkids would suit me just fine."

She would have rolled her eyes, but after their conversation Elle felt happier and lighter than she had in forever. All she wanted to do tonight was sit with her father, knowing she was going to be sitting with him for a long, long time.

hundred yada ahead, ... out of her head. She wavered. As she wanted more time with him, but she'd given ... she was going to be alone with him for a good long time.

Chapter Sixteen

New couple alert. I have definitive proof that Ellie Owens and Cam Dumont have apparently been getting it on. Look for their debut at Jasper's birthday party tonight!

Elle climbed the steps of the Dumont estate promptly at eight o'clock. She was ushered inside by a maid and shown to the solarium.

There was a spring in her step that had nothing to do with the semi-uncomfortable, yet utterly fabulous sparkly heels she wore. Her good mood could mostly be attributed to her conversation with her dad the night before. The two-ton brick of emotions that had been weighing her down for ten years was gone and Elle finally felt at peace.

Well, almost, she reminded herself. She still needed to tell Cam that she'd made her decision. She'd called the Smithsonian that morning and declined the job offer. Elle was going to buy that space in town and open a gallery, and she couldn't wait to see Cam's face when she told him.

Entering the solarium, she noticed that tonight's gathering was a much more intimate get-together than the *Printemps* party. She saw Mr. and Mrs. Dumont and a few older people that Elle assumed worked with Jasper. For the most part, though, the crowd consisted of people her age—former classmates and others she'd seen around town.

The decorations were sparse but tasteful. The solarium was a beautiful room with large glass windows and French doors that opened up to one of the terraces. People spilled outside, laughter and music mingling with the scent of yummy food. Elle turned as a waiter passed by with a tray.

"Pancetta-wrapped scallop?" he offered.

She smiled and popped one of the appetizers into her mouth.

She spotted Riley, who was in deep conversation with her boss, Sawyer Wallace. It looked pretty intense, so Elle walked to one of the many bars set up around the room and ordered a glass of champagne.

Riley and Sawyer eventually made their way over and ordered drinks. Riley gave Elle a quick hug. "Love the dress, Elle," she said with a wink.

Riley had picked out the short lilac number while they were in DC. Elle indulged her by doing a little spin.

"I smell a shopping enabler," Sawyer said. "Riley has ruined many a friend's credit rating."

"Oh, aren't you just hysterical. Ha, ha, ha." Riley rolled her eyes.

Sawyer was incredibly good-looking, Elle thought. He was tall, with blondish-brown hair that might be a couple weeks past due for a cut. Not to mention he had an adorable smile and hazel eyes that appeared to twinkle right now as if he was in on some kind of joke.

Elle smiled and stuck out her hand. "I'm Elle Owens. We haven't officially met yet."

"Sawyer Wallace." He returned her smile and shook her hand. "Nice to officially meet you. Although, between Riley's daily recaps of your exploits and the Bayside Blogger's columns, I feel like I know you."

At first Elle gritted her teeth at the mention of the Bayside Blogger. But suddenly, she pointed a finger at Sawyer. "Wait a minute. You know who this Blogger is. Why don't you tell me?"

Sawyer made a gesture like he was locking his lips. "I wish I could, but I've made a solemn vow."

"And he won't break it for anyone," Riley added. "Don't bother, Elle. I've tried."

But Elle was undeterred. "What do I have to give you? Money? A new car?"

Sawyer laughed and took a long swig of his beer. "Trust me, you are not the first to make me such offers. And you probably won't be the last. The truth is, I get more revenue from advertisers who specifically request to be in her section in the paper or on her page on the website than any other place."

Elle sighed. "She's your bread and butter right now."

"Just a bit." Sawyer must have noticed someone come in because he gave a little nod toward the entryway. "Cam's here. I'm gonna go say hi. Oh, and congrats, Elle. I think you and Cam make a really nice couple."

She blinked. "What did he just say?" she whispered to Riley, as Sawyer crossed the room and slapped a hand on Cam's back.

Riley turned her away from the crowd. "Um, I didn't want to say anything, but…"

Elle's eyes rolled back so far they were practically on the second floor. "Let me guess how this sentence is going to end. You're going to ask me if I've seen the Bayside Blogger's column today, aren't you?"

Riley looked sheepish as she nodded.

"Give it to me straight. What did she say?"

But before Riley could fill her in, Elle heard a couple standing nearby talking rather loudly.

"Ellie Owens and Cam Dumont are together. Like, together-together. As a couple."

"I think it's awful. What about Jasper? Ellie just led him on."

"Whatever! I'd take either of those brothers in a heartbeat."

Elle's stomach sank.

Riley leaned closer. "She said you and Cam were in a relationship now."

Oh, God. Elle peeked around the room. Cam was making his way toward her, a big grin on his face. At the same time, hushed whispers and curious glances occurred all around her.

"Great. Just great," she muttered.

Riley rubbed Elle's arm. "I'm sorry, Elle. I'll let you and Cam talk."

Elle thanked her friend and greeted Cam with a scowl.

"Hey, gorgeous," he said, oblivious to the latest gossip.

"Shh," she urged. Then she snatched his hand and pulled him to the far side of the room and a quiet, dark corner.

"What? What's going on?" he asked, eyes darting around the room.

"The Bayside Blogger outed us."

Cam appeared stricken. "She said we were gay?"

Elle rolled her eyes. "No. She said we were dating. That we're together. In a relationship."

Elle waited, but Cam didn't respond. Understanding flooded his face, only to be replaced by a red blush that covered his neck, his cheeks and even the tips of his ears. But he wasn't embarrassed, she quickly realized. He was angry.

He grabbed her arm. "Dammit, Elle. We *are* in a relationship."

Her pulse picked up. "That's not what I meant."

"Yes, it is." He ran a hand over his face and then let that hand fall in frustration. "I can't do this anymore."

Pure, unadulterated panic washed over her. Her throat was tight as she asked, "Can't do what?"

He gestured between them. "This. That." He pointed to the rest of the room. "I'm glad the Bayside Blogger put that in her column. I don't want to keep us quiet anymore. Hell, I should have thought to tip her off myself."

His voice had grown louder and quite a few heads turned in their direction. But Cam didn't seem to notice or care. Instead, he pulled her close to him. "I want to be with you in front of these people. I want to kiss you. But I'll tell you what I don't want to do—what I'm not going to do anymore. Hide."

He released her and abruptly turned his back. As he made his way through the room, an icy feeling spread throughout her body. She couldn't let him leave like this.

Running after him, she called out, "Cam, please wait." Then she reached for his arm, but he shrugged her off.

They were in the middle of the room. Cam shook his head. "I'm done waiting." After a last long look at her, one filled with regret, he fled the party.

Tears welled up in Elle's eyes, but she did her best to keep them from spilling over. Her cheeks were hot and she was aware that the music had stopped and everyone was openly staring at her.

"Elle?" She felt a hand on her back and turned to find Jasper's kind eyes. "What happened? Where did Cam go?"

"I, um, I think he left. I think I really messed up." She pointed to the door and then back to Jasper.

"Ooh, look! Now Ellie and Jasper are together."

"Wait. Which one is she into?"

"Did Ellie and Cam just break up?"

"Were they together? I thought she was in love with Jasper."

The whispers and questions poured in, and that's when she realized that she'd totally and irrevocably erred. She'd treated Cam like some dirty little secret, when in reality he was the best thing that had ever happened to her.

She'd pushed him away because she was so afraid people would gossip about her. Elle glanced around the room. That was happening, anyway. And now Cam wasn't by her side.

She stepped back from Jasper and fought the urge to start biting her nails. Her heart hurt.

Her gaze whizzed around the room, from one decked-out partygoer to the next. Who was this damn Blogger and why was she so intent on making a mockery of Elle's life?

Cam had been right. She needed to put a stop to this now. Right this very minute. The Elle Show had to come to an end.

She grabbed a champagne flute and a knife from a nearby table. When she clinked the knife against the glass, the room slowly quieted down and everyone turned in her direction.

Elle experienced a brief moment of terror at having so many people look at her at the same time. But then she remembered the *Printemps* party, and how she'd gotten through it. Because of Cam. Cam, who she'd just massively pissed off.

"Are you giving a toast?" someone in the crowd called out.

"Yes. Sort of," she said, her voice wavering. "I have a few things to clear up." She projected so everyone in the solarium could hear her. Her palms began to sweat when she noticed that people were even making their way inside from the terrace to listen.

She saw Jasper move forward on her left side. Riley and Sawyer were standing in the middle of the room, a curious expression on both their faces. Mr. and Mrs. Dumont were watching from their seats at one of the high tables near the French doors.

"Are you going to sing 'Happy Birthday'?" someone else asked.

"No. But happy birthday, Jasper. Thanks for having us," she said lamely. She cleared her throat one more time. "I know I was the star of a really bad video in high school, where I declared my love for the birthday boy."

"And then you jumped in the bay."

"Thank you, Tony," she called out, making a mental note not to tip him the next time she went to The Brewside.

"That video wasn't my fault. A couple girls spiked my drinks at a sleepover. I had no idea they did that, or that I was being filmed that night." A shocked murmur filtered through the crowd. She even thought she heard a *poor Ellie*.

Continuing, Elle said, "I didn't throw myself in the bay back in high school. Or last month. I simply slipped. Both times."

Since she was holding a glass filled with alcohol, and she wasn't much for public speaking to begin with, she downed the drink, the bubbles filling her with liquid courage.

"I stayed away from Bayside for ten years because of that video." A collective gasp roared through the crowd. "But you know what? I'm not running away again. This is my home, and I'm back to stay."

A couple claps were mixed with calls of *good for you* and *awesome*.

"And furthermore, I'm in love with Cam Dumont." Gasps, sighs and a loud whoop sounded throughout the room at this revelation. "Only I may have messed it up pretty bad."

She sighed. "Except for my dad, Cam is the greatest man I've ever known. Cam was the only person who really listened to me when I first got back. He's honorable and hardworking. He started his own company without any help or support."

Elle thought she spotted Cam's parents sit up straighter at that comment. They definitely exchanged a glance. She met Jasper's gaze. "And he worries about his brother all the time."

Jasper cocked his head, his formerly amused expression morphing into confusion.

It occurred to her that she probably shouldn't be revealing so much about other people, but she couldn't seem to stop. She veered back to herself.

"So that's what I have to say." She nodded firmly.

"Well done, Ellie," someone called from the back of the room.

She held up a finger. "Okay, one more thing." A few laughs rang out. "My name is Elle, not Ellie. Ellie is a little girl's name and I am a grown, accomplished woman. So, from now on, I'm Elle Owens, daughter of Ted Owens. I'm hopefully opening an art gallery down near the water. If you'll excuse me, I have to go."

With that, Elle turned toward the exit with her head held high. Applause and cheers followed her out the door as she went to track down the man she loved.

Chapter Seventeen

Ugh… Even bloggers get hung over after big soirees. What was your favorite part of Jasper's party? I think a certain speech made by our town's own prodigal daughter takes the cake. Don't believe me? Check out the best video I've taken in a while…

And PS. I think it's time we all start calling her Elle.

Cam was brooding. Full-on feeling sorry for himself, considering drinking himself into a stupor, forget this damn day and anything that had to do with Elle Owens brooding.

He stalked from the living room to his kitchen. He opened the fridge, grabbed a beer, then put it back on the shelf and slammed the door.

Restless, irritable and tired as hell, Cam contemplated going for a run, doing a little boxing at the gym, cutting some wood or just blasting hard rock.

In the end, he went for the music.

The only problem was that the heavy bass exacerbated the headache he had from not sleeping well. He sank into his favorite leather recliner. But the chair did nothing to soothe his mood. Or calm his nerves.

Because what he really needed to do was turn off his brain. The brain that was running a loop of Elle at the party last night. Elle refusing to admit they were in a relationship. Elle once again declining to stand up for herself.

And that's what really got to him. If she'd only tell everyone what was what, they'd probably back off, leave her alone. Because once she could be honest, there'd be nothing to gossip about.

And yeah, he wouldn't have minded being acknowledged as her boyfriend. Or at least someone she was sleeping with.

Still, as angry as he was today, he wondered how she was doing. He couldn't help but worry over what might have happened after he made his getaway. Cam knew he'd do just about anything for her.

Except pretend. He no longer would—or could—pretend there wasn't something between them. He loved her.

Then, without warning, his loud music stopped. The hard guitar riffs and pounding beat of the drums ended.

Cam looked over at his stereo and saw his brother standing there, watching him with his arms crossed over his chest. "What's the matter?" Jasper asked.

Cam shrugged. "I don't know." But he did know. He raked a hand through his hair and the floodgate simply collapsed. "I'm in love with someone and she can't even muster up the courage to admit we're dating. I guess I don't know her as well as I thought."

To Cam's amazement, Jasper grinned.

"What in the hell is so funny?"

"You are a clueless Neanderthal."

Cam could feel his headache returning even stronger. He pinned his brother with a hard stare.

"Hold on. Let me explain," Jasper said quickly.

Cam went to the kitchen and returned with two bottles of beer. "Here. Drink. Talk."

Jasper made himself comfortable in one of Cam's chairs. After a long swig of beer, Jasper met Cam's gaze. "You're in love with her."

"I already told you that."

Jasper let out a big sigh. The kind of sigh you give to a kid who says something stupid and you're trying to remain patient. "I noticed how you were around her the first time I saw Elle. Remember that day in the town square? I didn't recognize her at first. You had it bad back then."

Rising from the chair, Jasper walked around the room. "But I had no idea exactly how bad until I saw your face last night. It really hurt you when she didn't acknowledge you were in a relationship."

"Again, I've already stated this. Do you have a point?"

Jasper grinned, but the smile didn't reach his eyes. "Several. First off, don't give up on Elle. Seriously."

Cam downed the rest of his beer and considered grabbing another one. "After last night, I don't think there is anything to go back to. I won't pretend."

"Okay, let's table the Elle situation for a moment. There's something else."

"There always is," Cam groaned.

"Elle said something after you left last night." Jasper shook his head. "It…surprised me."

"What did she say?" Curious, Cam sat back and waited.

Jasper didn't speak at first. He seemed to be having an internal debate before he finally looked at Cam. "Are you worried about me?"

Of course. But Cam couldn't bring himself to say that out loud. "You're my brother," he said instead.

Jasper got up and stood right in front of Cam, crowding his space. "I'm going to ask you something and I want you to be brutally honest with me. Seriously," he added, when Cam shifted in his seat. "Do not lie or try to protect me or do whatever it is you big brothers do."

"Okay, fine."

"When I took over your spot in Mom and Dad's company," he began. But then he paused. "You've said some things in the past. Do you think I'm unhappy working there?"

Cam moved to get up, but Jasper blocked him. He settled for staring out the window and running a hand over the stubble on his chin.

"Come on, Cam," Jasper urged.

Too exhausted to fight or even to lie, Cam finally let it out. "The guilt I feel…"

"Guilt? Guilt over what?" Jasper asked.

"I made you take the job at our parents' company."

Jasper backed up. "No, you didn't."

"I mean, I didn't force you, but if it hadn't been for me, you wouldn't have stepped up. And you and Dad are at each other's throats all the time."

"That's because Dad can be really stubborn. So can Mom when it comes to it."

"I love my business and my job. But I feel guilty every single day." Cam sighed when Jasper cocked his head. He was going to have to spell this out for him. "If I hadn't been selfish and quit, you wouldn't have had to stand in for me."

Silence filled the room for a full minute. Then Jasper sat next to Cam on the couch. "Do you know what it was like to be born second in this family? To be the younger son?"

Cam shook his head.

"It sucks." His brother scrubbed a hand over his face. "Every single thing I ever did was discounted. Didn't matter."

"That's not true." Loyalty swelled in Cam for his little brother.

"Afraid it is. You were the one who mattered. You were the coveted heir, the future of the company. I was the spare."

Jesus. Was that how it had really been? "Don't ever say that again. You know you were loved."

"I do. But I wasn't respected." He stood up once more and began to pace. "I love real estate. I love crunching numbers. I love making deals. I love coming up with new ideas to expand the business. I love all of it."

"You do?"

"Yes. I always have. Why do you think I spent so much time following Dad around when I was little? Why do you think I spend so much time talking with Mom now? I worked my butt off to get into great schools and prepare myself for a place in the family business. When you told me you didn't want to work for Mom and Dad, secretly I was thrilled."

"I'll be damned."

"I'm sorry to say this, Cam, but I'm the one who's a selfish bastard. I didn't step in to help you out of a jam. I stepped in because I was finally getting exactly what I wanted."

Cam walked over to his brother. "Are you serious?"

"Yep." Jasper nodded firmly. "So you don't owe me anything."

Overwhelmed with emotion and feeling lighter than he had in years, Cam did something he hadn't done since they'd been young. He grabbed his little brother in a tight bear hug.

"Thanks, you little snot."

"Anytime, bro." Jasper pushed away. "Now, back to Elle. You gonna go after her or what?"

Exhaling a long, frustrated sigh of breath, Cam sank back onto the couch.

"You haven't visited the Bayside Blogger's column today, have you?" Jasper asked.

Cam rolled his eyes. "Oh, yeah, I checked it out right after I did some online shopping and watched a chick flick."

"Look, I know you're not a fan. But if there's one day for you to make an exception, today really should be that day."

"Why? Is she talking about who wore what to your party last night?"

Jasper chuckled. "Oh, she's definitely talking about my

party." After reaching into his pocket, he threw his phone over to Cam. "Pull it up. There's a video blog today."

"I really don't care about—"

"Watch the freaking thing already," Jasper said, impatience dripping from his voice.

Fine, Cam thought. When Jasper wanted something, he was like a dog with a bone. Even though he was in no mood to watch—what? Probably two people making out at the party, or someone wearing the wrong kind of outfit. But since he was having a moment with his brother, he figured he'd go for it.

Pulling up the website on Jasper's phone, Cam felt his heart drop when an image of Elle in her purple dress filled the screen. He pressed Play on the video clip and also saw Jasper, and could tell they were talking, but he couldn't hear anything.

"Turn up the volume, Einstein."

Offering his brother a finger of choice, he increased the volume and sat back to watch Elle Owens, the woman he was in love with, go nuts on the entire town. By the end of the video, his heart had stopped and he hadn't taken a breath.

He flicked hopeful eyes up to Jasper.

"She loves me"

His brother merely nodded.

Cam threw the phone back at him and jumped off the couch. "I gotta go."

"About time," Jasper called, as Cam ran in search of his keys. He had to find Elle.

He heard Jasper settle on the couch and flip on the television as he headed for the door. Cam burst through it and almost ran smack-dab into his father.

"Dad," he said, surprised. "What are you doing here?"

Collin Dumont was an older, more mature version of Cam. They were the same height, had the same dark looks and tanned skin. The only difference besides their choice of occupations was that Collin could nail his sons with the most intense fatherly stare. From the time Cam had been a little kid, one look from his dad and he would stop in his tracks.

At thirty-two, the same could still be said.

"I need a minute," his dad said, walking to the railing of the porch Cam had built himself. Collin stroked the finished wood and gave an appreciative nod. "This is good work."

Cam stayed quiet.

"This your work?" he asked.

Cam nodded and joined him at the railing. "Yep. The place didn't come with a porch, and with a setup like this, it was screaming for one."

Collin leaned back and seemed to take in the small Cape Cod house that Cam loved.

Leaning a hip against the railing, Cam tried to clamp down on the urge to brush his dad off. He desperately wanted to find Elle.

"I wanted to tell you something." Collin said. "Elle stated a lot of things last night. That's why I'm here."

When Elle finally decided to speak up, she really let loose, Cam thought with a grin.

"You do good work, Cam."

Surprised, Cam blinked. "Um, thanks."

"I don't tell you enough." Collin gave a short chuckle. "I don't tell you ever."

"I noticed," he replied.

"I wanted you to take over the company the same way I had from my father."

"Dad," Cam began, hearing the angst in his voice. "We've discussed this to death."

His father held up a hand. "I was stubborn about it. Perhaps too stubborn."

Cam shot him a look. A very surprised look.

To his credit, Collin appeared ruffled. He ran his hand through his hair the same way Cam often did. "You are your own man. You started a successful business without any help from me." His voice broke as he said, "I'm so proud of you, son."

Around a very tight throat, Cam replied, "Thanks, Dad."

Not one for overly emotional scenes, Collin slapped a hand on his back. "Very proud. I need to come look at some of your work soon. Not every man has such a talented son."

"You actually have two talented sons." Cam nodded toward his house, where Jasper had no doubt found one of the many movie channels Cam subscribed to.

Collin peered inside, as well. "I know."

"Wouldn't hurt you to tell him from time to time," Cam suggested.

"I know that, too. His time will come. Jasper still has a little more to learn."

Cam figured this would probably be the biggest Hallmark moment he ever had with his dad. But he still wanted to get to Elle.

"Where were you running off to when I interrupted?" Collin asked quite perceptively.

"Actually, I have to go talk to someone."

"Is someone a very attractive brunette who caused quite a stir last night?" He offered a rare grin.

"Seems like it. Not sure how you're going to feel about this," Cam said, as he walked down the porch steps. "I'm about to do something kind of risky."

"All good businessmen take risks," Collin said.

"I'm in love with Elle Owens and I'm going to try and win her back."

Collin crossed his arms over his chest and gave him a

steady, yet supportive, stare. "Well, if one of you didn't go after her, I would have thought I'd raised two idiots."

Elle had been all over Bayside. Her feet were sore, her head was pounding and she was exhausted.

She'd begun her day with her dad, who let her accompany him to his doctor's appointment. Even though she'd barely slept and wanted to talk to Cam immediately, she couldn't be happier that her dad was finally letting her in, so she'd tabled her get-Cam-back plans.

After the doctor's visit, she'd had to postpone finding Cam again, for another good reason. She'd visited the bank, spending hours going over paperwork and interest rates and preapprovals. Just thinking of it made her head swim. Although not as much as the fact that she was going to be a business owner.

Elle smiled. If all went well, she was going to be the owner of Bayside Gallery. She still couldn't believe it. She was going to stay in her hometown and be close to her dad.

And close to Cam. Who currently hated her.

She let out a long, frustrated sigh. She'd been everywhere looking for him, even his parents' house. She'd left no less than twenty messages on his cell phone. But he hadn't answered and he wasn't in any of the usual places she thought she'd find him. Not at The Brewside or Max's. His house had been empty, except for Jasper, who'd made himself comfortable with a big bowl of popcorn and Cam's big-screen TV. He'd been no help, though, just grinning at her like a loon.

Her next step was to drive down to Cam's cabin. But first she needed a moment.

Looking out at the bay, she took in the serene water, so calm today. So different from how she was feeling.

Why hadn't she taken his hand last night? She wanted him. She...loved him.

Instead, he'd run out and she'd completely lost her mind. Although he may have been on to something with the whole sticking-up-for-yourself bit. Perhaps it was all in her mind, but people were acting differently toward her today.

And Elle liked it.

With a final exhalation that did nothing to relax her, she stood, smoothed down her bright orange blouse—a Riley selection—and turned back toward the street. That's when she froze.

Cam.

There he was, running toward her. As if she'd wished him into existence.

"Elle," he called. In a few long strides he was at her side.

"Cam!" She released a long breath. "I've been looking for you all day. I'm so sorry about last night. You have no idea." The words rushed out of her. It felt like if she didn't get them all out immediately, she would burst.

"I've been so stupid," she continued. Cam opened his mouth, but she shook her head and put a finger to his lips. "No, you were right. You were so right about everything."

She shoved her hands into the pockets of her jeans and bit her lip. She had to go on. "You were right about sticking up for myself, and I finally did after you left last night."

He shifted and she could tell he was going to try and say something, so she kept going. "I had a long talk with my dad the other night. I've been an idiot with him, too. He's so happy I'm going to stay in Bayside."

Cam lifted an eyebrow and she laughed. "Yes, I'm staying. Depending on my preapproval, I'm going to open the gallery. Of course, I'll still do nursery murals and other side jobs, too."

His face softened and that was exactly what she needed to see. "Thank you," she said with a long sigh.

Cam grinned. "What are you thanking me for?"

"Thank you for believing in me. Thank you for not

judging me." She took a step toward him. "Thank you for pushing me." She gave him a little shove for emphasis. "Thank you for being my friend." Clutching his hands, she met his eyes. "Thank you for being more than my friend."

"Anything else?" he asked.

She nodded. "Most important, thank you for calling me Elle."

He laughed and pulled her to him for a long, overdue embrace. Their lips met and she melted. Elle didn't know how long they stayed like that and she didn't care. The only thing that mattered was that they were together.

Cam lifted his head. "That was a lot to confess," he said.

"There's one more thing I have to tell you."

"Oh, yeah? I'm intrigued."

She framed his face with her hands. "I love you, Cam Dumont."

He growled and crushed his mouth to hers. But the kiss quickly went from passionate to sweet and ended with Cam kissing the tip of her nose. "I watched the video of your speech on the Bayside Blogger's site. I'm so proud of you, Elle. I love you, too."

"So kiss me again and prove it."

He did just that, walking her backward until she felt the railing against her legs. All of a sudden, a creaking noise rang out and next thing Elle knew, she could no longer feel the railing on her skin. She didn't feel anything except that heady sensation of free-falling.

And with a big splash, they both went into the bay.

Yet again.

When she surfaced, Cam grabbed her. They stared at each other as they treaded water. After a moment, they burst into laughter.

"What is it with you and this water?"

"I just can't get enough."

"And I can't get enough of you." He kissed her again.

Funny, Elle thought. Everything seemed to have started with a video and her falling into the bay that night in high school. She looked at Cam. "You really watched the Bayside Blogger's video?"

"Yep. That damn gossip may have just saved us."

"Too bad she wasn't around a couple minutes ago. Maybe she could have saved us from falling in. I thought you fixed the railing?"

"I must have missed a portion. I'll have to come back tomorrow."

"With me. We'll fix it together."

As the sun began to set over their heads and water lapped around them, Elle wrapped her arms around Cam and kissed him. Perfectly content with her life and her man, all thanks to the meddling of a certain blogger.

Epilogue

Smiling, the Bayside Blogger powered off her laptop and flipped the lid closed. She did love a happy ending.

Rising from the table in The Brewside, she sneaked a glance around the room. As always, everyone was oblivious to her identity. Just as she liked it.

She knew her blog had upset people initially, but in the end, they had to realize she was only reporting the truth. And if you stuck to the truth, no one could really say anything bad. Her mother always said she had a talent for reading people and their emotions. Of course, her mother had wanted her to go into psychology or some other prestigious field. But she was happy right where she was.

She pretended not to be interested as people poured into the coffee shop, gossiping about Elle Owens and Cam Dumont falling into the bay. Again.

"I tried to give them a hand, help them out," someone was saying. "But they just kept making out."

She laughed along with everyone else. If she was alone, she'd pat herself on the back. In her mind, she'd definitely helped Elle and Cam along. Sometimes people just needed a little push.

But secretly, what she really wanted was a happy ending of her own. Maybe someday soon, she'd find that special person…

Until then, she had a feeling someone else needed her attention. As if conjured from her thoughts, Jasper Dumont strode into The Brewside. He greeted a couple friends and chuckled at the story of his brother and Elle.

Yes, Jasper needed some help. She was sure of it. And then maybe, perhaps, after that, she could take some time to find her own happiness.

Shaking her head, she reminded herself that just by giving them a few mentions here and there, she'd given Elle and Cam their happy ending. For now, that would have to be enough.

"Bye, Tony," she called with a friendly wave.

Her work here was done. Two more people saved by the blog.

* * * * *

Don't miss Jasper Dumont's story,
The next installment in SAVED BY THE BLOG,
from Mills & Boon Cherish

Coming soon!

MILLS & BOON®

Cherish™

EXPERIENCE THE ULTIMATE RUSH OF FALLING IN LOVE

0617/23

MILLS & BOON®

EXCLUSIVE EXTRACT

When Charlotte Aldridge tells CEO Lucian Duval
she's pregnant, the handsome billionaire is adamant
his child will have the one thing he never did – the
love of two committed parents…

Read on for a sneak preview of
THEIR BABY SURPRISE

'I want to be a part of this baby's life on a daily basis.'

The knot of anxiety inside her twisted. 'That's not
possible, you know that, I'm moving away from London.'

'Don't move away.'

Charlotte gestured around her apartment. 'I need more
space. I need to be near my parents. To have family
close by.'

'I agree, that's why I believe you should move in
with me…and for that matter, why we should marry.'

She sank down onto the window seat below the open
window. 'Marry!'

'Yes.'

A known serial dater was proposing marriage. This
was crazy. Lucian had the reputation for being impulsive
and a maverick within the industry but his decisions
were always backed up with sound logic. And that quick-
fire decision making, some would even say recklessness,
often gave him the edge over his more ponderous rivals.
But he had called this one all wrong. She gave an incred-

ulous laugh. 'I bet you don't even believe in marriage?'

He rolled his shoulders and rubbed the back of his neck hard, his expression growing darker before he answered, 'It's the responsible thing to do when a child becomes part of the equation.'

This was crazy. She lifted her hands to her face in shock and exasperation, her hot cheeks burning against the skin of her palms. 'Have you really thought about what it takes to be a father? A child needs consistency, routine, to know that they are the centre of the parent's life. Have you considered the sacrifices needed? Your work life, the constant travel, all of the partying—everything about the way you live now will be affected. Are you prepared to give up all of that?'

Stood in the centre of the room, he folded his arms on his wide imposing chest, his eyes firing with impatient resolve. 'I don't have a choice. This child is my responsibility and duty, I will do whatever it takes to ensure that it has a safe and happy childhood.'

Don't miss
THEIR BABY SURPRISE
by Katrina Cudmore

Available July 2017
www.millsandboon.co.uk

Join Britain's BIGGEST Romance Book Club

2 in 1 GREAT VALUE

MARINELLI

50% OFF
your first parcel

- **EXCLUSIVE offers every month**
- **FREE delivery direct to your door**
- **NEVER MISS a title**
- **EARN Bonus Book points**

Call Customer Services
0844 844 1358*

or visit
millsandboon.co.uk/subscriptions

MILLS & BOON®

Why shop at millsandboon.co.uk?

Each year, thousands of romance readers
find their perfect read at millsandboon.co.uk.
That's because we're passionate about
bringing you the very best romantic fiction.
Here are some of the advantages of
shopping at www.millsandboon.co.uk:

* **Get new books first**—you'll be able to buy
  your favourite books one month before they
  hit the shops

* **Get exclusive discounts**—you'll also be
  able to buy our specially created monthly
  collections, with up to 50% off the RRP

* **Find your favourite authors**—latest news,
  interviews and new releases for all your
  favourite authors and series on our website,
  plus ideas for what to try next

* **Join in**—once you've bought your favourite
  books, don't forget to register with us to rate,
  review and join in the discussions

Visit **www.millsandboon.co.uk**
for all this and more today!